The Rosetti Letter

Christi Phillips

POCKET BOOKS

LONDON • SYDNEY • NEW YORK • TORONTO

First published in the USA by Pocket Books, 2007
A division of Simon & Schuster Inc.
First published in Great Britain by Simon & Schuster UK Ltd, 2007
This edition published by Pocket Books UK, 2008
An imprint of Simon & Schuster UK Ltd
A CBS COMPANY

1 3 5 7 9 10 8 6 4 2

Simon & Schuster UK Ltd
Africa House
64–78 Kingsway
London WC2B 6AH

Simon & Schuster Australia
Sydney

www.simonsays.co.uk

A CIP catalogue record for this book is available from the British Library

ISBN: 978-1-84739-076-9

Printed and bound in Great Britain by
Cox & Wyman Ltd, Reading, Berkshire

Christi Phillips lives in the San Francisco Bay Area. Her interest in European history has led her all over the continent. *The Rossetti Letter* is her first novel.

Praise for Christi Phillips' debut novel *The Rossetti Letter*:

'Reading Christi Phillips' lush, beautifully written novel is like enjoying a sumptuous meal in the Venice it describes with such loving detail. You want to savour every moment' Ayelet Waldman, author of *Love and Other Impossible Pursuits*

'Phillips spent weeks in Italy researching this, her debut novel, and the result is a rich mix of history and romance . . . Modern-day and 17th-century love stories collide as Claire travels to Venice to complete her research and confront her rival. The author seamlessly weaves suspense and misunderstanding in this fascinating read. An easy blend of fact and fiction' *She*

'An enthralling debut. *The Rossetti Letter* has plenty of pace and conjures vivid period interest' *Financial Times*

For Brian

List of Historical Characters (in order of appearance)

Alessandra Rossetti, a young courtesan

Nico, Alessandra's manservant

Bartolomeo Cattona, a Venetian banker

La Celestia, née Faustina Emiliana Zolta, Venice's leading courtesan

Taddeo da Ponte, a young spy working for Batù Vratsa

Arturo Sanchez, a Spanish *bravo* in the Spanish ambassador's service

Jacques Pierre, a French mercenary

Nicholas Regnault, a French mercenary

Alphonso de la Cueva, the marquis of Bedmar and Spanish ambassador to Venice

Bianca, Alessandra's housekeeper

Moukib, La Celestia's gondolier

Gabriele, La Celestia's lover

Dario Contarini, a Venetian senator

Paolo Calieri, gondolier for the marquis of Bedmar

Ippolito Moro, Sant' Alvise sacristan and spy

Batù Vratsa, a Venetian assassin and spymaster

Girolamo Silvia, a Venetian senator

Luis Salazar, a Spanish spy

Antonio Perez, the viscount of Utrillo-Navarre and an assassin in the duke of Ossuna's service

Piero de Pieri, a Venetian admiral

Giovanni Bembo, Doge of Venice

Giovanna and Lorenzo Donatella, Alessandra's cousins

The entire city is dedicated to Venus.

—Alphonso de la Cueva, the marquis of Bedmar
and Spanish ambassador to Venice, 1608–1618

Two lone women in an unknown city—
now that's what I call an adventure.

—E. M. Forster, *A Room with a View*

The Hanged Man

3 March 1618

HER HANDS LOOKED unnaturally pale in the moonlight. For a moment, Alessandra forgot the bitter wind that kicked up an icy spray off the lagoon, and regarded her hands as though they belonged to someone else: a conspicuous ridge of bone-white knuckle, with pallid veins that were faintly visible through milky flesh. As they approached the Ponte San Biagio, she realized how tense she was, how tightly she gripped the edge of the gondola. Calm yourself, she thought, and released her grasp. *You must be calm.* She reclined against the seat cushions, assuming a relaxed posture she did not feel, and the coarse fabric of her costume bunched uncomfortably against her back. She chose to ignore it. *If Nico sees that you are uneasy, he will insist that you return home.*

Her manservant steered them into the Rio dell' Arsenale, leaving behind the lagoon where they'd hugged the shore since leaving her house at the southeast end of the city. The canal was empty and quiet, devoid of movement and light, save for the silent passage of the gondola and an occasional torchlight that trembled in the black water. The houses along both sides were shuttered and dark. They would remain that way until morning, while the inhabitants celebrated elsewhere: in the Piazza, in the smaller public squares, in the palaces along the Grand Canal. The end of Carnival was only three days away. After weeks of celebration, the revelry had built to a frenzy, as in the tale of a bewitched princess who danced for days and nights without rest. When morning dawned on Ash Wednesday, fragile and silver fogged, all of Venice would fall into a limitless sleep, as if under an enchantment.

They turned into the Rio di San Martino, then into a narrow waterway that circled west toward the Piazzetta dei Leoncini. In their wake, small waves gently slapped against stone foundations smothered in clumps of thick, glistening moss. She could reach out and brush the damp stone with her fingertips if she desired, so close were the buildings, and she inhaled their familiar grotto scent with a kind of reverence. Traveling through Venice at night always filled her with a rising excitement, but tonight her anticipation was tinged with fear. Alessandra tried not to think about what waited for her at the end of her journey, which was quickly approaching.

Already she could hear strains of music. Then came an indeterminate cry—of fear, passion, or laughter?—that echoed off stone walls and was abruptly silenced, leaving once again the oar's rhythmic squeak and splash. Soon there appeared a harbinger of the celebration at the city's center: a single gondola with a red lantern at its bow glided slowly toward them. Seated within it were two velvet-breeched men wearing the masks of pagan gods, and two elegant courtesans with feathered headdresses that resembled exotic birds, whose ruby lips and bejeweled throats gleamed in the rosy light. As the gondola passed, these fantastic creatures turned to regard her with a languid curiosity; then one of the strange, hybrid women wet her rouged mouth with her tongue and reached out her hand in silent invitation.

Alessandra felt as if she were merely a spectator at a passing show. Then she and Nico were swallowed by the shadow of a bridge and disgorged again, and all at once they were enveloped by music and light and laughter, a riot of color and strange costume, as the crowds along Calle Canonica pressed into the Piazza. Nico halted the gondola and exchanged a wordless look with Alessandra before she stepped onto the *fondamenta* and rushed away.

The Piazza was bright with torchlight, alive with music and revelry, but she could not join the general high spirits; the sinister maw that waited for her in the dark courtyard of the Doge's Palace filled her with dread. The *bocca di leone,* the lion's mouth, was a special receptacle created by the Venetian government to receive letters of denunciation. Into this bronze plaque went accusations of theft, murder, or tax evasion—the last a particularly heinous crime according to the Great Council, the Republic's ruling assembly of two thousand noblemen. Alessandra had never imagined, until recently, that she would ever avail herself of it. Behind the *bocca di leone*'s grotesque, gaping mouth lurked every terror hidden within the depths of the palace, the prison, and the Republic itself; surely unleashing that terror was a fearsome act not to be done with indifference.

As she pushed her way through the crowds, she was aware of the letter tucked inside the small purse tied at her waist. It bore both her personal seal and her signature. The Great Council paid no heed to anonymous letters, to discourage using the *bocca di leone* as a way of striking at one's enemies. Soon the marquis and his co-conspirators would know who had exposed their plan, and her life would be in danger. But how could she do other than what she had set out to do tonight? The Republic was in peril. It was her civic duty to place the letter in the lion's mouth, to set the wheels of justice in motion. If she failed, more lives than just her own would be lost.

Alessandra summoned her courage and moved toward the Porta della Carta, the dark archway that led to the palace courtyard, then abruptly stopped, startled by something that had caught at the edge of her vision.

Between the two great marble columns at the foot of the Piazzetta, a dead man hung limply against a background of starless sky. His limbs were broken, his face bloodied, his bruised flesh barely covered by dirty, tattered rags. Although he was suspended on a gibbet directly above the gaming tables that crowded the space between the two columns, not one of the many costumed revelers below took notice of him.

Stirred by a gust of wind, the hanged man turned slowly on the cord that had snapped his neck. Light from a bonfire below animated his blank, staring eyes; flickering shadows played across his mouth and turned his death's grimace into a grin. Alessandra stood transfixed, as it appeared that the hanged man was still alive. She imagined that he spoke to her, his warning delivered in a harsh whisper: *It could be you at the end of this rope, if you do not deliver that letter . . . but here is the fate of the one you love if you do.*

I am damned with the Devil's own choice, Alessandra thought, but as for the one I love . . . she looked again at the hanged man, and it was suddenly clear that all life had left him. Just a body at the end of a rope, no more, no less, not common, but not uncommon, either. She had seen hanged men before in this very place; she knew well they did not speak. She shook her head to rid herself of the apparition and turned away. The sooner she got on with her task and was away, the better.

As for the one she loved . . . well, he did not love her, did he? Still, her step was slow as she walked toward the Porta della Carta. *The Devil's own choice,* she thought, and slipped through the archway into the shadowed, silent courtyard.

Chapter One

". . . BY 1618, VENICE was past the apogee of its empire," Claire Donovan said as she shuffled an index card to the bottom of the stack, resisting an urge to fan herself with it. The Harriot Historical Society meeting room felt stiflingly hot. From her position at the podium, Claire saw that her audience was also suffering from the unseasonably warm weather. Program notes doubled as fans, and handkerchiefs were dabbed at brows and throats.

"Although the Republic was still a major power, it was surrounded by enemies: the Turkish Empire, France, and, most notably, Spain, the richest and most powerful country in the western world, and the dominant force in Italy. Italy was not the united country we know today, but a disparate group of territorial states, many of them under Spanish control, ruled by a Spanish viceroy or governor. The Venetian Republic stood alone in its independence; along with its fabled wealth and beauty, this vulnerability only served to tantalize those determined to conquer her.

"The duke of Ossuna set his sights upon Venice soon after assuming the viceroyalty of Milan in 1616," she continued. "But he knew he could not take the Republic on his own. He enlisted the help of the Spanish ambassador, the marquis of Bedmar . . ." She paused, distracted, as a bead of perspiration slid down her neck and underneath her collar. God, she was hot. It didn't help that she'd dressed up for the occasion of her first public lecture, exchanging her usual T-shirt and khakis for a skirt, blazer, and blouse; or that her long, fawn-colored hair was hanging loose instead of tied back into a neat, and much cooler, braid. She glanced at her notes on the 1618 Spanish Conspiracy against Venice, trying to regain her place and her rhythm.

"The marquis of Bedmar," she began again, then stopped as she heard a soft, wheezing whisper from somewhere in the audience. It was followed by the creak of metal folding chairs, the rustle of bodies, a few dry, muffled coughs. They weren't exactly enraptured, Claire realized, feeling a sudden flush of self-consciousness. One instant her thoughts had been on her scribbled notes, the words in her mind, and the images she envisioned: seventeenth-century Venice, Alessandra Rossetti on her fateful trip to the *bocca di leone*. The next instant she was just someone standing in front of a small group of people she hardly knew, feeling much too hot and not quite sure of what she was doing.

This didn't bode well for her future success. If she couldn't give a captivating talk to the members of the Harriot Historical Society, how would she ever present her doctoral dissertation to her adviser, the notoriously caustic Claudius Hilliard, and the rest of the Harvard committee who would watch her with judgmental, silent stares?

She took a sip of water from the plastic cup on the podium and looked up from her index cards. Elroy Dugan was fast asleep, but the other audience members still seemed interested. They were all women, all well over seventy years old, and they all looked up at her with expressions of encouraging expectation. Maybe her lecture wasn't going quite as badly as she'd imagined.

Claire smiled at them and brushed the perspiration from her brow. "The marquis of Bedmar, Spanish ambassador to Venice . . ." she said, her voice trailing off. Odd. Her notes were blurry. Her ears suddenly seemed to be stuffed with cotton. Her legs felt shaky, her head woozy. She gripped the sides of the podium to steady herself.

In the front row, Mrs. Branford Biddle, the historical society's director, leaned forward, looking concerned.

"Venice . . . ," Claire began once more, and wondered why Mrs. Biddle seemed to be lunging straight at her.

* * *

"Miss Donovan." A woman was speaking to her. Why couldn't she answer? "Miss Donovan, please stick out your tongue." It seemed an odd but perfectly reasonable request, so she complied.

Claire not only heard but felt someone walking toward her. She understood then that she was lying on the floor, which was rather uncomfortable. Why was she lying on the floor? And why was she sticking out her tongue?

"Why is she sticking out her tongue?" Mrs. Biddle asked. Even in Claire's confused state, Mrs. Biddle's voice was unmistakable: it had the grating edge of a woman who was accustomed to having things her own way.

"I was afraid she might swallow it," the first woman answered. "It can happen when people faint."

I fainted? Claire opened her eyes. The historical society's secretary, Adela Crenshaw, was kneeling beside her, gently patting her left hand. The other society members stood behind Adela in a concerned semicircle.

"Can it?" asked Mrs. Biddle, entirely unconvinced.

"I learned about it from a CPR course on the internet." Adela turned back to Claire and saw that she was conscious. "Ah, there she is."

"I fainted?" Claire asked. Adela smiled radiantly at her. But it was Mrs. Biddle, still standing over them, who answered.

"Yes, you fainted. Passed out cold and toppled like a ton of bricks. Good thing I caught you. And very good thing I spent my youth breaking in wild Arabians"—horses, Claire wondered, or people?—"or I would be a frail old lady lying underneath you with a broken hip. Okay, everyone, show's over. She's fine. Please help yourselves to iced tea and cookies in the reception area."

The others moved away to the vestibule as Adela and Mrs. Biddle helped Claire to her feet.

"This will make a very interesting story for the next newsletter," Mrs. Biddle said. "Wouldn't you say, Adela?"

"Very interesting. No one's ever passed out at the podium before," Adela explained.

Not for the first time did Claire reflect on the drawbacks of living in a town with fewer than a thousand inhabitants. Although she loved its Cape Cod locale and waterside ambience, loved that she could walk to the post office and the library and the General Store (and that there was a store actually named General Store), it was not possible to live an entirely private life in Harriott. Claire was certain that everyone would know she'd fainted while giving a talk to a small group of geriatrics, long before the historical society newsletter came out.

"Even Joshua Deerbottom," Mrs. Biddle broke in on her thoughts, "who is ninety-three years old, made it through his entire lecture on the Battle of Buzzards Bluff without once falling over. You're such a young thing, we did expect you to be able to stand for at least twenty minutes or so. You seem to be well enough."

If she were to rate her level of embarrassment from one to ten, Claire figured that she was hovering right around a nine.

Mrs. Biddle looked her over carefully. "Are you pregnant?"

And this was ten. "No."

"Well, there must be a reason."

"I think I just got too hot."

They had started toward the vestibule when Adela exclaimed brightly, "I almost forgot. We have something to show you." Claire followed them to the historical society office.

"Bitsy, do you know where I put it?" asked Adela, addressing Mrs. Biddle as Claire marveled that the petite but formidable woman should ever be spoken to so familiarly.

"Put what?" Mrs. Biddle said.

"The printout of that article I found on the internet. The one about Venice." Adela rifled through a few stacks of paper on her desk. "Oh, here it is." She handed two pages to Claire. "It seemed very much like the subject of your lecture."

VENICE CONFERENCE TO FEATURE NEW STUDIES IN VENETIAN HISTORY, the headline read. The article, from the online edition of the *International Herald Tribune,* announced that the upcoming five-day conference was being hosted by the Department of History at the University Ca' Foscari and would be attended by historians from all over Europe.

"Look at the second page, dear."

Claire turned to the second page of the article. Adela had kindly bracketed the crucial paragraph:

"Highlights of the conference include visiting history professor Andrea Kent of Trinity College, Cambridge, whose book in progress, *The Spanish Conspiracy of 1618,* will provide the subject matter for two lectures."

"Oh my god," Claire gasped. She would have sat down in shock except for the fact that there was only one chair in the room, and Adela was already in it.

"Maybe you should go and reveal passages from your book, too," said Adela encouragingly.

Even if she could afford a trip to Venice, there wasn't a chance she'd be asked to give a paper there. She wasn't a professor; she didn't even have her doctorate yet. But that wasn't her most important concern. What would happen if Andrea Kent's book was published before her dissertation was completed? She had believed the Spanish Conspiracy to be so obscure that her dissertation was unique—a crucial quality if she were going to stand out in the crowd of new Ph.D.s competing for a handful of teaching positions. This book was disturbing news indeed; its very existence could ruin her life.

"Do you have any more information on this conference?" Claire asked.

"I'm sorry, no," Adela replied. "I just happened to come across this while I was looking for something else."

"I can guess what you were looking for," Mrs. Biddle harrumphed.

"And what's wrong with it? I've met some very nice gentlemen on the internet. In fact, I have a date for brunch on Sunday."

"That's five dates in three weeks," Mrs. Biddle said indignantly. "You're an eighty-year-old nymphomaniac."

"I am not," Adela protested. "I'm seventy-nine."

Chapter Two

Claire stood on the grassy oval in the center of the four-hundred-meter track at Forsythe Academy, an exclusive preparatory school located at Harriot's west end, on Harriot Harbor. She looked out across the water, where small boats with brightly colored sails glided as swiftly and smoothly as skaters on ice.

She was waiting for the arrival of her closest friend and jogging partner, Meredith Barnes, Forsythe's assistant dean. Fourteen years before, Claire had been studying in her Columbia dorm room when Meredith had stepped through the open door. She'd paused for just a moment, as if she were one of those chic 1930s movie stars who needed to remove her gloves and hat before delivering her lines. Then Meredith said she'd "heard about her" and wanted to meet the only person who'd aced McNulty's ancient history class. Meredith was a philosophy major, an occasional Maoist (her current boyfriend had radical tendencies), and a self-described "inveterate theorist." Claire soon learned that this meant she could talk for hours on almost any topic. They'd immediately become friends and had remained so ever since.

Tall and willowy, Meredith was naturally and devastatingly glamorous, even now, walking toward Claire in a pair of baggy shorts and a gray jersey with GO, FORSYTHE FOXES! emblazoned on the front.

"Sorry I'm late," said Meredith, pulling her sleek, dark hair into a ponytail and securing it with a barrette. "I went home to change and on the way back I ran into Connie Sherwood. I had to talk to her, of course, because she's my boss's wife, but she's simply infuriating. She's always gossiping, but she doesn't understand how to make it interesting."

"You might be grateful for that if she starts gossiping about you."

"Listen to this. She said, 'Did you hear that Deirdre Fry shot her ex-husband in the foot on the eleventh hole of the Back Bay Golf Course?'"

"That's what I call a handicap."

"Apparently it was an incredible scene—paramedics and police and the whole golf course shut down for hours."

"Why did she shoot her ex-husband?"

"That's what I asked. And Connie just shrugged and said, 'I don't know. Don't all women want to shoot their ex-husbands at one time or another?'"

"Good point. But why in the foot? Why on the Back Bay Golf Course? Why on the eleventh hole?"

"My questions exactly, but she had absolutely nothing more to add. She's exasperating. I'm a twentieth-century creature—I like a little psychological insight with my gossip, even if it's superficial. What's the point of dishing if you can't pick apart someone's psyche?"

"Who is Deirdre Fry, by the way?" Claire asked. Along with Meredith's job as assistant dean came an immense social circle that included her colleagues, their spouses, important (meaning generous) supporters of the school, hundreds of Forsythe alumni, and the current crop of four hundred students, their parents, and (more often than not) stepparents.

"She's the mother of one of the students, a freshman," Meredith replied as they walked onto the track and began jogging. "Wealthy, and a notorious clotheshorse. Every time I've seen her, she's been decked out in the most amazing designer outfits. Apparently the owners of the golf course weren't too happy that she wore a pair of stiletto-heeled Manolo Blahniks as she was stalking her ex—she left tiny divots all over the fairway."

"And the ex?"

"Some big investment banker in Boston. Richer than God."

Claire told her about the events at the historical society the day before. "I don't understand what happened. One moment I was talking, and the next I was on the floor with ten of Harriot's most illustrious citizens staring down at me. What if I faint every time I try to give a lecture? Or during my oral exam?"

"I agree it's not an auspicious beginning, but I'm sure you'll do better next time."

"I couldn't do any worse."

"Exactly. You've got nowhere to go but up. Besides the dramatic finish, what was the reaction to your lecture?"

"'Underwhelmed' is the polite word for it. The frustrating thing is that I see the Spanish Conspiracy just as if it were a story, but when I talk about it, it doesn't come across that way. Later, when I looked at my notes, I realized that I was just reciting facts and dates and footnotes. It's amazing I didn't put them all to sleep."

"Isn't that what a dissertation is—facts and dates and footnotes?"

"I suppose so, but I want it to be more compelling than that. Anyway, that isn't the worst part. Another historian is writing a book on the Spanish Conspiracy. A Cambridge professor, no less."

"Cambridge?"

"Cambridge, England, not Boston. Trinity College." Claire paused for a minute to retie a shoelace and Meredith jogged in place. "You know how few jobs there are for historians. I thought if my dissertation was really good, and original, I could get a teaching position. If a book on the same subject is published before my paper's completed, that isn't going to happen. I drove up to Harvard this morning and met with Hilliard, and according to him it's nothing less than a disaster. He said the only way to succeed is to write something original, and as soon as that book comes out, my dissertation's going to be as original as mud."

"When's the book coming out?"

"I don't know."

"Maybe you can finish your dissertation before it's published."

"That's what Hilliard said. This professor's going to be speaking at a conference in Venice soon, and Hilliard advised me to go and find out everything I can. Keep abreast of the competition and all that. Although he wasn't quite clear as to whether I should befriend her or push her into a canal."

"I don't know about that, but I think he's right about going to Venice."

"I can't afford it."

"What about that grant?"

"I won't know until August, and even if I do get it, the money's not available until September."

"There must be a way." Meredith stopped by the water fountain at the north end of the track, bent down for a brief drink, then straightened. "It doesn't seem right that you've been writing about Venice for at least two years and you haven't even been there. Not to mention"—she paused for a few more mouthfuls of water—"there are Italian men in Venice."

"You don't say?"

Claire began running again, and Meredith trotted to catch up.

"Hordes of them, all gorgeous. You must see this to believe."

"I believe you already."

"But you can't understand what I mean when I say 'Italian men' without actually experiencing it. Didn't I tell you about the two weeks I spent in Rome?"

"Sure, but that was years ago."

"I don't think anything's changed. They're the most fabulous flirts on the planet. You read Ovid's *Ars Amatoria.* An Italian literally wrote the book on seduction. They make you feel like a woman."

"I already feel like a woman."

"Like a goddess, then."

"Oh, come on."

"I'm not kidding. Why do you think that almost every man I've dated since then has had an *o* at the end of his name?"

That was true. Claire could recall, in Meredith's past, a Riccardo, a Pietro, and an Enrico.

"Although," Meredith continued, "once they're transplanted to the U.S., something bad happens. Perhaps they spoil on the flight over. But while they're in Italy, they're amazing. I don't know what it is, exactly, but it has something to do with the way they look at you. American men think they can seduce women by being cool and distant, and they couldn't be more wrong. If American men knew what Italian men seem to know from birth, we would all be having sex all the time. Which reminds me—"

"I don't want to discuss it."

"You haven't had a date in what, two years?"

"Of course I have. A couple, anyway."

"I don't remember any."

"Sure you do." It took Claire a moment to remember them herself. "There was the guy who wore those weird orange pants." Her brow furrowed as she tried to recall his name, and couldn't. "He drove a Jeep Cherokee. And don't forget Jungle Boy."

"The one who spent six months in the Venezuelan jungle eating rats and snakes?"

"It wasn't a lifestyle choice, he was some sort of special forces guy in the army."

"Claire, don't you think it's time?"

An attractive man smiled and waved as he jogged past them in the opposite direction. Meredith smiled and waved in return.

"Time for what?" Claire said.

"To get out there again."

"Out where?"

"You know what I mean. To start dating again. Look at you—you're gorgeous. Didn't you see how that guy was checking you out? You've never looked better in your life and you've just shut yourself away."

"I haven't shut myself away."

"Two dates in two years?"

"Okay, so my love life hasn't been very exciting since . . . since . . ."

They passed the four-hundred-meter marker for the fourth time and stopped. Claire doubled over and put her hands on her knees, breathing heavily.

"Why don't you just say it?" Meredith gasped.

"Say what?"

"Since my husband left me on the day of my mother's funeral." She took a few deep breaths before continuing. "Look, Claire, I'm not trying to hurt you. I just think it would do you good to say it out loud sometimes. Whenever you start feeling sentimental about Michael, for instance. It would help you move on."

"At the moment," Claire said, "I need to move on to the hardware store."

"If you don't want to talk about it . . ."

"The kitchen sink's leaking again, and I've got to replace the curvy part of the pipe."

"The curvy part? Is that the technical name for it?"

"It is as far as I'm concerned."

"When did you get so handy around the house?"

"When plumbers started charging seventy-five dollars an hour."

A cloud passed overhead, blocking the sun and shadowing most of the track. A humid breeze rose off the ocean and chilled Claire's perspiring skin. She picked up her sweatshirt from where she'd dropped it on the grass and pulled it over her head. Did she really feel like a woman? she wondered as she and Meredith crossed the field. At the moment, she felt elated, calm, and sweaty, but not exactly feminine. What precisely did it mean to feel like a woman? The concept seemed to belong to her past, as something she dimly remembered that no longer had relevance.

Chapter Three

Claire scooted out from under the kitchen sink and stood up. It was almost dark, and a sky full of woolly gray clouds cast a deepening chiaroscuro twilight into the room, softly illuminating the white-tile counters, a few unwashed dishes, and the wallpaper that was beginning to curl at the edges. Like everything else in the house it was showing its age. She'd get around to replacing it after her dissertation was finished—that and about a million other things.

When Claire's mother Emily bought the house, Claire had agreed that it was charming, in a cottage sort of way, but after living there for two years she'd become unhappily familiar with its every idiosyncrasy. There wasn't a true right angle anywhere, and it wouldn't do to look too closely at the corners. Not that you could if you wanted to. Claire had moved her belongings in without moving her mother's out, and the result was a cozy—some would say messy—jumble of furniture and knickknacks and way too many books.

The clutter helped to fill up a house that had felt empty ever since Emily died. Her mother was only fifty-four when she'd been diagnosed with ovarian cancer. Claire had been in the doctoral program at Columbia University in New York, and she'd taken a leave of absence from her studies to look after Emily following the first surgery. As her mother's disease progressed, what began as a three-month hiatus from school turned into two years. Two years of hospitals, of surgeries, of chemotherapy and its debilitating aftermath, of watching her mother become frail and listless and in constant pain. Two years during which she and her husband, Michael, spent many nights apart. Claire had worn his favorite sweater, the brown one with the light tan stripes, when she slept in the tiny bed in her mother's guest room, just so she could have the scent of him surrounding her.

Ex-husband, Claire reminded herself. Most of the time she didn't allow herself to feel sentimental, but every once in a while—seeing a young couple holding hands on the commons, a swaddled baby in a stroller—she was painfully aware of everything she'd lost.

They had fallen in love six years ago, soon after being accepted into their respective Ph.D. programs: Claire in European history, Michael in ancient history—the Greeks and the Romans. She cringed to think of it now but, in a move highly uncharacteristic for her, she'd gotten his attention by "accidentally" dropping her books at his feet. Not only had Claire never done anything so obvious before, she had acted in defiance of an intuitive voice she heard the moment she first saw him: *He's too good looking to be trusted.* She'd ignored that voice through a whirlwind courtship, a wedding less than a year later, and three years of marriage. After all, what other man had ever understood her passion for the past, her overwhelming desire to bury her nose in books? Old, arcane books, at that. Michael was the first boyfriend she'd had who didn't accuse her of being "out of touch": his interests were even more obscure than her own. But the things that had brought them together hadn't been enough to keep them together, not with the strain of her mother's illness and their repeated separations.

Three months after her mother died, Claire transferred from Columbia to Harvard and resumed work on her dissertation. Soon she'd fallen into a routine: once or twice a month she went up to the university and spent a day in the library, but more often she worked in the guest room that she'd turned into a home office. She seldom bothered to change out of her favorite flannel pajamas and rarely left her office except to make a cup of tea or a quick sandwich that later she couldn't recall making or eating. Her dissertation filled her thoughts so completely that sometimes it was a shock, at the end of the day, to find herself returned to her mundane, uneventful, twenty-first–century existence.

Claire supposed Meredith had a point; she had sort of shut herself away, she thought as she rummaged in the fridge for something approximating dinner. But only because it was so important to finish her dissertation as soon as she possibly could. Her mother's illness had set her back more than two years—two years during which her peers had gone on to get degrees and jobs. Michael already had a prestigious position as an assistant professor of classics at Columbia.

With an avocado and tomato sandwich in hand, she went into her office and sat down at her desk. She glanced at the nearest bookshelf, filled with reference books and the two previous volumes on the Spanish Conspiracy. Both had been written in the late seventeenth century. Except for some scholarly papers published in Italy and Spain, the Spanish Conspiracy had not been explored in depth for a few hundred years. Until now, she thought ruefully. What would happen if Andrea Kent published before she did? Perhaps it shouldn't have surprised her that someone else was writing about her chosen subject. After all, the Spanish Conspiracy was one of the more exciting episodes in Venetian history, full of intrigue, espionage, and murder.

In 1617, the duke of Ossuna, the Spanish viceroy who ruled Naples, and the marquis of Bedmar, the Spanish ambassador to Venice, concocted a scheme to violently overthrow the Venetian Senate and make the Venetian Republic a dependency of Spain. Their attack was planned for Ascension Day 1618—the day when all of Venice would be celebrating the Serenissima's marriage to the sea. They intended no less than the complete sacking and pillage of Venice. One source credited Bedmar with charging his band of soldiers to "cut off the limbs of those senators who resist." Those who didn't resist would be held for ransom. The considerable loot and ransom money would be divvied up among the conspirators, a group of mercenaries that included French corsairs, English privateers, and the Spanish viscount of Utrillo-Navarre, Antonio Perez, a notorious assassin in the service of the duke of Ossuna.

Known for his recklessness and dissipated habits, Ossuna began a campaign of hostility toward Venice after assuming the viceroyalty of Naples in 1616. He built a squadron of galleys that attacked Venetian ships in the Mediterranean and the Adriatic, but apparently these spoils were not enough for him. Soon he set his sights on Venice itself, and found in the Spanish ambassador a willing accomplice.

The marquis of Bedmar was an intriguing figure; every source Claire came across revealed a new, often contradictory, facet to his character. His reports to the Spanish king were sharply observant and laced with an acerbic wit; he was described as "cultivated and charming in society," but also as "one of the most potent and dangerous spirits Spain ever produced." Like Ossuna, he was implacably dedicated to the conquest of Venice. They were matched in ruthlessness only by their adversary, the Venetian senator Girolamo Silvia, who was equally determined to thwart the Spanish threat.

But Claire was most captivated by a person who, in previous chronicles of the conspiracy, had been relegated to a footnote. Alessandra Rossetti was a young courtesan who wrote a secret letter to the Great Council exposing the plot. Known as the Rossetti Letter, it was mentioned in most accounts of the Spanish Conspiracy, but was never fully examined, as Alessandra's role had remained a mystery. No one knew how Alessandra had learned of the conspiracy; with the exception of the Rossetti Letter, there was no documentary evidence linking her to it.

Claire hadn't found any evidence, either, but she believed it existed somewhere—most likely in Venice's Biblioteca Marciana, which she hadn't yet been able to visit. She suspected that past historians had overlooked it simply because they didn't consider it important enough. They'd written about Ossuna, Bedmar, and Silvia at length, but Alessandra's life and contribution to history were largely ignored. A few had even stated that the Rossetti Letter was incidental, that the Spanish Conspiracy would have been discovered without it, but Claire thought they were missing the point. As soon as she'd learned of the young courtesan, her imagination had been captured. Who was this woman? How did she become involved? No previous historian had looked at the conspiracy from Alessandra's point of view, had placed her at the center of events, had given her adequate credit for helping to maintain the Venetian Republic's independence. Claire thought of Alessandra as a sort of Italian Joan of Arc, and she harbored a secret hope that her dissertation would elevate the courtesan to a more prominent place in history.

If Andrea Kent doesn't beat me to the punch, she thought as she brushed the last crumbs of her sandwich from her lap. That the Cambridge professor was a woman was especially worrisome; there was a greater possibility that she, too, would write about the conspiracy from Alessandra's viewpoint, making Claire's dissertation completely redundant. Her only hope was that Andrea Kent was having as much trouble finding information on Alessandra Rossetti as she was.

Two years and countless hours of research, and still Claire's knowledge of the courtesan was sketchy, full of holes that she could fill only with question marks. In general, even the most illustrious Venetians of the time did not leave behind numerous records, documents or other accounts of their personal lives—and women, generally, left behind fewer than men. By researching wills, tax declarations, and an odd collection of personal correspondence, Claire had been able to piece together a biography of sorts. She took out her notes and looked them over once more.

Alessandra Rossetti: born 1599, died?

daughter of Fiametta Balbi, of a noble family; and Salvatore Rossetti, a Venetian citizen. No confirmed birth dates for FB or SR. F. Balbi died circa 1608?, cause unknown. A merchant specializing in goods from the Levant, Salvatore Rossetti died 1616 (with Alessandra's elder brother, Jacopo, born 1597) in shipwreck off Crete.

With the deaths of Salvatore and Jacopo, Alessandra was left alone at the age of seventeen. The only honorable options for a woman of her station—a Venetian citizen, from a well-to-do merchant's family—were marriage or the convent, but Alessandra didn't choose either. The mystery of why she didn't marry was easy enough to solve; when the sea claimed her father and brother, it also took her family's fortune, including her dowry. As for the convent, Venetian girls rarely chose it of their own accord. Claire was fairly certain that Alessandra had entered into a close relationship with a man named Lorenzo Liberti, her father's business associate and the executor of Salvatore's diminished estate. Claire had come across a letter by Liberti in which he'd written that Alessandra had "bewitched" him, not only with her beauty but with her agile mind. Barely a year after their liaison had begun, Liberti was stricken with cholera and died.

Not long after Liberti's death, Alessandra became a courtesan. By some accounts, she was one of the most sought after women in Venice. It must have been a momentous time for her; less than twelve months later, in March 1618, Alessandra wrote the letter exposing the Spanish Conspiracy.

And then she disappeared.

The Rossetti Letter was the last known document written by Alessandra Rossetti, even, from what Claire had found, the last document that referred to her. So far she hadn't been able to discover Alessandra's fate. Had the letter placed her in danger? Had she died during the bloodbath that followed the revelation of the Spaniards' plot? If she'd managed to escape with her life, why couldn't Claire find any mention of her after March 1618?

Claire set her notes on her desk and sighed. Sometimes she worried that she'd never find the answers to the questions that preoccupied her: How did Alessandra learn of the Spanish Conspiracy? And what had happened to her after the conspiracy was revealed?

The Wheel of Fortune

18 April 1617

THE BELLS OF San Salvador were ringing as the gondola left the narrow confines of the Rio San Giovanni Crisostomo and sailed into the Grand Canal. Alessandra leaned out from the *felze,* the black baldachin that covered the boat's midsection, and looked up at the lowering sky. April, and yet it still felt like winter. Last night's scattered clouds had converged into an unbroken canopy of gray, and she half-expected to feel raindrops on her face. Instead, only the chill spring air greeted her, carrying with it the briny scent of the sea and the pungent odors of the bustling fish market on the opposite bank.

Her gondolier steered the craft to the middle of the great waterway, dodging a fruit-laden barge that sent a shower of frigid water over the bow. *I had the dream again last night,* Alessandra realized with a shiver. The same dream she'd had too many times in the past year, the one that caused her to wake up gasping and crying, that caused her to snap at her good, loyal Bianca for no reason, that left an emptiness inside her that she feared would never pass. She'd forgotten it as soon as she awoke, but now it came back to her in an instant: her father and Jacopo sinking down into the deep, cold ocean, descending into the murky darkness until only their pale, still faces were visible, their wide eyes blank, mouths open in mute surprise.

Keep safe from stormy weather, O Lord, all your faithful mariners . . . Each year on Ascension Day, the Doge repeated this invocation during the Sposalizio del Mar, Venice's ceremonial Marriage to the Sea. As far back as she could remember, Alessandra had, along with all of Venice, watched proudly as the *Bucintoro* was rowed across the lagoon and into the Adriatic. The red and gold ship of state was as ornate as a Mandarin dragon, and the Doge rode on its crest in his golden chair surrounded by the six scarlet-robed members of his private counsel, the Signory, and a hundred liveried oarsmen. When he threw the gold ring into the sea, and spoke the words dear to every Venetian's heart ". . . keep safe all your faithful mariners, safe from sudden shipwreck and from evil, unsuspected tricks of cunning enemies," she had recited them along with him.

What a child she'd been, to believe that gold rings and prayers to the sea would keep her family alive. Alessandra felt bitter tears rising, as they did too often, and she brushed them away with the back of her hand. There was no time for that this morning; her father's banker had summoned her. At last, her father's legacy, such as it was, would be in her hands. The shipwreck that claimed Salvatore and Jacopo Rossetti had left her nearly destitute; Alessandra's father had staked everything he owned on his last voyage. During the past year, the executor of her father's estate, Lorenzo Liberti, had invested what remained. Now that Lorenzo was dead, it would be up to her to manage it. No doubt the banker had some advice for her.

She disembarked at the Rialto steps. Mornings were the market's busiest time, and the lanes all around the Erberia and the adjacent church known as San Giacometto were crowded. She slowly made her way through the throngs of shoppers carrying baskets of asparagus from Sant' Erasmus, artichokes from Sicily, or wriggling burlap sacks filled with live crabs or eels. The last time she'd been here, she'd been fifteen, and on her father's arm. It wasn't entirely proper for a well-bred young woman to be in the market unescorted, but then, she thought wryly, she'd given up being entirely proper a year ago when she'd become Lorenzo's mistress.

She unfolded the banker's letter. The top was imprinted:

Banco Cattona
at the Rialto
on the Filled-in Canal of Thoughts

Below that was a note in a precise hand:

Signorina Rossetti:
It is of the utmost importance that you see me at once regarding your account.
I remain your obedient servant,
Bartolomeo Cattona

She stopped a young man pushing a tumbrel stacked with bread and asked for directions to the bank.

"Straight ahead, then left after the goldsmiths," he said, pointing the way along the Ruga degli Speziali. He took a second look at her before he walked on, and Alessandra saw his interest, his uncertainty, his confusion. He doesn't know what to make of me, she thought. An unmarried girl would wear a veil, but I do not, nor do I wear the neck pearls of a married woman. As for the third possibility, I am too modestly dressed. I am neither maid, nor matron, nor *meretrice.*

She followed his advice and soon was beyond the bustle of the markets, in a quiet cobblestone lane lined with shops. The Banco Cattona was considerably less impressive than she had imagined it. A squeaky door opened into a tiny anteroom in which sat a young clerk with ink-stained fingers and a pained, cachectic appearance. Alessandra presented her letter and the clerk led her to the banker's office, a windowless chamber lined with leather-bound ledgers, each with a gold-engraved name on the spine.

Bartolomeo Cattona sat behind a desk that took up much of the room, squinting through half glasses at a wide sheet of paper upon which he scratched a row of figures. He looked up distractedly as they entered, and the feathery end of his quill came into contact with one of the tapers on his candelabrum and caught fire. He extinguished the burning feather with a gruff exhalation, and a plume of white, acrid smoke rose in the air.

"Sit down, sit down," he said, waving away the smoke and pointing at the only chair in the office aside from his own. "So you're Rossetti's daughter? All grown up, I see."

"Yes," Alessandra replied, although it seemed odd to say it.

"Terrible what happened to your father, just terrible," he said. "I warned him never to set sail without insurance, truly I did, but he knew better, of course." He took off his spectacles and rubbed the bridge of his broad nose, grimacing as he put them on again, and regarded her with a thin-lipped smile. "But again, these days there are many like him, the high costs of shipping being what they are, many who are willing to risk it all just like your father did, in the hopes of undercutting the Turks, and the Portuguese, and the English. In better times," he went on, tucking a silver curl back under his silk cap, "no one would have set foot off the Molo without a long list of underwriters; why, I recall voyages that were complete disasters and still managed to turn a handsome profit! If only he'd taken my advice, your misfortunes would not be so great, my dear."

Alessandra suspected that Signor Cattona wouldn't have dared insult her father like that if he were still alive; he probably wouldn't have made such a pompous statement even to Lorenzo. She tried to conceal her displeasure at the banker's patronizing manner. "My father and brother died on that voyage," she said. "No amount of money could make up for their loss."

The banker must have heard the suppressed anger in her voice, for his cheeks brightened with color. "Of course," he said, coughing uneasily. "Forgive me."

"Signor Cattona, perhaps you could tell me your reason for this letter."

"Ah, yes. But first, please, allow me to offer my condolences on the passing of Signor Liberti." He spoke with a formality that should have been reserved for Lorenzo's widow, not herself, Alessandra thought. Was he aware of the nature of their relationship? "From the flux, was it not?" he asked, regarding her warily.

"Yes."

He leaned forward and spoke in a confidential tone. "Was he stricken here in Venice?"

"He was in Florence when he became ill."

"Ah." The banker sat back, visibly relieved. "One can never be too careful. You're too young, of course, but no one who survived it can forget the plague of 1575." Cattona shivered, and with a seeming effort brought his thoughts back to the present. "Were you aware that as executor of your father's estate, Signor Liberti made a number of withdrawals from your account?"

"Yes, of course. He made investments on my behalf."

"I see. Did he deposit the returns at another bank?"

"No, the profits were to go here."

"Signorina Rossetti, I am sorry to say that never happened. Signor Liberti made many withdrawals, but no deposits. I'm afraid there is very little money left in your account."

Her stomach sank. "How little?"

Cattona turned in his chair. Alessandra saw that it was cleverly fitted with wheels on the bottom so that he might easily navigate the shelves full of ledgers lining the room. He rolled along the back wall until he came to a ledger marked with her name, took it from the shelf, and pressed it open on his desk. He turned a few pages, running his index finger along the columns of figures, then stopped and looked back at Alessandra.

"Twenty-eight ducats, fourteen *soldi,* three *piccoli,*" he stated solemnly.

"But that's impossible." Twenty-eight ducats was barely enough to feed herself, Nico, and Bianca for two months.

He turned the open ledger toward her. "My figures are correct."

Alessandra looked down the row of entries, withdrawal after withdrawal, each signed by Lorenzo. "I can't believe this."

"I assure you that my accounting practices adhere to the highest standards," said Cattona, offended. "Every three months, Banco Giro itself audits my books—"

"I didn't mean to imply any misconduct," Alessandra said. "I just don't understand how Signor Liberti could have done this." She looked at the dwindling figures in her account with confusion and dismay. Had Lorenzo deceived her, or had this been accidental, brought about by his sudden illness and death? She would probably never know.

"Signorina Rossetti, have you any other means?"

"No."

"Have you given any thought to what you will do now?"

"I've had no time to think."

"I know that your father left you a fine house in Castello, near the lagoon. Perhaps you might consider selling the house to raise the money you'll need to enter San Sebastiano."

Alessandra stared at him, openmouthed. She was appalled by his assumption that her only option was to take holy orders at San Sebastiano, the Venetian convent founded by the poet and courtesan Veronica Franco as a refuge for "fallen" women. Obviously Cattona knew about her relationship with Lorenzo, or had guessed, but his presumption was rude beyond belief. The only thing worse than being a mistress, Alessandra realized, was being a former mistress; no doubt the banker's disrespectful treatment was what she could expect from now on.

"I could help find a buyer, if you like," the banker continued. "In fact, I might be interested in purchasing it myself . . ."

So that's it, Alessandra thought. Not only am I unworthy of respect, but he has no inhibitions about taking advantage of my misfortune. "Did you think you could frighten me into selling my home to you?" she asked. "No doubt you expect to purchase it for much less than its true worth."

"I assure you, I can offer a fair price."

"I dread to think of how peacefully you would sleep in my house, while I was walled up in a nunnery." Alessandra stood up. "I'd like my money, please."

"Pardon?"

"My money. I'd like to withdraw my money."

The banker was silent for a moment. He looked down at his ledger, perhaps trying to think of a new, more successful approach. But when he looked back at Alessandra, he must have seen that he was defeated. "Very well, then," he said brusquely. "How much?"

"All of it." She untied her purse from her waist and set it on the desk.

"Our deposits are not kept here," he replied with an aggravated wave at her purse, "but in the strong rooms of the Palazzo Camerlenghi, the state Treasurer's Office. It's the tall white building right next to the Rialto Bridge. Take this chit to the main counter"—he took a small paper from the desk drawer and wrote on it as he spoke—"and they'll compensate you." He held out the receipt with a dismissive glance. "Good luck to you, Signorina Rossetti," he said, but Alessandra knew very well that he did not mean it.

The clerk at the Palazzo Camerlenghi finished counting out fourteen *soldi,* then unlocked the largest of the three small chests on the table facing him. He glanced down at the chit from Banco Cattona, then up at Alessandra.

"Twenty-eight ducats, is that correct?"

"Yes," Alessandra said. Her voice sounded hollow. *Twenty-eight ducats. How will we survive with only twenty-eight ducats?* She drew in a ragged breath and brushed her fingers across her tear-stained face. This had to be the worst day of her life, except for the day nearly a year ago when she'd learned of her father's and brother's deaths. Lorenzo was the one who'd told her. Once he'd related the terrible news, he'd dropped to his knees and confessed his great admiration—no, he could no longer deny it, he said—his ardent love for her. He had begged her to allow him to help and protect her. He'd promised to take care of her, and she had believed him. Had she been deceived?

No, Alessandra decided, that could not be true. Lorenzo had loved her, she was sure of that; many times she had regretted that she could not return his passionate feelings. What had happened with her money must have been a mistake or simply bad luck. She only wished that knowing this made her present circumstances easier.

"That's twenty-eight ducats," the clerk said loudly, and Alessandra realized from his tone and vexed expression that he'd already spoken once or twice, but she hadn't heard him. As she took the neatly stacked gold coins from the table, a commotion at the front of the palazzo turned both their heads.

The guards had opened the wide double doors and the noise from the street echoed inside the marble-floored room. A great crowd had gathered outside, and the calls and shouts that arose from it soon captured the attention of everyone in the treasury. Alessandra strained to hear, but she couldn't understand what they were shouting.

The clerk stood up, his eyes riveted on the door. The other clerks had risen, too. Even the other patrons—all of them men, she noticed—were turned toward the door in anticipation. But of what?

Within seconds her curiosity was rewarded. Four bearers carrying an open palanquin entered the Palazzo Camerlenghi. Atop the palanquin, a woman more stunning than any Alessandra had ever seen was comfortably ensconced amongst a collection of silk and velvet pillows. Outside, the shouts grew louder as the doors began to close behind her. "La Celestia!" Alessandra heard quite clearly now.

La Celestia. Even Alessandra had heard of Venice's reigning courtesan, reputedly the most beautiful in the city—a reputation that was well deserved, Alessandra thought as she stared at her. The courtesan's heart-shaped face was framed by a mane of glossy dark hair that spilled around her bare shoulders and her generous breasts, which were almost fully exposed above the low neckline of her gown. Her eyes were large and thick lashed, as exotic as a cat's, her skin as pale and luminous as the moon. She was surrounded by a bewildering number of servants and admirers who pushed their way into the treasury. Judging by the size and sound of the crowd outside, La Celestia's appearance on the Rialto had nearly caused a riot. The courtesan seemed unfazed by the commotion she had created. As the guards shut the heavy doors, she smiled and waved at the men outside who were still calling her name, clearly enjoying the attention, as serenely happy as a beloved queen among her subjects.

The manager of the treasury rushed over to greet her. La Celestia's admirers, a dozen young noblemen, filled the room with their self-importance, talking and laughing among themselves. The bearers set the palanquin down, and two of the noblemen rushed to offer their hands to the courtesan. After a second's hesitation, she settled on the fairer of the two, who gave his rival a smug look as he helped her step down to the floor.

Alessandra gathered her purse and started toward the doors. She was making her way through the crowd when the nobleman whom La Celestia had rebuffed grabbed Alessandra by the arm. Apparently the blow to his pride hadn't been permanent. He wore a stylish blue tunic under his knee-length coat and a self-assured grin.

"What's this?" he said, smiling at her but speaking to the friend at his side. "A young miss out alone, without a veil?"

"This is a pretty problem," his friend said. He was not so well favored nor so fine, but his attitude was equally mocking. "Maid or matron, which do you think?"

"Whether I am married or not is none of your concern," Alessandra said.

"The lady has a tart tongue," the blue dandy said.

"Matron, then, I'd wager, for maids are sweet."

"You are both very rude," Alessandra said. "If you were gentlemen, you would let me pass."

La Celestia turned to face them. "What trouble are you two causing now?" she asked. A smile played across her lips, but her expression was kind. "Can't you see the girl's in mourning?" she chided her friends. "Leave her be."

"Thank you." Alessandra headed toward the doors.

"A moment," La Celestia called. Alessandra turned around. The courtesan moved closer, seeming to glide toward her instead of walk. She cocked her head, eyes questioning. "Haven't I seen you somewhere?"

"No," Alessandra answered without hesitating. Surely she would know at once if she'd met this woman before.

"My mistake," La Celestia said, turning away.

The guards opened the doors for Alessandra and she walked outside. The crowd had dissipated, but a few gawkers still remained, craning their necks to get another look at the courtesan. Alessandra moved quickly past them, clutching her purse, thinking firmly of home.

Death

22 April 1617

The Lane of Broken Vows was a fetid back alley, perpetually cloaked in shadow and strewn with refuse, that burrowed between the tumbledown warehouses of the Cannaregio waterfront. In the most silent hour of the night, under the light of a half-moon, a boy slipped into a dark doorway at the end of the lane. He was a street urchin with pinched features, red-rimmed eyes, and a small, pointed nose that twitched, rodentlike, in moments of uncertainty. He appeared to be no more than eight or nine, but he had been on this earth at least twelve years; or so the nuns of Santa Maria dei Miracoli, whose meager charity had kept him alive, had assured him.

His name was Taddeo da Ponte, and he was a spy.

He sank deeper into the shadows as he heard footsteps approaching. Three men walked single file along the *fondamenta,* then crossed an arched bridge spanning the slender canal known as the Rio della Panada. Moonlight glinted off bobbing sword hilts as the men's shadows flitted across the silvery surface of the water below. Two were French corsairs—Barbary Coast pirates—and one a Spanish *bravo,* a hired man-at-arms. Taddeo had determined at the tavern that they weren't the usual sort of layabout mercenaries who frequented Agostino's tiny pub; the corsairs were men of rank, and the Spanish *bravo* looked a cut above the common thug: tall, strong, with a stony gaze and a silver hoop that dangled from his left earlobe. Taddeo had even been close enough to the Spaniard to see the insignia on his sword hilt: a fox, the mark of Toledo steel and the emblem of the finest rapiers in the world. See where they go and come right back, Agostino had said, but Taddeo had a hunch that he might discover something Batù Vratsa would find worthy of reward.

He wrapped his short cape closer to ward off the damp and glanced up at the mist-shrouded moon. He waited until the men had disappeared into the darkness on the other side of the bridge before leaving his sanctuary, then followed them, soundless as a ghost. Before Agostino had given him work at the tavern, he'd been a link boy, leading the lost and weary through Venice's back streets and alleys. He could move along the *fodere*—the linings—as stealthily as the stray cats and scurrying rats that showed him their secret pathways.

He carefully approached a small *campo* and watched as the men unlocked a fortified door and went inside a warehouse that opened onto the Rio di Cabriotti. He inched around the side of the building and dashed to the edge of the canal just as a gondola glided past and turned into the warehouse's wide, arched canal door.

Taddeo steadied himself against the wall as he carefully stepped sideways along a stone ledge that extended from the alley to the portal. He stooped as he entered, then fell to his hands and knees and crept along the warehouse's back wall. In the dim, flickering torchlight, Taddeo saw that the large room was filled with wooden crates, barrels, and coils of thick rope. The air reeked of damp wood and rotting hemp.

The two corsairs and the Spanish *bravo* stood in an open space at the center of the warehouse, watching as the gondolier secured the boat. The gondola's lantern light reflected off the water and ribbons of yellow undulated on the walls and ceiling. Taddeo slipped down behind one of the crates as a man climbed out of the gondola. He was dressed in the Spanish fashion and very grand, his black velvet doublet embroidered with silver thread, a short fur-lined cape draped over one shoulder. Like the others, he wore both sword and dagger. A thick gold chain, ending in a large medallion, lay across his broad chest.

The Spanish *bravo* bowed briefly. "Your Excellency." He turned to the other two men. "It is my honor to introduce you to my lord, the marquis of Bedmar, Spanish ambassador to Venice." He looked to his master. "May I present Captains Jacques Pierre and Nicholas Regnault."

"Your Excellency," they said in unison, bowing low.

The Spanish ambassador? Taddeo's nose twitched and the tips of his ears tingled, as they always did when he felt excitement, apprehension, or fear. In the two years he had worked as the eyes and ears of the state, he had never spied on anyone other than a few lowly mercenaries, some local tradesmen, and the tavern whores, and for a moment Taddeo considered running away; he had a sudden premonition that something bad would come of this. Then he thought of Batù Vratsa and knew he had no choice but to stay.

Friend to orphans and outcasts, Batù had said when he'd introduced himself, fixing Taddeo with his chilling reptilian gaze; but no one would claim friendship with Batù, you simply did what he asked. *And Batù will ask about this. How will I look into those cold pale eyes and lie?* Taddeo rubbed his quivering nose and trained his ears on the exchange.

"Do you agree to our terms?" Bedmar asked. His trim, pointed beard had a few streaks of gray in it, but he possessed the vigor and confidence of a much younger man.

The French corsairs exchanged a careful glance. Pierre spoke. "We will of course have to propose it to our men. As I told Monsieur Sanchez . . ."

Pierre, Regnault, Sanchez, Taddeo memorized. Pierre was slight and dark, with a hawkish nose and nervous hands; Regnault was fair haired, ruddy faced, and beefy.

"I'm sure that the entire crew of the *Camarata* will follow me, but we are less certain of the sentiments among Captain Regnault's men," Pierre finished.

"We're offering better pay than you receive from Venice."

"It isn't just the money, Ambassador. They'll want to know they're not being led to a slaughter."

"This is a weak city, unaccustomed to battle," Bedmar replied. "The Republic's forces are heavily engaged elsewhere. Surely your men are not afraid of a few *arsenalotti.*"

Arsenalotti? The shipbuilders at Venice's Arsenale did double duty as the Doge's bodyguard in case of attack.

"There will be spoils for those who are valiant," the ambassador went on. "Think of it, the treasures of Venice. Unlike any they've ever . . ." His voice dropped to a murmur.

They're talking about an attack on Venice. He must tell Agostino . . . must tell Batù. Taddeo placed his palms on the floor and leaned forward, straining to hear. A fat, wet rat scuttled across his hands. He jumped and fell back against the crate.

"What was that?" Bedmar said sharply.

Taddeo froze.

"Search the room," the ambassador ordered. Three pairs of feet started off in three different directions.

Taddeo quickly backed away from the crate and crawled toward the canal door. He was inches from his escape when a meaty hand grabbed him by the neck and pulled him to his feet. Regnault gripped Taddeo's wrists and marched him to the center of the room, where the other men had gathered again.

"It's just a boy," Regnault said, holding him out like a fish on a line.

"It's the serving boy from the tavern," Sanchez added. His tone was suspicious; any second he would denounce Taddeo as a spy.

Taddeo countered his hostile stare with a practiced wide-eyed innocence. "Yes, my lords"—he bowed awkwardly, as his hands were still restrained—"my master sent me after you, to return the money that you overpaid for the wine you enjoyed in his humble inn."

"This is nonsense," Sanchez said. "What tavern owner turns away silver?"

"My lords, I assure you, I have the coins in my boot. If you'll unloose me," he said to Regnault. Bedmar nodded once and the corsair released him. Taddeo knew that surprise and speed were his only allies. He reached into his boot, straightened, and plunged his short dagger into Regnault's sword hand. The captain bellowed more loudly than an angry bull. Taddeo bolted while the others were still baffled by Regnault's sudden outburst, and was out on the ledge before they had drawn their swords and started after him.

Blast the moon, he thought as he ran frantically, making his way through the smallest and darkest of Cannaregio's warrenlike streets. Along the Alley of the Curly-Headed Woman, to the Street of the Seven Virgins, through the tiny, malodorous passageway behind the butcher and the tallow maker. His mind raced as he ran. *Must tell Agostino . . . must tell Batù. Stick to the shadows, blast the moon.*

He ran across Ponte Arrivosa and through the Calle Volto. Sanchez appeared at the end of the lane, running toward him. Taddeo turned back, only to discover the ambassador blocking his escape. Taddeo collided with him, the cold metal of the ambassador's gold medallion striking his cheek. Bedmar gripped his arm with one iron hand and looked down on him with an enigmatic smile. Sanchez trotted up to them.

"You should know better than to wag your tongue in a tavern," Bedmar scolded. "This little gutter rat can listen and speak the same as a grown man, and you've led him right to me."

"Forgive me, Excellency. It won't happen again." Sanchez hefted his sword and gestured at Taddeo.

They were going to kill him, Taddeo realized. He felt faint. His heart was beating faster than a rabbit's.

"No need," the ambassador said, and sheathed his sword.

Taddeo nearly collapsed with relief. "Your Excellency," he exclaimed, "you are a man of great mercy . . ."

There was a flash of steel in the moonlight, then excruciating pain. Bedmar's dagger sliced through his larynx with a searing, burning agony, an unholy baptism of fire and ice. Taddeo tried to scream but couldn't; his throat had instantly filled with blood. It was like a nightmare he'd once had in which he'd been cornered and desperate and yet unable to make a sound. He clutched his throat, feeling as though he were drowning, and his hand came away slick with blood, glistening and black in the moonlight. Taddeo looked up at the ambassador, his mouth open, his eyes pleading. Bedmar looked past him as if he were no longer there. But I'm still alive, aren't I? he thought, confused. *Must tell Agostino . . . must tell Batù . . . an attack on Venice . . .*

Bedmar released his arm and Taddeo fell to the ground. He heard the two men hurrying away, their footsteps on the cobbled lane gradually becoming fainter. He was vaguely aware of the gushing wetness at his throat, of his life streaming from him, his warm blood pooling on the cold stone. *Must tell . . . he must . . . what?* He couldn't remember. Taddeo turned his face heavenward. The moon rocked wildly in the sky, the stars whirled in circles, blurred, and grew dim, until at last they disappeared altogether.

The Empress

26 April 1617

PERCHED IN FRONT of her easel, Alessandra skillfully drew the scalloped edges of a budding rose, putting the final touches to her charcoal sketch. A small, snowy flower drifted down from the pear tree that shaded her. She glanced up at the tangle of white-blossomed branches outlined by clear blue sky, then out at the surrounding garden, a riot of new growth and bright blooms. It was a spectacular spring day, warm enough that the cool breeze off the lagoon brought welcome relief.

"My lady!" Bianca, her housekeeper and cook, burst out of the back door and walked along the garden path as quickly as her plump, aging body allowed. She waved a letter in the air. "From Padua!"

Alessandra eagerly took the letter from her.

My dearest Alessandra:

My father has told me of your request for help and his reply. I regret that he has so little to offer—at present he thinks only of his two daughters yet unmarried and in need of dowries. As for his suggestion that you take holy orders, I can only hope that you will, in time, forgive him. For a man with a wife and three daughters, he has little understanding of a woman's heart and mind. Although I have a few friends who have found peace in their vocation, I know very well that you would not be happy in the convent.

There is another possibility, which I have already discussed with my husband. We both want you to know that you are welcome to live with us in Padua for as long as you may need. I suspect your first impulse will be to say no, but I beg you to please consider it.

Your loving cousin,
Giovanna

"Well?" Bianca prompted as Alessandra folded the letter and set it beside her on the stone bench.

"They cannot help," Alessandra said. "Unless we're willing to go to Padua."

"Padua," Bianca repeated without enthusiasm.

"I would not force you to go with me."

"Did you think you would leave me behind?"

"No, I only thought you did not care to go—"

"If it's to be Padua, then so it is," Bianca said philosophically. "I will not leave you, my lady."

"Thank you, Bianca."

Bianca and her husband, Nico, had been with Alessandra's family for years, ever since her mother had died. They'd suffered with her the tragedy of her father's and brother's deaths, and stayed with her even after she had become Lorenzo's mistress. They were discreet and they did not judge, and in spite of their advancing years—Nico was almost fifty—they were hard workers, dependable, trustworthy, and always concerned for her care.

"You think about it," Bianca said. "I've got our supper to get on."

Giovanna's offer was kind, but Alessandra could not imagine leaving Venice, or leaving her home. In this very spot she'd spent many of the happiest moments of her life, drawing, reading, studying with Jacopo. Everything she cherished was here, in her house and garden overlooking the lagoon. From here she could watch ships sailing from the port at Malamocco to the Molo, the dock near the Doge's Palace, or gaze upon the shimmering lagoon as it changed with the seasons. Even though the view from the parlor was better, Alessandra preferred the garden, where she could feel the sun on her skin, could smell the salty Adriatic and revel in the earthy, sweet scents of the roses, the blackberry vines, the herb garden that Bianca had planted.

And yet everyone, even Giovanna in her own way, was telling her that it wasn't proper for her to remain in this house by herself. She was an embarrassment—a woman alone, not married, not widowed, not a virgin with a dowry. It wasn't suitable. She thought of a popular adage: *Aut maritus, aut marus:* If not a husband to govern her, then a girl needed a wall to contain her.

In Venice, this was more than a saying, it was common practice: hundreds of Venice's daughters had been consigned to the convent. Few of them went willingly, for it had nothing to do with religious vocation. In true Venetian fashion, it was a matter of money. The typical marriage portion settled on the daughter of an aristocratic family was twenty thousand ducats; few families could afford to marry off more than one daughter. The not-so-marriageable girls—the sick or lame, the unlovely, the obstinate or ungovernable—were forced to take the veil. The cost of putting a girl in the convent—for even convents required a dowry—was substantially less than a marriage portion, only a thousand ducats. The religious orders had kept many a Venetian aristocrat from financial ruin.

In the fifty convents scattered around the city and the islands of the lagoon, a few thousand women whose names were listed in the Libro d'Oro, the register of Venetian aristocracy, were immured for life. There they lived behind walls intended to separate them from society, urged by the patriarch to meditate on the glories of their virginal state.

The reality was somewhat less lofty than that, Alessandra knew. Most of these women had no true calling for the monastic life and performed their vows with little enthusiasm. They spent their time embroidering, gossiping, and socializing with visiting friends and family members in the convent parlor: a place open to visitors but accessible to the nuns only through grated windows. It was an insignificant life of trivial pleasures. No wonder the convents were rife with flirtations and romances—stories of affairs between nuns and priests were commonplace, so much so that Patriarch Priuli had condemned the convents as being no better than brothels. But who could blame the sisters, for what of life was left for them to live?

In her own case, the convent would be even less tolerable. Alessandra wasn't nobly born, and without money for a conventual dowry, her only option was to become a *conserva,* a lay sister who carried out the menial chores that the more privileged nuns did not want to do. The thought of spending the rest of her life behind convent walls, the servant of women who were less educated than herself, without books, without music, without freedom, was unbearable to her. Perhaps she had too much pride, but Alessandra saw the convent as a living death, an entombment. Better she had been born a man; she would have rather taken her chances with Jacopo on the open sea than kiss the stony ground and take those irrevocable vows.

But if not the convent, then what? Alessandra lay back on the bench. The dappled sunlight made her feel warm and drowsy. She would have to do something about money—what little she had wouldn't last past August. She'd already made economies: Bianca had made over her winter dresses for the summer, and she'd had to dismiss Zuan, her gondolier. Nico would have to suffice as gondolier from now on. Perhaps she'd send him to the Ghetto tomorrow with an item for the secondhand shops. What would she sell first? The painted chests, the tapestries, the lute made in Verona? It pained her to think of it; these were not just her belongings, but her mother's, her father's, Jacopo's. But it was either that or starve. She had a vision of herself, Nico, and Bianca living in the house as it slowly emptied, hanging on until there was nothing left. And what then? It was an impossible question to answer.

She awoke to the sound of a monkey chattering and the feeling that someone was watching her. Alessandra opened her eyes and gasped. Above her towered a blackamoor, the darkness of his skin accentuated by the bright blue sky behind him. He had a long, lugubrious face and was dressed in a gondolier's uniform of striped jerkin and scarlet tights.

"Signorina," he said, bowing low. His voice was very deep, and oddly accented. "My mistress wishes a word."

Alessandra sat up. Into her view walked La Celestia, resplendent in a gown of gold cloth so brilliant it was as if a second sun had come into the garden. In flagrant disregard of the sumptuary laws, she was dripping with jewels. Her throat was circled by a half dozen strands of pearls, her earlobes weighted with diamonds, her bodice studded with rubies and emeralds. Behind her stood a pert young maidservant and a boy trailing a small monkey on a leash. The monkey was outfitted in a purple silk jerkin and a tiny, tasseled cap. When he saw Alessandra, he jumped up and down and screeched, then scampered up to perch on the boy's shoulder, chattering all the while. Alessandra was tempted to pinch herself. Surely this was the strangest dream she'd ever had.

"Charming," La Celestia said as she took in the garden, the lagoon, the four-story house with its pointed Moorish windows. She came closer to Alessandra and studied her face with a curious but pleased expression. "As I thought, you're very pretty when you're not crying." She squinted at the sky. "Shall we go inside? The sun is ruinous to my complexion."

Alessandra stood up. "Of course." She was burning with questions, but she knew it wasn't polite to ask. She led La Celestia upstairs, to the parlor on the second floor. The room was shaded and cool, the thick damask curtains drawn against the afternoon sun. The courtesan looked over the furnishings and the wood-paneled walls with a practiced eye.

"It's a bit plain for such a well-situated house, but with some work it could be handsome enough," she said. "I know some very clever artisans who could help you with the decor."

"Thank you, but—"

"No Petrarch?" La Celestia asked as she inspected a row of books lining the fireplace mantel. Alessandra watched her fingers pass over the volumes: Virgil, Aristotle, Ovid, Boccaccio, Dante. "You should always have a pocket Petrarch at hand. The finest ladies always carry a copy." She looked over at her maid. "Isabella?"

Isabella curtsied and help up a small, beautifully bound edition of Petrarch's poems.

"See? I always carry one." La Celestia looked back at the books. "Have you read all of these?"

"Yes."

"Including the Latin and Greek?"

"Yes."

"Hmmm . . ." Her expression was inscrutable. "There is such a thing as being too well educated." She turned to the lute in the corner. "Do you play?"

"Yes."

"Sing and dance?"

"Yes . . . a little," she added honestly.

La Celestia stepped over to the best chair in the room, spread her skirt, and sat down. She nodded at Isabella and the girl silently slipped out the door, apparently heading downstairs to wait with the gondolier, the boy, and the monkey. "Your manners as a hostess could use some improvement," the courtesan said. "Aren't you going to offer me a refreshment?"

"Forgive me, but I don't understand why you're here," Alessandra said.

"To discuss your plans for the future, of course. What are you going to do now that Signor Liberti is dead?"

"You know about Lorenzo?" Alessandra was so astonished that she blurted out his Christian name.

"Very little goes on in Venice that I don't know about." Apparently La Celestia took some pleasure in surprising her, for she wore a self-satisfied smile. "It took a few days, but I finally remembered where I'd seen you—at a *comedia* at Ca' Pesaro that you attended with Signor Liberti. You turned no small number of heads there, though you seemed to be quite unaware of the effect you had. As you were the other day at the Palazzo Camerlenghi." Her expression grew serious. "I've heard that you are now without means, but surely

Lorenzo left you with something: jewels, houses, land, livestock?"

"No . . . well, some gold earrings, and he paid the taxes on this house." That Lorenzo may have paid the taxes with her own money was something Alessandra chose not to say. The courtesan's tone made her feel defensive.

"Is that all?" La Celestia asked.

"Yes."

"You mean you have nothing put away?"

Alessandra shook her head.

"I was told that you were smart. Have you so immersed yourself in those books that you've given no thought to your future?"

"How could I possibly have known that Lorenzo would die?"

La Celestia burst out laughing. "My girl, he was a man. Men die all the time. They're positively geniuses at it, always running off to war or some such thing. It's a woman's destiny to be abandoned by men, in one way or another. Tedious, but you must admit it's true. Your mistake was to rely on a man to take care of you."

"But you yourself . . . ," Alessandra ventured.

"You're thinking that I'm a living contradiction of my own advice. There you're wrong. I don't rely on one man, I rely on many. That way, if one of them dies, the effect is not felt so strongly. A wiser course for you to follow in the future."

The future? Alessandra thought. *What future?* La Celestia waited patiently for Alessandra to comprehend her meaning.

"Are you suggesting"—Alessandra knitted her brow; she would be embarrassed if she had misunderstood—"that I become a courtesan?"

"I admit that was my intention in coming here. However, I'm concerned about your lack of business acumen. You sold yourself very ill."

"Sold myself?" Alessandra felt her cheeks flush.

"You might not like the sound of the words, but the difference between being a kept mistress and a courtesan is only one of degree. You bartered away your most precious commodity, your maidenhood, for a few baubles and back taxes." La Celestia clucked softly. "Not even a pearl on those earrings?"

"No," Alessandra admitted.

"It grieves me deeply," she sighed. "With your pretty face, you could have sold your virginity for a very high price. *Numerous* times." She shook her head. "But no regrets, I always say—there's no profit in them. So, what will you do? I take it the convent doesn't appeal to you."

"No."

"Any suitors on the horizon?"

"No."

"Yet you hesitate."

"You make it sound as if being a courtesan is easy. But I've heard of women who are beaten, or have their faces slashed, or worse. And what of the French disease?"

"There are dangers, that is true. But life is full of danger, whether or not one is a courtesan. There are ways to avoid those problems. I'll teach you myself. You do realize this is a highly unusual offer. Most women would pay dearly for my secrets."

"Why are you offering to do this for me?"

"Something you will learn soon enough is that even the most beautiful women grow old." A shadow crossed La Celestia's eyes and for a moment Alessandra caught a glimpse of the woman behind the courtesan's polished facade, and realized that La Celestia was indeed older than she first appeared. The sunlight that slipped through the curtains revealed tiny lines around her eyes, deepening creases at the corners of her mouth.

"There will come a time when men will no longer pay so handsomely for my favors," La Celestia went on, "but I refuse to make the mistakes that other courtesans make. Instead of ignoring the future, I'm planning for it. For my instruction, and for introductions to the richest and most distinguished men in Venice, there is a price: twenty-five percent of your earnings."

"That seems rather high."

"Does it? Why don't I put it to you as my mother put it to me: 'You can become a courtesan—not a prostitute, mind you, but a *cortigiana onestà*—and enjoy riches the likes of which you've never imagined, or you can sell candles on the church steps and live in poverty and filth.' You don't seem to have many more alternatives than I did."

"Perhaps not, but—"

"Tell me, why did you choose to become Lorenzo's mistress instead of taking orders? You must have known that you would not be accepted in most society, that it would make it much more difficult for you to marry well."

"I wanted my freedom."

"Exactly. 'Freedom is the most precious gem a courtesan possesses. Given this privilege, even infamy seems honorable to her.' Francesco Pona wrote that. Once you're accustomed to freedom, it's impossible to give it up. And believe me, there is no freedom in poverty."

"I believe I have more choices than what you're offering."

"Do you? I see only three: you can become a nun, you can become a courtesan, or you can join the whores on the Bridge of Tits and sell yourself for cheap. If you're smart, you'll be at my house Wednesday at noon." She stood up and walked to the door. "Tell me, did you love him?"

"Lorenzo?" It seemed shameful to admit that she had never loved him, that she suspected she would never love anyone. "I don't know."

The courtesan gave her a penetrating look. "That's good. It's better if you don't love them. You must take my word on this."

Chapter Four

CLAIRE PUSHED OPEN a heavy glass door and walked into Forsythe Academy's main corridor. Meredith had called her that morning and insisted that Claire meet her at the school at one o'clock. As she turned right off the corridor and into the suite of offices where Meredith worked, she was still unsure as to why she'd been summoned.

"Good, I was hoping you'd get here first," Meredith said as Claire entered. Her office was reminiscent of her well-furnished home, with floor-to-ceiling bookshelves, decorator lamps, and two upholstered chairs facing an antique mahogany desk.

"First?" Claire asked.

"Someone's going to be joining us."

"Who?"

"Why don't I start at the beginning?"

"Fine."

"The father of one of our students is getting married next week. His second marriage, obviously. He and his new wife will be honeymooning in the south of France. Originally, his daughter was going to stay with her mother for the summer, but her mother is . . . well, she's not well. She's in the hospital, in fact. This morning he called to ask if we knew anyone, perhaps a teacher, who could take his daughter to Paris for a week. That way, he and his new wife can enjoy their honeymoon, then go back to Paris, pick up the daughter, and spend another week *en famille* before coming home. But summer school begins in a week and I'm shorthanded as it is."

"Are you suggesting that I take this kid to Paris?"

"No! To Venice. The dates of their trip and your conference coincide perfectly. I spoke to him already and he said it was fine as long as Gwendolyn is in Paris in time to meet them. I get the feeling he's desperate. Apparently the new wife isn't keen on having a stepdaughter along for the entire honeymoon."

"And what am I supposed to do with her while I'm at the conference?"

"Take her with you. She's not a child, she's fourteen. Tell her to sit still and shut up for the duration, then do something fun together afterward."

"I don't know how to have fun with kids," Claire protested.

"You don't like kids?"

"I didn't say I didn't like them, it's just that I haven't been around teenagers since . . . since I was a teenager."

"I'm around teenagers all the time, and they're not any different than we were. Most of them are really quite nice. Gwen's a normal kid. Perfectly normal. But the thing that's most important to remember about this plan is that Gwendolyn's father is very well off, and he's going to pay for everything. He may even cover the cost of the conference and throw in a little extra for your time."

"You're joking."

"I'm completely serious." Meredith was grinning, her eyebrows raised in a positive slant, but the pen in her right hand rapidly tapped the desk, revealing her anxious energy.

"What is it you're not telling me?" Claire asked.

"There was an incident that you'll have to be discreet about. In other words, you can't discuss it with Gwendolyn. Her father injured his foot a few days ago in a . . . a golfing accident."

"Someone ran over his foot with a golf cart?"

"No, someone punctured it with a bullet."

"This girl's father is the guy who got shot by his ex-wife?"

"Yes."

"Which means that this girl's mother is the woman who shot him."

"Yes."

"But you just said she was normal, perfectly normal. Having a mother who shoots people is not normal!"

"Keep it down, he's going to be here any minute. You have to pretend that you don't know anything about this."

"I thought you said her mother was ill, that she was in the hospital."

"She is. She's in the psych ward at Mass General." Meredith shrugged in reply to Claire's perturbed glare. "Temporary insanity is an illness. At least, that's the position her attorney is taking."

"You must be temporarily insane to think that I could be a chaperone."

"You don't want to do this?"

"No, I don't want to do this."

"Then let me lend you the money for the trip."

"No, I couldn't accept it." The night before she'd tried to estimate how much it would cost to go to Venice; once she'd added up airfare, hotel, food, and incidentals, it had been well over three thousand dollars. Even at tony prep schools like Forsythe, assistant deans weren't highly paid. The money Meredith was speaking of was probably everything she'd managed to save. "I don't know when I could pay it back," Claire continued. "What if I'm never able to pay it back? It would ruin our friendship. And that would be much worse than not going to Venice."

"I'm not so sure."

"What does that mean?"

"It means that I'm worried about you. You've hardly left your house in two years. Except for the nights we've gone out together, which I can count on one hand, I don't think I've seen you dressed in anything other than sweats and those ridiculous flannel pajamas."

"You think my pajamas are ridiculous?"

"When you wear them for days at a time, yes."

"They happen to be comfortable and it cuts down on the laundry."

"How you dress is not really the point. What I'm saying is . . . look, I might not have the husband and the kids and the picket fence and all that, but I do have relationships that last longer than one dinner."

"The only thing that's important to me right now is finishing my dissertation."

"Claire, you know I love you, and I think it's great that you're so passionate about the seventeenth century and care so much about what people were like then, what they thought, what they ate, what kind of fork they used—"

"It's interesting you should mention that. Forks were almost unheard of outside Italy in the early seventeenth century. Travelers to Venice often remarked on their use, they were so unusual."

"See? That's what I mean."

"What's what you mean?"

"You know about stuff from four hundred years ago, but most of the time you don't seem to know what day it is. You need to get out of your house, and you need to go to Venice. Your adviser said it was vital to learn everything you could about that competing book. If you don't, aren't you risking everything you've worked so hard for?"

Claire sighed. Meredith was right, of course, as usual. "This girl's father has agreed to pay for everything?" she asked.

"Everything," Meredith said, nodding.

Suddenly Venice wasn't out of the question, and Claire realized how desperately she wanted to go. In just over a week, she could be on a plane, on her way there. There'd be some kid sitting beside her, but so what? She could find out what this Cambridge professor had written and, even better, she could spend the rest of the week in the Biblioteca Nazionale Marciana, Venice's library, doing research. A week wasn't much time, but it was better than nothing. She'd be able to check the original documents for some of the sources she'd already cited; best of all, Alessandra Rossetti's diaries were there.

"And, as I told you the other day, there are Italian—" Meredith stopped as they heard a man's voice calling out an uncertain "Hello?" from the reception area.

Meredith stood up as Edward Fry appeared at the door. Claire made a quick appraisal: tall, medium build, vaguely athletic. About forty-five, she guessed, with a golfer's tan and attractive crinkles around his eyes when he smiled. He was casually attired in jeans and a polo shirt. The most remarkable thing about him was the plaster cast on his left foot and his hospital-issue cane, and Claire was reminded of why her assistance was being sought. It occurred to her that he might have done something truly terrible to deserve his ex-wife's fury. She was somewhat surprised to discover that Edward Fry was a pleasant man, and Claire soon realized that she'd made up her mind: she would go to Venice as his daughter's chaperone.

Honestly, how bad could it be?

Fortitude

21 May 1617

"ONCE MORE, ALL the way across the room," La Celestia said.

Alessandra hitched up her skirt and took a tentative step in her new *choppines,* the high, platform shoes favored by Venice's style-conscious women.

"Don't pull at your dress, it looks awkward. Your arms should rest gracefully at your sides, like so." La Celestia waved Alessandra back. "Start again."

Again? Alessandra sighed impatiently. La Celestia was a bigger tyrant than Signor Ligorio, her old Latin master.

"I heard that," La Celestia said. "Any time you're ready to give up, just remember that the convent awaits."

Alessandra tottered back to the end of the room. La Celestia stood at the other end, a good distance away. The courtesan's bedchamber was larger than most salons; it was easily twice the size of Alessandra's largest room at home. In the three weeks since she'd first come here, she hadn't quite overcome her astonishment at the luxuriousness of La Celestia's palazzo. Each day she found another detail at which to marvel: soaring ceilings painted with clouds and angels or scenes from mythology; endless mosaic tile floors, layered with sumptuous carpets; a *camera d'oro*—or chamber of gold, with walls coated in gold leaf—adjacent to the *portego* that glowed in the afternoons with a light so rich it appeared almost liquid. The walls were covered with tapestries, ornate mirrors, and portraits of La Celestia—Alessandra had counted eight so far. On the top floor was a lavish room just for bathing, containing a huge tub where the courtesan took her daily ablutions, in water steeped with fragrant herbs, or, twice a week, in milk.

The entire house was filled with sunlight, fresh flowers, and, in the afternoons, the sweet melodies of La Celestia's young daughters, Caterina and Elena, at their music lessons. Peacocks strutted on the *altana,* the rooftop loggia; finches, parakeets, and larks in gilded cages twittered and filled the air with their song; the courtesan's pet monkey, Odomo, had his own small room furnished with a tiny canopy bed and brocade chairs. Servants of every sort appeared and disappeared as effortlessly as apparitions, always ready to fulfill the slightest request. If Alessandra had not known otherwise, she would have thought that a princess lived in this palace.

Alessandra started across the room again, trying to imitate the graceful, gliding walk La Celestia had shown her. Why was it impossible to hold her arms elegantly while she was thinking about them? The harder she tried, the more they felt like two sausages dangling at her sides. And her dress, one of La Celestia's that had been fitted for her, was so tight that it itched unbearably. She reached up to scratch her back, and in the instant she took her mind off her feet, she tripped and fell in a heap on the floor.

"By the Virgin!" La Celestia exclaimed.

"It's this dress," said Alessandra, exasperated. "Is it necessary for it to squeeze the life out of me?"

"It's not the life I'm trying to squeeze out of you, it's your bosom. Little good it will do you, though, if you can't manage to walk like a lady."

"If my faults are so pronounced—if even my breasts are inadequate—then what on earth am I doing here?"

"Great beauties are not born, they are made. There isn't a woman in the world who wouldn't benefit from a bit of paint or a more flattering fashion."

Alessandra rubbed her ankle. A bit of paint? Clearly, in her case it required substantially more than that. In La Celestia's adjoining dressing room, there was an array of lotions, powders, oils, and unguents, each with a specific use, that La Celestia insisted she learn. La Celestia's maidservants, under her supervision, had primped and prettied Alessandra to the point that she hardly recognized herself. A few sessions on the sunny *altana* had lightened her hair to a golden blond; she'd been bathed in rosewater, had had her nails trimmed and buffed, her legs and underarms depilated, her hair and skin massaged with perfumed oils, her eyebrows shaped. She'd been fussed over so much that sometimes she felt like one of Bianca's game hens, plucked and trussed.

"Ready to try again?"

"I feel as if you want me to be someone other than who I am."

"Precisely. To be a truly successful courtesan, you must be more than a woman. You must be a goddess."

"Is that all?" Sarcasm laced Alessandra's voice.

"Do you believe that men think of me as just another woman?"

"No, but you're . . . you. You're La Celestia. You aren't like other women."

"How do you think that came to be? Luck? A happy accident? Did you imagine that I was born to the life I have now?" She sat down in one of the chairs near the marble fireplace and motioned for Alessandra to sit next to her. Alessandra dutifully slipped out of the *chopines* and, dragging her skirts, limped over to the empty chair.

"Not many people know what I'm going to tell you," La Celestia said. "I wouldn't like it to be repeated. Do you understand?"

"Yes." She'd already learned that La Celestia's angelic countenance concealed a calculating mind and an iron will. It would be foolish to cross her.

"Good." La Celestia smiled, but there was little warmth in it. "I was born in Treviso, not Venice. My mother was a prostitute. My father was a French soldier who never married my mother. The way we lived was . . . mean. Squalid. It was nothing like this," she said with a gesture that encompassed her luxurious bedchamber and its furnishings: the numerous carved and gilded chests and the palatial bed covered with gold-embroidered white silk linens.

"My mother was uneducated, but she was shrewd. By the time I turned five, she could see that I was going to be beautiful, and she used every resource at her disposal to groom me for the life she knew I could have. She made sure that I learned to read, that I studied music, singing, and deportment, that my manners were impeccable.

"When I was fourteen, we came to Venice for the sole purpose of launching my career as a courtesan. My father was long gone, but my mother had managed to save enough money to pay for our journey here and board and lodging for two weeks. Only two weeks. If her plan did not work, we would be out on the streets, poor, begging, and alone in a city where we knew no one.

"Even though we could barely afford it, we took rooms at an expensive inn on the Grand Canal, near the Rialto, so we would be close to the place where all the richest and most influential men in Venice congregated. On the very first morning after we arrived, my mother went out for a few hours, returning with a blue silk dress more beautiful than any I'd ever seen. She'd gone to the Ghetto and pawned her only piece of jewelry so that I would have something pretty to wear. Once she'd fitted the dress, and oiled and combed my hair, she bade me stand by the window overlooking the canal.

"After a while, a gondola came by and stopped under the window. In it was a young lord, dressed very fine." La Celestia smiled faintly. "I even remember what he wore: red hose and a red feather in his *biretta.* When he saw me, he burst into raptures.

"'Oh, my glorious lady!' he called. 'My heart is aflame! Your beauty is such as I have never seen! From whence do you come? Are you a stranger to this city? You must be, for certainly you are an angel, not a woman! Speak to me, my angel! If you cannot speak, show me a sign and I shall be yours forever, for your loveliness is beyond compare!'

"And on and on he went. Everyone nearby was curious to see the great beauty who had captured this young lord's heart. More gondole came to the window, and soon there were men of all sorts staring up at me. They shouted at me to step farther out on the balcony, to show myself, to let them feast their eyes. I grew afraid and went inside instead, to ask my mother what to do.

"And I saw something I'd never seen before, and would never see again. My mother's shoulders shook with mirth, and tears rolled down her face: she was laughing and crying at the same time. I said, 'Mother, why do you laugh? Why do you cry?'

"She replied, 'I cry because I know now that everything is going to be fine, and we will not end up begging in the streets. I laugh because in singing your praises, that ridiculous boy has become a lyric poet—he babbles on far beyond what I paid him to say!' "

Alessandra's eyes grew wide. "She paid him?"

La Celestia laughed. "My mother didn't believe in leaving anything to chance. However, this young lord kept coming back to see me, even without further recompense. But no matter; soon he was just one among many.

"Every day thereafter, all the men in Venice came by to get a glimpse of the new beauty who had just arrived in town. And a glimpse is all they got—for as I said, my mother was shrewd, and she played upon their curiosity like a fine musician plays an instrument. One day they might see a bare arm, or an ankle, or my hair cascading down my back, or my face in profile. I'm not saying I wasn't pretty—I was—but this mystery combined with the imagination of men's minds was incredibly powerful. Soon it was all over Venice that I was the most beautiful woman ever to grace the city. That I was also a virgin and destined to be a *cortigiana onestà* created a frenzy that surprised even my mother. Men sent their servants bearing all sort of gifts: fruit, flowers, jewels, expensive cloth. Poets wrote sonnets about me, and artists pleaded to paint my portrait.

"One day, one of the men who was courting me recited a poem in which he called me 'La Celestia.' In it he wrote that I was as beautiful and as remote as the heavens, and somehow the name stuck. From then on, I was no longer little Faustina Emiliana Zolta from Treviso, but only La Celestia. Even my mother began calling me La Celestia because she understood the benefits immediately: I was transformed from a pretty girl into something akin to a goddess. My new name only added to my mystique; men became absolutely crazed with passion for me. Fights broke out in the gondole that gathered under my window. When the passions were at their most fervent, my mother began the bargaining. She sold my virginity six times. Amazing what you can do with gum Arabic, rosewater, and sheep's blood, and, most of all, men's ardent desire to believe." The courtesan's eyes sparkled with irony as she looked at Alessandra through her thick, dark lashes.

"My point is this: being a great courtesan isn't simply a matter of beauty, charm, or even sexuality. It's about desire and fantasy. If men wanted only sex, then any common prostitute could satisfy them. You must ask yourself why the same man who would toss a few *soldi* to a tavern whore would bring me precious jewels. What men really want, and what they rarely find, is a woman who captures their hearts, minds, and souls. And no less important, a woman who flatters their vanity. Men know that when they conquer a woman whom every man covets, they are raised higher in other men's esteem."

"And how am I going to be all that?"

"I'll help you as my mother helped me. You know, to this day I seldom allow my feet to touch ground in public—it helps to preserve the illusion of my otherworldly nature. We'll have to think of some way to present you."

"Are you going to make me stand in a window?"

"No, we should try something new, something no one's done before. In the meantime, you still have a lot to learn."

The voyeur's chamber was as elaborate as one of La Celestia's jewelry chests, with walls swathed in a patterned red silk and cleverly disguised to conceal the closet-size alcove hidden between the bedroom and hallway. Alessandra peered through the peephole to the bedchamber, where La Celestia would soon arrive with one of her lovers. The scene that met her eye was superbly arranged for seduction. Except for a few candles that flickered in the far corners, the room was lit only by the roaring fire. Its welcoming corona illuminated the thick rug that had been placed in front of the hearth, and the small table set with a bowl of fruit, a carafe of wine, and two glasses. La Celestia's extravagant bed waited, tantalizingly, at the very edge of the firelight, its white silk sheets glowing with a warm, subtle sheen.

"Did you enjoy sex with Signor Liberti?" La Celestia had asked Alessandra earlier that day.

"I suppose," she had answered slowly, wishing that she didn't feel embarrassed by the question. If she were going to be a courtesan, she would have to overcome her reserve. "It wasn't terrible."

La Celestia laughed. "Not terrible? That isn't much of an endorsement. But accurate, as I recall. Sex with Lorenzo was rather . . . uninspired."

"You and Lorenzo?" Alessandra said, astonished.

"I'm very popular," La Celestia replied with a coy smile and a shrug. "The thing is, at eighteen you're too old to pass for a virgin, and I'm probably not the only one who knows about Signor Liberti, so that method of captivation is closed to us. It would behoove you instead to learn more of the arts of love. Since I'm certain that Lorenzo didn't teach you, I suppose I'll have to do it myself."

"Is that how you learned, from another courtesan?"

"My mother showed me a few things, but most of it I learned on my own. As it turns out, I am very well suited to my profession. I have a natural desire for love that is not easily satisfied. While this isn't an absolute requirement for a courtesan, it certainly makes life more pleasant." She looked at Alessandra searchingly. "Did you ever feel pleasure with Lorenzo?"

"Sometimes . . . not always."

"I'm not surprised. I don't think he gave much thought to a woman's gratification. Happily, though, not all men are like that. In fact, this evening I'm seeing one of my current favorites—he's young, vigorous, and quite remarkable in bed, as you'll see."

"As I'll see?" The shocked look on Alessandra's face must have been extreme indeed, for La Celestia burst into laughter.

"You won't be in the room with us," she said, and then she'd taken Alessandra to the voyeur's chamber. "He'll never know you're here," she promised. "Tonight you will stay, watch, and learn."

Alessandra smoothed her nightgown over her thighs and kneeled on the upholstered bench beneath the peephole for a better view. As to her own inquiry of La Celestia—what more was there to sex beyond what she'd done with Lorenzo?—the courtesan had remained infuriatingly silent. "What you'll see tonight will be far from usual," she had replied, "but I think you should know what is possible. Your life as a courtesan can be full of pleasure, if you want it."

La Celestia and her lover entered the room clad in long robes, having just come from the bath. They said not a word, but stood on the rug in front of the fire, facing each other. La Celestia looked up at him with a sweet smile as he slipped her robe over her shoulders and let it fall to the floor.

The courtesan was even more beautiful naked than she was when dressed. The roseate points of her breasts and the flourish of dark hair at the juncture of her thighs were the only touches of color on her exquisitely pale body. Everything about La Celestia was round and supple: her full, high breasts, the inviting curve of her stomach, and her buttocks, so round they appeared as halves of a perfect globe. It was easy to understand why men wanted so desperately to possess her.

Her lover—Gabriele, La Celestia had called him—stood a head taller than the courtesan, and his thick gold hair brushed his shoulders as he bent to kiss her. La Celestia unbelted his robe and, as he'd done to her, slipped the robe over his shoulders and to the floor. A quiet gasp of wonder escaped Alessandra's lips. She'd never seen such a man, except in paintings of Adonis or Hercules. Where La Celestia was composed of curves, Gabriele was sharply drawn, with muscular, well-defined legs and a broad chest. His tawny skin contrasted dramatically to La Celestia's own.

As they drew apart, Alessandra saw that he was already aroused, something that was not lost on the courtesan, who reached down to stroke what Alessandra could see was much larger than her hand. Then La Celestia sank to her knees in front of her lover.

What could she be doing? Alessandra wondered. For a second she thought that La Celestia glanced at the voyeur's chamber with a brief, mischievous smile just before she took Gabriele's penis in her mouth. Alessandra's jaw dropped in amazement. She had never done that with Lorenzo; she hadn't even known it was something that lovers did. But La Celestia's actions didn't seem to surprise Gabriele at all, and it was clear that he was enjoying it. He rested his hands gently on La Celestia's head as she caressed him with her lips, tongue, and hands, and his head fell back with what appeared to be intense pleasure.

La Celestia raised her eyes to his and stood up. Gabriele ran his hands over her body, then brought his mouth to her breasts, suckling each one in turn. After a moment, he knelt down, too, and for the second time Alessandra looked on with astonishment as he buried his face between her legs.

The effect on La Celestia was immediate and even more remarkable than the effect she'd had on him. She moaned with delight, her hands briefly on his head before they restlessly moved over her own body, fondling her breasts and her lips, the touch of her own fingers adding to her gratification. Gabriele clutched her hips and pressed his mouth more firmly into the tender spot he'd found. La Celestia moaned again, louder this time, her legs trembling. Then her lover, without forsaking his post, braced her back with one hand and placed the other on her buttocks, and lay her down before him, continuing to bite and lick her with the most spectacular results. The courtesan writhed on the floor, her legs bent, her back arched, her hands on Gabriele's head as if to more closely embrace him in this extraordinary kiss. Shocking sounds issued from her lips. If Alessandra had not been a witness to the scene before her, she would have thought that La Celestia was in tremendous pain, with piteous cries that were rising to a crescendo. At last, with a long and terrible moan, the courtesan sat up and, pressing her lover's face to her most sensitive part, rocked back and forth as if being shaken by an unseen force, then collapsed back upon the rug.

Never with Lorenzo had Alessandra ever experienced anything

like that, certainly; La Celestia's satisfaction was almost frightening in its intensity and yet undeniably compelling. It had affected Alessandra more deeply than she could have imagined: the flush she felt in her face, her fractured breathing, the spreading warmth at her very core all testified to it.

The lovers sat back, La Celestia leaning against her hands, her lover on his haunches, smiling contentedly at each other. So Gabriele had liked what he'd done; but was this it? Alessandra wondered. Then Gabriele stood up and walked to La Celestia's side, leaned over, and took her up in his arms. No, of course there was more, Alessandra realized as he carried La Celestia to the bed and placed her on the edge, facing him. The bed was of a height for them to be perfectly positioned as he stood before her. He gripped her ankles and raised her feet in the air as she sank back, stretching her arms out. She rested her ankles upon his shoulders, gazing up at her lover with a look of unashamed delight. Gabriele grabbed her hips and pulled her closer, and the passionate struggle began.

The lesson went on for more than an hour. Alessandra would not have imagined, before this, that the act of love had so much variety. For the first time since entering into her agreement with La Celestia, she looked forward to her new vocation with something that felt like anticipation.

The Lovers

7 June 1617

ALESSANDRA PEEKED OUT from behind the door of the *camera d'oro* to the *portego,* where La Celestia's guests were seated around an immense banquet table, finishing the last course of the feast she had provided. All of the guests were men, all of them were considerably older than she, all of them were wealthy and influential. Two wore the scarlet togas that signified their membership in the Senate, one was a vestment-clad prelate, the others were dressed in the best aristocratic fashion, with somber-hued garments made of the finest fabrics money could buy. None was conspicuously handsome, but none, she noted with relief, was markedly hideous, either.

Alessandra stepped back as La Celestia entered, closing the door behind her. "Are you ready?" she asked.

"I suppose so."

"You don't sound very enthusiastic."

"I'm of two minds," Alessandra admitted. "One part of me can't believe that I let you talk me into doing this. The other part knows that you're right—it's the best way."

"Of course I'm right. First impressions cannot be erased. To be revered and respected, you must be thought special—and after tonight, you'll be considered extraordinary. People will talk about this, mark my words."

"At the moment, I'd prefer to be standing in a window."

"Don't worry, you're going to enchant them." La Celestia led her to a table, at the center of the room, on which sat an enormous silver platter with a domed lid. "Alvise," she called, and a sturdy male servant came forward. He clapped; three others were soon at his side, and together they lifted the cover off the platter. Inside was a huge, gold-leafed papier-mâché seashell, large enough for Alessandra to lie down in.

"Hand me your robe and Alvise will help you up," La Celestia said.

Alessandra was glad it was night and the room not too brightly lit. Underneath her robe, she was practically naked, though not in the least unadorned. Her neck, wrists, and ankles were wrapped with pearls; slender gold and silver ribbons were interwoven in her hair, which fell in waves around her shoulders and down to the middle of her back. A sheer tunic hung to midthigh, though it did little to conceal the parts of her body it covered—as she looked down she could clearly see her nipples, which had been carefully painted gold, and the triangle of gold fabric that hid her sex. For the crowning touch her skin had been coated with a combination of gold dust and sugar, and she gleamed and sparkled as if she were made not of flesh, but of gold.

"You look ravishing," La Celestia said, arranging Alessandra's hair around her shoulders as she settled into the shell. "Perfect, in fact, like Venus just risen from the sea. Now don't forget to smile, just a little. You want to seem inaccessible but not *too* inaccessible, understand?" She nodded to Alvise, and the servants placed the cover over Alessandra, shutting her inside what felt like a giant silver egg.

The seashell was created for dramatic appearance, not for comfort, Alessandra realized as the four bearers picked up the platter and carried it into the *portego*. Thank goodness she wouldn't be in it for very long; it took only a few moments to reach the banquet table. From inside the enclosed salver, she could hear the chatter of La Celestia's male guests, then the courtesan's voice ringing out over them.

"Gentlemen—now, for the reason you have all joined me here tonight . . ."

The chattering stopped. Alessandra's heart was beating so loudly it seemed to echo inside the dome. She was going to stand up naked in front of a room full of men. It was the most shameful thing she had ever done. "You mustn't think that," La Celestia had said when Alessandra confessed her reservations about this debut. "You have no reason to feel ashamed, or to be embarrassed. You will be one of the most beautiful women these men have ever seen. There is great power in that, and you must not forget it. Until you become rich, the power of your beauty is the only power you have. If you use it well, you can live life in whichever way you see fit. If you do not use it, you will be at the mercy of fate."

Alessandra felt a slight jolt as the bearers set the platter down at one end of the banquet table and then, as they'd rehearsed, waited until La Celestia spoke.

"Gentlemen, may I present"—the four bearers slowly lifted the lid—"La Sirena!" La Celestia finished with a flourish as they removed the cover.

At first, there was a profound silence that seemed to Alessandra to go on endlessly. She looked down the table at the two rows of men who stared back at her, apparently not entirely comprehending what they were seeing. She glanced at La Celestia, who prompted Alvise to go to her. Alessandra took his offered hand and stood up. As she did, the august assembly seemed to realize that she was a living, breathing woman—and gave a collective gasp of surprise, then burst into applause.

"So, did you get a good look at any of them?" La Celestia asked.

"No, I was too nervous," Alessandra replied. They had returned to the *camera d'oro;* outside, a trio of musicians played while the men talked in small groups scattered around the *portego*. "So many faces—it was all a blur."

"I'm happy to say that the reverse isn't true." La Celestia regarded Alessandra with pride. "I don't think any of them will ever forget seeing you rise up out of that shell. It was brilliant. They were struck dumb, which is astonishing. Not one of those men ever shuts up voluntarily. You were a resounding success. They're lining up for you; truly, you have your pick." She motioned Alessandra to the door and peered out. "So, which one strikes your fancy?"

"I couldn't say."

"Choose three, then, and I'll help you decide who should be your first lover."

"Three, is it?" Alessandra studied the men along with La Celestia. "To begin with—*not* the bishop."

"I understand your disinclination, but eventually you'll want a high-ranking man of the church as one of your lovers. Every courtesan, at some point, needs protection from those who would cast doubt on her moral character."

"Ahh. I see."

"In the meantime, may I suggest Dario Contarini, in the senator's toga, and Sebastian Valier, over there by my portrait. Both are of excellent families, rich, and generous, both in and out of the bedroom. As for the third . . . what think you of that man standing with the bishop?"

"The dark-haired one?"

"Yes. An interesting man. I suspect he is wealthier than he lets on. Quite unusual in Venice, where everyone claims to have more than they've got. And he is very ambitious—rumor is, he'll be a duke before long. I remarked on his face when he looked at you. I know desire when I see it, and I would say that he had a serious case."

Alessandra looked at him more carefully, noting his muscular jaw, powerful neck, sensual mouth. His eyes were his best feature: they regarded everything with an amused irony and a certain dispassion, and it seemed that there was little that escaped his attention. He exuded power and authority, and she suspected that he could charm or threaten with equal success. "There is something about him . . ."

"Yes, I agree. He is attractive, is he not?"

"Yes."

"Come on, then, I'll introduce you."

Alessandra, wrapped in her robe once more, followed La Celestia across the *portego.* The bishop and his interlocutor turned as they approached. "La Sirena"—La Celestia gently offered Alessandra's hand to her intended—"may I present Alphonso de la Cueva, the marquis of Bedmar and the Spanish ambassador to Venice."

Chapter Five

"TURN LEFT ON Hollis," Claire said to the airport shuttle driver. From her perch in the front-passenger seat, she watched Harriot's sunlit, tree-lined streets pass by the windows and brooded a little. What in the world was she going to talk about with a fourteen-year-old? She couldn't discuss Gwendolyn's parents, obviously. The poor kid. Claire envisioned a sad-eyed, waiflike girl. How had Edward Fry described his daughter? Sweet and kind of shy, he'd said.

The shuttle stopped in front of the Forsythe dormitory known as Chesterfield House. Assuming that she would be meeting Gwen inside, Claire barely glanced at a girl sitting on a short stone wall facing the street. With a second look and growing dismay, she saw a suitcase on the ground beneath the girl's dangling feet, a bulky backpack beside her on the wall, and knew that she could be none other than Gwendolyn Fry.

Perfectly normal? She wished Meredith were there to explain precisely what she'd meant by that. Claire hadn't been around Forsythe students much, but she was pretty certain there weren't any others who looked like this. The girl's waist-length hair was dyed a color that didn't occur in nature, burgundy with a purple cast to it, which covered a much prettier, light coppery red revealed by the roots at her scalp. Her green eyes were rimmed by so much liner and mascara she resembled a silent film star or a raccoon. She had a full but narrow mouth that Claire knew at once had an unfortunate tendency to hang open. A small silver ring pierced her left eyebrow and a matching hoop studded her navel, which was clearly visible above the pair of tight, bell-bottom jeans she wore. Her blouse—a diaphanous, pink and red paisley chiffon thing—gathered under her breasts and then was split right down the front, revealing her entire midriff.

The outfit was much too sexy for a fourteen-year-old; at least it appeared as if it were intended to be sexy. On Gwendolyn Fry it simply looked awkward, as if she were wearing someone else's clothes. First of all, they were too small for her. Waiflike she was not; the blouse plunged past deeper cleavage than Claire would ever see on her own chest.

"Are you Gwen?"

"Yes." Her eyes revealed a different response: *Duh. Who else would be sitting out here?*

"Hi, I'm Claire."

"Oh."

No "hello," no "nice to meet you." Clearly the girl had no manners, but Claire was already, within seconds of meeting Gwendolyn Fry, thoroughly unsurprised by this.

"Where's Mrs. Randolph?" Claire asked. The dormitory housemother was supposed to meet her with the final paper to sign, one stating that she would be Gwen's legal guardian for the next week.

An almost imperceptible movement of the head. "Inside." Gwen slid down from the stone wall and grabbed the waistband of her jeans with both hands and hitched them up, an automatic reflex that appeared to be a requisite part of wearing such low-cut pants. She was taller than Claire by an inch or two, which Claire felt was unfair somehow. It put her at a disadvantage. She'd been expecting a girl—no, if she were honest, she'd been expecting a child—and instead got one of those fourteen-going-on-twenty types. That Gwendolyn Fry seemed graceless, awkward, and (in spite of her risqué apparel) wholly unsophisticated did not in the least mitigate Claire's negative first impression. Although it wasn't very nice to dislike someone so much younger than herself, was it? It wasn't very nice at all, she grudgingly admitted, at the same time acknowledging that there didn't seem to be anything she could do about how she felt.

Claire knocked on the front door of the dormitory and turned to glance back at the girl. She'd been under the impression that Gwen had wanted to go to Europe to be with her dad and new stepmother, but now she wasn't so sure. The teenager didn't look like someone who was excited to be going on a trans-Atlantic trip, she looked like a kid who was being trundled off to a distant relative's house because things were bad at home. Which was, Claire reflected, not far from the truth. For a moment she felt something like sympathy, and thought about the strange event that had precipitated their meeting: Why had Gwen's mother shot her father? Why in the foot? On the Back Bay Golf Course? On the eleventh hole?

Claire felt a sudden, nagging sense of dread. It settled in her stomach, where she feared it would remain until the moment she handed the kid back to her father.

The seat belt light came on with a muffled, bell-like chime and the airplane's engines throbbed. Claire looked out the window, where the long, slanted shadows of early evening stretched across the tarmac. Inside the cabin, the passengers were seated, and flight attendants cruised the aisles, checking seat belts and overhead bins in preparation for takeoff.

"I wasn't going to steal it," Gwen said for the fifth time.

"You were about to leave the store," Claire replied, also for the fifth time.

"I was going to pay for it."

They'd been browsing at an airport boutique when Claire had seen Gwen slip a pair of silver earrings into her backpack. "The next time you're in a store," Claire offered, "I suggest that you hold your items in your hands or place them on the counter until you've finished shopping." Her voice sounded even more schoolmarmish than she had intended. She sighed and tried to lose the judgmental tone; it seemed to inflate Gwen's sense of being wronged and misunderstood. "If only to stop having this conversation," Claire continued, "I will accept that you had simply forgotten the jewelry was in your backpack. But if I had let you walk out that door, you would have been apprehended, and we would have missed the flight, and I couldn't allow that to happen. So can we just drop this now?"

Gwen didn't answer, but she was pouting so powerfully it charged the atmosphere around them. This was a good example of why she preferred to be alone, Claire thought; other people's emotions could be so disturbing.

She turned in her seat and peered through the open curtains to coach. The plane was about half full. She and Gwen sat in business class, Claire in the right-side window seat, Gwen on the aisle, a luxuriously short row of two spacious, black leather seats that opened up like Barcaloungers, with small footrests at the bottom. It was clear that Edward Fry was not a parsimonious man. Two business-class seats to Italy purchased a week before the departure date? It must have cost a small fortune.

A female flight attendant stopped and leaned over to speak to Gwen. "All electronics need to be turned off and stowed away until after takeoff," she said with a smile that included Claire, and a look in her eyes that discreetly assumed and conferred mother/stepmother/aunt status on her. That Claire was technically old enough to be any one of those just made it more objectionable. Gwen switched off her iPod and reached under the seat for her backpack, then sorted through the contents of her pack with the resolve of someone who knew this would be her only salvation from boredom for the next eight hours.

Claire reached into her tote bag for a pen and the books she'd brought along, taking out Marmont's *History of the Counter-Reformation.* She could read and make notes, at least. She wiggled her toes and thought about taking off her shoes. Once she'd finished reading, she could relax for a while, maybe even get some sleep. After all, the girl couldn't get into any trouble on the plane.

The Emperor

15 September 1617

THE MEAT WAS tough and the wine—malmsey, the Venetians called it—was too sweet, Bedmar groused to himself as he ate alone in his private rooms at the Spanish embassy. He was the ambassador, by Christ; why was he served the same fare given to his legion of *bravi* belowstairs? It was time to trade in the old Castilian who'd come with him from Madrid for a chef versed in the local cuisine, although these Venetians could sometimes take creativity to curious lengths. He'd been to a banquet at Ca' Barbarigo the week before where all the food had been gilded—the fruit, the pheasant, even the bread had been covered in a thin layer of gold. It had occurred to him then that the only thing Venetians loved more than money was flaunting it. Odd as it was, though, it had been a better meal than this one.

He pushed his tray away and stretched out his legs toward the fire. At his feet, his wolfhound whimpered and turned in his sleep, firelight gleaming on his coppery coat. The sight of it calmed him, and the ambassador closed his eyes for a moment.

His apartment on the top floor of the embassy was the only place he could find any peace. Day and night, the embassy was swarming with Spaniards of every stripe, each of them desiring his attention, patronage, influence. Sometimes he thought it was the busiest place in all of Venice: the anterooms and corridors were full of slouching figures whispering together in groups, waiting for an audience with him. Even as a commander of Phillip III's regiment, Bedmar had never felt so harassed in his life. He'd taken a villa in the country so he could escape it from time to time, but the crowd of hangers-on simply followed. He swore that when he was viceroy, he'd have an entire palazzo to himself.

Viceroy of Venice. Most of the time, these were pleasant words that brought him a deep satisfaction. Venice was the only major power in all of Italy that hadn't yet surrendered to Spain's domination, and it would be Spain's crown jewel; no other city could boast of the riches that Venice possessed. Once he'd taken Venice, a good portion of the city's wealth would be his, and the king would surely reward him with a dukedom.

The conquest of Venice was the final step toward his lifelong ambition of restoring his family's reputation and position. He'd spent three decades repairing the damage his father had done to the name of de la Cueva, to their lands, to their wealth. It had taken years to regain his place at court, but at last he was on the verge of getting everything he desired. No, Bedmar corrected himself, everything he deserved. But tonight he felt the strain of the plan that he and Ossuna had devised.

Unless he obtained more money for arms and men, the success of their enterprise was far from certain. The French corsairs had been tough negotiators, and he would require a few hundred more recruits. For days he'd agonized over writing to the king, and he couldn't put it off any longer. But how to proceed? An outright request wouldn't do. Even if the king responded favorably, the duke of Lerma, the king's powerful minister, would be loath to do anything to further Bedmar's aims; their antipathy went back many years. But if he could compose it in such a way that the king felt compelled to act, in such a way that Lerma could not oppose it without opposing the king, he might be successful.

He stood up and crossed to his desk. A breeze rattled the windows, carrying with it the ever present stench of the canals and a presentiment of autumn. Bedmar felt his insides turn. From the pestilential marsh that surrounded it to the innumerable waterways that laced it together, the entire city was rank. Even within the grandest palazzi, he could smell the decay. It seeped up from the foundations into the stones and the mortar and the brick, into the filigreed plaster and the marble, into the mosaic tile and the ornate, gilded rooms. Not for the first time he wondered what had possessed men to build these opulent treasure chests on top of a swamp. Was it solely for the pleasure of their beauty? He'd never before encountered a people so concerned with appearances, with the surface of things.

"The entire city is dedicated to Venus," he'd written to the king soon after he arrived. Even now, years later, Bedmar wasn't certain if his words revealed condemnation or fascination. Was it possible to be simultaneously repulsed and attracted?

Since his posting to Venice, he sometimes had the odd sensation of being unsure of himself. At times he imagined that he looked different than he used to and was surprised to see his familiar face in the mirror. In outward aspect he was the same, but he felt himself a changed man. After years of soldiering, after decades of discipline and deprivation, how quickly he had discovered his appetite for Venice's epicurean delights: food, women, and all the trappings of wealth, from the finest fabrics to the most luxurious furnishings. He never admitted it, but in Venice he felt a constant unease: it brought forth the half-buried knowledge that he carried within himself the same weaknesses that had contributed to his father's disgrace.

The city exerted a hold over him that he was powerless to deny. At night, when he saw the light from gondola lanterns shining upon the water, or heard the tinkle of music and a courtesan's contralto laughter, the fever would come on him again, and he would feel the need for a woman's musky perfume upon his mouth and fingers, for a pair of limpid eyes that opened and closed with desire, for budding lips that sighed their satisfaction in his ear. Venice certainly had the advantage over any other city when it came to those particular pleasures, and La Sirena was the latest and most extraordinary example. Venice gilded its food and its women, Bedmar thought with an ironic snort. When he'd first set eyes on her, he hadn't even realized that she was real; he'd thought she was a golden sculpture of the most perfect woman ever imagined. Now it was La Sirena more than any other who lured him out into the Venetian night.

Nocturnal Venice was a place unique to itself, a strange aquatic realm ruled not by Poseidon but by Morpheus, god of dreams and delusions. For only Morpheus could conjure the spell that transformed Venice into the shimmering, ethereal world it became once the sun had set: a place where flickering torchlight turned solid stone into rippling illusions of water and light, where bejeweled sirens on silently gliding barks exposed their breasts to the night, and the fevered moans of masked liaisons echoed from dark doorways. Only in the cool wash of dawn did reason return, and the truth become apparent: the real Venice was not so much a seductress as an eternal Narcissus reflected in a thousand watery mirrors, an aloof divinity made all the more vulnerable by vanity. The enchantment faded and he felt in possession of himself again, poised to pluck his prize. Becoming viceroy of Venice would be his greatest victory in a lifetime of victories. Neither Ossuna nor even Lerma could touch him then.

At his desk, the ambassador opened a slender drawer and withdrew quills, ink, and paper. In another drawer he found a brass key, which he used to open a small, lacquered *damaschina*-style chest, painted with intricate red, blue, and green arabesques. The chest contained only one item: an untitled book, which he also placed on the desk.

The morocco-bound book was rare, only one of two copies. The other was in the possession of Philip III's secretary, who used it in the same manner as Bedmar did: to code and decode letters between the ambassador and the king. The method was a simple one: the words of the message were substituted with a numeric code consisting of the page number, line, and position of the corresponding word in the book. Simple, but effective; even the code breakers who worked round the clock at the Doge's Palace could not decipher his letters without the book. First he would write the letter, then with the book create the encrypted copy.

Bedmar sat down and sharpened a quill. He considered an opening line, but quickly discarded it. No pleading, no begging, he reminded himself. If he could raise the king's ire against the Venetians, however, the king might offer help of his own accord and Lerma would not be able to argue against it. The ambassador dipped the quill into the ink and began to write.

Your Majesty,

The crimes of the Republic against your Crown and against the Holy Church become more insidious with each passing day. Venice has always sought to slander the name of Spain, but at present they respect no bounds of decency . . .

Bedmar stopped suddenly, surprised by the appearance of a servant who'd come in to pick up the dinner tray. "What in God's name are you doing here?" he grumbled angrily.

"Pardon me, Your Excellency. I knocked, but there was no answer. I thought you'd gone." He was an ungainly sort, with a pockmarked face, a scrawny neck, and a large Adam's apple that bobbed up and down when he spoke. His eyes ranged over Bedmar's desk.

"As you can see perfectly well, I haven't. Announce yourself next time." Bedmar looked at him more carefully. "Who are you? Where's Pasquale?"

"He's taken ill, Your Excellency. Tomás Esquivel, at your service, sir."

"To whom do you report?"

"Don Rodrigo, same as Pasquale, Your Excellency."

"Tell Don Rodrigo never to send up a new man without telling me first, you understand?" Bedmar didn't wait for an answer. "Now get out."

Bedmar's gondolier rowed into the Rio di San Martino, heading toward the Grand Canal. The marquis leaned back against the gondola cushions and slowly ran his hand over his beard, as if his thoughts were far away.

"I'm looking forward to tonight's performance," Alessandra said, less because it was true than to break the silence.

"The baronessa's entertainments are always diverting." Bedmar looked at her as he spoke, but he seemed preoccupied. More so than her other lovers—of whom there were now five—the marquis was an enigma. Alessandra wondered what he thought of her and realized that she might never know. Bedmar was an intensely private man who seldom shared his thoughts. She suspected that he regarded her as a kind of pretty trinket, a possession, a china doll without a soul. Perhaps that was how he thought of all women—the ones who caught his notice, at any rate. With another man she might have felt resentful, but with Bedmar it felt safer to play the role he wanted her to play. Though he'd never threatened her with any harm, she sensed that he was dangerous.

Even though La Celestia had often told her that men were generally simple creatures, Alessandra suspected the ambassador was not. He could be charming or taciturn by turns, and at times she witnessed a brooding anger that made her uneasy. But then he was Spanish, not Venetian, and perhaps his foreignness made him more difficult for her to fathom. She felt an easier intimacy with her Venetian lovers than she felt with the marquis. They regaled her with their long-ago exploits in war and their more recent successes in business and politics. Bedmar deflected any personal inquiries with polite firmness.

But when Alessandra had expressed her concerns to La Celestia, the courtesan had breezily dismissed them.

"I know he does not flatter and give trinkets as much as other men," La Celestia said, "but he has been more than generous with his purse. And does he not express his delight with you in other ways?"

She'd told La Celestia about that, too. Bedmar's desire for her was fierce, and he was a skilled lover, with a sure touch that never failed to arouse her.

The marquis turned to his gondolier. "Take the Rio della Fava," he said, and the gondolier responded with a flourish of his hand. He was a young man a year or two older than herself, thin but apparently strong, with deep-set eyes circled by shadows.

"Your new gondolier—is he mute?" she asked.

"Yes, thankfully. Paolo's the one man in Venice who cannot reveal my secrets."

"Such as?"

"Such as the name of the lovely courtesan in my gondola tonight."

"Did you know that gondoliers take an oath never to reveal anything they witness in a gondola? The penalty for breaking the oath is death."

"I have heard that. I've also heard that gondoliers have webbed feet, and that to a man they are born on a mysterious island during a full moon."

They were getting closer to the Grand Canal and the Rialto. "There's still time before we reach Palazzo Erizzo," he said, drawing her closer. One hand cupped her breast as he brought his mouth to hers; the other slipped down under her skirts and slowly moved higher. He ran his fingers along the inside of her thighs, then pulled her underneath him. She felt herself acquiescing, her body rising to meet his. The marquis reached up and drew the curtains, enclosing them inside the *felze.*

"I see you don't believe in your gondolier's discretion," Alessandra said.

"I don't believe in fairy tales. Gondoliers are men like any other. After all, this is Venice. There are spies everywhere."

The Hermit

9 October 1617

In the dusky, intimate hush of Sant' Alvise, a gnomelike figure, clad in a tattered wool robe and worn leather sandals, loitered near the altar and looked out at the empty church. Roast pheasant, perhaps, or duck stuffed with cherries and apples, Ippolito Moro thought wistfully. Apulian wine, crayfish, and quail, followed by sugared almonds and marchpane with cinnamon . . . oh, the feast he would enjoy tonight, just for being Batù's eyes and ears.

Any moment now, the secret assignation would begin, as it had once a week for the past three weeks. The last Mass of the day was done, the priests had gone, and the nuns had disappeared from the choir balcony, the sequestered site of their devotions. All that remained were the lingering odors of smoky incense, sour unwashed bodies, sweet beeswax candles that flickered and hissed. And Ippolito, waiting, anticipating, his robe still dotted with bits of straw from his afternoon nap.

"Ippolito!" Priest Domenico, impatient and entirely lacking in the spirit of tolerance on which he had just pontificated, called from the vestry. "Ippolito! Hurry up, now!"

The dwarf snatched the Bible and the chalice from the pulpit, cradling the hallowed items in his arms as he hobbled over to the vestry door where Priest Domenico stood, looking disgruntled. The priest's face grew fatter every day, Ippolito noticed with disgust; eventually his eyes would look like two tiny black olives surrounded by pink flesh, just like a suckling pig. *Hmmm. Roast pork might be tasty, too.*

"Take care this time," Domenico said as Ippolito pushed past him. "If I find that chalice on the floor again, you won't be sacristan any longer."

A pox on you, Ippolito thought as he watched the priest's retreating figure. He wasn't worried by Domenico's threats. He'd been at Sant' Alvise for more than twenty years, long enough to see many priests come and go, long enough to lose the esteem he'd once felt for them. *Parasites all, sucking up the bounty of the convent.* The sisters routinely used up their rations of flour and eggs to bake bisquits and cakes for the rapacious priests, while he, Ippolito their faithful servant, got nothing but scraps. But whose fault was that? The uppity nuns were hardly generous themselves. Only Sister Brodata—homely Sister Brodata, of the ample bottom and the unfortunate mustache—was friendly; but now, he reflected sorrowfully, even she was shunning him. But it was the priests' fault, not his! Brodata herself had complained that they ate all the food, and Ippolito had sniggered, "Be careful or they'll take your virginity, too . . . unless, of course, you've already given it away."

Brodata knew at once he'd been talking about Priest Fabrizio, whom he'd seen fawning over her, even though the old goat already had a mistress over at San Sepolcro. Brodata refused to speak to him now, but Ippolito knew she was only pretending to be angry; in truth she was flattered and secretly pleased. She wanted people to believe that the priest was sweet on her, no matter what cost to her honor. But what did these nuns care about honor?

He shook his head vigorously, as if to clear it. If Brodata didn't want to be friends anymore, he would simply stop thinking of her! He had more important things to attend to, certainly. He would be a rich man tonight, if all went well; rich enough, at least, to buy himself a decent meal; even, perhaps, Ippolito thought as he returned to the nave, rich enough to take a stroll over to the Bridge of Tits, where the gentle *meretrici* would consider his money as good as any man's, regardless of his shrunken form and bandy legs.

He wondered what old Brodata would say about that. No doubt she'd deliver a sermon on the sins of the flesh, he thought darkly, along with dire threats of the *morbo gallico,* the French disease. He remembered a priest from long ago who'd tried to convince Ippolito to give up lusting after whores; why gamble on those pox-ridden prostitutes, he'd said, when love between men is as good or better? I'd rather take my chances with the *gallico* than with the gallows! Ippolito had cackled, pleased with his own wit. Everyone knew that sodomy was a hanging offense, and a sin against God, and that was why the wise men of the Republic encouraged the *meretrici* to expose their breasts in public: to remind men of the proper expression of their desires.

Ippolito waited near the altar once again. In the church's echoing quiet he heard the sound of water slowly dripping, then a sudden trill of conversation from the courtyard. It occurred to him that if things did not happen as he'd said they would, that blue-eyed devil, Batù Vrats, would make his life a living hell. He'd heard that Batù was not forgiving of mistakes. Ippolito wondered if he were nearby, watching and waiting. The thought made him shiver.

Just as Ippolito was beginning to lose hope, the first man arrived. This was the one he thought of as the traitor, for the man was Venetian, Ippolito was sure of it. "Not noble, no, nothing like that," Ippolito had said when he'd described him for Batù, "someone from the lower orders, a guildsman perhaps, a weaver or a glassblower." Yes, that had intrigued Batù; more so than most, Batù knew that the secrets of Venetian glass were sought by foreign courts using the most devious means. And even though it was Venetian policy to hunt down and assassinate any glassblower who plied his trade outside the Republic, a breach of the Venetian monopoly still happened occasionally. Only last year the French king had wooed one of Venice's premier mirror makers with promises of money and women, and the Council of Ten was still agonizing over its inability to get to the turncoat, who was happily sequestered at the French court.

Ippolito watched from the altar as the Venetian sat down in the same pew he'd sat in for the past three weeks, and he witnessed the traitor's false ritual of piety. First he knelt and briefly prayed; then, almost imperceptibly, he placed a small, folded paper into a crack in the wooden pew in front of him. He stayed only a moment longer, then slipped out of the church.

This was the crucial moment. Batù had explained that they would let the first man go—for now—in order to capture the second. The Spanish spy, as Ippolito thought of him, for he dressed in the Spanish style of doublet and hose, and one day Ippolito had followed him all the way to the Lista di Spagna and the Spanish embassy. He desperately wanted to go to the pew and make certain that the paper was there—they must catch the Spanish spy with the note, Batù had said—but he knew he must stay where he was, remain silent and still. If it did not go as Batù said it must, well . . . Ippolito was afraid to think of what might happen. Going hungry would be the least of his troubles.

Ippolito felt his breath catch as the Spanish spy entered the church and proceeded to the same pew. Yes, he was certain it was him: the Spaniard sported a thin black mustache that did little to cover the scar that had split his lip and left his mouth with a permanent sneer. He wore the same dusty brown doublet he'd worn the week before. Like the first man, he briefly knelt, appeared to pray, then took the slip of paper from its hiding place in the pew. He'd walked only a few steps toward the door when four men, brandishing swords, blocked his exit. He whipped around toward the altar, his eyes wild, in a futile search for another way out. The Spanish spy looked right at him and Ippolito gasped, afraid for his own life, but the instant soon passed because the Spaniard drew his sword and turned back to fight his attackers.

Within seconds the church was filled with the sound of clashing steel. "Don't kill him," one of the four shouted to the others, and Ippolito saw the Spaniard fight with increased zeal, as if he would prefer death to the alternative they had planned for him. A better end than that which comes in the Court of the Room of the Cord, Ippolito agreed as he watched the battle from behind the pulpit. Soon enough the Spaniard was disarmed, his sword flying in a glittering arc across the nave and clattering along the floor. The four men pounced on the spy, pinioning his arms and legs and hustling him away. Ippolito watched them through the open door as they moved across the *fondamenta* to the tiny canal outside and a waiting gondola. The scuffle was over in minutes, and the church was deathly quiet once again.

What about me? Ippolito wanted to cry out. Where is the reward Batù has promised? He curled his tiny hands into fists and felt as though he might burst into tears. Without the money as proof, Brodata would never believe he was responsible for the capture of a spy, that he had risked his very life! For all his fantasies of sumptuous meals and courtesans, he'd done it only for Brodata, to win back her friendship. He'd never felt quite so bereft before. He was about to shuffle away from the altar when a shadow, as black and sinuous as a viper, filled the church doorway.

Throwing back the hood of his cloak, Batù Vratsa entered the church and walked down the aisle toward Ippolito. He was strong and graceful and, Ippolito knew from the stories he'd heard, as dangerous a man as ever lived. Friend to outcasts and orphans, Batù had said when they'd first met, but the blue-eyed devil was one of the few people in this world who terrified him. He came from far away, the land of the Rom. They must be a bizarre race, for certainly Ippolito had never seen anyone like Batù before: a face strangely flat, with cheekbones that jutted out like wings; skin the color of dried tobacco, and eyes so light they appeared as empty as the most distant, colorless part of the sky. A blue-eyed devil. When he asked you to be his eyes and ears, how could you refuse?

Batù Vratsa looked down on Ippolito and handed him a leather pouch filled with coins. "You did well, my little friend," he said, smiling, causing a tremor along Ippolito's spine. "And how are you going to spend it all?" he asked, still with that smile that made the dwarf feel cold inside. "Perhaps there's a nun here who's your particular friend?"

Ippolito gulped, speechless with fear. Had the blue-eyed devil been watching him, too? Luckily he didn't have to answer, for Batù Vratsa had disappeared as mysteriously as he'd arrived.

The Magician

12 October 1617

"WELCOME TO THE Court of the Room of the Cord," Senator Girolamo Silvia said. He put his ax blade of a face close enough to the Spanish spy to see the dueling scar on his upper lip and the nervous sweat beading his brow. "No doubt you've heard of it: it's the most feared place in all of Venice. The cord from which it takes its name is this one here." Silvia reached up to touch the rope that hung from the ceiling and was tied to the prisoner's wrists, bound behind his back. "We call it the strappado, and its purpose is to rip your shoulders from their sockets, something it does with remarkable efficiency. Of course we hope this will not be necessary. If you cooperate with us, you may still be able to lift a sword when you leave here. If you don't cooperate, this may be the last place you'll ever see."

Buried deep within the Doge's Palace, the Court's thick, windowless stone walls admitted no light and deadened all sound: even the most horrifying scream could not be heard outside its solid fortifications. In the dim light cast by the wall-mounted torches, the bloodstained floors appeared black and the mice that scrabbled along the edges were little more than small, swift shadows. Silvia took a breath and the oppressive smell of the room filled his mouth and lungs. It was a smell you could taste, heavy and unpleasant on the tongue, a charnel odor of blood, vomit, piss, and fear so pervasive his clothes still reeked of it after he left. Because of that he never wore his scarlet togas in here, only the black. When prisoners were brought in, they often gagged and retched, but Silvia was inured to the smell; he had even begun to associate it with a sense of triumph.

In the Court of the Room of the Cord, Silvia had become privy to some of the most closely guarded secrets of Venice's many enemies. Secrets that had often provided the Republic with an advantage in waging war, negotiating treaties, or outwitting their rivals in business and trade. One hundred hours of so-called diplomacy produced less good effect than what he and Batù could achieve in an hour in the Court. Here, Silvia discovered the hidden designs and true intentions of foreign kings and their dissembling minions, the shifting alliances and secret policies that determined the fate of nations. In a world of lies and deception, the Court of the Room of the Cord was a temple of truth.

He stepped away from the prisoner as Batù entered, slipping out of his cloak and turning to the plank table where various instruments of wood, leather, and metal were arranged in rows. His angular face and ice blue eyes appeared feral in the torchlight. He looked at the Spaniard with contempt and Silvia was reminded of the first time he'd seen him.

It had been more than twenty years ago now, belowdecks on a Turkish carrack docked in Constantinople. After four years on an official tour of the republic's colonies, Silvia needed a servant to take back with him to Venice, one young enough to train properly. The slave auctions once held at the Rialto had been banned since 1366, but owning a slave or two was not uncommon among noble Venetians, nor was it illegal. The Turkish captain was a round little fellow with a gravelly voice. "I've got a boat full of pilgrims on their way to Mecca," he said as he led Silvia down into the grubby hold where the slaves were kept. Most of them were Greek or from the lands surrounding the Black Sea. "The slaves not sold here will be unloaded at Alexandria. See anything you like?" The captain gestured at a group of boys huddled on the floor and Silvia's gaze settled on a child of six or seven with golden skin and black hair.

Even then his blue eyes were unsettling; they seemed to pierce right through the grimy darkness.

"What about him?" Silvia asked.

The captain guffawed and spit. "Not that one, sir, he's wild and vicious as a cat."

"Still, I'd like to get a better look at him. Could you ask him to stand up?"

The captain went over to the boy and kicked him, but he did nothing except glare at them with even greater ferocity. He grabbed the boy's arm and dragged him to his feet, but as soon as he let go, the boy defiantly sat down again. The captain pulled him up once more, this time adding a hard smack across his face. "See what I mean? He's incorrigible. An orphan, and a strange half-breed, too—Romanian by way of the Golden Horde. Named for the grandson of Ghengis Khan, Batù Khan, who laid waste to all the lands between Mongolia and Bohemia. He's got the blood of demons in him."

Red welts were rising on the boy's cheek, but he hadn't flinched when he was hit, hadn't even uttered a sound, and his eyes were as dry as bone. Silvia looked for a tear without finding the least glimmer of one.

"I'll take him," he said.

He'd brought him to Venice ostensibly as a houseboy, but Batù's intelligence and extraordinary physical agility were soon apparent. His unruliness had subsided once he realized that he wouldn't be abused; in Silvia's household the servants were treated well. Observant, silent, and unafraid, Batù became Silvia's favorite. The unspoken affinity between them grew and Silvia began to think of him as the son he'd never had—the son he couldn't have. He saw to it that Batù was schooled in the things he was best suited to, and by the time he was twenty, there was no better sword fighter in the city. Even in cosmopolitan Venice, his exotic appearance drew notice; he was often challenged, but never bested. Batù was lightning fast and fearless—because, like Silvia, he was oblivious to pain. Which also made him the ideal partner for Silvia's work in the Court of the Room of the Cord. Like his mentor, he had a particular skill for extracting the truth.

"The prisoner's name is Luis Salazar," Batù said in a low voice. "That much at least we learned from the traitorous *arsenalotto* before he died."

"Anything else?"

"Very little. He was injured during the arrest. He didn't last long."

The note they'd found on the Spanish spy had nothing to do with glassmaking, as Batù had first thought, but was in fact detailed information about the Arsenale, Venice's shipbuilding factory, passed to him by a Venetian Arsenale worker.

Silvia went back to the prisoner. "Luis Salazar, state secrets regarding the defense of the Arsenale were discovered upon your person. Being in possession of this information is punishable by death. However, I'm offering you a chance to save your neck—all you have to do is tell me who you are working for."

Silvia spoke in Italian, and he saw comprehension in the prisoner's eyes, but less trepidation than he would have imagined. Usually three days in the Doge's Prison was enough to make men prey to their own fears; by the time they got to the Court of the Room of the Cord, they were half finished already. This one apparently had more mettle. Silvia could see the pulse in Salazar's throat as his heart quickened its rhythm, and the increased sheen of anxiety on his face, but he did not move a muscle or utter a sound.

"Is it the governor of Milan? The viceroy of Naples? Or are you working for the Spanish ambassador and King Philip III himself?"

The prisoner held his silence. Silvia repeated himself in Spanish, just in case, but saw no difference in the spy's countenance. He doesn't look sufficiently afraid, Silvia thought. His eyes shone with a dull, heavy-lidded defiance, as if he'd just been awakened by the guards before being brought here. But who slept in the Doge's Prison, knowing what terrors were in store for them? In a flash, Silvia realized the source of the Spaniard's bravado.

"If you thought that taking opium would see you through this, you were laboring under a serious misapprehension." Salazar must have hidden the palliative in his clothes; perhaps he should insist on having prisoners stripped down in the future. "Batù?"

At the mention of his name, Batù turned the crank that hoisted the strappado. The Spaniard groaned as his arms were pulled up behind his back and his feet left the floor. The weight of his body put excruciating stress on his shoulders. Sweat began to stream down his face. Batù raised him a few meters from the floor, then let him drop suddenly and quickly snapped the rope taut. The spy's wrists were jerked high above his head. Silvia heard the familiar crack as his shoulder joints split apart, and Salazar's piteous scream.

The senator approached the spy once more. "I will ask you again. Who are you working for?"

Salazar was sweating profusely. Tears ran from his eyes and his breath came in shuddering, heaving gasps. But still he did not speak.

"If you do not talk to me, I will get very angry," Silvia said. "You don't want to make me angry. I'm all there is between you and Batù. There are many ingenious devices here in the Court and Batù is familiar with them all. I can tell him to start and I can tell him to stop. The only way to convince me to make him stop is to tell me the truth. You will discover that nothing else—not your tears, or your screams—will have any effect on me." Silvia paused for a moment, then turned away. "Batù? What think you next?" He looked back at the prisoner as he listed the possibilities. "There is the garroting chair, in which a steel point at the back of the chair is slowly driven into your neck. There is the rack, for the systematic dislocation of every joint in your body. There are a few other, how shall I say, more prosaic devices, such as the thumbscrew, the head crusher, or hot pincers, which can tear off nipples, ears, noses, tongues, and genitals.

"If you think we will simply kill you, you are wrong. You will wish for death, but we will not give it to you. Men can withstand a great deal more pain than you have and continue living. I know this from personal experience. When I was fifteen, I was trampled by a bull. My legs were broken, my pelvis shattered. No one expected me to live, but I did, although I suffered more pain than most men could endure. You might think I boast of my strength, but in truth I confess a personal failing: since that time I have had little sympathy for the pain of others. You might say that I am a connoisseur of pain, and that Batù is a connoisseur of inflicting pain. Between the two of us, you will have no mercy. Now, I ask you once more: who are you working for?"

The Spanish prisoner looked him in the eye, then spat in his face.

"You will regret that," Silvia said.

Chapter Six

A JOLT OF turbulence shook Claire awake. The cabin was dark, quiet, slumbering. She felt groggy and a little nauseous, the lingering aftereffects of some very disturbing dreams. No wonder, she thought as she looked down at the open book on her lap. *Common Torture Devices in Use in the Sixteenth and Seventeenth Centuries,* she read. *The Spanish Inquisitors developed something they called the Pear, a metal instrument which was inserted into the . . .*

Ugh, she groaned, closing the book and stowing it away. The seat next to hers was empty. Gwen had said something about getting a soda, but Claire reckoned she'd gotten up more than two hours ago. She removed her headphones—she'd fallen asleep listening to a Vivaldi concerto—and put them down on Gwen's seat, along with her portable CD case. Then she stood up, stretched, and quietly walked to the forward galley, which was cluttered with the used coffee cups of the after-dinner service. A painfully bright overhead light bounced off a row of chrome microwaves and a stainless-steel beverage cart. There was no one in the galley or the aisle.

Gwen must've sat down in another seat—there were plenty of vacant ones—and stayed there, Claire decided. It wasn't surprising that Gwen didn't want to sit beside her the entire flight; no one could accuse them of bonding. Maybe once she'd sat down somewhere else, she'd fallen asleep. Claire scanned the nearest faces, but Gwen wasn't in business class.

She knew, of course, that there was a perfectly rational explanation for Gwen's disappearance, but she felt a dull ache in her stomach again. Exactly how do you tell a man that you've lost his daughter somewhere over the North Atlantic?

She ducked past the curtains separating business class and coach and slowly walked down the aisle, searching for Gwen's uniquely colored hair. She reached the end without seeing her. The rear galley was empty, and in a worse state of disarray than the one up front. The drinks cart looked like it had been ransacked; empty soda cans and tiny liquor bottles littered the counters. A few flight attendants relaxed in the rows at the very back of the plane. Claire was stepping toward them, intending to ask if they'd seen Gwen, when the plane shuddered and lurched and she fell against the lavatory door. It opened inward with a thud and the surprised "Hey!" of the boy standing inside.

He wasn't alone. Claire had a clear view to the bathroom's mirrored wall, in which she saw the reflection of the boy's narrow, plaid-shirted back, his closely shaved head covered with dark stubble, and Gwen's dumbstruck, lipstick-smeared face.

Then Gwen saw her, too. Her eyes went wide. "Oh, shit," she said. The door slammed shut. "Shit," the boy muttered.

"Get out of there right now," Claire hissed.

There was a flurry of movement inside. She was relieved not to hear any zippers zipping. At least they'd been fully dressed.

"Is that your mom?" asked the boy, his voice cracking.

"No," Gwen replied. "But I better go."

Claire stepped back as the door collapsed inward again and the boy appeared, brushing past her without meeting her eyes. He couldn't have been more than fifteen, she noticed with relief. Then Gwen slowly extricated herself and stepped into the aisle.

"We were just talking."

"Don't insult my intelligence, just get back to your seat." She'd almost ended with "young lady," and was surprised by her automatic parental reaction. The desire to take the girl firmly by the arm, march her down the aisle in double time, and put her in her seat with a grim, "You're grounded," felt programmed into her

DNA, the impulse was so strong. Of course the grounding idea probably wouldn't be very effective, being, as they were, currently airborne.

She couldn't imagine what her own mother would have done in the same situation, probably because her mother hadn't had to face anything like this. As a teenager, Claire actually had been sweet, shy, and perfectly normal, a description that fit Gwendolyn Fry about as well as the jeans that were currently cutting off circulation to her pelvis. If Gwendolyn Fry was a perfectly normal teenager, Claire was going to have a tubal ligation the moment she got home from Italy. "Devil spawn" would be a more fitting description, she thought as she squeezed past her and sat down.

Gwen immediately launched into her defense. "He was just showing me his tattoo, that's all."

"I don't want to know about it. Gwendolyn, this isn't going to work out. We'll be landing in Milan soon and when we do I'm going to call your father and tell him I'll take you to Nice, or he can come to Milan to pick you up, but one way or another we are not going to continue traveling together."

Gwen pondered this outburst with a thoughtfulness Claire hadn't seen before, as if she were carefully weighing her options. "But if you do that," she replied, "you won't get to go to Venice. He's only paying for your trip because you're with me."

The girl was right. Claire's anger had made her overlook a rather important fact; she hadn't thought beyond handing Gwendolyn back to her father. Her plane ticket would still be good, she supposed, but what about the hotel, the food, the other expenses?

"No me, no Venice." Gwen smiled loopily and giggled, and Claire got a whiff of her breath.

"Have you been *drinking*?"

"Just a little rum and Coke. No biggie."

"Oh, Christ," Claire groaned. *No biggie.* She thought of something else she would do as soon as she got home: kill Meredith. Then she'd have her tubes tied.

Gwen opened up Claire's CD case. "Still using the old technology, I see," she said. "So, what kind of music do history teachers listen to?" Gwen flipped the plastic sleeves. "Vivaldi, Bach, Vivaldi, Bach, Mozart, Vivaldi, Bach. All ancient, just like I thought. Oh, look at this. The Beatles. Well, these guys are pretty old, too. They're so old," she snickered, "half of them are dead."

"Not funny," said Claire, snatching the CDs away from her.

The line for passport control at Venice's Marco Polo Airport stretched the length of the terminal. Claire, with Gwen following wearily, took a place at the end. Up ahead—which seemed an endless distance from them, one filled with two hundred other travelers—were six Plexiglass booths, but only two were occupied by fresh-faced officials. They sat under interrogation-style lamps, heads solemnly bowed, as they carefully studied each passport.

"You'd think there would be more people working here," Claire remarked to Gwen. "It's high season in one of the most visited cities in the world."

"Uhhhh," Gwen replied, and burped.

Claire peered ahead impatiently. Gwen's intoxication had caught up with her at the Milan airport. They'd spent a joyless hour in the women's bathroom while Gwen was sick, had missed their flight to Venice, and had had to wait over an hour for the next one. Claire checked her watch. If they managed to get through this line in less than a half hour, she just might make it to the Biblioteca Marciana before it closed.

Ten minutes passed and they didn't move forward so much as a foot. This is what Ellis Island must've been like, Claire thought, when it was filled with the huddled masses. At this rate she wouldn't get to the Marciana at all that day. An entire day wasted!

Two people broke away from the line Claire and Gwen waited in and went to stand in the much shorter line in front of the passport-control booth marked EU. If they held European passports, Claire wondered, why had they waited in this endless line before moving over?

Perhaps they knew something she didn't. Perhaps it was okay for non-EU citizens to go through the EU passport control when, as now, there was such a disparity between the two lines. And why not? Soon the EU guy would be sitting there with nothing to do. If you put your American passport in front of him, and it was clear that you were a law-abiding kind of person, he would probably stamp it and wave you through, wouldn't he?

"Gwen, pick up your pack." Claire lifted her carry-on onto her shoulder.

"Huh?" She was still in a stupor, which her lunch of cheeseburger and coffee had done little to ameliorate.

"Your pack. We're moving."

They walked across the terminal to the end of the other line. From here, Claire could actually see the face of the passport-control officer. He looked young and friendly. Surely he wouldn't mind if they went through the EU passport booth. And this line seemed to be moving, unlike the other. She felt a little of her tension dissipate.

Gwen noticed the sign above the booth. "What's the EU?"

"The European Union."

"What's that?"

"It's a group of European nations that have joined together because they have more economic and political power as a group than they had individually. It's kind of like when the thirteen colonies became the United States of America. Now the countries in the EU have a common currency and, well, other stuff"—Claire didn't want to admit that she was stumped about the other stuff—"like this special line at passport control, for instance."

"All of the European countries are in it?"

"Most of them, I think." Claire envisioned a map of Europe and started at the top left. "The UK, Sweden, the Netherlands, Denmark, Belgium, France, Germany, Austria, Switzerland, Italy, Spain, and Portugal."

"You've forgotten Finland, Luxembourg, and Greece," said the man standing behind them.

Claire turned. The possessor of the unmistakably English voice regarded them with a cool disdain, as if he were peering through a microscope at a dead insect. "You've also left out the ten countries that have recently joined, which include Poland, Slovakia, and the Czech Republic," he added.

His speech seemed more like a lecture than a friendly interjection, and Claire wasn't entirely certain if she should be offended or not. She searched for a clue in his appearance, which was at odds with his manner. Perhaps he believed that superciliousness compensated for his lack of sartorial splendor. His brown slacks, green wool sport coat, and light blue button-down shirt appeared well-worn and quite possibly slept in, in addition to being a combination of hues agreeable only to the color-blind. In his left hand, he carried a saddle-colored leather satchel; in his right, a black umbrella. *That* was what was strange about him; the weather outside in Venice was, reportedly, eighty degrees and sunny, and he was dressed for London fog.

His face was pleasant enough, in an unremarkable sort of way. He had dark wavy hair, which apparently had not been combed or even looked at recently, for then he would have been aware that it was sticking up oddly on the left side. He hadn't shaved in a while, and the hollows of his cheeks and his upper lip were marked by a blue-tinged shadow.

"Well," Claire said, with a vague feeling that she had been put down or snubbed in some way, "you certainly are a font of useful information."

"Thank you," he replied. "However, as I am also quite certain that America is not a part of the EU, and as I can tell from your accent that you are an American, I believe that you're in the wrong queue, and should be standing"—he pointed his umbrella at the huddled masses—"over there."

For a moment, Claire was too stunned to reply. "But there must be two hundred people over there," she sputtered.

"At least."

"And you think we should move anyway."

"We've already established that you are not a citizen of the EU."

"That sign," Claire pointed at the passport control booth, "does not say EU *only*."

"You regard it as just a suggestion, do you?"

"It could be."

"Well, isn't that just like an American."

"What exactly do you mean by that?"

"You Americans seem to believe that the entire world belongs to you. What the sign actually means is that no one but EU citizens are allowed in this queue, and that everyone else, including you, must go over there." Again, he pointed the umbrella.

"Excuse me, but are you a customs official? Or in any way affiliated with the policing apparatus of the Italian state?"

"No."

"Then why don't you mind your own business?"

"Because the European nations have spent billions of dollars so that we can more easily cross the borders of our neighboring countries, in addition to 'other stuff,' as you so cleverly put it. If we let everyone else in the world use our border facilities, then there was little point in creating them in the first place."

Gwen had witnessed their exchange with complete bewilderment. She nudged Claire and nodded at the passport booth. "That cost billions of dollars?"

"No. Shush." Claire addressed the Englishman once more. "Since you seem to feel that we're inconveniencing you, why don't you take a place in the line ahead of us?"

"Thank you, I will." He stepped forward and stood in front of them.

Claire fumed. "You know, a real gentleman wouldn't have done that. Instead, if he felt that I was doing something unconventional, he would assume that it was necessary to bend the rules a bit in my favor, and that I was in need of assistance."

He turned back to them. "Are you in need of assistance?"

"This girl"—Claire grabbed Gwen by the arm and pulled her closer—"is very ill, and she needs to get to our hotel as soon as possible."

"I'm sorry to hear that. What is her problem?"

"I have a hangover," Gwen said.

"Ah," he said, in a high, clipped voice. He noted Gwen's tender age, more obvious now that her face was washed clean of makeup.

"I see." A brief, disapproving glance at Claire. "Right." He turned his back to them again.

Claire glared at Gwen.

"What's the matter with you?" Gwen asked.

"I believe," the Englishman said, barely turning toward them as he spoke, "that a gentleman would warn an American that she was in the wrong queue, and tell her to go to the correct one, before the official in the booth up ahead has an Italian militiaman escort her there, or to one of those rooms for questioning." He nodded at a row of spartan offices that lined the far side of the terminal. "I've seen it happen before."

He walked to the booth, leaving them at the front of the line.

"Come on." Claire pulled Gwen back to the end of the other line, still over two hundred strong.

"Why are we moving again?"

"We either go of our own accord or have a military escort, apparently. Insufferable British. If it weren't for Americans, he'd be speaking German."

"Really?" Gwen asked. "Why?"

"Because of the war, of course."

"There was a war? What war?"

"Never mind."

"But I don't understand. Why would he be speaking German?"

"Oh, shut up," Claire said.

Chapter Seven

THE WATER TAXI rounded the eastern end of the island and the heart of Venice came into view. Even at a distance, Claire could see the distinctive shape of the Campanile, its pointed green and white rooftop towering above the Piazza San Marco, and the Gothic facade of the Doge's Palace. As exhausted as she was, she still felt excited: at last, she would be in the city where Vivaldi had composed his greatest works, where Palladio had revived classical Roman architecture, where Titian and Tintoretto had ushered in the Venetian Renaissance. Where Alessandra Rossetti had saved Venice from the evil machinations of the Spanish Conspiracy.

"Isn't it incredible?" Claire said. Gwen sat next to her, gripping the rail and looking down into the water with a glassy-eyed stare. A dead rat floated on top of the short, choppy waves of the lagoon.

"I think I'm going to be sick again," she replied. "We should have taken the bus."

"It would have taken too long." Making up for lost time wasn't her only concern. For centuries, before the causeway that joined the city to the mainland was built, the only approach to Venice was by boat—a boat directly to the Piazza San Marco, as they were headed now. She'd wanted her first sight of the city to be the same as if she'd been arriving four hundred years ago. "We're almost there," she said, prodding Gwen to make her look up at the view.

The unbroken line of buildings facing the Riva degli Schiavoni, the waterfront walk along the lagoon, glowed with the honey-colored light of the late-afternoon sun. Tourists crowded the promenade, to stroll in the sunlight, browse at souvenir kiosks, or dine in the open-air cafés facing the lagoon and the island monastery of San Giorgio Maggiore. The thickest throng covered the bridge just east of the Piazzetta, and as their water taxi motored past, Claire could see what had drawn them there: fifty yards behind the bridge, suspended above the canal, the Bridge of Sighs connected the Doge's Palace to the prison directly behind it.

The boat glided into a slip adjacent to a row of gondolas. The pilot, an older man with a sympathetic smile and a striking profile, helped Claire lift her luggage onto a narrow dock, then offered his hand as she climbed out of the boat. She looked up to see the twin marble columns, topped by the Lion of San Marco and the statue of San Teodoro, which marked the entrance to Venice. Four hundred years ago, the Piazzetta had been as much of a tourist mecca as it was today, filled with market stalls and people from all parts of the world, alive with exotic costume and custom. Games of chance flourished in the space between the two columns, which was also the traditional spot for executions. Four hundred years ago, Claire reflected, some of the Spanish conspirators had died in this very place. Superstitious Venetians didn't walk between the Lion of San Marco and the statue of San Teodoro, even now.

They stepped onto the Piazzetta. The white, two-story Sansovino library, which housed the Biblioteca Marciana, fronted the west side and faced the Doge's Palace. But it was already past six o'clock and the library was closed. With their wheeled suitcases trailing behind them, Claire and Gwen reached the base of the Campanile. According to the map the travel agent had provided, their hotel was located just beyond the northwest corner of the Piazza San Marco. Dodging people and pigeons, Claire started diagonally across the square, Gwen plodding along after her.

An hour later, they entered the lobby of the Hotel Bell'acqua, a hostelry that was only a ten-minute walk from the Piazza San Marco, when one knew where one was going. Happily, their labyrinthine path was well rewarded: the small but luxurious hotel was qualified to please in every way, with its picturesque location near two intersecting canals, its elegant lobby, and, not least of its charms, a front-desk clerk who, Gwen insisted as they ascended to the top floor in a tiny elevator, was *really* cute.

Their fourth-floor suite elicited a yawn from Gwen and a feeling of gratitude from Claire, whose budget would never have included such a room, one that was as delicately pretty as a rococo music box. Its Wedgwood blue walls were crowned by elaborate white molding; from the high ceiling hung not one but two Venetian glass chandeliers. The two beds were covered by blue brocade duvets and fluffy down pillows. A small sofa, two chairs, and a hand-painted writing desk occupied a spacious alcove off the main room. Four shuttered windows faced an enchanting panorama of canals, stone bridges, and quaint shop fronts. At the bend of the larger of the two canals, a group of gondoliers stood watch on a row of gondole. It was almost too perfect to be real; it looked like the stage set of a fantasy Venice.

"You've got to see this," said Claire, turning back from the window.

Gwen lay facedown on one of the beds, arms flung wide, snoring softly. She hadn't even bothered to take off her shoes.

At nine o'clock that evening, Claire and Gwen were wandering the narrow lanes near the hotel in search of a restaurant recommended by the cute front-desk clerk. He had directed them to a place only a few blocks away, and had drawn their route on a map. Even so, Claire wasn't entirely sure that the restaurant they eventually found was the restaurant he'd mentioned; but as it had the appealing ambience of a vintage trattoria, she decided it would do quite well.

An elderly waiter wearing a knee-length white apron gave them each a menu as they sat down. Gwen didn't even look at hers.

"I want a cheeseburger," she said.

"But that's what you had for lunch." Or was that breakfast? Their meal in the Milan airport seemed as if it had occurred days ago instead of hours.

"So?"

"Don't you think it's a good idea to vary your diet a little?"

"I vary my diet," she replied. "Sometimes I eat pizza."

"I don't think this place has cheeseburgers."

"What kind of restaurant doesn't have cheeseburgers?"

"A good one." Claire scanned the menu. "Why don't you try the *margherita*? It's pizza, more or less."

"I want a cheeseburger."

A waiter walked over to their table. "*Buona sera, signorine,*" he said. "I am Giancarlo. What can I bring you tonight?"

Claire looked up from the menu. *Holy* god. Standing next to them was one of the most breathtakingly handsome men she had ever seen. He was an inch or so over six feet, with broad, muscular shoulders, slim hips, and sun-streaked brown hair that fell in ringlets to just above his shoulders. His skin was a beautifully burnished golden brown, his mouth generous and full, with the kind of sublime definition she'd seen in Renaissance paintings. His nose was large but refined, with, it seemed, more planes and angles than are usually found on noses. It kept his symmetrical face from being too perfect or too pretty.

How was it possible that in Italy men who looked like this just walked around like normal guys, being waiters, or boat pilots, or hotel clerks? If Giancarlo ever went to the U.S., a giant photograph of him in nothing but Calvin Klein briefs would be dwarfing Times Square faster than he could say "sun god."

"Hi. I mean, *buona sera,*" Claire said.

"*Buona sera,*" Giancarlo said again. This time he said it with a smile and a gaze that held hers for much longer than was necessary to establish a congenial diner/waiter relationship. His eyes were large and hazel, a shimmering combination of green and gold. As he smiled, his eyes seemed to smile, too, as if they could communicate all on their own. Isn't that what Meredith had said about Italian men, that their allure had something to do with the way they looked at you? Now she understood, because Giancarlo appeared to be saying many things with just one glance: that he thought she was attractive, that he was as surprised and delighted to meet her as she was to meet him, and that, if it were up to him, he would get to know her better. Much better.

Claire finally broke their gaze. Holy god, Holy god. No one had looked at her like that since . . . maybe no one had *ever* looked at her like that.

"Gwen?" she prompted. The girl was staring up at Giancarlo with her mouth hanging open. "Do you know what you want to order?"

"Oh." Gwen composed herself. "That thing you said."

"She'll have the *margherita,* I'll have the spaghetti *alle vongole,* and we'll each have a green salad," Claire said.

"You speak Italian," Giancarlo said.

"Not well, I'm afraid," Claire said, switching back to English.

"It sounded very good to me."

"Grazie."

"Would you like some wine with dinner? I can recommend the pinot grigio."

"Yes, that would be lovely."

Giancarlo returned to the kitchen. Gwen batted her eyes. "Yes, that would be lovely," she said, imitating Claire.

"Knock it off."

"Don't you think he's a little young for you?"

"No. Not that it's any of your business." Claire had been wondering about Giancarlo's age herself. Twenty-eight, twenty-nine perhaps? Not a lot younger than herself, but still . . . younger. Meredith might be comfortable going out with younger men, but Claire wasn't so sure that she would be. Not that he was asking. Not that she would have time! And what would she do with Gwen, in any case?

A few tables away, a man speaking accented Italian startled Claire from her thoughts. She hadn't noticed anyone new come into the restaurant. The elderly waiter who had first greeted them stood at attention next to his table as he ordered the osso buco and a glass of cabernet.

Something about the timbre of the man's voice was familiar, but Claire couldn't see him, as the waiter blocked her view. Then the waiter nodded, took the diner's menu, and walked away.

"Look," whispered Gwen, "it's that English guy from the airport. You know, the one who was mad at you."

It was him. A little less rumpled, with combed hair, a clean shirt, and a shave, but unmistakably him.

"He wasn't mad at me. He was officious and rude. Just ignore him." It was hardly necessary, as he didn't notice them. Instead, he noisily unfolded a newspaper, spread it on the table before him, leaned over it, and began to read. She squinted at the masthead: *Il Gazzettino,* the Venice daily. Of course he'd make a show of reading an Italian paper.

Giancarlo returned with a bottle of white wine, a basket of bread, and two salads. "Are you here on holiday?" he asked. Even his voice was beautiful: deep, contented, sensual.

"No, for an academic conference."

"The Ca' Foscari conference?"

"You know of it?"

"Yes, very well. You are giving a lecture?"

"Just attending."

"But you study Venetian history?"

Claire nodded. "My dissertation is on seventeenth-century Venice."

"So you have been here before."

"This is my first time, actually."

"Mine, too," said Gwen.

He turned to Gwen. "You are lucky that your sister brings you along, yes?"

Claire saw dismay in Gwen's eyes and was quietly pleased. Thank heaven he hadn't said mother.

"You are staying in Venice?" Giancarlo continued.

"At the Bell'acqua," Claire replied. "It's not far from here."

"Ah, yes. It's very nice."

From the kitchen, someone called for Giancarlo. "Excuse me, please," he said, hurrying away.

"Sister," Gwen muttered. "You're too old to be my sister."

"I could be your half sister," Claire offered.

"I just don't understand why."

"Why what?"

"Why men like you."

"What do you mean?"

"Men like you. They look at you, they smile at you, they flirt with you."

Except for Giancarlo, Claire hadn't noticed anyone flirting with her, and said so.

Gwen ticked them off on her fingers. "The guy on the boat, the guy at the hotel, and this one, John whatever. I don't get it. You're not, like, wicked hot or anything."

"Thanks very much."

"I don't mean that in a bad way."

"Is there a good way?"

"I mean, you're pretty, but not obviously pretty."

"Maybe some men don't like obvious. The subtle approach can be effective, too."

"It's just that you don't use any makeup, and it looks like everything you're wearing comes from L.L. Bean. Bor-*ring*."

Claire refrained from telling Gwen that nearly every article of clothing she owned came from the L.L. Bean catalog. The clearance catalog.

"So, do all men like you?" Gwen asked.

Claire thought of Michael. "No."

Their conversation was silenced when they saw Giancarlo approaching them again. For a second, Claire wished she were more obviously pretty. Clearly, there were times when it offered a distinct advantage.

Her eyes followed the waiter as he set their dinner on the table, then picked up the bottle of pinot grigio. As he leaned across her to refill her wineglass, her face was only inches from the small, half-hidden concavity at the base of his throat. His warm, golden skin smelled of rich, exotic spices. Maybe she could lean in a little closer, and brush his throat with her lips . . .

"That's enough wine, thank you," said Claire, abruptly coming to her senses.

Giancarlo smiled and stood there for a moment, as if he were going to say something, then seemed to think better of it. "*Buon appetito,*" he said, nodding, and left them alone once again.

"Do we really have to go to this conference thing tomorrow?" Gwen asked.

"Yes."

"Maybe you could go and I could just hang on my own."

"Not a chance."

"But history is so boring."

"How could you possibly think that history is boring?"

"Doesn't everyone think it's boring?"

"Of course not. History is fascinating. It makes the world come alive."

"But it's all about stuff that doesn't even exist anymore."

"That's not true. History is all around us. Especially here. It's in architecture, in art, in social customs and laws . . ." She picked up her fork. "It's even in this. History is much more than memorizing dates or wars or presidents. It's about people—what they accomplished, what they invented, what they imagined. History is—well, it's stories. You like stories, right?"

"Sure."

Claire thought for a moment. What kind of story would capture Gwen's interest? "Have you heard of Casanova?"

"You mean the guy with all the girlfriends?"

"Yes." Close enough, anyway. "Casanova was born here in Venice, in 1725. Apparently, you've heard of his amorous adventures, but there's something else he's famous for. He's one of the few people ever to escape from the Doge's Prison, the one we passed by earlier."

"How did he escape?"

"Carved a hole in the ceiling of his cell, climbed over the roof of the prison, and jumped into a gondola. He'd left Venice before anyone even knew he was gone. In his memoirs, he wrote that he'd had so much experience sneaking in and out of women's boudoirs that escaping from prison was easy by comparison."

"Why was he in jail?"

"For debts, most likely. Casanova was also the inventor of a vanishing ink that disappeared after a few days. He said it was perfect for signing bills—and for writing love letters."

"He was jailed for suspected espionage." The Englishman, a few tables away, spoke as if he'd been a part of their conversation from the beginning. "It was never proved, however. In fact, there was never even a trial."

Claire stared at him, slightly aghast. She still felt embarrassed by their encounter at the airport and had hoped that they would avoid his notice entirely. Unfortunately he was the only diner, besides themselves, who remained in the restaurant. After a few seconds, it dawned on her that he didn't even remember her. He was simply the kind of person who felt entitled to butt in on any conversation he happened to overhear. She wasn't sure which of these things she liked least.

"A fascinating story, though, as you tell it," he went on.

"It's not just a story," Claire replied. "It's a fact."

"Are you sure? I suspect that Casanova was as much a liar as he was a lover." As he spoke, he seemed to be looking toward her, but not quite at her, which Claire found annoying.

"I'm a historian," she replied. "I study early modern Europe."

"Pardon me, I didn't realize I was speaking to an expert. Exactly how do you define 'early modern'?"

"End of the Renaissance to the beginning of the Industrial Revolution."

"Really?"

It was amazing how much a person could say with only one word, Claire marveled. His "really" sounded as if it were a terse code that, deciphered, meant: you are ignorant, unintelligent, and possibly insane as well.

"That seems a rather broad scope of time," he continued. "I thought that historians studied meaningless, obscure bits of history, like, for instance, how the third battle of the Boer War affected the wool industry in early twentieth-century Scotland, or some such thing that no one in their right mind gives a rat's ass about."

It was startling to hear him swear, and oddly funny; when he said "rat's ass" it sounded like "rot's oss." Gwen stifled a guffaw, but Claire didn't feel like laughing. He'd belittled her life, ridiculed her entire existence. Her face felt flushed and hot.

"It's true that many historians, myself included, write on lesser known subjects and events," Claire said, "but even historical events that seem small and obscure can be considered important if they change the course of history or if they help us to understand . . ."

Suddenly she was at a loss for words. What exactly was she trying to say? Something about how stories from the past can help us understand personal motivations, our inner selves, the human heart. Yes, to understand the human heart. Oh, crap. She couldn't actually say that. Not to him, anyway.

"To understand the human condition," she finished weakly. If he said "Really?" again she would attack him with her cutlery.

"Well," he mused thoughtfully, "perhaps you're right." He stood up, glanced at the check lying on the table, and counted out some euros. "I must admit that I was much more intrigued by your Casanova story than I was by your pithy analysis of the EU." He looked at Gwen. "Are you feeling better?"

"Yes," she answered in a small voice.

"Well then," he said, nodding, "have a good evening." The bells on the restaurant door tinkled merrily as he walked out.

"You were right," Gwen said.

"About what?"

"Not all men like you."

"I don't like him, either, so it doesn't count." She discreetly looked around for the man she did like. Where was Giancarlo? Their dinners were finished, but there was no sign of him. The elderly waiter came over to remove their plates. By all appearances he was a sweet man, but he was no substitute for a sun god.

"May we have the check, please?" Claire hoped that her request would inspire Giancarlo's reappearance from the kitchen, but the elderly gent brought the check, and the change that remained after she'd paid the bill. She scanned the restaurant as she pulled on her jacket and walked to the door, but it was clear that Giancarlo had already left for the night.

Claire sternly reminded herself that Giancarlo was beautiful, yes, but he was just a waiter. They'd had a little flirtation and nothing more. He probably flirted with any number of women every night, and it was silly of her to imagine that she might see him again in different circumstances. Certainly they would have nothing in common, nothing to talk about. The whole idea was ridiculous.

Why then did she feel so disappointed?

Chapter Eight

THE SUN WAS up but the Piazza was still in shadow. In a few more hours, the cavelike chill produced by so much stone would dissipate, but as she walked into the gray, empty square, Claire could feel the cold seeping right through her workout clothes.

She had planned to jog a few laps under cover of the arcades before heading for a more important destination at the eastern end of the island near the Public Gardens, but the Piazza's lack of light made it less appealing than she'd imagined. She thought it was lovely to be there so early, though, and so completely alone. The shops and cafés were still closed, and there wasn't another soul in sight. Poetic justice demanded that her footsteps echo as she crossed the silent, unoccupied expanse, but her Nike Air soles only squeaked a little as she headed toward the Piazzetta and the Riva degli Schiavoni.

She turned right at the Campanile and encountered the sight of San Giorgio Maggiore, glorious in the morning sunlight and rising from a blue lagoon that glistened with a jewel-like brilliance. Bobbing on the water's shimmering surface, a row of gondole at the Molo gently tugged at their moorings; farther east, at boat docks spaced along the waterfront, unmanned vaporetti waited patiently for the day to begin.

Thank god for jet lag. Otherwise she wouldn't have woken up at six A.M., and wouldn't have seen Venice like this, unpeopled and pristine. Not surprising, Gwendolyn had still been fast asleep when Claire had quietly sneaked out of the room. She'd left a note, but Claire suspected that she'd be back before Gwen was awake to read it.

With its wide, sunlit sidewalk, picture-postcard views, and small, stair-stepped bridges, the Riva turned out to be the perfect place to run. At least it was perfect in the early morning, before the crowds arrived. The only other people Claire saw, at first, were a few fellow joggers. As she made her way along the promenade, signs of the city coming to life gradually appeared: a suited man carrying a briefcase stepped out of a doorway; a woman carrying a baby on her back traipsed steadily along in the opposite direction. There were unseen signs, too: in the air drifted the tantalizing aroma of baking croissants.

She jogged past the Hotel Danieli, where George Sand's passionate affair with the poet Alfred de Musset had ended with appropriately operatic fury: after he became ill from drink and debauchery, she decamped with his Italian doctor. Farther along she passed La Pietà, the church belonging to the orphanage where Antonio Vivaldi taught music for most of his life. The orphan girls of La Pietà were the first to perform many of his compositions, in concerts that drew audiences from all over Europe. The church was already open for visitors, but Claire didn't stop. The place she most wanted to see was a bit farther on.

A small but lush garden in front hid the house from view. Only when Claire reached the top of the last bridge before the Public Gardens could she see its distinctive lancet windows, set off against the Moorish-style, terra-cotta colored house by thick, white crenellated sashes. Claire stopped and consulted her map just to be sure: yes, the canal flowing beneath the bridge was the Rio di San Giuseppe.

She unfolded a Xerox of a black-and-white photograph from a forty-year-old book and compared it to the scene before her. Nothing had changed: not the four-story villa overlooking the canal and the lagoon; not the water-level entryway and candy-striped boat mooring on the canal side; not the overgrown garden bursting with plum-colored bougainvillea that lay between the house and the Riva dei Sette Martiri. As she'd suspected when she'd first seen the photo, nowhere else on the canal offered a view of the eastern tip of the island.

This had to be Alessandra Rossetti's house; every piecemeal bit of information she'd been able to find added up to it. A letter written in 1617 by an unknown Venetian mentioned the "comforting establishment" of the Signorina Rossetti, who lived on the Rio di San Giuseppe; in one of her letters, Alessandra mentioned seeing the eastern tip of the island from her parlor as she watched ships sailing into the lagoon. Where else on this canal would she have had the view she wrote of? The Rio di San Giuseppe was wider than the average Venetian waterway, lined on both sides by a narrow sidewalk, or *fondamenta,* and colorful houses dotted with flowering window boxes. It looked essentially the same as in the photograph. In a sixteen-hundred-year-old city, Claire reflected, forty years didn't mean much.

Four hundred years was a slightly different story: then, the wide, paved Riva and the bridge she was standing on didn't exist. There would have been a very simple wall or dike between the garden and the lagoon, a wall that was probably buried under the present-day fortifications. Of course, that would fit perfectly with Salvatore Rossetti's account of a flood in 1612, one that had necessitated his family's hasty removal from the premises.

Claire wondered what Alessandra's daily life had been like. During her childhood, she'd been surrounded by family, of course, her father, her brother, and her mother. There'd been lessons in Latin, rhetoric, and mathematics, music played on the lute and the virginal, visits from family and friends, annual celebrations and festivals.

All that must have changed for her when her father and brother embarked on their fateful journey to Crete. How long did Alessandra wait, watching the lagoon for their return? Claire could imagine her waiting forever, through endless, stormy winters and dew-dappled springs; through late summer and its poignant harvest of sweet, tangy berries; through the ripening autumn as the sun faded into mist and the lagoon turned cold and gray as stone.

Even on such a bright, sunny morning, Alessandra's house felt lonely and remote, as if her ghost still stood on her widow's walk, looking out to sea.

Claire wondered how Alessandra felt about being a courtesan. She preferred to think that her heroine was happy, or at least complacent, knowing that she'd made the best of what life had offered her. But was it possible to be happy living the life that Alessandra lived? Or even content? Perhaps the demands of simple survival made those kinds of questions immaterial; maybe happiness and contentment were concepts that people thought less about, then.

And what about love? Nothing Claire had read indicated that the courtesan had a deep emotional attachment to any of her suitors. Perhaps romantic love hadn't mattered to Alessandra. Perhaps it was enough to be independent, to be mistress of her own fate. Or was she? Claire watched the bougainvillea rippling in the light wind. She realized that upon seeing Alessandra's house, she'd hoped to experience some insight, a revelation. Instead she felt longing and despair. Was it really possible to discover what had happened almost four hundred years ago?

The Prince of Swords

11 November 1617

BIANCA HAD LET him in unwillingly, then hurried upstairs to tell her mistress of their unexpected visitor. Alessandra put aside her sketch, picked up the candle that illuminated her drawing table, and gathered her skirts to go down to the parlor. She resented the intrusion at so late an hour, but her study of the nautilus shell had annoyed her. She could not seem to capture the gleam of the shell's pearlescent interior, and she wasn't completely unhappy to quit it.

Her mysterious caller stood facing the fire, his black cape dripping on the parquet floor. He turned at the sound of her approaching footsteps just as a bolt of lightning split the sky and lit up the room for one earth-shaking, shattering second. Face-to-face, in that first moment, Alessandra believed she was looking into the cold, glittering eyes of a madman.

But when the lightning and the crash of thunder had passed, he introduced himself with the curt bow of a young gentleman. "Antonio Perez, viscount of Utrillo-Navarre. I bear a letter for the marquis of Bedmar."

"He isn't here," she replied. "I'm surprised you did not go to the Spanish embassy. Anyone can direct you to it."

"My instructions were to bring the letter here and to wait for him if necessary. I come at the order of the duke of Ossuna, viceroy of Naples."

"I do not expect the marquis for another four days."

"Then I must presume upon your hospitality."

"You presume too much. This is my home, not a lodging house. There are plenty of taverns in Venice should you need a bed."

Antonio Perez seemed distressed by her refusal. In the dark room, lit only by the fire in the hearth, assorted candelabra, and the occasional flash of lightning as the storm moved south across the lagoon, Alessandra did not notice the way his skin seemed drawn tight over his temples, or the faint blue shadows beneath his eyes, or the bright, feverish blush on his otherwise pale cheeks.

"Signorina Rossetti, I have just spent hours in that storm and I am soaked to the bone." He didn't add that the inclement weather had provided excellent cover for being smuggled into Venice. "If it is your desire that I go out in it again, I will do so, but I must tell you that the men who brought me here have already departed and shall not return. I have no transport."

"My manservant will take you to a nearby inn."

"Then may I impose upon you for a hot brandy before I go? I fear I have caught a chill."

Alessandra disliked his presumption but she could see that he was shivering in spite of his attempts to conceal it. "Yes, of course," she said, turning away. As she moved toward the doorway to summon Bianca, the viscount of Utrillo-Navarre collapsed on the parlor floor.

With considerable effort, Alessandra and Nico managed to carry him upstairs to one of the bedchambers. The young nobleman was more robust than he at first appeared. Even after his soaked garments were stripped away, his strong, athletic physique had an unusual solidity that made it difficult for the two of them to lift him onto the bed. Although Antonio Perez had a gentleman's manner, his nakedness revealed the hard musculature of a soldier. He had the sort of figure Alessandra rarely saw, at least not among the men of her intimate acquaintance, accustomed as they were to lives of luxury and ease. With the exception of Bedmar, she corrected herself, though he was shorter and more stout than this viscount, but still a powerful man for his age.

"Do you think it wise to let him stay?" Nico asked.

Alessandra saw the concern in his soft, weathered eyes. "No, I am not certain there is wisdom in it, but he is ailing. What else can I do?"

"I could take him to La Pietà. The convent sisters will take care of him."

"I fear that would put him in as much danger as this fever." She took her hand away from the young man's hot forehead.

"What if he carries the pestilence? We don't know where he is from."

"He comes from Naples. I have not heard of any sickness there." Alessandra gathered up the viscount's wet clothes and handed them to Nico. "Please take these down to the kitchen to dry, and bring up some firewood. Let's give him a day or so and see. He looks strong—perhaps he will pull through quickly."

"As you wish."

After Nico left, Alessandra studied Utrillo-Navarre's few possessions: an elegant sword and scabbard; a dagger that hung at his waist and another that had been artfully hidden within a pocket inside his sleeve; a modest purse, with Neapolitan and Venetian coins; and a letter encased in a waxed parchment envelope. She took the missive from its waterproof enclosure and turned it over in her hands. The cream-colored vellum was of the finest quality, but carried neither direction nor name, only a seal of bloodred wax, stamped with an intricate, interlocking design. She quickly tucked it into her pocket when she heard footsteps on the stairs.

Bianca entered carrying a basin of water and some clean towels. Alessandra motioned for her to set it down on the bedside table, and pulled two chairs nearer the bed. Bianca dipped a cloth in the basin, wrung it out, and gave it to Alessandra, who placed the cool compress on the viscount's brow.

"Perhaps we should call a doctor," Bianca suggested. "I should not like to see you with a fever, too."

"Don't worry, you know I am never ill. If our patient is not better by tomorrow, I will send for Benedetto. He may not be the best physician in the world, but he is discreet." She looked at Bianca meaningfully. "As we all must be."

"Yes, my lady."

"In the meantime, I will nurse him."

"As you will. I should know better than to advise you. God's truth, he is a handsome one."

"Bianca!"

"I only say that if a stranger is going to fall ill in your house, he should look exactly like this young gentleman." Bianca's expression was grave, but her eyes sparkled. "Look at the way his raven hair curls about his brow, and his skin, like lilies and roses—"

"That is the fever."

"But fever does not account for his lush, firm lips, or the pleasing contours of his face. And he is young, unlike the others," she said with a knowing glance. "'Tis a shame he will not open his eyes."

The viscount's closed eyes had not so much as fluttered since he had fallen, but Alessandra remembered with remarkable clarity the moment she'd first seen them, as the lightning had struck. She'd been shocked by how black they were, as raven black as his hair.

"I know you speak only to provoke me," said Alessandra, smiling, "but I will grant you he is not unsightly. For a Spaniard, that is."

It was a hand. Antonio squinted and focused on a glass-fronted curio cabinet against the wall near the bed. Yes, prominently displayed on the top shelf was a human hand, cut off just above the wrist, blackened with age, wizened, clawlike, grotesque.

He had seen many repugnant things in his twenty-six years: mutilations, amputations, decapitations, even seen men gutted and tripping over their own entrails on the battlefield—nevertheless this desiccated, disembodied hand unnerved him. It provoked, from the fog of his recent memory, a disturbing recollection of what may have been an unholy ritual, complete with incense and chanting and the sound of tinkling glass, performed at his bedside by a hideous, birdlike creature. Antonio lifted his hands to eye level just to make sure: yes, he still had the requisite number, one at the end of each arm.

He pushed back a thick coverlet, rolled on his side, and tried to sit up, but the effort was too great. There was a profoundly bad odor in the room, the smell of something dead. He fought back a wave of nausea as he surveyed his surroundings.

The bedchamber was very fine, larger and more elegantly furnished than his rooms at Ossuna's palace in Naples. The canopy bed's brocade draperies were drawn open, letting in the heat from a well-tended fire in the manteled hearth on the right. To the left, a wood table was covered with small ink and charcoal sketches of seashells and plant life, with some of the drawings pinned to the wall above. Ahead, muted light shone softly through a row of Moorish windows, through which he could see the delicate tracery of barren tree branches and, beyond that, water and sky, both a misted silver-gray. It was an austere yet pleasing prospect. The time was either early morning or late afternoon; he couldn't tell which.

He was at Signorina Rossetti's, he realized. The last he could recall, he was standing in the parlor. He remembered the fire, the roar of the storm raging outside, how he had tried to stop his teeth from chattering but could not. Although why he should be so vain in the presence of a courtesan, he knew not, except that she'd been so much different from what he'd expected. From what he'd heard, Venetian courtesans were akin to mythic sirens who ensnared men with a glance and a sweet song and who existed solely to charm a man's purse from him.

But this one had been ready to toss him out into the storm again, in complete defiance of Ossuna's wishes! She hadn't been impressed by him in the least. Surely, though, he would've been more impressive if he'd left the parlor under his own power. Obviously someone had carried him to this room, but he remembered none of it. How many hours—or days?—had he slept in this comfortable bed? In truth he could not tell; he knew only that sometime between the moment of his insensibility and his awakening was a dark night of chanting and incense, and a vision of a huge, horrific bird.

He studied the curio cabinet again. The hand was not the only curiosity on display; it was set among other artifacts and relics equally strange, although generally less repulsive. Antonio noted a flat stone etched with hieroglyphs; numerous coins, Roman and Greek; a few rough nuggets of carnelian, onyx, and crystal; and pieces of amber with insects entombed. One, shaped like a heart, contained within it a tiny but perfectly formed salamander. One shelf was wholly given over to the natural treasures of the sea, with shells of diverse shapes and sizes, a family of starfish, opaque bits of colored sea glass, a few pearls, and a handful of small, polished rocks.

The door slowly opened, and Alessandra peeked in. She caught his eye, smiled, and entered. "I see the patient is restored to life."

"How long have I been here?"

"Two days."

"Oh, no. I must get up . . ." Antonio raised himself on one elbow and grimaced.

"You are too weak," she protested.

He sank back, dizzy from the effort. "I fear I am in your debt."

"It's too soon to worry about that. First, you must get well." She held her hand to his forehead. "You have improved. The fever broke a while ago, and I thought it best to let you sleep."

"Is it morning or night?"

"Night, in a few hours. I have come to inquire as to whether you would like some supper."

"I'm not certain I can stomach a meal just yet. I don't mean to offend, but there is a terrible odor in this room."

Alessandra laughed. "You are the source of that odor."

"I beg your pardon."

"Please allow me to explain. The doctor was here last night—"

"By any chance does he resemble a large bird? Or was that a nightmare?"

"You remember his mask. It is commonly used for protection against the plague. As you are still alive, I think we can assume that you have not carried the pestilence with you."

"You did not do well to summon anyone."

"I am well aware that your visit to Venice is—how shall I say?—a private matter. But what would you have me do? If you had died in my house, I would have had a body to dispose of. A doctor's visit is easily explained, but a dead body is not."

As he had been on their first, brief meeting, Antonio was impressed with Signorina Rossetti's remarkable self-possession. He'd never known a woman to speak so calmly about such things. Although he was not yet certain, he suspected that their meeting was not completely incidental to his task, but yet another part of Ossuna's grand design. The duke thought Bedmar a fool for consorting with a Venetian mistress; facing her now, he reckoned that Ossuna had more reason to be worried than he knew. In Signorina Rossetti were beauty and intelligence combined, and Perez intuited that she would not be easily frightened. If the courtesan could not be intimidated, then her fate was dark indeed. For a moment he felt something like regret, if he should be chosen as the instrument of that fate.

"In Spain we do not associate doctors with increased health, but with death," he said.

"Perhaps our Venetian physicians are more enlightened. After all, you appear to be on the mend. Benedetto bled you, and he recommended some ointment of his own design, which he rubbed on your chest and the soles of your feet. That is the source of the odor of which you complain."

"It is truly quite foul."

"He assured me of its curative properties. It is the distillation of marmot."

"Marmot?"

"The oil from the creature's skin, he said, can relieve every suffering."

"Are you of this same opinion?"

"I believe that paying the doctor well for the opportunity to test his medicine has bought his silence. How do you feel?"

"I cannot yet tell you. But be assured that this ointment has cured me of one thing—my appetite."

"It is that bad?"

"Can you not smell it?"

"I didn't say it was pleasant, but I thought you might be able to bear it until you are better."

"I believe I shall be ill as long as I am thus anointed."

"Very well then. Nico will bring a basin for you to wash in." She walked toward the door, stopped, turned around. "I have not sent to the marquis to tell him of your arrival. I thought it better to wait until you were well, and seek your counsel on the matter."

"You are prudent as well as accommodating."

"Shall I send Nico with a letter?"

"Do you often send messages to the marquis?"

"Never."

"I was instructed not to approach him directly. If you do something out of the ordinary, it may attract notice. Perhaps we should delay, until he arrives at his customary time."

"As you wish."

As Alessandra left the room, Antonio saw that his clothes had been dried and neatly folded in a stack on a chair at the end of the bed, and realized to his chagrin that he was, underneath the coverlet, completely naked.

Alessandra sat in front of the large, gilt-framed mirror in her bedchamber, powdering her exposed shoulders, finishing the last of her toilet. Bianca had hired a girl, Luisa, who came in every afternoon to curl and arrange her hair. Tonight it was swept up with a diamond comb in back, the curls framing her face, a style that Luisa said was being worn by the most fashionable women in town. Her maquillage was exquisitely pale, though a bit more dramatic than usual. She preferred a light hand when it came to face powders and lotions, but tonight would be spent with Senator Contarini. He was the type of man who liked the look of a painted woman, as long as it was not overdone.

Sometimes Alessandra thought that she spent more time getting ready for her liaisons than having them. Not long ago, she never would have imagined that she'd spend so many hours staring at her own reflection, carefully considering how a lock of hair was set or if the color of a fabric complemented her skin. In some ways she found it tedious, but the act of preparing for her lovers was often reassuring; the time it took for her physical transformation provided the opportunity for her emotional transformation, too. She became a creature who was not quite herself, a chameleon who could embody whatever fantasy her clients desired: a seductress, a virgin . . . a boy, even, she thought with a wry smile, thinking of Signor Vespaccio's unusual proclivities. She'd discovered that younger men generally preferred more artifice, older men tended to care little for powder and rouge: unadorned youth was evidently more beguiling as one aged, and she dressed and made herself up accordingly. Contarini was, at forty-two, one of her younger clients, and he expected to see Alessandra at her glittering best. She surveyed herself carefully one last time: kohl-lined eyes; deep red lips; her newest and finest dress, a flattering green silk heavily woven with gold thread. For the finishing touch she clipped on a pair of diamond earrings and fastened a matching necklace around her throat. It wouldn't do to go out without them: the jewels had been given to her by Contarini himself.

"You should be in bed." Alessandra stopped by to check on her patient and found him attired in his shirt and slops, the loose breeches worn by Spanish soldiers. He was peering through the glass of her curio cabinet. The tray that Bianca had brought up earlier had only crumbs left on it, and Alessandra surmised that he had discovered his appetite after all. The bath and clean linens had no doubt helped; the room smelled fresh again.

"I was admiring your collection." His white shirt glowed in the firelight, and orange points of light gleamed in his dark eyes. "Is that truly a human hand?"

"It's the hand of an Egyptian mummy. My father was a merchant who used to visit many exotic ports."

"He no longer travels?"

"He and my brother were lost in a storm. But while he was alive, he never failed to bring back interesting presents."

"A mummy's hand seems a strange gift for a girl."

"Perhaps I am a strange girl." She laughed at his surprised expression. "Originally it was an entire mummy. But then the crew was apprised of its worth, and their avarice reduced it to this."

"What would you have done with an entire mummy?"

"I don't know. Propped it up in a corner to scare away thieves, I suppose. It would have made a wonderful study," she said wistfully.

"Those are your drawings, I take it?"

"Yes, but they're not meant for others to see." Alessandra hoped he did not see the flush in her cheeks. This was her private sanctuary, a place where guests were not invited, which was why she had hidden him here. It hadn't occurred to her that he was a guest, too; but then, he hadn't been conscious at the time.

"I think they're quite good." Antonio swayed a little as he spoke, and Alessandra realized that he had remained standing out of politeness.

"I insist that you rest," she said, and this time he didn't hesitate to return to the bed. She took the tray away as he climbed under the coverlet.

"Where are the things I carried with me?" he asked.

"You mean the letter? It is in the bed-table drawer."

"Thank you for keeping it safe. And for keeping me safe. I'm sure your generosity will be rewarded."

"I require no reward, but an explanation would be welcome. Why were you instructed to come here instead of going to Bedmar directly?"

"I cannot tell you."

"I have a right to know."

"I cannot tell you because I do not know. I'm not privy to the contents of the letter or to the duke's reasons for such secrecy."

"You're just the messenger, then?"

"In this instance, yes." He searched her expression for a sign of trust and found none. "You don't believe me."

"I don't know what to believe, except that I am being used for some end in which I have no part."

"Perhaps your lover, the marquis, can explain."

In the viscount's comment she discerned a snide insinuation and a coldness in his voice that she didn't in the least like. She moved toward the door, taking the tray with her.

"You're leaving?" he called.

She turned to face him. "I'm called out for the evening."

"Is that why you're dressed so handsomely?"

"It is a courtesan's duty to beautify and entertain." She curtsied with an irony she suspected was lost upon him.

"What mask will you wear?"

"None at all. Masks are worn only during Carnival and other festival days."

"So your beauty will be on display for everyone to enjoy."

"Is that a compliment, or a slight? Your words, like your sword, can cut both ways. In your blundering attempt to win a woman's heart, you may harm yourself."

"I thought a courtesan's heart could not be won, only bought. And as you no doubt have seen from my purse, I have not the means. I am but a poor viscount, reduced to soldiering."

"That is a shame, indeed. Perhaps the next time you come to Venice, you shall be better equipped."

Alessandra was determined to ignore Utrillo-Navarre entirely, but by the next evening her resolution had wavered and she sent Bianca with a message asking him to join her downstairs for supper, if he were well enough.

Still pale but steady of step, Antonio appeared in the parlor at the appointed hour, and escorted Alessandra into the dining room. Nico had lowered and lit the chandelier that illuminated the gold cloth-covered table, on which Venetian glass goblets and an array of exquisite Florentine china sparkled and shone.

"I thought that this evening you would once again be summoned to a party of pleasure," Antonio said as he pulled out Alessandra's chair, then took a seat across from her.

"It's true, I am unexpectedly free. It seems that one of my patrons has found other company he desires more."

"I hardly know how to respond to such a new and unique challenge to my gallantry. Should I congratulate you for relinquishing one of your weekly sins or condole with you for losing a portion of your keep? I confess I am confused. Although I must say you don't seem unhappy."

Alessandra laughed. "No, I'm not unhappy, strangely enough. As for your predicament, I require neither your congratulations nor your condolences."

"And how was your evening? Was it magical? Was your gown a success?"

"So many questions! You must have been terribly bored."

"On the contrary. While you were out making conquests, I was praying for your soul's salvation."

He spoke so solemnly that at first Alessandra believed he was sincere, then she saw the mischievous glint in his eyes. "You're jesting."

"But you believed me for a moment."

"Only a moment. You don't have the look of the saint about you. I'm certain that if you were feeling better, you would join in the revels."

"Perhaps. But if I did, I would claim to be unduly influenced by a certain Venetian courtesan."

Bianca carried in a tray with dishes of olives and bowls of soup.

"I believe you find delight in thinking me wicked," Alessandra said after Bianca had gone.

"You mistake me. I simply want to understand your character."

"'Venetians first, Christians second,' is what we say here, and I suppose that applies to me as well as anyone."

"So you do not consider your way of life sinful?"

Alessandra's hesitation was barely noticeable. "No, I do not." She had never felt the need to share her private misgivings; why did she have to suppress an impulse to do so now?

"Tell me, how is it you are without children? Is it not a mortal sin to prevent their conception?"

"What the church may call a sin I call a kindness. I have no desire to produce more fatherless babes for the orphanage. But lest you think that all Venetian women are as sinful as I, please let me assure you otherwise—there are many bastards in Venice." Alessandra smiled. "Some of whom were not even born here."

Antonio laughed heartily. "I deserved that. I must confess, I have never been devout. I did not like church at all when I was a boy. My family belonged to the grandest church in Pamplona, and I thought it was fearsome. Often enough they had to drag me there, kicking and screaming."

"You were afraid of church?"

"When I was a boy, yes. When I got older, I simply slipped out the door as soon as it was convenient."

"You're not afraid any longer?"

"No." He smiled. "But I always carry my sword, just in case."

"It does not seem as if fighting and praying are all that compatible, anyway."

"You'd be surprised. There is a great deal of praying on a battlefield."

"Do you like being a soldier?"

"I suppose. I don't think about it much. It was the path that was chosen for me, and yet I think I am well suited to it. Although there was no indication I would be. My father, may he rest in peace, always said I was undisciplined, but that changed when I went into the duke's service."

"The duke of Ossuna?"

"Yes."

"Are you pleased to be under his command?"

"In what way do you mean?"

"It's a simple question. Your refusal to answer tells more than you would wish known, I suspect."

"On the contrary, I do not refuse. The duke is a man of vision who reigns supreme in Naples."

"We Venetians have a different view. He is a rogue who challenges our fleet without provocation, and it is rumored that he is living too well off the riches of his fiefdom."

"He assumes the privileges of power as does any lord."

"You defend him."

"Of course."

"You believe in unquestioning obedience, then?"

Antonio's jaw tensed. "That is a soldier's duty. And, I might add, a courtesan's duty if she cares to keep the patronage upon which her subsistence depends."

"My mind is no one's possession but my own." She rang for Bianca. "I find I am no longer hungry. Please continue, if you like." Alessandra hurried from the room.

Antonio hesitated a moment, then stood and brushed by Bianca as she entered the dining room. He caught up with Alessandra on the stairs leading to her bedchamber on the top floor.

"Forgive me," he said. "I don't know how to talk to you."

"You could begin by answering my questions."

"To reveal my thoughts could imperil both of us."

"Your presence here already does."

Against his better judgment, Antonio decided to take her into his confidence. "The duke of Ossuna is not a completely rational man," he confessed reluctantly. "I cannot respect him, yet I must serve him or my life is forfeit. He rules with an iron fist and, in doing so, foments rebellion. He concocts grandiose schemes by which I fear he will bring himself and others to ruin."

"And the marquis? Do you serve him, too?"

"In a manner of speaking, I suppose I do."

"And what is your opinion of him?"

"Ambitious, ruthless, even cruel at times. But he's also a masterful politician, a brave soldier, and a strong leader."

"But is he a good man?"

"You perhaps know better than I." He smiled ruefully. "Now that I have shared such private beliefs, I am completely in your power."

"You have no reason to distrust me."

"I have no reason to trust you, either."

"Need I remind you that you arrived in the middle of the night with a letter for the Spanish ambassador, a letter you could not freely take to his door. By this I can surmise that either you or this letter is unwelcome in Venice, and yet I have not given you up. Do not mistake my tolerance for naiveté. Just tell me—what secret business does Ossuna have with the marquis? Is he a spy?"

"You go too far." Antonio angrily turned away and stamped down the stairs.

"Is he a spy?" Alessandra called after his retreating figure, but she got no answer.

Alessandra was seated at her writing desk when Antonio entered the parlor the next morning. He stopped in the center of the room. "I have no wish to disturb you if you are busy."

"On the contrary, I'm just finishing a letter to my cousin in Padua." They had not spoken since their argument of the night before and the air between them was strained. "Please, sit down."

Antonio perched on the chair near the fire. He still looked pale, and as if he'd had little sleep. "You will be happy to know that soon I will be on my way back to Naples."

"I agree it is best." Alessandra paused and looked away before meeting his eyes again. "You said you wanted to understand my character. I do not wish you to leave thinking I am without morality, or without any religious feeling. But even when I was young, I knew that I had not those raptures that others professed to feel during Mass. It's not that I had a competing philosophy; I was simply unmoved. The singing, the incense, the chanting meant little to me. I have always preferred the natural treasures of this world to the presumed rewards of the next. When I look at a seashell, or a rosebud, or the intricate veins of a leaf and see the order and the patterns of nature, I have a sense of my soul being taken and lifted by God, the same feeling that my friends claimed was inspired by the holy mysteries. Does that seem strange to you?"

Antonio shook his head. "I have often felt such things myself, yet I have never been able to put it into words."

"My father used to say that contact with many creeds must dilute belief in just one. Perhaps it is that which contributes to my lack of Christian fervor, but I cannot regret it. If I were a man, I would be a sailing man, and travel to distant ports, and learn many strange customs."

"A sailor? You?"

She smiled. "Not just a sailor—a pirate."

"A pirate!"

"Yes." She flourished her quill like a sword and pointed it at his throat, grinning mischievously. "I'd take my treasure off men like you—dainty, lily-livered dogs who faint from a little fever . . ."

Antonio sprang toward her, tore the feather from her hands, and threatened her in turn. Laughing, Alessandra led him on a merry chase through the parlor, until Antonio caught her and lightly imprisoned her between his two outstretched arms, his palms firmly planted against the wall. Panting and smiling, she looked up into his face. All at once she did not feel like laughing anymore. For a moment, as their lips slowly moved closer together, neither seemed to be breathing at all.

Bianca rushed in and curtsied nervously. "The marquis of Bedmar is arrived, my lady," she said, her eyes darting between Alessandra and Antonio as they quickly stepped away from each other and prepared themselves to receive him.

The Fool

14 November 1617

BEDMAR TIPPED OSSUNA'S missive toward the hazy light from Alessandra's parlor windows and read it again. *Damn and blast.* The letter brought him nothing but trouble.

. . . surprise is one of the greatest weapons in our arsenal and to delay any longer than necessary could mean defeat. I will have new ships ready to launch at the end of April; the fleet could reach Venice before Ascension Day. Indeed, there seems no better time . . .

He skimmed over the remainder: *no more delays . . . fully prepared . . . ready to strike . . .* it was full of the saber rattling so typical of the duke. And foolhardy, as well—it left them only six months to prepare for an all-out attack.

Bedmar wondered if the count of Segovia's regiments, still fighting in the Netherlands, would be able to get to Venice in such a short time; in all his calculations their experienced support was an essential element of success. *Mother of Christ, six months!* As usual, the duke had asked the impossible; but the marquis had managed to achieve the impossible before. And damn if he would show his displeasure in front of Utrillo-Navarre.

The young viscount stood nearby as Bedmar read Ossuna's letter and mulled over his reply. The message, the marquis reflected, was not entirely contained within the text. Antonio Perez was an unusual choice for a messenger, but Bedmar knew better than to let on that he was aware of this. When he had first entered Signorina Rossetti's house and seen the viscount there, his eyes, well trained to conceal his thoughts, had fleetingly betrayed his surprise.

Only once before, at Ossuna's palace in Naples, had Bedmar been face-to-face with the duke's most trusted and lethal assassin, whose swordsmanship was known throughout Italy and Spain. Utrillo-Navarre was still young, but Bedmar could see a bit of his father, the old viscount, in the boy's tall, solid form and confident expression. Now *there* was a man in the grand old tradition—they'd once crossed swords, fought until neither could stand, then called it a deuce and gone away friends. The marquis had been sorry when he'd heard of his passing. But the son? It was unlikely that a similar camaraderie would develop, given the circumstances.

Utrillo-Navarre's presence in Venice brought everything into question; Bedmar had recognized at once the threat he embodied. First, to Alessandra; Ossuna had more than once made it clear that he thought her a danger to their security. Second, to himself. Ossuna had managed to bring Antonio Perez into Venice unnoticed. *Next time,* the duke seemed to be warning him, *even you won't know that he is there.*

What was behind the duke's sudden need to launch their assault a full two months ahead of the date on which they'd earlier agreed? It made no sense to strike before Bedmar could assemble all his troops—unless the duke planned to strike at him as well.

It was no secret that Ossuna was unpopular in Naples. Did he have designs on the viceroyalty of Venice, Bedmar's intended post after the victory? The marquis stole a glance at Perez. Perhaps the duke's new scheme was that Bedmar would not survive the battle—and no doubt Utrillo-Navarre would be close at hand to make certain of it.

If Ossuna wanted to play the blackguard, he would be the one to lose, Bedmar thought darkly. The duke's warning was meaningless to him, and irritating as well. It would have to be answered in just the right manner, and in a way that Ossuna would never expect. At once Bedmar hit on the perfect reply, a reply that had begun to take shape as soon as he'd seen Perez, and sat down at the writing desk.

Your Excellency—

It would be my pleasure to oblige your new instruction. I will accelerate readiness on all fronts and will send maps as soon as they are complete.

So generous of you to send your esteemed viscount to Venice. Indeed, his return is required, as he can be of much service here. I will of course see to it that his visit is unnoted and that he is without want for as long as he is in my care.

Brilliant, Bedmar thought, and signed his name with a flourish. In his own way, Bedmar was letting the duke know that he was fully aware of his black intent, yet was unafraid. Ossuna would certainly take the bait, believing that his assassin could carry out his orders successfully in spite of Bedmar's foreknowledge. But the marquis had many times discovered that youth and strength were no match for experience and cunning. Bedmar folded the letter and sealed it.

"I wish you good journey," he said. "My gondolier waits below. He'll take you to a small boat at the end of the island; from there you will be rowed to a ship anchored at Malamocco. If need be, let Captain de Braga speak for you. Don't say a word until you're safely at sea."

"Your Excellency." Antonio bowed. "I look forward to our next meeting."

"As do I," Bedmar replied.

So that's how it will be, Alessandra thought. She stood at her bedroom window, looking out at the lagoon, at the Rio di San Giuseppe that flowed along the east side of the house, and at the fallow garden below. In the canal, Bedmar's empty gondola was tied to a red-and-white-striped post next to stone steps that rose from beneath the water's surface and led to the garden gate. Any moment now the viscount would appear, progressing from the back door along a curving path of stepping stones, then out through the gate and into the waiting gondola. She supposed that he and Bedmar had not much more to say after she had taken her leave of them.

Not a word, not even a meaningful glance did he leave her with. She had come into the parlor as Bedmar handed his reply to the viscount, then threw Ossuna's letter onto the fire. Utrillo-Navarre had said nothing to her, except to ask that his cape be brought to him. Then he'd made a slight, formal bow, not even meeting her eyes, although she suspected that if he had, she would have found no sentiment there.

She'd excused herself and gone up to her room, intending to read or to write in her journal. But once she'd come upstairs, she had done neither of those things. Instead, she'd been drawn to the window, the one at the very corner of the room, the one with the best view of the gondola that would take him away.

Now she reproached herself, because of course there hadn't been any true intimacy between them. They'd talked a bit, was all, and had seldom agreed. Perhaps his seeming charm was due to circumstance. He'd been dependent on her protection, but now that he was not, he no longer needed to keep up the pretense of an amiable nature. She decided she should not give him the pleasure of knowing she was watching him depart, but still she could not pull herself away from the window.

The fire in the hearth sizzled and popped, and Alessandra strained against her dress. The best brocade in the city and still the fabric chafed. The room was too warm, in fact it was stifling, she noted with irritation. It was Bianca's doing, always insisting that Nico stack the grate with so much wood. Always worried she would get a chill, always hovering, always fussing. For a moment, Alessandra inwardly railed against Bianca's solicitude, as unfair as she knew it was for her to do so. She only wished that . . . she didn't even know what she wished. She felt a longing for something, but it was a mute longing, inexpressible. To be free of it, she thought, and instantly mocked herself: to be free of what? *To be free of this dress, for a start.* She moved closer to the window, pressed her fingers to it. Moist, cold air seeped through the mullions with a faint keening whistle. The glass felt like ice. She rested her forehead against it and felt some relief.

Although it was not raining, the sky was filled with gray, roiling clouds. Even at midmorning, Alessandra could sense the night coming on, and with it another storm. For the moment, everything felt timeless and still, as if under this somber light the world had stopped turning. In her view, nothing moved save for the flight of a solitary seabird and the constant, shallow rippling of the water. It was as quiet as a day of mourning. She heard the crackling of the fire at the opposite end of the room, and vague noises from downstairs: indistinct, low-pitched male voices, the dull thump of heavy boots across creaking floorboards. In the distance, carried along on the thin stream of air blowing between the windowpanes, came the muffled toll of a church bell. *Sailors panic if they hear bells while at sea,* her father had once told her. *They believe it a bad omen.* She wondered how it must feel to be on the deck of a heaving ship, far out to sea, with nothing but wind, and sea spray, and the pounding waves as companions. She briefly closed her eyes and tried to imagine the freedom of it: the sheer, incredible freedom of it.

Paolo, Bedmar's gondolier, appeared at the side of the gondola—he must have walked along the *fondamenta* from the kitchen, where he'd been waiting—and boarded the boat. Utrillo-Navarre emerged in the garden a moment later. The gondola's *felze* had been removed, and Alessandra could see him plainly as he sat down, but he faced the lagoon, and she could not see his expression. He wrapped his cape tighter, as if he were cold.

Paolo untied the rope that moored the boat, then coiled it and placed it behind the gondola seat. Before he took up the oar, he glanced up to where Alessandra stood. It was as if he'd known exactly where to look, had known that her solemn face would be framed by that particular window. She had thought the viscount would be the one making the backward glance, but he stared resolutely ahead.

Paolo looked up at her with a sober, unwavering expression. He was gaunt, with dark hair and large eyes, a young man of twenty-one. He was often around, especially when Bedmar was away. Whenever the marquis was gone from Venice, Paolo made himself available to Nico and Bianca; he rowed Alessandra's gondola for them, brought melons and fresh fish from the markets, carried in the heavy kegs of wine that arrived by cargo boat. They rewarded him with a few coins now and then, as was proper.

A few weeks before, she had unexpectedly found Paolo in the spare bedchamber, the one in which Antonio had just stayed. As she'd walked up the stairs, she'd noticed that the door was slightly ajar. A glimmering candle shone softly within.

She had pushed the door open and discovered Paolo standing next to her drawing table. Clearly she had startled him, as he had turned suddenly to face her, at the same time concealing something behind his back. He was silent, of course, but his expression betrayed his guilt.

"What are you doing here?" She did not expect a reply, but the question had been prompted by anger. Paolo was welcome in the kitchen, but he had no leave to be wandering about her house. She moved closer. "What do you have in your hands?"

Paolo had stood very still, his eyes trained upon her, apparently without fear. It occurred to her that he might not know that the consequences for stealing were severe. She glanced over to her curio cabinet, but the room was too dark to see if anything was missing from it. What would have caught his fancy? "Give back what you have taken and you can go. I won't tell anyone," she offered, holding out her hand.

He looked pained at her words, but slowly brought his hands from behind his back and held out a small square of paper. On it was a sketch of a seashell, one that at first she took for her own. Alessandra held the paper closer to the candlelight and saw that it was not her drawing. Every detail of the nautilus was perfectly rendered, with a clarity and precision she had never seen before, and yet it was more than an objective view: the essence of the shell had been captured as well.

"Did you draw this?" she asked.

Paolo nodded.

"Just now?"

Another nod.

"It's beautiful. You have a rare talent."

He made no response, just kept his steady eyes locked upon hers. "But you do know that you are not allowed to be in this room, or to take my things?" Alessandra spoke gently, as she was not sure of the depth of his understanding. She held out the drawing. "You may keep this, though."

"I d-don't w-want it," he said. "I d-drew it for you."

She'd been surprised to hear Paolo speak; hadn't the marquis said that he was mute? Alessandra wondered why the gondolier allowed the ambassador to think he was incapable of speech. Was Paolo embarrassed by his stutter, or did he have another, more sinister, reason for feigning silence?

Now, as Paolo looked up at the window, it occurred to her that he'd been watching her for days, perhaps weeks. But he soon turned away. He pushed the gondola away from the canal bank, and his steady rowing quickly brought it into the open lagoon, where it veered east, toward the point. As the boat bobbed over the small, rippling waves, traveling farther and farther away, Alessandra waited for Antonio Perez to turn around and look at her one last time, but he never did.

Chapter Nine

"VENETIAN COURTESANS WERE legendary," Claire told Gwen after she returned to their hotel room. "Thomas Coryat, an Englishman who visited Venice in 1612, wrote, 'So infinite are the allurements of these amorous Calypsos that the fame of them hath drawn many to Venice from some of the remotest parts of Christendom.' It's estimated that there were approximately ten thousand courtesans in Venice at the time, in a city with a population of only one hundred sixty thousand. That means that one of every eight women was a courtesan of some kind."

Gwen had evinced little interest in Claire's adventure of the morning or her tale of the conspiracy until she'd mentioned Alessandra's profession—and then explained what a courtesan was.

"You're writing about a prostitute?" Gwen asked. She sat cross-legged on her bed, attired much as she had been the day before, in tight, flared jeans and a 1960s-inspired shirt. This one, at least, covered both abdomen and chest. The contents of her backpack were scattered in front of her: iPod, headphones, tubes of makeup, half-eaten packages of candy, gel pens in assorted colors. She'd been writing in a small, leather-bound journal when Claire walked in, and had quickly snapped the book shut and stuffed it into her backpack. A diary, Claire surmised. Full of a fourteen-year-old's secrets.

"A courtesan is not exactly a prostitute," Claire explained.

"But she had sex for money, right?"

"It wasn't just about sex. Rich families didn't want their fortunes to be diminished by dividing them among all the children, so they generally allowed only one son to marry. The other sons had few options other than a relationship with a courtesan," Claire informed her. "And because there weren't many options for women, either, the men offered financial support. It was a mutually beneficial arrangement."

"So a courtesan would sleep with anybody?" Gwen seemed rather subdued this morning, Claire noticed, and wondered if yesterday's behavior was typical. Was Gwen completely wild, or was the previous day's drama just a single, isolated ride on the hormonal roller coaster of adolescence?

"Some weren't so choosy, but a *cortigiana onestà*—which means 'honest courtesan,' or, in a sense, high-class courtesan—tended to have a select group of steady, long-term lovers, each with a designated night of the week. Alessandra was one of these. She was well-educated—more so than most noblewomen, in fact, who often weren't given much education at all. A *cortigiana onestà* entertained her clients with music, dance, and conversation, and she often married and gave up the courtesan's life."

Gwen yawned and stretched. "Where do we get breakfast?" she asked.

The lobby's pale marble floors and high, white walls seemed to dance with the bright reflections off the canal just outside the hotel's large picture windows. From the top of the first-floor staircase, the illusion was surreal, as if the lobby were underwater, and they were walking into a dazzling grotto filled with ormolu accents and gilt-edged furniture. Halfway down, Gwen grabbed Claire's arm. "Oh my god," she gasped.

The very moment that Claire saw Giancarlo sitting in one of the lobby chairs, absently reading a newspaper, he looked up and saw her, too. She and Gwen descended the last of the steps and walked toward him, and he put the paper aside and stood up. Claire would have felt nervous except that his smile was so warm and welcoming, and the expression in his eyes so unabashedly admiring, that she was instantly put at ease and smiled back. Just as she was about to ask Giancarlo why he was there, he spoke.

"Please forgive me," he said. "I must leave so suddenly last night that I didn't have the chance to ask your name."

"Claire Donovan."

Gwen nudged her.

"And this is Gwendolyn Fry, my . . . student."

"Giancarlo Baldessari," he said, with a slight bow that managed to convey a sense of formality and irony simultaneously. "It is a pleasure to meet you both. I'm hoping you're free this evening to join me for dinner at my house."

There was probably some sort of cocktail "meet and greet" thing at the conference that she should attend, Claire thought, but . . .

Giancarlo misunderstood her hesitation. "My family will be there, as well."

Gwen nudged her again, harder this time. "Say yes," she whispered.

"We would be delighted," Claire said. All right, so he was a waiter, but when she looked at him, she didn't care about whether they would have anything in common or not. Giancarlo was so handsome, he made her feel a little woozy. Staring directly into his eyes was like being zapped with a stun gun; it temporarily suspended her power of speech.

"I won't be able to meet you here in advance, as I would like, but I have a map with the directions marked." He took a small piece of paper from his pocket and gave it to Claire.

"Thank you. I'm sure we'll be able to find it."

"I'm not," Gwen muttered.

"I'm sorry, but I must leave you now; I'm late for an appointment. I've been waiting for some time hoping to see you." Giancarlo smiled at her again, and she felt her heart skip a beat. "I will see you tonight, yes?"

"Yes."

"Seven o'clock. *Arrivederci!*"

Claire and Gwen watched as Giancarlo bounded out of the lobby and then waved as he walked by the windows. Claire was suddenly filled with a sense of well-being, and gratitude for all of the surprises life held.

"You are *so* going to get your groove back," Gwen said.

"Excuse me?"

"Your groove. You know, you're an older woman, he's a younger guy, you lost your groove, he's going to help you get it back."

"First of all, I'm not old, and he's not that much younger. Second of all, I have not lost my groove. But if I had, and if I get it back, and how and with whom I get it back is none of your concern." She turned and walked toward the dining room.

Gwen trotted to catch up with her. "He's such a hottie."

"I'm not going to discuss this with you."

"If he can't help you get your groove back, no one can."

"There will be no more groove talk, understood?"

"I can't believe we're going to a *library,*" Gwen complained as they passed a group of empty gondole in the small canal outside the Bell'acqua. "I want to go on one of the boats." She turned to flash a smile at a young gondolier.

"The gondole are very expensive," Claire said, urging her along to the Piazza.

"It's my dad's money."

"That money is meant for necessary things, not tourist traps."

"But it looks like fun."

"We don't have time for fun today." Indeed, as yesterday had been a total loss, she was going to have to pack two days' work into one.

The conference began at eleven, but Claire had already realized that she wouldn't be able to attend all of the conference events and work on her dissertation, too, not with only six more days in Venice. One was going to have to give way to the other, and making the choice had been easy: her research took precedence. In fact, this morning when she'd perused the schedule (which was merely a hard copy of the no-frills Web page devoted to the conference), she saw only a few lectures that directly pertained to her subject. Andrea Kent's first talk was in the Ca' Foscari main hall at three o'clock that afternoon. She'd highlighted it with a yellow marker and ruminated on the strangeness of seeing in print what was very nearly the title of her dissertation—"The Origins of the Spanish Conspiracy of 1618" (A. Kent)—with someone else's name attached to it.

"Did you know that Armani, Missoni, and Valentino all have stores here?" Gwen asked as they strode past Caffè Florian and caught a glimpse of the three-hundred-year-old café's bordello red interior.

"How nice for them." Claire understood that Gwen was talking about fashion designers, even though she was only marginally aware of who they were.

"My mom says that Valentino is the most romantic designer. She loves his clothes. Did you know that practically every designer in the world has a store in Venice? I read it in one of your guide books this morning. Maybe after the library we could go shopping."

"I have a ton of work to do."

"I thought teachers didn't work in the summer."

"I'm not a teacher yet."

"Tyler says that in the future no one will actually have to go to work anymore, we'll just do everything from a Palm Pilot."

"Who's Tyler?"

"He's my, um, friend."

"Your boyfriend? So he isn't going to work, is he? Just what is he planning to do with his life?"

"He's going to be a senator, like his dad." Gwen looked with longing at a jewelry-store window. "I don't see why we can't go shopping. This is supposed to be my trip, too."

"Yes, an educational trip. That's what you're getting."

"Hold on a minute, I just got out of school. I didn't come here to actually learn anything."

"Consider it a bonus."

"What's so wrong with doing something fun?"

"I think you had enough fun yesterday to make up for the entire week, don't you?"

"I don't remember having any fun."

"You've already forgotten Tattoo Boy and the rum and Cokes?"

"It may have looked like fun to you, but trust me, it wasn't that great."

"I was being sarcastic."

"That doesn't change the fact that I'm still not having any fun."

"After the library, we're going to go sightseeing, okay?"

"And see what?"

Claire pointed ahead. "The Basilica and the Doge's Palace."

"We're going to look at *buildings*?"

"They're not just buildings." Claire offered a compromise. "I need to do this today, but tomorrow we can do something that you want to do, okay?"

They passed the Campanile and the entrance to the Biblioteca Marciana came into view. Claire recalled that Cardinal Bessarion, a Greek monk who had devoted himself to the preservation of Greek civilization, founded the library in 1468 when he donated his collection of ancient Greek literature to Venice, which he saw as the heir to Byzantium. Architect Jacopo Sansovino began work on the library in 1537; in 1560, it was opened to the public. Now the Marciana housed nearly one million volumes, including thirteen thousand manuscripts, nearly three thousand incunabula—books printed before 1501—and over twenty-four thousand books from the sixteenth century. The prospect of having this venerable collection at her disposal made Claire pick up her pace with excitement. They walked up a wide staircase framed by a vaulted hall of gilded stucco, which led to an ornate antechamber, its ceiling a mosaic of Renaissance paintings. In the middle of the room, two huge globes on pedestals stood nearly as high as Claire herself.

"Are you sure this is the right place?" Gwen asked. "It doesn't look like a library. There aren't even any books."

"I think we have to go back here." Claire led the way through a set of double doors to the main hall, a cavernous room that opened to a ceiling of skylights, three stories above. Long, solid wood study tables were arranged in two rows in the center; around the perimeter were three floors of arched arcades constructed of gray stone. A wall of windows at the far end yielded views of the lagoon and slanting shafts of dust-mote-speckled sunlight.

A young, blond woman presided over the counter at the back of the hall. As they approached, Claire read the nameplate on the desk: Francesca Luponi.

"Are you the librarian?"

"Yes. May I help you?" Francesca smiled prettily. She was very sleek and stylish, Claire thought; certainly she looked nothing like the librarians at Harvard, who generally favored baggy sweaters in shades of mouse-brown and mushroom, and Birkenstocks paired with woolly socks. Claire handed over her university ID and her list of requested documents and books. Francesca donned a pair of dark-framed glasses and peered at both. Somehow the glasses made her appear even more stylish. Was it because she was Italian that she could pull that off? Claire had worn glasses much like that in high school, before she got contact lenses, and they'd made her look even more nerdy than she already did. Some women had style, she supposed, as did this rather self-assured librarian, as did Meredith. And some women, Claire thought ruefully as she tried to smooth out the wrinkles in her L.L. Bean clearance-catalog skirt, didn't.

"Ms. Donovan, yes, I remember your e-mail. You're working on the Spanish Conspiracy, yes?" Her voice had a charming lilt to it. "I've already set aside a few items for you," she said, turning away to the shelves of books and documentary materials behind her. Each stack was tagged with a name. At the top of the small collection Francesca handed her was a thin, cloth-bound volume with a bit of art nouveau decoration on the spine and cover and a gilt title: *Diary of Ettore Battista Fazzini, volume IV, 1615–1618.* Interesting, but she hadn't requested it. She looked up at the librarian, who anticipated her question.

"Fazzini was a chronicler of the early seventeenth century," Francesca explained. "Rather like Marino Sanudo in the sixteenth, although not so well-known or so comprehensively published.

There are just six volumes of excerpts from Fazzini's diaries extant. They were first published in Venice in 1785, and then this 1891 English edition, published in London."

"This is the first I've heard of him."

"Fazzini is out of favor. His recollections are colorful, but not considered entirely credible. But I believe he mentions Alessandra Rossetti once or twice, so I thought you might like to read it. You did say you had an interest in Alessandra Rossetti, yes?"

"Yes."

"Your other requests should be available later today or tomorrow morning. Just ask for them here at the desk—they'll be on the shelf."

"Excuse me," Gwen piped up, "is your dress a Missoni?"

"Gwen . . . ," Claire chided.

"It's all right." Francesca leaned on the counter. "I have a little secret. It's not exactly a Missoni, it's just a very good copy." She shrugged and smiled. "It's not so easy to buy designer clothes on a librarian's salary."

"Wow, it looks like the real thing."

"There's a shop near the Merceria San Zulian where you can find many items like this. But we don't tell this to too many foreigners—only those like you, with a good eye for fashion."

As Gwen and Francesca debated the merits of various fashion designers, Claire found an empty table nearby and eagerly opened Fazzini's diary. This was exactly what she had hoped to find in Venice: the long forgotten book, document, or manuscript that other historians might have overlooked. She flipped through the yellowing pages, running her finger down the lines of text, searching for Alessandra's name. One hundred and eighty-eight pages later, the book ended and she hadn't found it. She turned back to the beginning, this time going more slowly and reading a few of the anecdotes of seventeenth-century Venetian life that Fazzini related with a breathless delight.

"My dear friends, I must relate the most astonishing piece of gossip. The esteemed lord Constantin Vasari has taken the courtesan Beatrice dalle Crosette as his wife! Although she is without doubt accomplished, with the singing voice of an angel, and so blessed with beauty that she can vie with any in Venice, she has continued her disgraceful habits and has licentiously given over her body to many men. Recently she had another lover in addition to this Vasari, but the latter seems not to have minded. Well, love knows no limits! . . .

"The dashing abbé de Pomponne is the source of a scandalous feud between the abbess of Santa Chiara and Sister Eugenia, one of the nuns in her charge. The two women fought over their mutual lover in a poniard duel held in the convent courtyard late at night. No one is shocked that the women should fight—but to fight on consecrated ground! That is the scandal . . .

"La Celestia owns a monkey which runs loose over the rooftops, sometimes entering into the open windows of other palazzi. One day he stole a diamond ring from Signora Grafia Corsa next door, and wore it about on his finger. Lorenzo Giambatti saw the monkey with the ring and confronted the courtesan: 'Did you know your monkey stole Signora Corsa's ring?' he asked. 'Why, no!' she said. 'But haven't you noticed him wearing it?' he asked. 'Of course,' she replied, 'but I thought it was his!'"

Claire looked up from the book as Gwen sat down next to her. "How long are we going to be stuck here?"

"Not much longer." She'd spend another half hour on Fazzini, then take a glance at the other books Francesca had given her. The *Diary* wasn't so promising after all, but it was easy to become engrossed in, and quite different from the texts she was accustomed to reading. Venetian history could be surprisingly dry, a seemingly endless litany of doges and wars. The Republic's aversion to anything approaching a "cult of personality" meant that intimate details about Venetian leaders, nobles, and citizens weren't in great supply. Piecing together the personal lives of those involved in the Spanish Conspiracy had taken some effort, and no doubt it would require quite a bit more. Fazzini was a welcome find. Although he might be unreliable, he offered some insight into the mores and interests of the time. She turned her attention back to the Diary.

"La Celestia's launching of a new *cortigiana onestà* in a most dramatic fashion at an exclusive banquet at her luxurious Ca' Aragona has spawned a trend among those women who desire to be elevated above their designation of 'sumptuous whore.' Ever since La Celestia's protégée La Sirena made her debut as a most delectable dessert, covered by nothing save the glimmer of gold dust, a few strands of pearls, and some well-placed gold leaf, courtesans have been adorning themselves in the most outrageous manner, clothed in nothing but jewels or bright feathers . . ."

That name again: La Celestia. A courtesan named the Heavens? Unusual for a Venetian courtesan to have a nom de guerre, as it were. It had been much more common in Rome a century earlier, when Imperia and La Dolce were the stars of the age. Venetian courtesans generally went by their given names: Bianca Saraton, Elena Balbi, Gaspara Stampa, the Ballerini sisters.

"I'm so sorry." Francesca stood beside the table. "I checked the records and it seems I've given you the wrong book. The mention of Alessandra Rossetti is in Fazzini's volume Five, not Four. But you're welcome to keep it, if you like."

"No thanks. It's entertaining, but there's nothing in it I can use."

Francesca took volume Four from her and put volume Five on the table. "It's on page twenty-four."

Fazzini's fifth volume covered the years 1619 to 1623—*after* the conspiracy. Did gossipy Ettore know what happened to Alessandra? She skipped to the page Francesca had flagged and began to read.

"Ever since Alessandra Rossetti's letter was passed to the Great Council, the presence of mercenary soldiers in Venice is greatly reduced, with both good and ill effects. It's easier to get a table in a tavern, but one mourns the loss of the nightly fights and skirmishes that made life so exciting . . ."

Claire sighed. That was it? She felt a pang of disappointment. Perhaps, she thought as she closed Fazzini's *Diary,* she should have known better than to get her hopes up so high.

Chapter Ten

"My feet are killing me," said Gwen, plopping down in a chair outside a café in the tiny Campiello degli Squellini with her usual lack of grace. She took off one of her sandals and rubbed her toes. "I didn't know we were going to walk all over Venice."

The journey from the Doge's Palace through the chic streets of San Marco, then across the Accademia Bridge to Dorsoduro hadn't seemed all that far to Claire, but it did feel good to sit down. To her dismay she'd discovered that there was no such thing as a truly accurate map of Venice. There wasn't one in her possession, at any rate.

A waiter appeared and she ordered a cappuccino, and a lemonade for Gwen. They weren't far from Ca' Foscari, but she needed a few minutes to relax and revive herself before she faced the conference. Her thoughts, as they often had in the past ten days, turned to Andrea Kent. Finally, she would meet the woman who was her closest professional counterpart, or perhaps her nemesis. Would she be friend or foe, ally or adversary? There was a possibility that Andrea would consider her a threat, even though, from Claire's point of view, Andrea held all the cards: she taught at one of England's oldest universities, and her work on the Spanish Conspiracy was about to be published. How could she even hope to compete? Not for the first time did she wish that Andrea Kent was a professor almost anywhere other than Cambridge. Why couldn't she teach at some obscure little college instead of at one of the few universities in the entire English-speaking world more illustrious than Harvard?

And how was she going to introduce herself, anyway? "Hi, just happen to be working on the same thing you are, how about we get together and compare notes?" Ha. While she was a teaching assistant at Columbia, she'd witnessed academic squabbles so vicious, one would have thought they were based on something intensely personal instead of professional.

All historians defended their territory; that's how careers were made and furthered. It was unlikely that Andrea Kent would share anything more than what she was willing to reveal in her lectures, so Claire would simply have to glean as much as she could from them. Perhaps it would be better to keep the subject of her dissertation and her particular interest in Andrea's work to herself. She imagined being introduced to the professor, complimenting her on her work, then making casual inquiries: What a fascinating subject! So you've written a book? When will it be published?

As soon as she thought of it, she felt disgusted. She hated dissimulation, and it was only partly because she had no knack for it. Which left her back at, "Hi, just happen to be working on the same thing you are . . ."

Gwen slurped the last of her lemonade through a straw. "It's weird, but it doesn't really look like the movie," she said. "I mean, sometimes it does, but a lot of times it doesn't."

"What in the world are you talking about?"

"Venice. It doesn't look like the movie."

"What movie?"

"It's this movie my mom watches all the time. It's like her favorite movie." Gwen scrunched her eyes as she remembered the title. "*Summertime.* With Katharine Hepburn."

Claire vaguely recalled seeing the film, years and years ago. She hardly remembered anything about it, except— "Doesn't Katharine Hepburn fall into a canal?"

"Yeah, and that's where she meets the guy—he's got this antiques shop. Oh!" Gwen exclaimed. "Could we go there?"

"Where?"

"It's called . . . Barnaba. I remember it 'cause the kid points it out to her: 'Ponte Barnaba, Campo Barnaba.' I *have* to go there before I leave. I promised my mom I'd take a picture of the store."

"So, it's your mom's favorite movie?" It seemed an unusual choice for a woman so familiar with firearms.

"It makes her cry," she said, nodding.

"Really? How come?" Maybe if she got Gwen talking about her mom, she'd divulge why she shot her dad.

Gwen shrugged.

"Does it make you cry, too?"

"No, it just makes me mad. Katharine Hepburn comes to Venice and she meets this Italian guy and they fall in love but then at the end she goes home."

"Isn't he married?"

"Yes, but he doesn't live with his wife anymore."

"I think the movie was made a long time ago—in the fifties or something—and back then, Italians couldn't get divorced. Ever. Maybe that's why she goes home."

"So why doesn't she just live with him? Honestly, I don't get it. All that's waiting for her back home is a boring life and a boring job."

"I don't think that's what you're supposed to be thinking about at the end of the movie."

"That's what I'm thinking about. Katharine Hepburn leaves Venice, leaves the guy she loves, and for what? It's the stupidest movie I've ever seen."

It may have been the stupidest movie Gwen had ever seen, but something about it obviously struck a chord. Claire hadn't seen her get so worked up about anything else; for a moment the terminally bored look in her eyes had been replaced with anger or even sadness. Perhaps memories of her mother had brought on the surge of emotion. The question was on the tip of Claire's tongue: So, why did your mom shoot your dad?

Then Gwen gave her a piercing look and said, "Why haven't you asked me why my mom shot my dad? I mean, that's all anybody at home wanted to talk about. I swear, everyone I've known since third grade called to ask me." Gwen's voice rose in mimicry: "'Why'd your mom shoot your dad?' 'Why'd your mom shoot your dad?' 'Why'd your mom shoot your dad?'"

"I got the feeling that you didn't want to talk about it," said Claire.

"I don't," said Gwen.

Ca' Foscari, the Grand Canal palazzo occupied by the University of Venice, was a prime example of the fifteenth-century Gothic style. In 1574, it had famously housed Henri III of France, on his way to Paris to assume the throne. A stone patio, bordered by low walls covered with climbing vines, marked the entrance on the landward side. A small banner announcing the conference hung above the palazzo door, and people stood about in small groups, chatting and smoking.

Claire stepped up to a folding table manned by a student wearing a red T-shirt with a picture of Karl Marx on the front. She handed her registration confirmation to him and in return got a name tag for herself and a guest pass for Gwen, whom she described, sotto voce, as her daughter. About Andrea Kent—she had decided that she would take the high road and hope for the best. She'd be honest and explain her dilemma. There was always the possibility that Andrea was a magnanimous person who would foster another historian's career instead of sabotage it.

They walked through a milling crowd in the foyer, up a massive staircase to the second floor—the *piano nobile,* traditionally the floor used by the Venetian aristocracy for entertaining—and stepped into the main hall just as a harried man placed a poster-size sign on an easel near the door.

The placard announced the name of the next speaker, along with the speaker's photo. It was someone both Claire and Gwen recognized at once, and they stood stock-still in front of it.

"It's that English guy," Gwen said, her voice breathy with bewilderment.

It was him. Unmistakably him. Just beneath the photo (in which he looked appropriately serious and scholarly, and was posed before an artistically blurred background that hinted strongly of classical columns and laurel leaves, as if he were the human repository of all knowledge dating from the Hellenic era) was his name: Andrew Kent. An*drew,* with a *w* not an *a,* Kent. Andrew Kent.

In the main hall, a podium on a two-foot riser faced eight rows of long, narrow tables and chairs. It looked much like other seminars she'd attended, except that the Ca' Foscari conference room had once been the *portego* of a wealthy fifteenth-century Venetian family. Large landscapes in gilded frames adorned the walls; the high, domed ceiling offered a celestial scene of gold-flecked clouds populated by larger-than-life-size mythical figures and rosy-cheeked cherubs.

Claire took a seat in the very last row. She wanted to be as far from Andrew Kent as possible. There was no hope now of any collegial cooperation between her and the other historian writing about the Spanish Conspiracy. How could there be? He was a supercilious English snob. He was rude and duplicitous. All that stuff he'd said the night before about how history didn't matter, pretending not to know what "early modern" meant—he'd been baiting her, trying to get her to say something ridiculous; worse, she'd fallen for it. He'd twice gone out of his way to make her feel like a fool. If, during either meeting, he'd acted in a civil manner, she would have been happy to stick to her original, honesty-inspired plan. But this was war, pure and simple.

She took out her notebook—no doubt there would be a transcript available later, but she wanted to record the key points now—as a tall, fiftyish man stepped onto the stage. His air of authority had an effect; voices hushed and people scurried to find seats.

He switched the microphone on and sent an ear-splitting jolt of feedback through the room. "Sorry," he said. "Has everyone found a chair?" he continued. "No? We'll have some more brought in and set up along the back."

There must have been at least sixty people setting down bags, laptops, and briefcases. Claire was surprised to see that a lecture on the Spanish Conspiracy had drawn such a crowd. She noted the moderator's attractiveness; he had a regal, rather leonine appearance, with slightly long salt-and-pepper hair and a trim, graying beard. He looked like the prototype for a modern European aristocrat, the kind of man who would sail a sixty-foot sloop around the Aegean or star in a luxury-car commercial. He waited until everyone was seated before speaking again.

"Our next lecturer comes to us from England, from Trinity College, Cambridge, and has, as is his usual way, something revelatory to share with us. But I'm going to give over the introduction to my favorite presenter of culture and art, Gabriella Monalisa Arianna Griseri, host of the popular television program *Time After Time.*"

It was clear from the enthusiastic applause that many in the audience knew who she was. Or perhaps they simply appreciated culture and art in the female form; even from the back row, Claire could see that the woman was a knockout. Her slim yet curvaceous figure was sheathed in a perfectly fitting sleeveless dress in which she looked effortlessly elegant. She had a face like a fashion model and lustrous black hair that was styled in a sleek chignon at the nape of her neck.

"What was her name?" Gwen asked.

"I don't know. I got lost after Gabriella."

"Thank you, Maurizio," Gabriella said, taking the stage with professional ease. "Thank you all. I am proud to have the honor of introducing our next speaker. I first met Andrew Kent at the Sorbonne six years ago, when we were both invited to speak at a seminar on the seventeenth century. His lecture on the death of King Charles, a controversial look at the demise of the Restoration leader, was the talk of the conference. I've taken great pleasure in witnessing his meteoric career since then. The Sorbonne lecture, as many of you no doubt already know, provided the basis for his book, *Charles II and the Rye House Plot,* which became a bestseller in the UK, and was subsequently published in thirteen countries . . ." She looked to her right, where Andrew Kent stood at the base of the stage, looking vaguely uncomfortable. "Is that correct?"

"Yes," he said, nodding, then clasped his hands behind his back and resumed his study of the floor.

"Published in thirteen countries and adapted for the highly acclaimed BBC series, *The Rye House Plot: The Attempted Assassination of Charles II.* Andrew has forbidden me to disclose anything about today's lecture or his second talk on Saturday, but I will say this: with this new work, lightning is going to strike twice!

"But what else could we expect from such an accomplished historian? Andrew Kent is a Fellow at Trinity College, Cambridge, and a lecturer in history at the university. He is the recipient of the Villier-Horschak Award for historical research and a two-time winner of the Prescott Prize. He's been a featured speaker at conferences in cities all over the world, including Stockholm, Naples, Tokyo, Barcelona, Warsaw, Dublin, and St. Petersburg. And now, for the first time, the University of Venice. I hope you'll all join me in giving a very big welcome to Andrew Kent."

Claire politely applauded along with everyone else in the room. During Gabriella's introduction, she'd felt her heart sink further, and further, and further, until her fighting spirit was beaten and broken. Andrew Kent was much too accomplished for her to compete with. A bestselling book? The Villier-Horschak Award? The Prescott Prize—twice? *A BBC series?*

Andrew Kent wasn't just a historian, he was a demigod of historians, one of the few who'd climbed—no, make that *soared*—out of the ivory tower and found fame in the larger world. She wasn't in the same league. No, that wasn't quite accurate—she wasn't even a player yet.

He stepped up to the microphone as Gabriella left the stage. The popular hostess of *Time After Time* flashed him a brilliant smile as they passed. He thanked her, then took a sip of water from a glass on the podium and cleared his throat a few times as the applause died down. He seemed self-assured, but not as confident as Claire would have expected from someone who'd just had the highlights of his illustrious career cited so sweetly. Certainly not bestselling author, BBC consultant, big-historian-in-a-small-pond assured.

As she studied him, she sensed that something was wrong; Andrew Kent didn't seem like his usual bristly, rather off-putting pedantic self, but more like a guy who was apologetic about taking everyone's time. Maybe this false humility was an English thing. Or maybe he didn't feel well. Whatever the cause, she had the distinct impression that he wasn't terribly excited about his own lecture. He cleared his throat once more and began to speak.

"One hundred years ago, Julian Corbett wrote, 'Of all the mysteries of Italian history, there is none more dramatic or difficult to probe in all its dark recesses than what is known in Venice as the Spanish Conspiracy.' I agree with him that it is one of the most enigmatic events in the history of Venice; its legend owes much to myth and rumor. I hope to retire some of those myths, silence some of those rumors. Why is this important? Because, as Horatio Brown has remarked, the story of the Spanish Conspiracy 'throws so strong a light upon the causes which first corrupted and then destroyed the Republic.'

"But I get ahead of myself. The origin of the conspiracy is the primary subject of this lecture, as I mean to show that the events of 1618 were by no means isolated; tensions between Venice and Spain had been building for decades."

Claire listened without taking notes while Andrew Kent gave an overview of what was, for her, familiar territory. By the sixteenth century, the Venetian Republic was in decline. Even so, at the beginning of the seventeenth century, Venice was the only independent power remaining in an Italy dominated by Spain, which achieved its dominion with its military might, its wealth, and its control of the papacy. In 1606, when Pope Paul V excommunicated the Doge and the Venetian Senate and placed all territories of the Republic under an interdict in retaliation for the arrest and conviction of two priests, Venice came into direct conflict with Rome and therefore Spain.

"By 1618, distrust between Venice and Spain was at its peak," Andrew Kent said. "Although treaties existed between the two countries, the reality, according to the Venetian ambassador to Madrid, was 'hostility and war.' In his report to the Doge, the ambassador wrote of 'fierce encounters and troublesome incidents' between Venice and Spain.

"But does this provide sufficient grounds for a 'Spanish plot'? Indeed, does the evidence even exist? It may help to review what we know for certain of the events of 1618.

"We know that the Venetian Senate wrote to its ambassadors: 'The insidious practices of the Spaniards never cease . . . such tricks and artifices have never before been seen'; we know that the Spanish ambassador, the marquis of Bedmar, was summoned to the Doge's Palace for a formal rebuke. We know that the duke of Ossuna, in Naples, was constructing a new fleet of warships. We know that a letter written by a courtesan named Alessandra Rossetti charged a group of mercenaries with plotting to overthrow Venice. We know that three men—two Spaniards and one Frenchman—were strangled in prison and their corpses hung from the gibbet on the Piazza San Marco.

"But these events do not add up to the account we have heard of the so-called Spanish Conspiracy . . ."

The *so-called* Spanish Conspiracy? Claire wondered. What was he getting at?

" . . . an account that has come down to us as history but frankly is based on testimony no more reliable than a child's bedtime story." Andrew Kent paused for effect before revealing his most important disclosure. "My research has revealed that what has been thought of as a Spanish conspiracy for four hundred years is, in reality, a Venetian conspiracy."

"What?" Claire said, so loudly that people in adjacent seats swiveled their heads to look at her.

"I believe that the 'Spanish' Conspiracy was a fabrication created by the Council of Ten," he went on, "a group of men known to have had the best spy network in Europe at that time, a group known to have used any means at their disposal, including hired assassins, to protect the sovereignty of the Republic."

Murmurs rippled through the room.

"Those enigmatic enforcers of state security, the Council of Ten and its deadly subcommittee, the Tre Capi, or three heads of the

Council of Ten, were so feared that they spawned a popular axiom: 'The Ten send you to the torture chamber, the Three to your grave.' The main architect of the Venetian Conspiracy, Senator Girolamo Silvia, was in 1618 the leader of the Three and as effective a spymaster as Walsingham had been in England. His network of informants included those from the lowest to the highest echelons of Venetian society. He used these informants, along with his own group of *bravi,* to wage a shadow war against the enemies of the Republic. He seemed to have a particular animosity toward the duke of Ossuna, but the advancement of his own political career was a significant motivating factor.

"Another issue raised by my research concerns the Rossetti Letter. For four hundred years, the mysterious Alessandra Rossetti has been considered a heroine of sorts, the courtesan whose letter to the Great Council exposed the plot and saved Venice from a brutal sacking and pillage. But if the Spanish Conspiracy is a fabrication of the Council of Ten, so, too, then is the Rossetti Letter. Indeed, Alessandra Rossetti was no heroine, but a pawn of the Three . . ."

"No!" Claire gasped.

" . . . their puppet, if you will, one whose false statements resulted in politically motivated deaths."

"Oh god," Claire moaned.

"I see that my time is up. Thank you all for attending. I hope you'll join me on Saturday morning for my second talk, when I'll elaborate on these issues."

Claire was in such a state of shock that she hardly heard the applause. She stood up and inched her way out of the hall with Gwen and the rest of the crowd. They walked to the *traghetto* crossing near Ca' Rezzonico in silence.

"Is something wrong?" Gwen asked.

There certainly was; it was even worse than Claire had anticipated. It was bad enough to oppose the opinion of an acclaimed historian, but if Andrew Kent destroyed the credibility of the Rossetti Letter, she might as well give up now.

"I've just discovered that I've wasted more than two years of my life, and that I'm going to have to throw my dissertation in the garbage and start all over."

"Why?"

"If Andrew Kent publishes a book saying that the Spanish Conspiracy was based on lies, no one's going to take my work seriously; in fact, it could be rejected entirely."

"But that's not fair."

"Who said life was fair? All that matters is that he's an authority and I'm not. Did you hear that introduction? He's won the Prescott Prize twice. The frustrating thing is that I know he's wrong. He's completely wrong."

"If you're right and he's wrong, you shouldn't care about his stupid awards. I mean, if you're right, someone else is going to know you're right, right?"

"Maybe. I don't know." At least she had the Biblioteca Marciana at hand to help verify what she believed to be true. "Look, do you mind if we just get a quick bite to eat and stay in tonight? I've got to go over my notes and make a plan for tomorrow."

"What about Giancarlo?"

"Giancarlo!" Claire stopped. "I completely forgot." Giancarlo would be a wonderful respite from everything that had occupied her all day: her research, the conference, Andrew Kent. "I did say we would go, didn't I? It would be terrible to disappoint him."

Gwen eyed her critically. "Is that what you're going to wear?"

"Why, is there something wrong with it?"

According to Gwen, everything was wrong with it. It was shapeless, wrinkled, colorless, boring: a verdict she handed down on nearly every article of clothing in Claire's suitcase. Then Gwen opened her own suitcase and began taking out blouses of a type that Claire had seldom seen: chiffons, silks, velvets, all of them fit for a gypsy or the cover of a romance novel, with low-cut necklines and fluttery sleeves, in a multicolored array of paisleys, floral prints, and rich jewel tones. Soon the beds and the chairs were covered with clothes.

"It looks like Stevie Nicks exploded in here," Claire said.

"You can wear this black skirt of yours with one of my tops to dress it up. That one maybe?" Gwen pointed to a black chiffon number with dark blue flowers on it. "Wait, this is better." She held up an emerald green velvet blouse with a low, rounded neck and long sleeves that gathered at the wrist. Claire slipped it on and Gwen nodded approvingly. "That's your color. Plus there's a tie in the back to make it a little tighter." She tied the ribbon, then stepped in front to regard her once more. "It works, more or less. Have you ever thought about buying a push-up bra?"

"No." Claire went into the bathroom to look in the mirror. She was pleasantly surprised. It was quite pretty, and romantic, in the sense that it looked like it belonged to a more romantic era. In fact, it reminded her of something Alessandra might have owned. In a certain way it suited her more than anything she'd ever worn, as if it revealed something secret about her—the part of her that lived in the seventeenth-century world. Not that she'd want to dress like this all the time, but for now, for tonight, for Venice—

"It's perfect," she said.

Chapter Eleven

AT SIX THIRTY, two transformed women walked west through the *sestiere* of San Marco in search of an address adjacent to a *campo* near the Calle del Dose. The slightly smaller of the two, in an anachronistic combination of Renaissance-inspired top and conservative low-heeled pumps, carried a brown bag that contained a bottle of white wine and a selection of *dolci* the confectioner had recommended.

Claire hadn't wanted to go to Giancarlo's empty-handed. She suspected that he'd asked her to his family's house because he couldn't afford a dinner out—the restaurants in Venice were outrageously expensive—and worried that she hadn't brought enough. On the other hand, if she brought too much, it might seem like noblesse oblige. As they walked the narrow lanes, she thought about what his house would be like, imagining a cramped living room with a view of the decrepit building next door. Her expectations for the flat of a waiter's family weren't high. Not that she cared in the least; she was more concerned that perhaps she and Gwen were overdressed.

Gwen was wearing black, flared pants and a black silk top with ridiculously large, witchlike sleeves and tottered along on shoes not vastly different from *choppines,* the high wooden platforms once worn by Venetian women. Not terribly practical, Claire had said when she'd first seen the outfit. Gwen had matter-of-factly replied that she wasn't planning to do anything practical in the next few hours.

She had to admit that tonight Gwen seemed different from the gawky, inarticulate girl she usually was and looked rather mysterious and exotic. Her sense of style didn't look as out of place here as it had in Harriot. Everywhere in Venice, Claire had seen women, young and not so young, fit and not so fit, who were squeezed into skintight, hip-hugging, bell-bottom pants. What had happened? Had someone decreed that all women must dress as if it were 1973? Or was it instinctive, something similar to whatever it is that inspires a flock of birds to suddenly turn as one, or that makes migrating monarch butterflies alight on the same trees as the generation that preceded them?

They reached the *campo* and consulted the map Giancarlo had given them. Following its instructions, they crossed a bridge over a small canal, turned three times into crooked, claustrophobic alleys, and kept walking until they got to a wrought-iron gate set into a high brick wall. The gate opened into an enclosed courtyard, across which was the main door to the building.

It was opened with sudden force only seconds after she knocked. Claire was surprised to be face-to-face with the tall, aristocratic man she'd seen earlier at the conference.

"I'm sorry, I must have the wrong house," she said.

"You're the Americans, yes?" he said brightly.

"I'm looking for Giancarlo Bal—"

"Yes, we're expecting you. Come in, please. I'm Maurizio Baldessari, Giancarlo's father."

They stepped into an elegant entry hall with open doorways at each side and a wide marble staircase directly ahead. A phone rang in the room on the right. A murmuring voice answered it.

"I saw you today at the Ca' Foscari conference . . . ," Claire began, still uncomprehending.

"I'm the director of the history department. Giancarlo did not explain? When he told me that he'd met an American who was attending the conference, I asked him to invite you."

A younger man stepped into the doorway. "Professor Franco is on the phone."

"Can you tell her I'll call her back in just a few minutes?" He motioned for Claire and Gwen to follow him up the stairs. "Allow me to show you in. Giancarlo tells me you're studying seventeenth-century Venice."

Claire nodded as they walked up the stairs to the main floor of what was clearly a palazzo, one that was decorated in an exquisitely refined, classic style. Even Gwen, her eyes wide and her mouth slightly agape, was dazzled, although Claire figured she was probably unaware that the furniture was eighteenth century, the Oriental carpets antique, the piano a rare Bösendorfer concert grand, the mammoth chandelier Austrian crystal, or that the age-darkened paintings were portraits of actual Baldessari ancestors. As Maurizio briskly led them into this grand salon, they were met by a woman who entered from a doorway at the far end.

"Renata, these are Giancarlo's guests," he said.

"From America, yes?"

Claire introduced herself and Gwen, all the while wondering at the way everyone said "America" or "Americans," as if they were special and rare, as if they'd just sailed from the uncharted New World and were about to relate strange tales of brown-skinned natives and wondrous crops of tobacco and corn. Or was this a feigned enthusiasm, meant to cover up a basic European dislike of them?

"We're delighted that you could join us," Renata said. She possessed a lush and timeless sort of beauty, accentuated by a simple black dress that displayed her voluptuousness to excellent effect. Her chestnut hair was swept back from her face and pinned up in a tangle of curls, showing off the delicate diamond and sapphire necklace circling her throat.

"Excuse me, please," Maurizio said, "but I must return that call. It's so busy right now with the conference."

"Maurizio!" Renata exclaimed. "You promised that you would be done with your work by the time the party started . . ."

"I will," he insisted as he rushed down the stairs.

"And don't keep poor Enzo here all evening," she called after him. "His assistant hardly ever has any time off," she confided. "But then Maurizio works too much. It is a very big mistake to put an office in your home." Renata shook her head with mock exasperation, then walked over to one of the room's two tall windows and opened the drapes.

There wasn't a window behind the curtain, but what Claire thought of as a French door (in Venice, she wondered, would it be called an Italian door?), which opened onto a balcony. Beyond the balcony was the Grand Canal. Claire had been completely disoriented by the time they'd arrived at the Baldessaris' house and hadn't realized where they'd ended up. They were in a palazzo on the Grand Canal. The palaces across the water gleamed under the warm brilliance of the evening sun as a few gondole bobbed in the wake of a vaporetto chugging its way toward the Salute. She had to make a conscious effort to keep her involuntary "wow" to herself. She glanced at Gwen who, now that her initial astonishment had passed, seemed to be taking it more in stride than she was.

"What a delightful surprise," Renata said, "that you should meet Giancarlo by chance, and also be attending the conference."

Was Claire imagining it, or did Renata's seemingly gracious welcome carry an undercurrent of insinuation, as if to imply that she had somehow engineered such a shocking coincidence? What Renata might suppose her motive to be, Claire couldn't even begin to guess.

"Funny, isn't it? I mean odd funny," Claire said. "We just happened to have dinner in the restaurant where he works, and here we are." Maybe she was being oversensitive, but suddenly it seemed important to make light of it all, especially her attraction to Giancarlo.

"How long will you be staying in Venice?"

Again, Renata's question seemed innocuous enough, but Claire had the distinct feeling it wasn't. "Until Saturday afternoon. I have to take Gwen to Paris to meet her parents."

"Oh!" Renata's eyes opened wide and ricocheted between them. "So the two of you are not—Gwendolyn is not your daughter?"

"I'm Gwen's chaperone for the week." Claire had rehearsed it, after deciding that this explanation would prompt the least number of questions in reply, unless she was speaking to someone unusually nosy or rude. Indeed, it seemed to stop Renata's intended line of inquiry; unfortunately their Italian hostess quickly adapted to the change and steered the conversation into even more treacherous waters.

"Then you have no children of your own?" Renata asked pleasantly.

"No, I'm not married."

"How sad. Years ago a study proved that if a woman wasn't married by the time she was thirty, she had as much chance of being killed in a terrorist attack as she did of ever walking down the aisle. But that can't be true anymore. There's so much more terrorism now, I'm sure that the odds must be *much* worse."

Claire managed to stammer, "Well, I was married, once . . ."

"You're divorced? So it's true that American women are perfectly happy without a husband and children? For me, it would be terrible, I would not—"

Gwen suddenly doubled over and began coughing uncontrollably. She straightened slightly and gasped, "I think I swallowed a bug."

"I'll get some water," said Renata, looking vaguely shocked.

The coughing attack stopped as soon as Renata left the room. "She hates you," Gwen announced.

"She has no reason to hate me."

"I didn't say she had a reason, I just said she hates you."

"You didn't really swallow a bug, did you?"

"Duh."

"Duh? That's a reply?"

"You know what I mean. She's never going to leave you alone with her precious son."

"You're only fourteen. You don't know anything about anything."

"At least I know when somebody doesn't like me."

"Had a lot of practice, have you?"

"Funny ha-ha. Not as much practice as you've been having."

Renata returned with a glass of water for Gwen, who drank thirstily, then used her sleeve to dab at her convincingly watery eyes. Claire shifted the brown bag to her other arm, regretting it as soon as she did, for it caught Renata's attention.

"May I take that for you?" their hostess asked.

The gift seemed rather meager, under the circumstances. "It's just a bottle of wine," Claire began.

"And dessert," Gwen added.

"How thoughtful," said Renata, without the slightest trace of sincerity. She turned toward the dining room and summoned a uniformed waiter. Good god, Claire thought, they have servants. Renata handed him the bag and instructed him to take it to the kitchen.

"I'm sorry my oldest daughter, Giulietta, is not here to meet you. She's in Rome now, at the university there. These young girls, they want to be so independent, but I tell Giulietta, you *must* have children while you're young, don't put if off, twenty-five at the latest. She'll be twenty-three next year and I'm starting to worry. I would just hate to see her wait too long—sometimes women are so old by the time they have their first child, you can't tell if they're the child's mother or grandmother!"

How would she endure an entire evening of this? Claire wondered. Was Giancarlo really worth this humiliation?

Renata seemed to think of her son at the same time. She glanced up at the clock as it struck the quarter hour and said, "Giancarlo should be here by now. He works too much, just like his father. His firm keeps him so busy. Currently they're supervising a big project in a palazzo near the Accademia."

"Catering it?"

"Renovating it, of course." Renata smiled as she realized the source of Claire's misapprehension. "Oh yes, you met him at the trattoria. He didn't tell you what he really does?"

"No."

"Giancarlo is not a waiter. He just helps out his friend Sergio, who owns the restaurant, sometimes. Giancarlo is an architect." The pride in her voice was boundless, as was the implication that he was much too good for her. No, definitely not worth the humiliation, Claire decided.

Then Giancarlo appeared at the top of the stairs, looking slightly flushed and out of breath and even more handsome than ever. *That hair.* There was something about the juxtaposition of the ringlets and his well-tailored Italian suit that was truly devastating. Giancarlo was almost superhumanly attractive, and possessed a kind of charisma that was even more noticeable here, in his native environment. All three women naturally turned toward him, like flowers toward the sun. So, what's a little humiliation? Claire wondered.

Giancarlo greeted his mother with a quick kiss on the cheek, then took Claire's hands in his. "I'm sorry I could not be here sooner, but I'm so glad you could make it. My mother has made you feel welcome, I trust."

Claire mumbled something that sounded like yes and felt Renata's eyes upon them, observing them with a curiosity not unlike that of a lioness watching over one of her cubs.

Chapter Twelve

"WHY DIDN'T YOU tell me last night that you were an architect?" Claire asked Giancarlo as the wine was poured.

"I didn't want to seem as if I was trying to impress you. And I wanted to know if you'd agree to come to dinner if you thought—"

"That you were a waiter?"

"Yes." Giancarlo smiled, and Claire felt her heart flutter again.

She took a breath and looked around the magnificent room in which they were to dine: the high, baroque ceiling; the candlelight; the soft lilt of Vivaldi in the background; the uniformed waiters who hovered in the shadows. Besides Maurizio and Renata, the dinner party included Gabriella, four professors from the conference, and Giancarlo's teenage sister, Stefania, who sat next to Gwen.

Only one thing marred this spectacular setting. Sitting directly across the table from Claire was the person she least wanted to look at: Andrew Kent. His presence at the Baldasarris' had come as a shock. Giancarlo, after introducing them to Stefania, had taken them on a brief tour of the palazzo. When they returned to the salon, she'd felt mortified to find her nemesis talking to Maurizio, who waved them over.

"We've already had the pleasure of meeting," Andrew said with an ironic but not unfriendly smile, "although not formally."

Claire tried to smile back, wondering if she would be able to get away before he asked—

"Maurizio tells me you're studying the seventeenth century," he continued. "What's the subject of your dissertation?"

"Well, it's the, um, rise of piracy in the Adriatic and its, ahhh, myriad effects on Venetian shipping."

"Myriad? One would think that piracy could have only one possible effect."

"It was bad, generally."

"As I suspected." He took a sip of champagne and stared at the floor for a moment, then looked in her eyes. "Do you think you'll shed any light on the human condition?"

He was mocking her again. Claire felt the anger rush to her face, and tried to formulate a few choice words that would convey her displeasure and still be considered polite. Fortunately Renata ushered everyone out of the salon and into the dining room before Claire said something she would regret. Then Giancarlo steered her to a seat beside his own, and as she sat down she realized that Andrew Kent was taking the chair directly opposite hers. She couldn't very well move; instead, she resolved to keep her eyes away from the other side of the table and concentrate on Giancarlo. Not that this was any hardship, she thought, stealing a glance at his profile.

"But why?" Claire asked him. "Why pretend to be someone you're not?"

"Venice is a small town," Giancarlo replied. "Here everyone knows me, they know my family, know my . . . situation. Sometimes people have liked me for reasons that had nothing to do with me at all. But then, Venetians have a reputation for being devious," he said, smiling.

From his spare details, Claire intuited an endless barrage of marriageable daughters sent by scheming mothers to conquer the Baldessari citadel, represented in the flesh by its male heir. The troubles of the wealthy and beautiful did not usually move her, but Giancarlo's revelation convinced her that at least sometimes he felt quite alone; and with that she felt an acute sympathy.

He also turned out to be a delightful conversationalist. They discussed his work (he'd been an architect for two years, with a firm that specialized in historic renovations), her work (Claire improvised a few pirate stories), the problems of living in Venice (flooding, tourists), the advantages of living in Venice (no cars), and the eternal question of just how long Venice would remain above sea level without intervention. Would the Italian government ever decide what to do about it? Claire asked.

"Every time we think something's going to be done, we elect a different government, and they start debating it all over again," Giancarlo said. "It is called, in a turn of phrase you will appreciate, 'Passing the bucket.'"

Renata turned to them and asked Giancarlo a question that seemed to be about the palazzo he was currently renovating. Claire's Italian was fair, but the Venetian accent made comprehension more difficult. She didn't even try to follow the conversation as Giancarlo spoke to his mother and Gabriella Griseri.

Renata's proximity certainly put a damper on what amounted to their first date, Claire reflected. She realized that she had refrained from laughing too much, or leaning too close, or from any of the other things she might do—or did, ages and ages ago, in the misty memory of her dating life before Michael—to indicate her interest. Giancarlo had seemed similarly careful, which suddenly struck her as odd. He wasn't the one who'd gotten the pre-dinner grilling. If he sincerely liked her, she reasoned, he wouldn't care what his mother thought.

As he continued to talk with Renata, Claire brooded a bit. What if Giancarlo's interest in her was of a more general kind? So far, he'd done nothing overtly romantic. Hadn't Maurizio said he had asked Giancarlo to invite her? Maybe Giancarlo's appearance at her hotel that morning had been prompted by his father, not himself. Why hadn't she thought of that earlier?

Then she remembered the way Giancarlo had looked at her when she was descending the stairs to the lobby, and his expression had seemed unmistakably enamored. Or had she just imagined it? Claire realized that she couldn't be certain. She'd been out of circulation for so long, she couldn't tell if a man liked her or not.

Hoddington Humphries-Todd, on Claire's left, leaned toward her. "Why, for a party of only eleven people, must we sit at a table roughly the size of a cricket field?" he asked with a good-humored grin. "I can hardly hear anything anyone else is saying. Damned annoying. Especially when there's so much of interest going on."

Humphries-Todd, or Hoddy as he'd insisted she call him when they'd been introduced earlier, was tall and elegant, with an attractive, chiseled face. As one of Europe's reigning experts on Pietro Aretino, the sixteenth-century writer, Hoddington Humphries-Todd was a regular feature of the Ca' Foscari annual conference, and of the Baldessaris' intimate, first-night dinner party. He nodded discreetly at the two women seated at the far end of the table. "It looks to me like my good friend Ines"—Claire knew he was referring to the dark-haired, gamin-faced woman, a professor of Venetian studies at the Sorbonne—"has taken up with Katarina von Krupp." He nodded at the woman sitting next to Ines.

Von Krupp, Claire recalled, taught at the University of Berlin. Her short, ice blond hair and man's white summer suit gave her a dashing if sexually ambiguous air.

"It's too bad, really, because her previous lover, a Welsh clog dancer named Gryffyd, was much more to my taste. *Fabulous* legs."

Claire studied the two women, both of whom were engrossed in a conversation with Maurizio. She didn't notice anything particularly intimate between them. "Are you sure?"

"Absolutely," Hoddy insisted. "I have a knack for detecting romantic liaisons. Especially those that are in the early stages or, better still, illicit, obsessively passionate, tragically doomed, or on the verge of breaking up, preferably in a dramatic way in a posh public place. Although every once in a while I can be caught napping. For instance, take Andy"—he glanced across the table at Andrew Kent—"and Gabriella. I didn't know about that until this evening, and apparently it's been going on for some time."

Claire had been surprised, too, to see Andrew Kent show up with Gabriella Griseri. They'd arrived last, Gabriella with her long hair unbound and falling like a silky black waterfall around her shoulders.

"She looks radiant in a suspiciously postcoital sort of way," Hoddy remarked. "And what about you and our lovely young Giancarlo?" he said with eyebrows raised.

"Oh . . . we just met," Claire replied, trying to think of something that would deflect Hoddy's interest in her private life. "Aren't you giving your paper tomorrow?"

"Tomorrow afternoon at four," Hoddy confirmed. "It's called 'The Three Amici: The Friendship of Aretino, Titian, and Sansovino.' It's mostly about Aretino, but I tossed in the other two because I thought I might draw a bigger crowd that way."

"You're not serious," Claire said, laughing.

"Completely. Conference organizers like a full house, and I like free trips to Venice. Works out well for all of us. Are you familiar with Aretino, or are you strictly seventeenth century?"

"I've read the *Dialogo,* his satire about courtesans."

"Ahh, the *Dialogo.* Ostensibly it is about courtesans, but Aretino manages to lampoon just about everyone in Venetian society. I think he actually felt a strong affinity with courtesans; he often compared their existence to his own, as a courtier. He lived rather magisterially with a group of women who were probably courtesans, who were called 'Aretine,' or 'Aretino's women,' although his relationship with them was somewhat unclear."

"Have you ever heard of a courtesan named La Celestia?"

"Sounds vaguely familiar, though I'm not sure why. Why do you ask?"

"I read about her in Fazzini's *Diary* today. Along with another called La Sirena."

"There was something, I seem to recall, but I can't quite remember . . . but then, Fazzini was early seventeenth century, quite a bit later than Aretino, so I never had any reason to study him. Although I have read some of the diaries. I'd say he was more of a scandalmonger than a satirist. Fazzini reports, while Aretino skewers."

"Yes, I got the feeling Aretino didn't like anyone much."

"True, although he could write the most obsequious drivel when it suited him. Generally, though, he spared no one, especially those in power." Hoddy warmed to his subject. "It's true he was a bastard, but I can't help being intrigued by a man who died of excessive laughter after hearing an obscene joke about his own sister. He was known as the 'Scourge of Princes' because his satiric verse was so popular, it could sway public opinion. Even kings lived in fear of him, and he became fabulously wealthy because they and other powerful men sent bribes so that he wouldn't write about them. Which one must admit is exceedingly clever. I don't believe there's another writer in history who's hit upon such an excellent method of writing. Anytime someone saw him pick up a quill, they threw money at him to put it down again."

"Nice work if you can get it," said Andrew Kent, raising his wineglass in tribute.

"Do I detect a note of jealousy?" Hoddy asked.

"Oh, not at all," Gabriella answered for him. "He's received three offers on his book already." She smiled at Andrew. "I insist that I have the first interview once it's published, of course."

"I'm all yours," he replied.

"Gabriella hosts a television program," Giancarlo remarked to Claire.

"I heard it mentioned at the conference." She spoke across the table to Gabriella. "What sort of topics do you cover?"

"Anything that involves history, culture, or art, so it's pretty far ranging," Gabriella replied. "I've interviewed most of the great artists of our age: Umberto Eco, Luciano Pavarotti, Roberto Begnini . . ." She shook her head to indicate that this was only a small sampling of her illustrious guest list. "Do you have similar programs in America?"

"Not that I know of, but I don't watch television much."

"Of course, it must be difficult to have such a program in your country, since you have so little history and culture."

"I'm sure there isn't a show like yours in America because there isn't anyone else like you, Gabriella," Hoddy interjected diplomatically.

"You're too kind."

"I think Hoddy has a point there," Andrew said. "Gabriella has more general knowledge about art and history than anyone else I know. How many degrees do you have? Three?"

"Three, yes, it's true, I'm terribly overeducated." Gabriella addressed her remark to Claire, speaking as if it were an embarrassing revelation, yet managing to brag about it at the same time.

Gabriella couldn't be much older than herself, Claire thought with dismay; at least, she didn't look it. Three degrees? She must be some kind of superwoman. Was it fair for anyone to be so beautiful and so smart?

"Of course, I'm not counting the one from the University of Vienna," Gabriella continued, "since it was an honorary degree."

"The last time I was in America, it seemed as if every chat show ended up with people fighting onstage," Andrew said. "I'm sure they can't all be that bad, but it does appear as if anyone can be a television presenter, and it doesn't really matter whether they know anything at all."

"Then I could easily be a star there, couldn't I?" Gabriella turned to Andrew with a dazzling smile.

"Anywhere, I'm sure," Andrew said gallantly, although Claire had the impression that he was embarrassed by Gabriella's shameless egotism; she behaved as if she were continually in the center of a spotlight. The poised yet bubbly personality that worked so well in a television studio was a bit much within the confines of a dining room.

"More wine?" Giancarlo didn't wait for an answer, just picked up the nearest bottle and refilled Claire's glass. "She's hard to take sometimes, yes?" he said softly, with a glance at Gabriella.

"I think she has too many names."

Giancarlo stifled a laugh. "I think it's pretentious, too. Around here, we just call her La Contessa."

"Because of her, ah, manner?" She left out the adjectives that had come to mind: conceited, self-absorbed, preening.

"No, because she is a contessa. But it's an Austrian title, not Italian," Giancarlo said with just the slightest disdain, as if there was something not quite legitimate about an Austrian countess. "But there are better things to talk about, yes?" he said softly, resting his hand lightly on her knee.

Oh my. That was a little more than just friendly, wasn't it?

Hoddy leaned forward to catch Giancarlo's eye. "So where's that gorgeous fiancée of yours tonight, Giancarlo? Natalie, isn't it?"

Fiancée?

Claire looked at Giancarlo, who appeared as though he'd swallowed his tongue. "She's in Milan on business," he replied. His hand slipped from Claire's knee as discreetly as it had arrived.

"Didn't you tell me that she works in the fashion industry?" Hoddy continued.

"She's a marketing manager for Dolce & Gabbana."

"How fabulous! Does she get a discount on those wonderful clothes?"

"Free samples, actually. They have to wear them when they're working."

"I thought she was exceptionally lovely. But then, I've always thought that Italian women were the most beautiful in the world."

Claire sat silently between the two of them, forced to listen as Hoddy waxed eloquent on the elegant attributes of Italian women, and assimilated this new information: one fiancée, gorgeous, named Natalie, who was apparently very well attired. She noticed that the mention of Natalie's name had piqued Renata's interest; her curiosity carried across the table like radar.

Claire glanced at Giancarlo, who looked as embarrassed as she felt. It must be true, as he hadn't denied it, but she had the distinct impression that he hadn't wanted her to know. Well, it explained a few things, anyway—no wonder she'd been getting mixed messages. She was left with only one question: how soon could she politely say good night and get the hell out of there?

Justice

30 November 1617

"WE WERE SAILING past the islands just south of Istria when we were set upon by pirates out of Dalmatia," Piero de Pieri said, with a glance down at the hat he held in his hands.

He's nervous, and rightly so, Girolamo Silvia thought. The Venetian admiral stood alone in the center of the Room of the Four Doors in the Ducal Palace, addressing the Doge, the Signory, and the Council of Ten. He guessed it was the admiral's first time reporting to the Doge—when ships returned safely, it wasn't necessary. But rumor had it that the admiral's last excursion had been a disaster, and he hadn't even left the Adriatic.

Silvia shifted in his chair and scanned the faces of the other members of the Council of Ten. He had a sudden intuition that the admiral's account would be in conflict with his own agenda. No one would be happy to learn of pirates so close to home, of course. But when the others knew what he knew, certainly they would be convinced of the larger threat facing them. Or would they? he wondered bitterly. Too often in the past, his wise counsel had been ignored by those less informed. Not this time, he vowed. The very survival of the Republic was at stake.

"They call themselves the Uskoks, the escaped ones," de Pieri said. He was a short man with wide shoulders and dark, leathery skin. He'd worked his way up through the ranks, and a lifetime at sea showed in his sturdy physique and the deep lines of his face. Although he faced Venice's supreme governing body, he seemed undaunted by the intimidating presence of so many scarlet robes. Only someone as observant as Silvia noticed the little twitch at the corner of his eye, the fingers that gripped his *biretta* too tightly, the tiny beads of perspiration at his temples. "They're Christian refugees from the parts of Dalmatia that were captured by the Turks," the admiral continued. "Although they're in the service of the Hapsburgs to help protect their borders from the Turks, they're seldom paid, so they survive by plundering passing ships. And a right good enterprise they've made of it, too. All of Segna grows rich from their piracy, including the churches and the monasteries. These Uskoks have hundreds of small ships, only ten oars to a side, very fast and easy to maneuver. They brought out dozens of these against us and soon we were overcome."

The Doge raised a frail hand and de Pieri fell silent. Like most Doges, Giovanni Bembo had been elected to office in the twilight of his life. He'd been Doge for two years now, and Silvia suspected he would not live to see out a third. "Could you not put to sail and get away?" he asked.

The admiral looked troubled. "Their women are witches, Your Serenity," he said with a wary glance around the room, fully aware of how preposterous his statement sounded to the learned and reasonable men of the Republic. "They congregate in caves along the shore, wailing like tormented souls in Hell, casting spells to bring the *boro,* the north wind, down upon us."

"Surely you don't believe . . . ," the Doge began.

"I would not believe, except that I witnessed it myself, Your Serenity. A frigid wind began to blow as soon as those women began wailing, then a storm arose and the sea pitched and tossed something fierce. That's when the Uskoks attacked. Their ships may be small, but they man them with ten men per oar, and they're strong as devils. Within two hours all four of our ships had been boarded. The crews on three of the ships were on wages and had no stake in the cargo. On agreement that their lives be spared, they stood down and the Uskoks looted the goods. The fourth ship fought back."

De Pieri looked down at the floor. "Many of our men were killed. And the captain . . ." He looked up again at the Doge, at the six-member Signory flanking him, at the Council of Ten seated along the walls. Silvia saw the glint of anger in his eyes. "The captain was flayed alive, right there on the deck of his own ship."

An uneasy murmur went around the room. "Flayed alive?" the Doge repeated softly. His papery eyelids slowly closed then opened again, reminding Silvia of an ancient tortoise.

"Yes, Your Serenity, just like Bragadin," the admiral said. "A trick they learned from the Turks, no doubt."

Damn them to hell, Silvia thought. The ghost of Marcantonio Bragadin would do his cause no good whatsoever. The dismal end of the Venetian commander of Cyprus was known to everyone in the room. After months of siege, in August 1571 Bragadin was forced to surrender Cyprus to the Turks. When he met with the Turkish pasha to ratify their agreement, he was seized and tortured. Then he was taken to the center of town, where he was stripped naked, tied to a stake, and skinned alive. The butchers began at his feet; it was said that Bragadin did not lose consciousness until they reached his waist. After the deed was done, his skin was stuffed with straw and paraded through the town. The fury this outrage inspired helped lead the Venetians to victory over the Turks in the Battle of Lepanto two months later, and now, Silvia was certain, the similar fate of the captain would stir up passionate feelings against the Uskoks.

The Doge dismissed the admiral and the room buzzed with comment. "Quiet, please," Bembo commanded. "Everyone will have his chance to speak."

Even before the other members of the council had offered their opinions to the Doge and the Signory, Silvia knew what they would say. Predictably, Senators Foscarini, Balbi, and Gradenigo advised an immediate strike against the Uskoks. Hotheads, Silvia thought, annoyed; they're always ready to go to war at the least provocation. Senator Corner, one of the Tre Capi, more temperately suggested finding allies before battling the pirates.

Allies? Silvia thought resentfully as he waited for Corner and the others to finish speaking. What had allies ever done for Venice? He looked at the wall opposite, where an immense painting commemorated the arrival of Henri III in 1574. Venice's welcome for the young French king was legendary. They had prostrated themselves and nearly bankrupted the treasury with specially designed triumphal arches and commissioned artworks, with a round of lavish banquets—including one for a crowd of three thousand, in which everything, even the napkins, had been made of spun sugar—and with the outfitting of Ca' Foscari with the most precious carpets, tapestries, paintings, and silk bedding. But what good had it done them? In the years immediately following, Venice had suffered a fire that nearly destroyed the Doge's Palace, and a plague that killed more than fifty thousand. Their alliance with the French king had helped them not one whit.

Finally the others finished speaking. All had recommended retaliation against the Uskoks. Not one, Silvia reflected with disgust, had considered a simple alternative: that Venetian ships avoid the Dalmatian coast. Why was it always up to him to be the voice of reason?

"Senator Silvia, what have you to say?" the Doge inquired.

Silvia stood to face Bembo and the Signory. "While the events that Signor de Pieri related to us are regrettable," he began, "it's a mistake to wage war against the Uskoks. There is piracy everywhere. Venetian merchants and sailors must cope with it as best they can."

"But this happened in our very own Adriatic!" Balbi exclaimed, unable to restrain himself.

"Which makes it easy to avoid them," Silvia said. "We know where they are. These small ships the admiral spoke of—surely they cannot venture far from their own coast. The Uskoks are an annoyance, yes, but not a threat."

"If we allow them to thrive in the Adriatic, we will appear weak," Gradenigo said.

"We are weak," Silvia countered, "and so we must choose our battles carefully. Gentlemen, we face a greater threat than that posed by a group of Dalmatian peasants. It has come to my attention that the duke of Ossuna is building a new fleet. As you all know, during the past year he's been harassing our ships in an effort to monopolize our trade. But these new ships of his are not merchant ships—they're warships. In addition, he's planted spies who have passed on secret information about the Arsenale."

The mention of spies set everyone talking again and Silvia had to raise his voice to be heard. "I believe that the duke has his eye on more than supremacy in the Adriatic. I believe he has designs on Venice itself."

At this, a few of the senators exclaimed loudly, and the council and the Signory began arguing among themselves. The Doge hushed everyone, then turned his tired eyes back to Silvia. "Do you have evidence that Ossuna is planning an attack?"

"No, Your Serenity, but there are indications . . ."

"Indications? Philip III may be half the man his father was, but Lerma is someone to be reckoned with, and Spain is still as rich as ever. Are you suggesting that we go to war with Spain on the basis of an indication?"

"I'm suggesting that we not squander our resources when we may very well need them right here."

The Doge placed his fingertips together and rested them against his chin, momentarily lost in thought. With barely a glance up, he said, "Contarini?"

By the bloody Virgin, Silvia swore silently. Dario Contarini was the Doge's favorite adviser and considered by some to be the embodiment of the Venetian ideal: robustly healthy, rich, virile, popular, and so politically astute that he'd been appointed to the Signory at the tender age of forty-two. It seemed to Silvia that he was the only one who saw Contarini for what he truly was: two-faced, equivocal, and always willing to bend with the prevailing winds, provided that it benefited him personally. But somehow his lack of respect for Contarini did not have the humbling effect that Silvia felt it should have; the younger senator simply shrugged it off and seemed to embrace every opportunity to oppose him. Even worse, he appeared to enjoy it. As Contarini stood to address the assembly, his fine-featured face could not conceal a slight smirk that Silvia knew was meant for him.

"Senator Silvia is right when he points out that we don't have the resources to wage war on two fronts," Contarini said. "But in the absence of an actual threat from Ossuna, we can't ignore the fact that the Uskoks are damaging Venetian profits and taking Venetian lives."

Damn you, Silvia thought as Contarini went on in that oh-so-reasonable tone of his, one that was tinged with just the slightest hint of condescension. As he expounded on the uncertainty of Ossuna's intentions, his unspoken message was clear: Silvia was an old crank who saw conspiracies everywhere. Silvia gritted his teeth to keep a rein on his fury. It would do no good to show it here.

"As the Uskoks are ostensibly in the service of the Hapsburgs," Contarini concluded, "we should look to Savoy for an alliance."

The Doge nodded in agreement. Silvia felt a piercing pain at his temples. The obtuseness of his peers was frustrating beyond belief. His only solace was that one day they would thank him for his foresight; they would thank him and, by God, they would elect him Doge.

"Ossuna could wish for nothing more than to have both Savoy's and Venice's armies off fighting on the other side of the Adriatic," Silvia said harshly. "If this be your decision, we may as well set up a welcoming committee for the duke at Malamocco."

"Stand down, Silvia," Bembo said. "We must put an end to the Uskoks' depredations, but your warning will not go unheeded. If the Three should discover more evidence of Ossuna's plotting, I trust you will inform us."

"Of course, Your Serenity." Silvia couldn't help but sneak a glance at Contarini. He didn't meet Silvia's eyes. By this small admission, Silvia was certain that Contarini had heard the Doge's implied command to Silvia to keep on with his intelligence gathering. Silvia allowed himself a smirk of his own. Of course he would keep on. And he knew just where he would start.

The Hierophant

17 December 1617

IN THE MARQUIS'S gondola, moored at the Molo, Paolo Calieri listened to the thunderous sound of rain drumming on the *felze*. The squall had come in from the east just before dawn, and by midday all of Venice was suffering the effects of the deluge. In torrents, rain streamed off the silent bell towers, cascaded from the golden spires and shining domes of the Basilica and the Redentore, and spilled down the stone walls of palaces and tenements, flooding cobbled lanes and turning unpaved alleys into mud. Rain gushed into the rising canals, where tufts of seaweed and moss swayed in the murky depths, and reduced the traffic on the Grand Canal to a single galleon, pregnant with spices and aromatic oils, that labored valiantly toward the Rialto.

He peered out from under the canopy at the forlorn scene before him: the Piazzetta and the Piazza San Marco were as tightly shuttered and empty as the deck of a battened ship. He thought about his collection of spiderwebs, tenderly preserved between translucent sheets of parchment and kept in the driest cupboard in his room. Even though he took such care, the webs' pearlescent threads never lasted through the wet Venetian winter, but their ephemeral delicacy contributed to their fascination. Paolo marveled at the way they disintegrated so slowly and beautifully, and left behind the bits of treasure they had caught: an iridescent insect's wing, a shiny beetle carapace. So tiny yet so exquisite; if only he had more time to study them.

Paolo got to his feet as the Spanish ambassador appeared from the arcade of the Doge's Palace and strode across the rainswept square. The marquis stepped into the gondola and shook his cape from his shoulders. It was wet through, just in the brief time it had taken him to cross the Piazzetta. He leaned back on the upholstered bench and looked up at Paolo, who stood unbowed against the rain, one hand gripping the oar, waiting for instruction. "To the embassy," he said, raising his voice over the sound of the storm. Paolo nodded and rowed them away from the dock.

The ambassador watched the Doge's Palace slip past, its multiarched, pink and white facade unusually solemn under the dismal sky. The rain depressed him. There was water enough in Venice already, too much water without more of it falling from the sky. He felt a sudden, sharp longing for the scent of earth in his nostrils, the familiar, spicy loam of the Spanish plains, instead of Venice's moldering mildew. His appointment to Venice was considered one of the most prestigious in the diplomatic corps, but Bedmar often wondered if Venice was fit for men like him, men who would rather be astride a horse than in a gondola, who preferred vast, silent vistas and barren mountains to this damp, cold rat-warren precariously balanced on the sea. It was nothing but water and stone, stone and water, a place of reflections and illusions, deception and guile. Someday the whole city would melt into the lagoon like stale bread in broth, and Bedmar wasn't at all sure he would be sorry.

Mother of Christ, he was ill-humored. For the first time since he'd arrived, Bedmar wondered if he was in over his head, lost in a maze of plots, feints, lies, and half-truths as confusing as Venice's watery streets. Just when his fortunes were improving—Philip III had come through with a shipment of silver and gold coin—Ossuna had suborned his own cousin, that young fool Javier, to gather intelligence on the Arsenale. Had the duke truly believed that Javier could outwit the Venetians at their own game? Bedmar had known from the beginning of their enterprise that the duke was dangerous, but he had thought their mutual need of each other would provide security against any betrayal. What was Ossuna up to? He was going to have to watch his back more carefully from now on.

Paolo executed an expert flip of the oar, and the gondola bobbed heavily into the heaving Rio del Palazzo directly behind the palace. Above them loomed the Bridge of Sighs, which connected the Doge's Palace to the prison. From the lion's den into the lion's mouth, Bedmar mused. He felt his bile rise again. These Venetians would be sorry if they tried to catch him in their voracious maw; he'd give them a case of indigestion they'd never forget. They called themselves noble, but they were nothing more than merchants, men without rank or title. This Senator Silvia had sent for him as if he were a lackey! He'd submit to it once, but not twice. He was a marquis and an ambassador of Spain. If Silvia meddled with him again, he would know his wrath.

The senator had received him in his chambers in the Doge's Palace. A moon-faced, slow-witted clerk led Bedmar into a richly furnished study, where a sickly light seeped through windows that appeared to be melting under the steady downpour. A blazing fire in the grate kept the chill at bay without illuminating the shadowy recesses of the room. From the dark places glinted the Eastern excess that crowded Silvia's private sanctum: gilded paneling, Venetian glass candelabra, a gleaming parquet desk, a row of jewel-studded gold goblets.

"Over here." A powerful voice, edged with impatience, sounded from the center of the room. Silvia sat in a brocade-covered chair near the grate, facing the fire. His wood-soled shoes poked out from beneath the hem of his toga. The right shoe had a sole at least an inch thicker than the left.

So the stories about the bull were true, Bedmar thought. But he hadn't known until now that it had left the senator lame, a crookback with a shortened limb.

The senator noticed the direction of Bedmar's gaze, and pulled his feet under his robe. He shifted and turned, and the marquis was nearly overcome with the aroma of frankincense that emanated from him and mingled with smoke from the hearth. His fur-lined scarlet toga appeared bloodred in the firelight, and his sallow skin glowed with a deceptively rosy hue. Girolamo Silvia was an unpleasing man, with a beaklike nose, sunken cheeks, and long, narrow hands that Bedmar suspected had wielded a stiletto more than once. But in spite of his lush surroundings and his princely attire, Bedmar sensed an austerity in Silvia that he might have, in a place other than irreverent Venice, thought of as priest-like. The association was not reassuring, however; Silvia's countenance reminded him too much of the grotesque bird mask, filled with prophylactic herbs, that physicians wore to ward off the black death. If the senator was a priest, he was a priest in the service of the Devil, if an ascetic, an ascetic with assassin's hands.

"Have a seat, Ambassador," Silvia said in the same gruff tone. "I trust I am not keeping you from your duties of office."

"Spain's good relation with the Republic is my duty of office," Bedmar replied smoothly as he sat down. "I am at your service, Senator."

His polite manner made little impression on Silvia, who dispensed with further amenities. "Do you know a man named Luis Salazar?"

Bedmar paused thoughtfully. "No, I can't say that I do."

"Odd, since he was a *bravo* in your employ."

"These men come and go. I know few of them by name."

"Perhaps you will recall his face. He had a dueling scar upon his lip, quite pronounced."

"No, I don't remember anyone like that." Bedmar cocked his head. "What is the point of your inquiry?"

"Luis Salazar was arrested some weeks ago. He was in possession of state secrets passed to him by an Arsenale worker."

"Why should this concern me?"

"Because it was Salazar who led us to the man responsible for bribing the *arsenalotto* who provided this secret intelligence. A man who was also employed by your embassy: Javier Diego de la Esparza."

Bedmar felt himself blanch, but his face registered no emotion other than mild interest.

"Do you know him?" Silva asked.

"We have a passing acquaintance."

"A passing acquaintance? I believe he is your cousin."

"A distant cousin."

"Distant or not, I thought you would like to know what he told us before he died."

"He's dead?"

"Javier was a delicate sort. Prison did not agree with him."

The oily bastard. Bedmar had a sudden desire to reach over and snap Silvia's neck. He could do it—he had done it, to heartier men than he. He had a swift, satisfying vision of leaving the senator slumped in his chair and walking out of the Doge's Palace without a backward glance. But then of course he'd have to keep going—all the way back to Spain. No, he'd never depart without the riches that were due him. No point in letting this crookback senator goad him into doing something stupid. Bedmar smiled. "Please go on," he said.

"Your cousin was in the pay of the duke of Ossuna. The duke is building a new fleet, with which he plans to attack Venice."

"Is that so?"

"Do you expect me to believe that this is the first you have heard of it?"

"You can believe whatever you like. But I am only an ambassador. I have no authority over the viceroy of Naples."

"Perhaps this statement of Javier's will interest you: 'The Spanish ambassador has his house full of *bravi* and assassins, and keeps a bank to receive bets on elections to the Great Council. The ambassador intends to blow up the Great Council, and he has stored in his house barrels of powder, which he pretends are full of figs and oil.'"

"These are statements made under torture—"

"But does that necessarily make them less true? Perhaps we should consult your Holy Inquisitors for their opinion on this. After all, Spain has been . . . instrumental, shall we say? . . . in developing new methods of uncovering the truth."

"It is God's wish for heretics to suffer."

"How convenient it must be to know what God wishes," Silvia said. "I myself am never entirely sure. Tell me, is it God's wish for you to emulate that English zealot Guy Fawkes? If you're not careful, you may end up like him, hanging from a scaffold. Your diplomatic immunity does not extend to acts of war against the Republic. The only reason you are still a free man is because your cousin did not implicate you in his crime. He insisted that he was working for Ossuna, not you."

"I am a free man," said Bedmar, "because I answer only to the king of Spain." He stood up. "Need I remind you that I am the official representative of the most powerful country in Europe. When you threaten me, you threaten Spain. That's a dangerous game, Senator, and one I suspect your colleagues would not like to play. I came here today out of courtesy, but should you summon me again, you will find me much less gracious." Bedmar turned toward the door. "You are welcome to search my house at any time," he called over his shoulder. "You will find nothing but figs and oil."

It was the senator's outright threat that had made him certain he had nothing to fear, Bedmar reflected as the gondola turned into the Rio della Fava. If Silvia had evidence of his and Ossuna's plan, he'd be brought up in front of the Ten or the Three without any warning or explanation. No, the senator was groping in the dark. A more astute tactician would have kept secret Javier's confessions, and let him wonder and worry. But Silvia had revealed all. Had he slipped up, or was there another purpose behind it?

Whichever it was, Bedmar made a mental note to send for Sanchez when he got back to the embassy and have him and his men move the barrels of powder to a new hiding place. They'd have to do it soon—perhaps as soon as tonight, Bedmar thought, as Paolo steered the gondola into an unfamiliar waterway. He leaned back and peered up from under the *felze* at his gondolier. "Where are you going?" he shouted.

A quick flurry of hands revealed that their new route was due to the rising tide. Such a peculiar youth. Sometimes, like now, in the driving rain, with his hair plastered against his face, his head low and his eyes wide, Paolo reminded the ambassador of a wet, hungry dog in the moment before one knew if it would wag its tail or bite.

The gondolier crouched low as they passed under the Ponte

Pinelli. On bright days, striated light from the rippling water reflected gaily on the rounded inner walls of the bridge. The Venetians, in their strange, slurred tongue, had a special name for the effect. But on this gloomy afternoon, the ancient arch pressed around them like a secret, abandoned cave, weeping with condensation, streaked with algae, rancid with decay. With a stink like a crypt, Bedmar thought, like the smell of death. As the gondola glided into the open canal, the marquis suppressed an involuntary shudder.

Silvia looked up as Batù stepped out of the shadows. As always, his eyes came into view first. Silvia studied their Asiatic contours, their ghostly blue irises.

"Well?" the master inquired of the disciple. "What did you think of him?"

"He's confident. He does not fear you."

"Not yet, perhaps, but he will." Silvia got to his feet and walked to his desk, where he opened a flagon of wine and splashed some into a goblet. "He knows of Ossuna's plans, I am sure of that. But he did not know of his own cousin's espionage—which means that he and Ossuna are not in complete accord. This could work in our favor."

"Why do you let him go free? Why haven't you arrested him for the crimes de la Esparza confessed?"

"As the ambassador pointed out, a move against him is a move against Spain. We have a treaty with them at present, a treaty neither country obeys to the letter, but an outright breach would call the Spanish army down upon us. No, we cannot move openly against the ambassador. To bring him and Ossuna to justice, we'll need evidence of their plot. In the meantime, though, we can move against him secretly. There's no reason why his life in Venice should be one of ease and pleasure. This is, after all, a very dangerous place."

The Sun

21 January 1618

SURELY IT MUST be called for what it was: madness. What Antonio had seen of Venice during Carnival, in the two days since he'd returned, convinced him that everyone in the city was possessed by folly. Masks disguised true identities, from the lowest servant to the highest noble, and Venice was alive with music and a thousand gambols: balls and comedies, gondola races, jousts and combats, goose catching and bull baiting. The three-month celebration drew people from all parts of the world, and the variety of costume, custom, and complexion was greater than he'd ever seen, even during his years in Sicily. The entire city had been transformed into an open-air bazaar: at every corner, mountebanks peddled their medicines in a dozen different tongues; sellers of beads and lace and glassware could be found in all the squares; foodstuffs of every sort were offered from booths or by vendors wandering the streets.

"Isn't it amazing?" Alessandra asked as they stood near the base of the Campanile on the Piazza San Marco.

Amazing was a tame word for it, Antonio thought. The Piazza looked as if it had been taken over by a throng of fools. The square was full of masked merrymakers, puppeteers, rope dancers, musicians, jugglers, gamblers, almanac makers and fortune-tellers, whose tables were set with globes and conjuring books. He watched as a soothsayer held up a long, tin pipe to whisper his augury into the ear of a curious monk.

"No need to answer, I can see that you're astonished," she went on.

"As astonished as you were when I arrived at your house this morning?"

"Maybe not as astonished as all that," Alessandra admitted.

Her gentle laughter provoked a strange sensation in Antonio's chest. He hadn't planned on seeing her again, but as soon as his errand was done, he'd found himself at her door. As he looked at Alessandra, he realized how often he'd thought of her, how he'd compared every woman he'd seen to her and found them all wanting. Even so, his memory hadn't done justice to her loveliness.

"Just how did you come to be in Venice again, by the way?" she asked.

"Does it matter?"

"You will not tell me?"

"Does it matter?" To tell her that he was once more a messenger for Ossuna, relaying letters between the duke and the marquis, seemed a confession that was beneath his dignity. And truly, it was better if she did not know of the communication between the two. Her suspicions had been aroused the last time.

"I see. No more questions, then," Alessandra said. "Let us continue with our tour. So far, you've seen the Rialto and the Merceria; now we stand at the very heart of Venice. Our renowned Basilica famously houses the remains of our patron, St. Mark, cleverly smuggled from Muslim lands in a basket of pork. It's also home to other relics sure to delight the faithful, including a small ampula of our Blessed Savior's blood, a goodly sized piece of the true cross, a part of St. Luke's arm, one of St. Stephen's ribs, and a finger once belonging to Mary Magdalene."

"Almost enough to build another saint, it would seem."

"The marble columns at the entrance to the Piazzetta were brought from Constantinople almost four hundred and fifty years ago and were erected by an engineer named Nicolò Baratieri. For his service to the city, Baratieri was granted rights to set up gaming tables, which as you can see are still there. And just above that is where criminals are executed—a gibbet is strung between the columns."

"You're clearly a learned guide, but there's no need to go on about that."

"The gibbet is for the common criminal," Alessandra continued, blithely ignoring him, "but high on the Campanile is a cage reserved for the punishment of wicked priests, where some have been confined and made to live on bread and water for weeks at a time. When I was a child, there was one such up there—I believe he became quite an attraction for visitors. There was even a popular song about him, 'The Lament of Father Augustine.' My brother and I used to sing it quite a lot, to the consternation of my father. It was a terrible, cruel song about how he was wasting away, but we thought it very funny. Soon after that, 'The Lament of Father Augustine's Woman' became even more popular. I recall it was most concerned with a particular pleasure she missed while her lover was strung up in that cage—quite scandalous. My father absolutely forbade us to sing that one."

"The true scandal is how Venice treats its priests," Antonio teased her. "When I leave here, I'm going directly to Rome to advise the pope to excommunicate the entire Republic once again."

"Another interdict? The Great Council will simply ignore it, as they did before, and order the priests to continue celebrating Mass in spite of the ban. There is a well-known story about a priest who was not sure, during the interdict, whether his loyalty lay with Venice or with Rome, and so announced that he would not perform the sacraments until he received inspiration from the Holy Ghost. He was immediately informed that the Holy Ghost had already inspired the Council of Ten to hang anyone who disobeyed them."

"More proof, I should say, of your irreverent city. Not that more proof is necessary." A group of revelers pushed past them, laughing and screeching. "This is like being in a house of lunatics."

"Would you like to go elsewhere?"

"Yes."

Alessandra's gaze alighted on a row of food stalls. "Shall we dine on the lagoon?"

* * *

On the unprotected shore the air was brisk, but the solitude and tranquility of the small island was a welcome change. Antonio and Alessandra sat on a sun-warmed spit of sand not far from where the water gently lapped at the island's edge. The gondolier Antonio had hired that morning stayed in his craft, looking out at the nearby island of Giudecca. Gondoliers must spend a great deal of time in their boats, Antonio thought, wondering how they occupied themselves when they weren't rowing. No sooner had the thought occurred to him than the gondolier provided an answer: he plumped a few cushions and lay back for a well-deserved nap.

"This seems a charmed place," Antonio said as Alessandra unwrapped the packages of food, revealing a roasted capon, sardines with lemon and herbs, a loaf of bread, a plum tart. A strand of hair blew across her bare face—they'd both removed their masks as soon as they were out on the lagoon—and he stifled an urge to brush it away.

"When I was a child, I used to come here with my brother and my cousins," she said.

"Not anymore?"

"My cousins moved to Padua some years ago."

Antonio remembered the sad fate of her father and brother. "Do you have any other family here?"

"No." She untied the narrow leather case she wore at her waist and took out a set of cutlery. "I hope you don't object to sharing," she said, handing him a knife.

"Not at all. Your mother is gone also?" Antonio asked. "Or perhaps you don't want to talk about it."

"No, I don't mind. It was a long time ago, or so it seems. She died when I was eight, in childbed. I witnessed it. I guess they thought because I was a girl I should know what birth was like, but it was terrifying. The child was breach, and my mother was frail—both she and the baby died. When you were here last, you asked me why I had no children. I didn't tell you the whole truth. I take precautions because I am afraid of being with child."

"Understandable, given your experience," Antonio said. "Dare I ask, while you are so unguarded, if you are partial to the life you lead?"

"There are worse fates than becoming a courtesan. I never cared much about being married, like other girls. I think that in some ways I am deficient—I have never loved, in the romantic sense. So perhaps the life I have chosen is best." She tore a piece off the loaf of bread and offered it to him. "And you? Do you have a family?"

"Three older sisters, all well married. But I have not seen them these nine years."

"That's a long time."

"Yes," Antonio agreed, though he did not explain.

"Have you a wife or mistress?"

Why was she asking? He gave Alessandra a sidelong glance, but her expression was as disinterested as ever. "Like you, I cannot love," he admitted. "For I know it only as the prelude to disaster."

"But how can that be?"

"It's a long story."

"I like long stories."

Antonio paused. In the past nine years, he'd not told anyone this tale. He had a sudden, vivid memory of his father, his mother, of the ancient oak tree that stood on a rise just outside his childhood home. Alessandra made him think of things he had not thought about in a long time, things he didn't necessarily want to think about, but he pushed aside his misgivings and began.

"When I was sixteen, I bested my father at swordplay," Antonio said. "He realized then that he had no more to teach me, and so arranged for my tutelage with Don Gaspar Ortiz y Vega de la Vasquez. He lived on the other side of Utrillo, the main town in my family's fiefdom. I had to ride two miles to the town, then another four miles past, then through a grove of walnut trees to get to his house.

"Don Gaspar was a successful sword master. He had helped train the king's guard, and he had written a treatise on sword fighting that was very popular in Spain. He had been away for many years, then come back to Navarre with his daughter. His small estate was approached by a gravel path that came out of the walnut grove and widened into a clearing where the house stood. It was a fine house of rose-colored stone, with a large arch at the center that led to an inner courtyard, and four large windows and balconies spaced along the second floor.

"The first day, when I rode out of the walnut grove into the clearing, I looked up to see a figure standing at one of the center windows. It was a girl, very solemn, staring down at me. She was the most beautiful girl I'd ever seen. I sat there on my horse, forgetting everything else, not moving, just staring at her for what seemed a long time. She was so beautiful, and yet if I describe her, you might say there was nothing so special about her: she had black hair, and rosy lips, and dark eyes that were uncommonly still and deep. What made her truly beautiful were her ears. Her hair was pulled back, so I could see them clearly, small and perfectly formed, like delicate shells. She was like a rare creature one seldom sees, reminding me of a doe I'd once come across in the forest. She had that same gentle, serious expression, as if I'd surprised her, but also as if she'd been expecting me. And she was equally skittish, for she suddenly stepped back from the window and disappeared from my sight.

"And just as well, as Don Gaspar had appeared in the courtyard and was striding toward me. He was older than I'd expected, with gray hair and a small, neat gray beard, but very trim and fit. He had an elegant manner, precise in its courtesy, and he was always attendant to the correct forms of address. He greeted me and showed me into the studio, which we entered from the courtyard. I could hardly hear a word he said, could hardly speak, because of the vision I'd seen.

"But as we began the lessons, I came to my senses. How hard I fought, thinking that she might be somewhere nearby, watching. How I suffered every time I made the slightest mistake, fearful that she had witnessed my ineptitude! It was glorious and terrible. Every time I rallied against my master, I felt a triumph unlike any other I'd ever known; and when I failed, I experienced such despair, as though I would never be happy again. Of course I did not know, on that first day, that Don Gaspar was going easy on me as he developed a sense of my skill and level of training, or that my new master had an inexhaustible supply of moves and feints, more than I could ever hope to learn. Thank the heavens for my ignorance; if I'd known how easily he could best me, I might never have come back. Or perhaps I should curse my ignorance, for if I had never gone back . . ." Antonio paused as his eyes clouded over, then shook his head and continued.

"This went on for months. Each day as I arrived, I would see her standing at the window, and all through my lessons I would be aware of her presence somewhere in the house, but never see her; she never came back to the window as I was leaving. I learned her name, Ephegenia, and I would find myself saying it over and over, savoring it in my mouth like a taste I could not get enough of. Sunday, when I had no lessons, was torture; I spent the whole day practicing in secret, waiting only for Monday to arrive. I grew jealous of any others who took lessons with Don Gaspar, jealous that they might see her and love her as I did. I began to despair. Some days I thought I was in love with a vision, not a woman, for although I spent almost every afternoon with Don Gaspar, he never once mentioned his daughter to me.

"After I had been his student for many months, he invited me and my family to his house for a Sunday supper. To celebrate and acknowledge my superior skill, he said. I was surprised because Don Gaspar could still best me; but he insisted that I was his finest pupil, and that my family should be proud of me. You can imagine how excited I was. Surely, on an occasion such as that, I would meet Ephegenia, we would be formally introduced.

"The great day arrived, and with my family I joined Don Gaspar in his home. But when Ephegenia was presented to me, she offered nothing more than the brief, polite comments she'd given to my parents and my sisters. For the rest of the afternoon, she did not speak to me or even look at me. By the time we left, I was devastated. I realized that I had only imagined the feelings she had for me. I thought I'd seen something in her eyes, as she looked down at me from her window, only to discover that it had been a boy's folly. I wasn't certain that I would ever recover from my own foolishness.

"I almost didn't return to my lessons. It was with a heavy heart that I approached the house the next day, not with the mixture of joy and anxiety that I had felt so many times before, a sensation that had become the most important of my life. She was not standing in the window, and I was almost glad of it, for surely she would have seen the sadness and disappointment in my face.

"I was terrible at my lessons that day, so clumsy and mindless that Don Gaspar gave me a good scratch without even trying. I think he was more upset about it than I was. I was so dispirited, I hardly cared. He yelled at me, saying that if I could do no better, I should leave.

"So I left, feeling as if I wanted to die: my mind was in turmoil, my heart in despair. I was untying my horse at the front of the house when a walnut fell out of the sky and landed at my feet. It was odd—the trees were too far away for the nuts to be blown hither, even with a strong wind. Then I realized it had not come from the grove, but from behind me. I turned and looked up, and there she was, in the window. She gave a barely perceptible nod, and I understood that she had thrown the walnut, and that I was to pick it up. When I did so, I saw that the shell was hollow. I pulled the two halves apart and inside found a bit of white cloth, folded very carefully into a tiny square. I unfolded it. In the center of the cloth was a beautifully embroidered heart of red silk.

"It took a moment for me to comprehend the significance of this. I looked back at Ephegenia. She stood as still and silent as ever, then she lightly touched her right hand to her heart. The expression on her face changed ever so slightly, not a smile, but somehow a brightening. This was all I needed to understand her meaning.

"She loved me. I wanted to leap into the air, to shout, to sing—but instead I tried to preserve my youthful dignity. I bowed low, then held the cloth to my chest, to show her I would always keep her heart next to my own. And for the first time, I saw her smile. In such a way did she transport me from death to life once again.

"I jumped on my horse and raced home. I couldn't wait to tell my father the news. I found him in his study and announced that I wanted to marry Ephegenia Ortiz. What he told me in return would lead to the destruction of all our lives.

"I could not marry her, my father said, because she was betrothed to another. And who was this man? None other than the duke of Girrón. I will not exaggerate and say he was our most hated enemy, but there was no love lost between us. The duke was our neighbor to the south; our lands and his shared a border. He had been unfairly claiming rights to some of our lands for years. At first, he had tried to convince my father to sell this land to him, but when my father would not agree, Girrón tried to take it from him. That he had not been able to do so made him angry and bitter, and our encounters with him in the town were generally less than pleasant. Girrón was much older than Ephegenia or I; he was a widower with two children, one of whom was nearly Ephegenia's age, fifteen.

"When my father told me that the duke was going to marry Ephegenia, I was overcome with jealousy and rage. When he pointed out that the duke was much richer than we were, with many men-at-arms, horses, fine houses, and so on, and could provide Ephegenia with things I could not, it just made me angrier. He also reminded me that the dowries for my three sisters had emptied his pockets, and that it would be necessary for me to marry a rich girl. 'Although Ephegenia is a fine girl, of a respectable family, she is not rich,' he said. 'Even if she were not already betrothed, I would have to advise against it.'

"I had gone from death to life to death again in one day. That my beloved father did not understand the depth of my love for Ephegenia only added to my despair. He thought I could be dissuaded by another suitor, or by the need for money, but I refused to be put off so easily. I would devise a way to speak to Ephegenia, to meet with her in secret. After all, she had given me her heart. Surely she despised this proposed marriage as much as I did.

"The next day, she was waiting at the window as always. I was prepared. I had written a note and put it in the walnut shell. When I held it up for her to see, she opened the window, and I quickly threw it inside. In the note, I'd written that I'd wait for her in the walnut grove after my lesson. I knew that Don Gaspar tutored another student after me, and would be occupied. Still, she would have to sneak out past her duenna and the servants. I told her I would wait there every day, until she came.

"Three days later, she finally arrived. Our meeting was so strange—at first it felt like a dream to hear her speak again, to be so close to her. I kissed her hand, and knelt before her, and told her I would lay down my life for her. She burst into tears when she spoke of her upcoming marriage to the duke. For a few weeks, we went on so: I would wait every day, and she would meet me when she could. Finally we could not bear it anymore, and we decided that we must elope.

"Sometimes now I wonder what I was thinking. It seems to me I wasn't thinking—for certainly our plan was only half a plan at best. I left my home in the middle of the night and rode to Ephegenia's house to find her waiting for me, as we'd agreed, in the walnut grove. She was shivering with cold and fear. But when she got on my horse, and put her arms around me, and we rode away, I believe we were happier than we'd ever been in our lives. And so we were, for the next few hours that it took to ride to Utrillo and then Pamplona.

"I had stayed at an inn in Pamplona with my father, and there we were headed—beyond that, I'm not quite certain what we proposed to do, except find a priest who would agree to marry us. I suppose we believed that if the deed was done, our families would be forced to accept it. But we had no sooner arrived at the inn than we were caught up with, first by my father and Don Gaspar.

"My father had noticed my absence soon after I'd gone, and quickly understood the reason for my late-night departure. My feelings were apparently not as concealed as I'd thought. He rode to Ephegenia's house and woke her father, who was ready to leave within minutes. Riding hard, they nearly overtook us on the road to Pamplona. They were angry and upset, of course, and we were heartbroken by such a terrible end to our escape. Ephegenia was crying hysterically as Don Gaspar took her away.

"But our bad luck did not end there. A few of Girrón's men had seen us when we had earlier passed through Utrillo. Not long after my father arrived, so did the duke, full of fury and demanding satisfaction.

"Although my father explained to the duke that he had discovered us before we had eloped, the duke insisted upon a duel of honor. I had despoiled his intended bride, he said. Although I hadn't done what he suggested, I was eager to fight him, but my father wouldn't allow it.

"'He is a boy of seventeen,' my father told Girrón, 'and you are a man of much experience. It will be easy for you to take him, and it will add no luster to your reputation. Surely there is another way for us to satisfy you.'

"My father offered the duke the lands he had so long been coveting. But the duke wouldn't have it—he wanted a fight. I argued with my father to let me fight Girrón, but he refused. And so my father and the duke drew swords.

"In his day, my father was an excellent sword fighter, but he had not been in a duel for many years. Girrón was a brute, always in one dispute or another, and rumors said that he had made many a man a corpse. It was clear, very quickly, that Girrón had the upper hand. I tried to step in to help my father, but his men held me back. And that is how I watched my father die: first with a jab to the stomach, then one in each arm—I think the duke was tormenting him, tormenting me—then the killing thrust through the throat. As my father lay dying, he could not even speak to me any last words.

"After my father took his final breath, I stood and drew my sword. Girrón's men moved toward me, but the duke waved them away.

"'Behold the new viscount,' he said. He wiped my father's blood from his sword and faced me. 'The last viscount of Utrillo-Navarre, I'd wager—and the one with the shortest rule.'

"I knew he was going to kill me, but I didn't care. My father was dead, on my account, and Ephegenia was gone—I knew I would never see her again. My life, as I'd known it, was over. But perhaps that—that and all I'd learned from Don Gaspar in the past year—

saved me, for I fought as I had never fought before, without fear of pain or death. And the duke was complacent; he did not expect such a fierce combatant. It seemed that every feint he made, I countered with a thrust, wounding him three times, even leaving a long cut along his cheek. Then, growing bolder, I stabbed him in each arm, as he'd done to my father. By this time, the duke was worried, and his men were getting restless. I realized then that I was all alone; even if I killed the duke, there would be four of them left for me to fight, should they choose to avenge their leader. And then Girrón made a foolhardy move. Perhaps he was tired, or perhaps I had wounded him more seriously than I'd thought. In any event, he left his chest unguarded, and I ran him through. He fell, clutching his heart, and expired in seconds.

"Just as Girrón's men were about to close in, other men who had been watching our duel came forward to my defense. One was the duke of Ossuna, who then and there took me under his protection. He had seen the entire encounter and would proclaim my innocence to any court; I had the right to avenge my father, he said. I could not but be grateful to him for this; and since there was little left for me in Navarre, I went with him to Sicily, where he was viceroy for a few years, and then to Naples.

"So all I know of love is how it can destroy people: my father, my mother, who did not long survive my father, Ephegenia . . ."

"What happened to her?"

"Don Gaspar sent her to a convent. From what I know, she is there still."

"And you? Did it destroy you?"

"I'm alive, am I not?"

"For the second time today, you evade my question."

"Yes." He turned to her with a thin smile. "Forgive me."

"You are forgiven, but only because that is one of the saddest stories I have ever heard."

"We both have such stories, it seems."

"Still, yours was an unduly harsh introduction to the ways of the world."

"I suppose. But you understand now why I owe my life to the

duke of Ossuna." He was silent while he thought of what he hesitated to tell her: how, when he saw his father and Girrón dead on the ground, it was as if all feeling had left him. How killing a man in practice was quite different from what one imagines: more difficult, messier, more agonizing than his brief description would imply. He'd never been able to forget the grimace of surprise and suffering in Girrón's face as he died. Or how every man he'd killed since seemed to look back at him with Girrón's eyes.

The sun was low in the sky. "We should go back," Antonio said. "Are you ready to join the festivities again?"

"Must we?"

"Yes, I insist. Carnival is most exciting at night. You must see it at least once."

The moon had risen and set before they made their way back to Alessandra's house. In companionable silence, Antonio and Alessandra rode facing each other in the gondola. She'd shown him the best of Carnival: the flotilla of decorated boats in the Grand Canal; tumblers, jugglers, dancing dogs, and puppet shows in every square; the midnight performance of the Flight of the Turk, in which an acrobat made a spectacular descent along a rope from the top of the Campanile to the door of the Doge's Palace. They ended the evening at an outdoor ball in the Campo Sant' Angelo, so packed with bodies that they never felt the chill night air. At first, Antonio had taken her hand with what appeared to be reluctance—perhaps he did not dance?—but soon the music and the gaiety inspired him, too, and they whirled around and around with the others until they were laughing and nearly breathless with the simple pleasure of it all. She looked away from him as she remembered it, a recollection based more on sensation than thought: the sudden charge of standing so close to him; the way her palm fit neatly in his; his lips as they brushed against her forehead; the warm, intoxicating feeling of his hand at her waist.

They turned into the Rio di San Giuseppe, preternaturally dark and quiet in contrast to the celebrations in the city center. As the gondolier steered their boat to the mooring post outside her garden gate, Alessandra was surprised to see that another gondola was already there.

"The ambassador is here," she told Antonio.

"You were expecting him?"

"No." She peered at the gondola. It was empty. "He must be in the house already. Wait here. I'll see why he is come, then I'll return." She had already offered Antonio her spare bedchamber for the night, and now she'd have to sneak him in somehow. She stood up to step out of the gondola, but Antonio held her back.

"The last time I was here you asked me about the marquis, and I could not answer," he said. "I have an answer for you now. He is an ambassador—which means, of course, that he is a spy."

"What do you know exactly?"

"Nothing that I am at liberty to tell you. But you must trust me when I say that I know something of the world in which he moves. I don't think it wise for you to be connected with him."

"And just what do you expect me to do? Tell him to leave me be?"

"That is one way . . ."

"You are not so wise if you imagine it will be so easy. Please, do not concern yourself." She looked back at the house, saw the glow of firelight in the parlor windows. "Wait here. I'll be only a moment."

Inside, Bianca was upon her as soon as she set foot in the door. "The marquis waits for you upstairs. Something is wrong—he is in a very bad humor."

Alessandra climbed the stairs and found the ambassador seated in front of the fire, a glass raised to his lips as he took a swallow of strong drink. As she approached, he turned his head. The firelight gleamed red in his eyes. Alessandra realized her heart was beating furiously; although she had shrugged off Antonio's warning, he'd made her afraid. She'd never seen the marquis looking so fierce. Alessandra steeled herself for an outburst.

"Do you sew?" he asked.

His question was so far from what she had expected, she wasn't sure she'd heard rightly. "Pardon?"

"Do you sew?" The ambassador's voice was deeper and more

gruff than usual. As he took another swig of brandy, Alessandra wondered if he was drunk.

"Yes, of course."

"You must help me." Bedmar put his glass down on the floor and slowly stood up. With his left hand, he fumbled with the buttons at his chest. "Help me off with this."

Alessandra unbuttoned his doublet, gasping when she saw the bloodstain spreading across his linen shirt.

"What happened?" she asked.

"I was set upon by some ruffians." Or so they were meant to seem, Bedmar thought. There was one who fought as if possessed by the Devil himself, with greater skill and agility than was common in a street hoodlum. A light-eyed creature with Mongol features who would have killed him if Sanchez and the others hadn't come to his rescue. When this devil had seen that his three cohorts had been mortally wounded and that he was outnumbered, he had clambered up the side of a building and away over the rooftops, escaping as easily as a bird taking flight. Bedmar would swear that he'd turned around and smiled triumphantly before he'd disappeared. No, they weren't common thugs; that crookback senator was behind the surprise attack, he was certain.

Alessandra helped the marquis remove his shirt and saw the wound that pierced his right shoulder, so deep it exposed the bone. "I'll send for the doctor."

"No doctors."

"He is discreet."

"No, you must sew it yourself. It will not do for anyone to know I have been wounded."

"All right, then. You should stay seated. I'll be back in a moment with something to bind your wound." She raced downstairs to the kitchen, where Bianca waited anxiously. "I'll need needles and thread and some dry towels," she said. "And ask Nico to prepare the spare bedchamber—we'll have more than one guest tonight."

Alessandra pushed past Bianca and hurried to the door. The viscount would surely be wondering what had kept her so long. But when she got outside, she discovered that Antonio had already gone.

Chapter Thirteen

"DAD!" GWENDOLYN SQUEALED. She held the hotel phone tight to her ear and sat down on her bed. "I was just going to call you!"

Claire had just returned from her morning jog on the Riva. She'd gotten back sooner than she'd planned. Halfway to Alessandra's house she'd spotted a man jogging toward her. As he got closer, she'd seen that it was Andrew Kent, and she'd turned back toward the Piazza. If she was going to (almost literally) run into the Cambridge professor, she'd much rather do it when well fortified by coffee and breakfast.

"The flight was fine," said Gwen, with a sidelong glance at Claire. "You mean the boats? No, not yet. But I met this really nice girl, Stefania . . ."

Claire knew what would follow. As they were leaving the Baldessaris' the night before, Gwen had asked if she could go to the Lido with Stefania in the morning. Claire had said no, of course, as she imagined how much trouble Gwen could get into if she were left for an entire day on her own. Gwen had sulked all the way back to the hotel, not forgetting to mention every five minutes that her parents would have said yes.

". . . and she asked if I could go to the beach with her today," Gwen went on, "and I really want to go but Claire said I couldn't and I was just wondering if you'd talk to her—not to Stefania, to Claire—and tell her I go places with my friends *all the time* . . ."

Claire wondered if she should tell Edward Fry why she had forbidden Gwen to go off with Stefania, but there was probably no way to do that without revealing a few of his daughter's more interesting proclivities. Of course, if Gwen went to the Lido, Claire would have the day to herself, an entire, uninterrupted day in the Marciana, and this was weighing heavily in favor of the girl's excursion. It was also true that during the past twenty-four hours, there had been no stealing, no drinking, no groping of tattooed boys. Yes, it was a vast improvement over the previous twenty-four, which clinched Claire's resolve: if Edward Fry gave his consent, then she'd happily go along with the plan, and whatever fate befell Gwen that day would be on his conscience, not hers.

Gwen held out the phone. "He wants to talk to you," she said, smiling triumphantly.

Behind the counter of the Biblioteca Marciana reading room, the sleek, chic Francesca checked a stack of books and documents against the list of requests Claire had left behind the day before.

"Minutes of the Great Council meetings, March 1618"—Francesca placed a large, leather-bound volume in front of Claire—"and the *Relazioni* of the marquis of Bedmar." This smaller book was the product of an eighteenth-century Italian publisher, with a faded, water-stained Venetian pressed-paper cover. Reputedly, this edition was a direct translation of Bedmar's original *Relazioni,* the official reports that, as ambassador, he sent regularly to the Spanish king. It was as close as she could get to the original, at least for the moment, as the original was in an archive in Spain.

Francesca carefully picked up a single sheet of antique parchment that was encased in a clear plastic sheet. "And Alessandra Rossetti's letter to the Great Council."

Claire regarded it with wonder. Almost four hundred years ago Alessandra had composed this letter, and put her life at risk to save Venice from the conspiracy. She looked over the letter's spidery black script and saw that she had a serious task ahead of her. She hadn't considered how much more difficult it would be to translate someone's handwriting than to work from a printed text. Alessandra's ornate, archaic penmanship looked about as decipherable as Sanskrit. She skimmed the page with growing concern; it hardly looked like words.

Francesca broke in on her thoughts. "I'm afraid that the diary you requested is not available."

Claire was so engrossed in the letter that it took a moment for the librarian's statement to sink in. "The diary?"

"Yes, you requested"—she checked Claire's list once more—"the diary of Alessandra Rossetti, January 1618 through—"

"But I have to I see it. Except for this letter, it's the most important document in my research. Are you telling me that you don't have it?"

"We do have it, but it's already been reserved by someone else. As you know, the materials can be checked out for one week. After he turns it in, we can make it available to you. That would be next Monday."

"I'm leaving Venice on Saturday."

"I'm so sorry. I know how disappointing it is, but he was here before you, and we must honor the first request."

"Who's 'he'?" Claire asked, with a sinking feeling that she already knew the answer.

Francesca checked another paper on her desk. "Andrew Kent."

Of course, Claire thought. He had arrived at the Marciana an entire day before she had because he had waltzed through the EU line at the Venice airport passport control while she was stuck in a mob of two hundred. Something for which, she now decided, he was completely to blame. His story about her being apprehended for not having an EU passport could have been a lot of baloney; it was almost as if he knew where she was headed and had deliberately misled her in order to get to the diary first. Claire understood that she was being irrational, but she was too angry to care.

"We have an earlier diary of Alessandra Rossetti's, if you're interested," Francesca said, holding up a small, battered journal bound with rust-colored leather. "This one covers the period from July through October 1617."

Claire nodded her assent. Although it didn't cover the crucial months of early 1618, it might provide some insight into Alessandra's life.

"Perhaps Dr. Kent will finish his work with the other diary soon," Francesca said, "and you'll be able to see it before you leave." She glanced at the shelves of books and manuscripts behind her. Near the middle was a large stack of books topped by a small, weathered, leather-bound book that looked identical to the one Claire held in her hands: Andrew Kent's stack, topped by Alessandra's second journal. There it was, so close and yet so far from her grasp, waiting not for her but for Andrew Kent to uncover its secrets.

"Can I take a look at it?" Claire asked.

Again, Francesca shook her head, softening her refusal with a sympathetic smile. "I'm sorry, but we have to keep very careful track of the materials. Once they've been reserved, we cannot give them to anyone else. There have been a number of thefts from Italian libraries recently, and we've been forced to institute stricter procedures." Francesca smiled confidentially and leaned closer. "Perhaps if you ask him, he will return it early so that you can see it. I'm sure you can be very persuasive if you choose."

Claire stared at the librarian, her mouth slightly agape with surprise. Francesca was suggesting that Claire use her womanly wiles to get the diary. After all, Francesca's subsequent shrug implied, that's what she would do—without any remorse, and certainly without regard for political correctness.

"That's—that's an incredible idea," Claire stammered.

"You are a woman, he is a man . . ." Francesca's pretty hands went palms up in the air.

Claire giggled in spite of her desire not to.

"You think I am a comic?" Francesca asked.

"I was just thinking that I can't imagine a Harvard librarian ever suggesting that I use my sexuality to coerce a manuscript from another historian."

"What's the point of having sexuality if you're not going to use it?"

"Ah. Well. You do have a point. But don't you think it's sort of . . . wrong? Most American women are philosophically opposed to that sort of thing, and the librarians would probably worry that giving out advice like that would make them vulnerable to a lawsuit."

"You Americans are much too serious. It's just a game, and it's so simple," Francesca said. "You are a woman. You should know how to get what you want."

All well and good, except that it was Andrew Kent they were talking about. He didn't exactly inspire her feminine instincts. Not to mention that she wasn't so sure she had any womanly wiles to call upon.

She gathered up her materials and walked off in search of a secluded spot in which to work. It was still early, and only two others—surrounded by books, heads bent, quietly industrious—sat at the reading room's massive wooden tables. She set her things down on a table at the back, far from the wall of windows. The day was so brilliantly beautiful, she was afraid that the alluring view of the lagoon would be distracting, and distractions she had more than enough of.

She decided to start with the *Relazioni* instead of Alessandra's letter. Her translating skills needed some polishing, and the book, with its printed text, provided a better way to begin. She took a copy of her dissertation from her tote bag and set it down next to her notebook, books, and documents. Small yellow Post-it notes marked with a "B" flagged the places in her paper where she had used quotations from Bedmar's reports, quotations she'd found in other published sources.

She had long hoped this moment might arrive, when she'd be able to confirm the citations in her work with books such as this, and with some of the primary sources. It was a huge step toward completing her dissertation. Before she left Harriott, she'd looked forward to the time she would spend in this room, immersed in books and papers, immersed in the past, lost in thought, her mind focused and humming. But as she opened the *Relazioni,* pen poised over notebook, she didn't feel the excitement she had thought she would. Now that she was where she had so long wanted to be, she couldn't concentrate.

The Marciana's slanting shafts of morning sunlight, its slowly drifting dust motes, its hushed silence: all conspired to increase the restlessness she felt. She had an overwhelming desire to be outside on the Riva, sitting at a table under a striped umbrella, drinking coffee and looking out over the lagoon. Or on a vaporetto chugging slowly along the Grand Canal. Or aimlessly walking through the narrow Venetian streets, stopping wherever she pleased to window-shop for things she didn't need: Venetian glass and carnival masks and high-heeled shoes of glove-soft leather. Or eating nothing but gelato for lunch and then spending hours in the Accademia, looking only at the paintings she loved and ignoring all the others, even if they were important. She could be with Gwen on the beach, soaking up the sun and the Lido's cheesy, retro glamour.

Gwen. An anxious sigh escaped her lips. It wasn't only the attractions of Venice that were making it hard for her to concentrate, it was the distraction of other people. Living, breathing people who crowded her thoughts and provoked too many emotions. It hardly seemed fair, now that she had the day to herself, that she should be worrying about Gwen. It was a constant, niggling kind of worry, like a mental ticker tape of every problem, disaster, or catastrophe that Venice could inflict upon the girl. Or vice versa.

And what about Giancarlo? She'd better not start thinking about him or she'd never get any work done; but she couldn't forget how estranged they'd been by the end of the previous evening, her questions unanswered, his discomfort evident. He hadn't exactly lied to her, but he hadn't told the whole truth, either, had he? She supposed it served her right for falling for a handsome face. She should have guessed that there was a woman in his life already—men like Giancarlo were always attached to someone. Often enough, they were attached to more than one someone.

He'd been embarrassed, and Claire knew that was enough, in itself, to keep him at a distance for the rest of her stay in Venice. She probably wouldn't see him again, and tried to gauge how she felt about that. Not happy, certainly. In other circumstances—for instance, if she'd been on her own, without a teenager tagging along, and if Giancarlo had not been engaged, she could imagine—what? A fling? A grand romance? She wasn't even sure. Maybe that's why it bothered her; it was over before she'd even had a chance to decide just what she wanted, or to find out what it might become.

That Andrew Kent would no doubt be arriving at the Marciana soon was another source of anxiety. Claire settled into her inconspicuous spot and knew she was being vaguely ridiculous—as she had been that morning, she supposed, when she'd turned back instead of running past him on the Riva. It was stupid to spend the rest of her time in Venice avoiding him.

No, she decided a moment later, it wasn't stupid. In fact, resolving to avoid Andrew Kent was the one thing that gave her a measure of relief. Although, she admitted, she would like to know more about his book: last night Gabriella had mentioned that it wasn't finished yet. But how far from completion was he? A month, a year, two years? How was she going to ask him about that? Before the request for Alessandra's diary, or after? If she were going to avoid him, how could she ask him anything at all? Damn!

Claire felt unsettled, emotionally disheveled, a stranger to herself. She was accustomed to being alone more. A line of description came to mind: "secret and self-contained, as solitary as an oyster." It must have come from one of the novels she'd read in the past year: Forster? James? Wharton? She couldn't recall, but the words were comforting, and vaguely reminiscent of a romantic heroine. *Secret and self-contained, as solitary as an oyster.* That's just the way she was, and she was perfectly happy being that way.

Why should she feel different in Venice than she felt at home? All she really needed was to concentrate and get focused again and she'd feel more like herself. She opened Bedmar's *Relazioni* with a renewed determination.

Work was the answer. Work was always the answer.

Chapter Fourteen

Gwen leaned over the rail of the vaporetto and drew in a deep breath of fresh, sea-scented air. She felt excited for no particular reason, in anticipation of exactly what she wasn't sure. It was sort of like everything—the rumble of the boat, the ocean spray that misted her face, the sight of Venice receding in the distance and the warm, bright morning sun that promised a day filled with possibility—contained in this one moment held all the best moments of all the best summer days she'd ever known.

"That's the Lido," said Stefania, pointing to the approaching shore. She had short, tousled hair and a cute, wide-eyed face, and she looked as vibrant as the morning, in a white cotton blouse and a pair of yellow capri pants. She glanced up and smiled, and Gwen noticed the smattering of freckles sprinkled across the bridge of her nose.

The crowd on the vaporetto pressed forward as the boat docked. Stefania and Gwen were first off, Gwen following closely as her new friend walked briskly along the road that paralleled the water. They turned right onto the Gran Viale Santa Maria Elisabetta, the Lido's main street, which led from the lagoon to the seashore, and soon they were seated on a couple of springy red seats at the back of a bus, peering out the windows at the tree-lined boulevard and the luxurious storefronts.

The beach stretched on for miles in a beautiful, unobstructed arc and was lined with two rows of blue-striped canvas cabanas.

Stefania led her along the golden sand to the Hotel Des Bains.

"These beaches are supposed to be for hotel guests, but my uncle is one of the managers here, so I get—how do you say?—a preference," Stefania said as she paid for a cabana rental. "Anyway, this is where my friends and I like to meet."

They changed into their bathing suits and spread their towels on the sand. Stefania's tiny, bright orange bikini glowed against her olive-toned skin. Gwen felt a twinge of envy at her figure. Stefania was a bit flat-chested perhaps, but she was slender, and had skin that tanned instead of burned. Gwen felt like a large, colorless blob next to her. She took a bottle of sunblock from her backpack and began slathering it on her legs; her skin was so pale in the bright sunlight that it seemed to have a faint blue tinge to it. The black bathing suit didn't help much. She'd bought it last year during the height of her Goth craze and now it was too tight—she was practically bursting out of it—and against her white body it made her look like one of the Undead.

This morning she'd promised herself that she'd spend the whole day being her new, improved, super-cool mysterious self, no more geeky Gwen, and three minutes in a bathing suit had eroded her resolve and every bit of poise she had mustered. I'll probably manage to do something stupid, Gwen thought darkly. Like trip as I walk along the sand, or drown when I try to swim.

Stefania shaded her eyes and gave Gwen a wise, appraising stare. "You know what you look like?" she asked.

Sure, Vampira, Gwen thought.

"Like a Hollywood starlet. Like one of those bombshells from the fifties who used to come for the film festival."

"I don't think so."

"Yes, you're very glamorous. Your long hair, your porcelain complexion—and you have the body of a woman," she added with genuine admiration. "You must have many boyfriends in America, yes?"

Gwen almost told the truth, but her more worldly alter ego moved tantalizingly within reach. "Just a couple," she said, trying to make it sound like there were tons of guys just dying to take her out.

"Only a couple? I don't believe you."

She could see that Stefania was sincere. It suddenly didn't seem very nice to pretend to be someone she wasn't, someone more sophisticated and cool.

"Where I'm from, guys don't seem to like girls who look like me," Gwen confessed. "I'm too . . . sort of plump. They like girls like you—skinny model types."

"Maybe we should change countries," Stefania said. "I get teased all the time because I have no curves. People say, 'Who wants a girl who looks like a boy?' All of my friends are going to worship you. They will think you are a goddess; even better, an American goddess."

"Really?"

"Wait and see. It's still early, but my friends—Giovanni, Pietro, Marco—will be here later. You can take your pick of any one of them. Except for Marco—Marco is for me," she said with a conspiratorial smile. "But I can tell you about the others. I know everything about them—I mean *everything.*"

Gwen settled herself in the warm sand, closer to Stefania. She took in the vista before her: the expanse of golden sand just beginning to fill with beachgoers; the shimmering blue ocean and the limitless blue sky; the rhythmic, percolating sound of the waves breaking then dissipating along the shore; the sparkle and shine of her silver navel ring and her purple-polished toenails. She sighed. She hadn't felt this happy in weeks.

Francesco was the boy in the red bathing suit who'd said he was a boxer and had flexed his muscles for her inspection; Giovanni and Giuseppe, two brothers who looked almost identical but were a year apart, had insisted on setting up a huge beach umbrella so that Gwen would be protected from the sun; Pietro, scrawny but cute, was a bit of a clown, quick-witted and full of jokes; Lorenzo didn't speak much English, but gazed at her with soulful eyes. Gwen looked at the boys gathered in a half circle at her feet, under the umbrella's shade, and hoped that she'd finally gotten all their names straight. One of the boys—she wasn't sure which one—had provided her with the low beach chair upon which she sat. Anyone passing by (anyone with a rather fanciful imagination) might have thought the scene resembled that of a young queen surrounded by courtiers; and, fanciful though it was, courtiers were no more eager for a queen's favor than Stefania's friends were for Gwen's.

"How do you say 'nose'?" Gwen pointed to her nose. Their impromptu Italian lesson—Gwen the sole student with five teachers—had already covered the sights surrounding them: beach, ocean, sky.

"*Naso*," they all replied.

"*Naso*," Gwen repeated. "How do you say . . . 'lips'?"

"*Labbra*," they said in unison.

"And how do you say . . . 'kiss'?"

"*Bacio*," they said, smiling and laughing. Pietro sprang to his feet. "I will demonstrate!"

"Pietro, behave," Stefania called. She and Marco were lying under an adjoining umbrella, face-to-face. They talked in low but excited voices, as if they were old friends who had been apart for ages, although Stefania had said that she'd seen him only two days before. Gwen could see that they were crazy about each other. Stefania hadn't exactly said so, but Gwen got the impression that her parents weren't quite so fond of Marco as she was. She wondered why; he seemed perfectly nice.

Pietro briskly saluted Stefania and plopped back down in the sand while the others laughed. They looked to Gwen for her next request. She thought about saying something like "love" or "sex" then decided against it. Although it didn't seem to matter what she said or did. Stefania had already told her that they all liked her; she just had to decide which one of them she liked.

They were all cute in their own sort of way but, like most boys her age, they seemed younger than herself. Not that she was complaining. They were still boys, and they were Italian, and they spoke with really cute accents, and they acted as if they'd never met an American girl before. Like Stefania had said, they seemed to think she was a starlet or a goddess or something. Boys at home would never bring a girl an umbrella or a chair, wouldn't say, right to her face like Pietro had the moment they met, that she was beautiful! Boys at home, Gwen thought, wouldn't be this nice even if you *paid* them.

Even though she had tried, Gwen couldn't stop thinking about Tyler. Tyler Daniels, *the* hottest guy at Forsythe. She'd had a crush on him for months. A few weeks ago, right before finals, she and some friends snuck out of their dorm after midnight and walked to the harbor. A group of boys, including Tyler, had been there, too. Somehow she'd been different that night—like, grown up, sort of. Everybody had seen Tyler flirting with her—and then he'd kissed her, really kissed her, in the shadows of the boathouse. She'd let him touch her boob, just over her shirt of course. He'd wanted to go further and there'd been a bit of wrestling, but that was normal, wasn't it? Tyler had said he thought she had a great body, and that he didn't like stupid anorexic girls. For two days, she was as happy as she ever remembered being. Then she'd seen him holding hands with Tiffany Havermeyer. Tiffany Havermeyer was so skinny, her arms looked like two twigs. Tiffany Havermeyer was probably anorexic *and* bulimic. But Tyler hadn't even looked at Gwen after that. It was horrible—everyone knew that they had made out, and then he just dumped her. One of Gwen's friends told her that Tyler had said that Gwen was too young and not experienced enough.

Too young! She wasn't too young—she was going to be fifteen in two weeks. The real problem was that she didn't have enough experience. If she wanted to kiss someone—and possibly more—she was going to have to choose one of the Italian boys.

Stefania declared that it was time for lunch. A great deal of excited Italian conversation followed (to Gwen it seemed that people were always excited when they spoke Italian), and Stefania explained that the boys were arguing about who was going to buy lunch for her. Stefania put an end to it by telling them that they would all buy lunch for her. Marco was also on his feet—obviously he was going to the café, too; this lunch ritual seemed to be routine.

What a wonderful country this was, where boys wanted to do nice things for girls. Maybe she could stay here forever and live with Stefania and her family, Gwen thought, as the boys, all of them except for Pietro, trudged off down the beach.

"Why are you still here?" Stefania demanded.

Pietro fell on his knees before Gwen and held his clasped hands to his heart. "I don't have so much money," he said, "and I am not a muscle man like Francesco, but you must love me the most because I have great personal charm." He batted his eyes comically.

"You are as charming as a snake," Stefania replied, "and you have plenty of money. Go to the café with the others. We want to be alone." When he had gone, she turned to Gwen. "Remember what I told you about Pietro. He seems harmless, but he isn't. My friend Carmela went to the movies with him and he was like an octopus—you know, with many hands."

"Ciao, Stefania." An older boy in black bathing trunks walked up to them, stopping just outside the umbrella's shade. He looked tall and deeply tanned against the bright sky. His dark hair fell into his eyes, and as he brushed it aside, Gwen saw the bulge of his biceps and the ripple of muscles across his abdomen and chest. Drop-dead *gorgeous* her best friend, Shannon, would've said. Gwen felt her breath catch in her throat. He kind of nodded in her direction, and in Italian asked Stefania a question that Gwen guessed meant "Who's your friend?" Then, while Stefania was talking, he looked back at her and their eyes met.

Gwen thought later that it was like everything stopped. Like the waves stopped breaking and the wind stopped blowing, like the children stopped running on the beach and laughing and splashing in the water. Like all the sound stopped, except for the sound of her heart beating. All she could remember of that moment was the sight of his face, and her heart pounding in her ears.

She barely heard Stefania say, "This is my cousin, Nicolo," barely heard Stefania mention her name, but, sort of like it was all happening in slow motion, she saw Nicolo's lips part and his mouth open to speak to her.

"Ciao," was all he said, but it was enough.

Chapter Fifteen

Something about it was odd. After a couple of painstaking hours, Claire had completed her translation of the Rossetti Letter. She read the pages of her notebook a second time, hoping that another careful perusal would reveal exactly what was bothering her.

Respectfully submitted to Your Serenity the Doge, the Signory, and the Great Council:

Venice is in great danger of attack by enemies from within and without. Every Venetian has seen how mercenaries increase their numbers daily in our city, but this recent influx of soldiers is not solely for the benefit of the Republic. The Spanish ambassador, the marquis of Bedmar, has been suborning these men for his own ends, to overthrow Venice and take the city for the Spanish crown. The mercenary leaders include Jacques Pierre, privateer and captain of the Camerata, *Simon Langland, Arturo Sanchez, Charles Brouilliard, Santos Delgado, and Nicholas Regnault. These Spanish and French adventurers are known* bravi *and artificers of Greek fire, who have been signalized in the armies and the fleets of the Republic and are dissatisfied with the rewards they have obtained. This plan has been conceived and abetted by the duke of Ossuna, viceroy of Naples.*

Letters exchanged between Ossuna and Bedmar in January of this year revealed the full extent of the ruin they have in-

tended for Venice. They plan their assault to commence on Ascension Day, when all of Venice will be celebrating and vulnerable to attack. As Bedmar's company of bravi, *led by Sanchez, begin rampaging through the city, setting fire to the Ducal Palace and the Basilica, burning and looting everything in sight, so then will come Ossuna at the head of his fleet, surrounding and tormenting all.*

By this their sinister plot they hope to make Venice subject to Spain, and for the Republic to be completely at the mercy of the Pope and the Spanish king.

I, Alessandra Rossetti, offer this account in accordance with my devotion to duty and the happy continuance of the Republic. I hereby swear by God in truth I have written this sixth day of March, 1618.

Claire had seen a few excerpts, but she had never read the Rossetti Letter in its entirety before, and the overall tone was different than she had expected. It seemed rather matter-of-fact, not like a letter written in panic or haste. If Alessandra Rossetti had been involved with the conspirators in some way, wouldn't she have been in danger? How was it possible that she could be so self-assured, so unafraid?

Unless—a dark, unpleasant thought came to her—unless there was some merit to Andrew Kent's theory that Alessandra had helped the Venetians frame the Spaniards.

Claire could see how the Rossetti Letter might have inspired that conclusion. It didn't seem like a missive composed in fear and delivered through the secret auspices of the *bocca di leone.* And there was something else, too, that she knew was wrong, but as soon as the idea was about to coalesce into something solid, it vanished just as quickly.

So—Alessandra as Mata Hari, not Joan of Arc? No. Claire refused to believe it. She opened the large, morocco-bound *Minutes of the Great Council, March 1618,* and ran her finger along the daily entries: March fourth, March fifth, March sixth. There it was. *Signorina A. Rossetti bocca di leone Palazzo Ducale.*

What else could this mean except that she had delivered a letter to the *bocca di leone*? That seemed clear enough, but what happened after? And why did Alessandra seem to disappear once the conspiracy came to an end? It seemed that the Rossetti Letter was destined to raise unanswered questions, the most persistent being, how did she learn of the conspiracy? It was assumed that she had ties to one or more of the conspirators named in the letter, but no evidence of a connection between her and any of these men had ever been found. Nor was there proof of a link between her and the Spanish ambassador, or the duke of Ossuna. And that phrase, "Letters exchanged . . ." How did she know about that?

Claire turned back to Bedmar's *Relazioni.* She'd already confirmed the accuracy of the quotations she'd used in her dissertation, but now she wondered if there might be a mention of Bedmar's correspondence with Ossuna in his reports to the king. It was worth a look, anyway.

She skimmed a report detailing recent appointments to the Great Council, and one about the Doge's failing health and the most likely candidates for his successor, then read Bedmar's portrayals of other diplomats in Venice. He went on at length about the English ambassador ("Sir Henry Wotton is at heart a heretic who hopes to persuade Venice to adopt his impious beliefs and has at his embassy both books and men to support him in this aim"). There were tidbits about Venetian customs, with an emphasis on recent crimes and the punishments meted out by the state, and some rather more tedious accounts of the management of the Spanish embassy and its expenses. Following that were a few reports of events he had attended, detailing social customs and conversations he'd had with people he'd met. Exhaustive, almost, but no mention of Ossuna anywhere. Claire began skimming faster, pausing only when her eye was caught by a familiar name.

". . . a midnight party and a sumptuous feast, again at Ca' Aragona." Ca' Aragona—where had she seen that before? In Fazzini, she remembered, in his anecdote about the courtesan La Celestia. So Bedmar was an intimate of this courtesan. She checked the date of Bedmar's report: June 10, 1617, and made a note to look up the date in the account by Fazzini about the debut of the new *cortigiana onestà*. What if they were writing about the same event? Claire's mind whirled. Lorenzo Liberti had died in the spring of 1617, and Alessandra had become a courtesan soon after. Could it be possible that she was the courtesan whose debut was made that night? That she was La Sirena? If she was, and if Claire could place Bedmar in the same place at the same time as Alessandra, it would help make her case for her version of the Spanish Conspiracy.

Claire almost laughed out loud. Numerous historians before her had tried to establish a relationship between Alessandra Rossetti and the Spanish ambassador, without success. If it was that easy, she reasoned, surely it would have been done already. She leaned back in her chair and massaged her temples as footsteps sounded at the other end of the reading room. They stopped in front of the librarian's desk and a familiar voice began speaking.

Andrew Kent's English accent was evident even when he spoke Italian. His voice was very deep, Claire realized. She wouldn't have thought, looking at him, that he had such a low-pitched voice. But even from across the room, even when he was talking softly, she could feel it resonate in her solar plexus, in the same spot where she would feel the vibrations of a bass drum.

With a sideways glance, Claire looked over at the library counter as Andrew Kent picked up his books, then walked to an empty table near the center of the room. He sat down, took a pair of glasses from his shirt pocket, opened Alessandra's other diary, and started reading, without any additional preparation. He didn't have any reference books with him; apparently he didn't need an Italian dictionary.

She sensed that he wasn't going to give up that diary too easily, in spite of Francesca's belief in the efficacy of feminine persuasion. Honestly, though, he didn't look as if he was all that receptive to feminine persuasion. Of course, he seemed to like Gabriella, but what man wouldn't? She was beautiful, intelligent, successful, and if last night was any indication, she flattered him almost incessantly. From his point of view, that would be pretty hard to dislike,

Claire admitted. That Gabriella was also self-absorbed and vain was no doubt a minor issue, considering the whole package. Men would forgive a lot worse in a woman who was so beautiful. The real question was, what did Gabriella see in Andrew Kent?

Claire was in a good position to study the professor without being observed, and he seemed too engrossed in his work to notice much of anything, anyway. His hair was a little too unkempt to be considered stylish. His glasses sat askew on his face, courtesy of a broken earpiece that was precariously stuck back on with a thick wrapping of Scotch tape. He was wearing that unfortunate blue shirt/brown pants combo again. Granted, Claire was focusing on the least attractive things about him, but it was pretty evident that Andrew Kent was not exactly a romantic fantasy man. Why was Gabriella acting like she'd just caught the biggest trout in the stream?

Maybe he was obscenely rich. Maybe he was a titled aristocrat, like Gabriella—maybe Andrew Kent was really Sir Andrew or Lord Muckety-Muck, with a big country estate and an entire village of domestic servants. That would appeal to a countess, wouldn't it?

Claire looked at Alessandra's diary, filled with page after page of four-hundred-year-old Italian script, which would take more time to translate than she had left in Venice. The task before her suddenly seemed overwhelming. She couldn't concentrate anymore, not with Andrew Kent in the room. Perhaps it was time to go out and do some of the things she'd thought about that morning: she decided on a gelato and a boat ride along the Grand Canal. Better to forget about her adversary for a while. Hadn't she made up her mind to avoid him, anyway? Except that she needed to find out about his book, and find a way to persuade him to give up that diary. She wondered what Francesca would do.

Probably not this, she thought, as she walked to the library counter by the least conspicuous route, left her books with an assistant, and escaped from the Marciana before Andrew Kent could realize she was there.

Womanly wiles. Good lord.

Chapter Sixteen

AS THE FINAL bars of the first act of *La Traviata* swelled and filled the theater, Claire decided that listening to Verdi in La Fenice was about as close to a vision of heaven as she'd ever been able to conjure up.

She and Gwen occupied a box, or *pepiano,* in the fourth tier of the round, five-tiered gallery, and the view of the stage and the theater was dazzling. With its ornate rows of gilded tiers, its celestial blue domed ceiling, its numerous crystal sconces and sparkling chandelier, it was rather like being inside a jeweled Fabergé egg.

What appeared to Claire as astonishing excess, a venue designed to host women in rustling silk and men in powdered wigs, was in fact a theater meant to embody republican values and symbolize the Enlightenment. Completed in 1792, the 175 boxes of the theater originally known as La Fantine were deliberately egalitarian in design; this lasted until 1807, when an impending visit from Emperor Napoleon had prompted the destruction of six of the *pepiani* to make way for the Imperial Box, which still faced the stage from its commanding position on the second tier. La Fantine had twice risen from the ashes, the first time in 1836, when its reconstruction had inspired its present cognomen, The Phoenix. In 1996, La Fenice had been gutted by fire once again, but years of renovation had resulted in a spectacular restoration.

Claire would have been content to remain in her seat during intermission, but as the houselights came up, Gwen complained of a severe thirst that could only be slaked by a trip to the lobby and the purchase of a soda that would probably cost ten times its usual price. They left the *pepiano* and joined the rest of the audience, who unhurriedly made their way to the Sala de Appollonia. As they slipped into the line at the refreshment counter, Claire spotted Andrew Kent at the opposite end of the room. He stood with Gabriella Griseri and a few people Claire recognized from the conference. To her enormous surprise, Andrew caught her eye, then briefly whispered something in Gabriella's ear and began making his way through the crowded lobby toward her.

"And I was having such a perfectly nice evening," Claire grumbled. "Come on, we're going back."

"What are you doing?" Gwen protested as Claire steered her out of the line.

"Avoiding Andrew Kent."

"Why?"

"It's one of my few pleasures in life."

"But you're not supposed to be hiding. You're supposed to be in the lobby."

"There's no rule that says you have to go to the lobby during intermission."

"But I want a soda. I'm really, really thirsty."

"We passed a water fountain in the hallway just a moment ago." They hurried through the lobby's red-velvet-draped door and ran into Hoddy Humphries-Todd.

"Hello," he said pleasantly. "Going back to your seats so soon?"

"We're hiding from the English guy," Gwen said glumly.

"I do hope you don't mean me."

"Oh, no," Gwen said. "The other one."

"You're hiding from Andy?"

"Not hiding, exactly, just avoiding," Claire said.

"I'm sure there's a difference, but in case there isn't, why don't you both stand behind this curtain and I'll keep a lookout," Hoddy said. He craned his neck and peered into the lobby. "He's heading this way . . . now he's stopping . . . looking around . . . appears confused. Ahhh . . . excellent. That git Nigel Carothers just started chatting him up. Fat chance Andy will get out of that in less than twenty minutes. He still looks bewildered, but I think he's given up the chase. You're safe, at least for the moment."

"Can I please go get a soda?" Gwen asked.

"Okay, but don't talk to him, all right?"

"Why would I talk to him?"

"Just don't."

"And don't talk to that Nigel, either," Hoddy called after her retreating back. He shrugged at Claire. "It's a bit of advice I feel honor bound to offer: never have anything to do with men named Nigel. They're always trouble." He paused. "Are you going to keep me in breathless suspense, or are you going to tell me why you were trying to lose the old boy?"

"It's hard to explain. We just don't hit it off."

"You wouldn't be the first."

"Do you know him well?"

"We were at Cambridge together. Still are, actually. I've always found him a nice enough fellow. A bit stuffy, is all. Honestly, I don't know why some people take an immediate dislike to him."

"Because it saves time?" Claire offered.

A grin stole over Hoddy's face. "I think I'm going to like you. Even though I didn't see you at my lecture today, which may be unforgivable."

"I spent most of the day in the Marciana. But then," she admitted, "I played hooky in the afternoon."

"Hooky? Is that some sort of game?"

"No, it's slang for skipping school. Instead of working, I went for a vaporetto ride on the Grand Canal, then found an empty table on the Riva and simply looked at the lagoon—"

"For hours," Hoddy finished the sentence with her. "It's remarkable, isn't it? Sort of hypnotic, the way the water shimmers and changes colors with the changing light. Don't feel guilty. The sudden lack of desire to place nose to grindstone is a common problem here. Researching my thesis took twice as long as I'd planned," he admitted. "By the end of two years in Venice, I was in a very bad state with my supervisor, quite dissolute, and exceedingly happy."

"Except that I have only a few more days left," said Claire. "I really can't afford to waste time." She turned to peek out the doorway. Andrew Kent was still talking to Nigel, and Gwen had moved to the middle of the refreshment line. Oddly, though, she was facing away from the counter and looking around the room expectantly.

"Last night, you asked me about courtesans," Hoddy said. "La Celestia and . . . what was the name of the other one?"

"La Sirena."

"Perhaps it was La Sirena . . . ," Hoddy mused. "I woke up this morning thinking about something I'd read in Fazzini, a terrible story about a courtesan who was murdered. I think it might have been one of the courtesans you mentioned."

"Which one?"

"I can't remember. I read this years ago. I only recall that it was a brutal murder, and the murderer was never found."

"When did this happen? Do you remember the year?"

"It was around the time of the Spanish Conspiracy, or just after."

"But I just read the volume of Fazzini's diary that covers those years. There was no mention of a murder." Claire thought back to her first day at the Marciana, when she had skimmed through the book page by page. "I don't see how I could have missed it."

"I'm not at all surprised you overlooked it. I recall that it was a huge tome. Fazzini was an obsessive diarist who recorded absolutely everything, including what he ate for breakfast every day."

"No, in fact it was a very small volume." Claire paused as the light dawned. "Did you read Fazzini in English or in Italian?"

"Italian."

"The English version must be abridged, then." With growing excitement, Claire wondered how many other extraordinary bits of information had been left out of the books she'd read. What if Fazzini mentioned who had attended the courtesan's debut that night? Or La Sirena's real name? She'd ask Francesca for the Italian edition tomorrow. Maybe there was hope for her dissertation after all, in spite of Andrew Kent's greater authority and head start. "Do you know much about the book Andrew Kent is writing?" Claire asked.

"On the Spanish Conspiracy? Obviously there's some publisher interest already. Not surprising, since his last did so well."

"But do you know if it's finished?"

"I don't know for certain, but I should think he'd be close to finishing it, otherwise why reveal his findings in these lectures?"

"That's what I thought," said Claire, disheartened.

"No doubt it will lead to another round of awards and accolades for Andy. Not that I'm jealous, mind you. It's good to see him so happy and productive."

"This is what he's like when he's happy?"

"I guess I should say 'happier.' He's had a difficult few years."

Claire recognized gossip when she heard it. She wrestled with her conscience for a moment and lost, something she decided she could feel bad about some other time. "Difficult?" she prompted.

"Andy's a widower. His wife died two years ago."

"I'm sorry," said Claire, chagrined. "I had no idea."

"No need to be sorry. I don't recall that anyone liked her very much. 'Cept Andy, I suppose, and I think even he was rather lukewarm toward the end."

It was impossible to tell if Hoddy was serious or not. "What was she like?" Claire ventured.

"She was an archeologist, an expert on Mesopotamian cave dwellings. Brilliant by any standards, but she had an unfortunate, droning sort of voice. That combined with an extensive knowledge of igneous rock formations made her one of the most horrific bores this side of Babylon. Bloody awful at parties—she used to simply stun people into a coma. Once, while she was lecturing, she put an entire class to sleep."

"How did she die?"

"A tragic accident. She was thrown by her horse."

"That's terrible."

"Yes, it was. They had to shoot the horse." Hoddy clucked and shook his head. "Seems you can't let a good horse live, not even a champion, if the damn animal kills somebody."

"How long has he been dating Gabriella Griseri?"

"About four months, I believe."

"They seem a rather odd couple."

"Not when you look beyond the surface. After that series based on Andy's book, he's the current darling at the BBC. They think he's going to be the next Jonathan Miller—popular history for the masses and all that."

"What's that got to do with Gabriella?"

"It seems that RAI just pulled the plug on her show. Apparently Italians are as wild for reality shows as Americans, and the high-brow programs are being sacked more viciously than the Goths sacked Rome. After all, who wants to listen to Luciano Pavarotti discuss opera when you can watch a group of attractive young people eat worms? The rumor is that she's looking for new opportunities and is quite prepared to leave Italy and take her lovely self north to be adored by the British viewing audience."

"That explains it, then."

"It also occurred to me that she just might be in love with him."

"Really?"

"Just because you don't fancy him doesn't mean that no one would. I know any number of students, past and present, who've had serious crushes on our poor Andy. And I can't help but notice that you seem to be awfully interested for someone who saved herself so much time by disliking him right away."

"It's not for the reason you think."

"I don't expect this affair with Gabriella to last, however."

"Why not?"

"Andy has a son. He's young, eight or nine, I believe, and a real terror. Somehow I can't imagine Gabriella playing stepmummy."

A bell chimed and the houselights dimmed briefly. Gwen rejoined them as everyone began returning to their seats for the second act.

"Do you ever get up to Cambridge?" Hoddy asked as they walked along the corridor.

Claire shook her head. "I've never been."

"That's too bad. You really should come visit us sometime. It's a lovely town. And there's terrific shooting in the countryside."

Claire and Gwen looked at Hoddy quizzically. "Oh, that's right," he corrected himself. "In America, you call it hunting. You don't have 'shooting' in America, do you?"

"Sure we do," Gwen replied. "In America, people shoot each other all the time."

"Look!" Gwen exclaimed as they walked down the steps of La Fenice after the performance. "It's Stefania and Giancarlo." The brother and sister were standing near a fountain in the middle of the square adjacent to the opera house. Gwen waved to get their attention.

"Good evening," Giancarlo said as the four of them met halfway. "May I talk to you for a minute?" he asked Claire, with a meaningful glance at the two girls. They moved a few feet away for more privacy as the two teenagers watched them with eager interest.

"About last night . . . ," he began. "I would like the chance to explain. Will you join me for dinner tomorrow?"

The Chariot

25 February 1618

VALERIA, THE UPSTAIRS maid, carried a tray set with Florentine china and breakfast pastries into the bedchamber. La Celestia lounged in a chair next to the crackling fire, still wrapped in her sable-lined dressing gown. The slight puffiness in the courtesan's face and her sleep-heavy eyes attested to the early hour. The maid glanced discreetly but with noticeable displeasure at the person who had disturbed her mistress's morning, a man in a crimson toga who stood at the window, looking out at the drizzling rain and the gray sky.

"Will that be all, my lady?" she asked, curtsying.

"Yes, Valeria." La Celestia smiled to herself as the maid left the room. She'd seen the look Valeria had given her guest. Her maid seemed to have a particular dislike of senators, though La Celestia didn't have the slightest idea why. With their robes off, they were just like other men.

Except for this one, perhaps. Not that she'd ever seen him without his toga, or had any desire to. An encounter might make him more amenable to her influence, of course, but that wasn't possible. He'd been unmanned years ago, before he was yet of age. Her most potent manipulative skills were of no use in this case. It made her uneasy in his presence and wary of his power.

La Celestia poured cups of wine as Girolamo Silvia turned from the window. His countenance never failed to distress her. In it, familiar features had been sharpened and narrowed, and the result was an unattractive, distorted reminder of another, morc handsome face she had once loved.

"I expected more from you," Silvia said as he walked to the chair opposite hers and sat down. In spite of his unpleasant appearance, the senator carried himself with dignity. His limp was noticeable only if one knew to look for it.

"Is it not too early to talk of such business?"

"Not for me," he replied. "But then, unlike you, I conduct my business during the day."

Not all of it, La Celestia thought. What about those secret meetings of the Three, the long nights in the Court of the Room of the Cord?

"I told you from the start what I wanted," Silvia continued. "I don't like being disappointed."

How dare he come here to threaten me? La Celestia felt her bile rise, but kept herself in check. As much as she would have liked to throw him out, she could not afford to make the senator her enemy. "I did what you asked," she said sharply. "I introduced Bedmar to a girl. The rest was up to you."

"You have a selective memory, I see. I expressly told you that I wanted a full accounting of the ambassador's actions."

"And I told you what I wanted in return. Until you make good on your promises, I see no reason for procuring this intelligence."

"I made you no promises. What you expect is impossible."

"Your own family bought its way into the aristocracy," she reminded him.

"My ancestors didn't purchase their nobility, they were admitted to the Libro d'Oro in recognition of their outstanding service during the War of Chioggia. And that was more than two hundred years ago."

"Contributing three thousand ducats to the state coffers didn't hurt, I'm sure."

"The fact remains that no new families have been admitted to the Venetian aristocracy for two centuries. The rules for inclusion in the Libro d'Oro are set. It's an impossibility for a courtesan who isn't even a Venetian citizen."

"You know it's not for myself. My daughters are of noble blood. All I'm asking is that you help Caterina and Elena become legitimized so that they can marry nobility, as they should."

"Large dowries will go a long way toward gaining entrée into the aristocracy. I know a few impoverished nobles who would gladly overlook the girls' illegitimacy for the gold."

"But if my daughters are not legitimized, my grandsons will not be entered in the Libro d'Oro, or be allowed to serve on the Great Council."

"Such grandiose plans for the future, La Celestia. Does the little courtesan from Treviso envision a Doge among her descendants?"

She knew it was unwise, but she couldn't curtail her sharp tongue. "At least I have descendants."

The sour look that crossed Silvia's face was a warning she'd gone too far, but was somehow satisfying. "Conferring legitimacy is not as easy as you imagine," he said.

"Surely you wield enough influence. Can you not see how important it is? By the Virgin, they're your brother's daughters."

"They're my brother's bastards."

"He would have married me if—"

"*If* he had come back from fighting the Turks. Or so you believe. I'm not convinced that he would have married you, had he lived. But we'll never know, will we? In any event, you are left with two daughters without patrimony. If you hold out hope for their future, you will do as I ask."

The senator wasn't going to give an inch. What made him such a hard-nosed bargainer? "Spy on Bedmar?" she ventured.

"The ambassador has something I need. This young courtesan, she stays overnight at the Spanish embassy sometimes, yes?"

"I believe so."

"I will tell you what it is, and where it is, and you will instruct the girl to get it for me."

"You want her to steal something? You've chosen poorly.

Alessandra's no thief. I'm sure you've already placed spies in the embassy. Why not use one of them?"

"The ambassador's rooms are locked when he is away and no one is allowed in. She's the only one with access."

"Except that he'll be there as well."

"And peacefully asleep, I should imagine."

"How am I to convince her to do something so foolhardy?"

"The Spanish ambassador plots an attack on Venice. It is not so far-fetched to believe that anyone so intimate with him would be an accomplice to his intrigue. I can easily imagine her hanging alongside her lover."

"So I'm to coerce her with threats?"

"It isn't a threat. If she does not cooperate, it is a promise."

"You might have appealed to her patriotism instead. I'm sure she would not like to see Venice sacked by Spanish forces."

"You may try that, if you think that will be more effective."

"You are a cynic."

"I'm practical. And I'm in a hurry."

"The marquis is a clever man. And dangerous. I'm not convinced this is a wise course. If he discovers the girl in the act, there's no telling what he would do. I've made a substantial investment in her and I would be very unhappy to lose such an excellent source of income. What's more, he'll know that she would not attempt something like this on her own, and he'll suspect me. No, I won't do it."

"I think you will. The ambassador may be dangerous—but you forget, I am equally so. Perhaps more dangerous, to you."

"Will you promise to help my daughters?"

"I won't promise anything, but you will do it nonetheless. If you do not, I will make it known that the men who play cards in your house are being systematically cheated."

La Celestia turned pale. "You cannot prove it."

"I can. It would ruin you, La Celestia. It appears your greed has overcome your common sense."

La Celestia held the senator's gaze for a long moment. If he were bluffing, then he was highly skilled at it; she did not want to challenge the certainty she saw in his eyes. She wondered which of her servants he had corrupted; only one, she hoped. As soon as Silvia left, she'd begin making inquiries of her most trusted staff, and with any luck she'd root out and dismiss the spy before the day was over. No doubt he or she would go back to Silvia for a rich reward, and placement in another courtesan's household. And so it went.

"What must I do?" she asked.

28 February 1618

"It's a morocco-bound book, with no title," La Celestia said. "I am told that Bedmar keeps it in a small *damaschina* chest in his study. The key to the chest is somewhere in his desk."

Alessandra met with the courtesan in La Celestia's sumptuous gondola, moored near the Broad Alley of the Proverbs on the Rio di San Martino. Inside the *felze*, only one small lantern was lit, barely chasing away the shadows. Outside, La Celestia's blackamoor gondolier, Moukib, sat at his post on the stern, keeping a careful watch.

"And who told you this?" Alessandra asked.

"Do not concern yourself, it's better that you don't know. Once you have the book, you must leave the embassy at once. Go to the Lista di Spagna, then to Ponte degli Scalzi. Moukib will be waiting under the bridge, and will bring you to me. I'll return the book to you a day later. You must replace it in the chest just as you found it."

"Replace it? That may prove even more difficult than taking it. I usually see the marquis only once or twice a week. Am I to invite myself to the embassy? I have never done so before. It will raise his suspicion."

"I don't know how you will do it, but it must be done. And carefully. Bedmar must never know that the book was missing."

"What is this all for? I deserve to know that, at least."

"The ambassador plots against Venice. He assembles an army of mercenaries with which he hopes to take the city, and colludes with the duke of Ossuna—"

"The duke of Ossuna?"

La Celestia looked at her sharply and Alessandra instantly regretted her outburst. "Do you know of the ambassador's dealings with the duke?"

"No." Alessandra tried to keep her expression composed as her mind reeled. Was the viscount involved in this plot? "Why is this book so important?" she asked.

"It's the key to the code he uses to write to the Spanish king. With a copy of this key, all his thoughts, all his movements will be exposed. But it will be successful only if the book is taken and replaced without his knowledge."

The marquis would surely show no leniency if he discovered her treachery. "What do you imagine he will do if he catches me?"

"Make no mistake. He will kill you."

"And you expect me to undertake this fool's errand?"

"You have no choice. If you do not do it, you could be implicated along with the ambassador and any others who conspire with him. You could hang."

She had chosen the courtesan's life for the freedom it offered; now, Alessandra realized, she couldn't be less free. "You introduced me to the ambassador just for this purpose, didn't you? From the very first day, when you came to my house, you knew it would lead to something like this."

"I did what I had to do. And now so must you or you will hang along with the Spanish."

"But I know nothing of any plot."

"You do know something, however—something you're not telling me."

"I know nothing."

"I think you lie. I hope you have a good reason for doing so. Do you protect the marquis? Can it be that you're in love with him?"

"No, of course not. Are you certain that he conspires against Venice?"

"It seems so, yes."

"How do you expect me to dissemble so completely?"

"I know that you are not suited to this, but you must find a way. I speak as someone who cares about you—"

Alessandra laughed bitterly. "Cares about me? When did you ever care about anyone but yourself? Tell me, La Celestia, what's in this for you? More money? Are you not rich enough yet?"

"I am not so coldhearted as you imagine. I do care about you, and I should not like to see you hurt. And think of this: the ambassador contrives a treacherous plot that places every Venetian in danger. You can help stop it. Is that not worthy?"

"Of course it is, but—"

"I know it's dangerous. I won't lie to you about that. You must believe I am sorry for this—but in this instance, neither of us has a choice."

"Someone is forcing your hand, too?"

"Yes."

"If I take the book and replace it without the marquis knowing, will we be safe?"

"Yes."

Alessandra was silent for a moment. "All right, then."

"You understand exactly what you must do?"

"Yes."

"Please, make sure he is quite soundly asleep first."

"He does not tire easily, and he is always on his guard. He will wake as soon as I rise from the bed."

"I feared as much. That's why I brought you this." La Celestia held out a small glass flask filled with an amber-colored liquid.

Alessandra did not reach for it. "Is it poison?"

"No, just a sleeping draft. A few drops in his wine should do the trick. But no more or you'll make him ill, and you don't want him to suspect anything untoward."

Alessandra took the flask, turned it in her hands. "Have you any other advice for me, La Celestia?"

The courtesan leaned back against the cushions, her mouth pursed in a concerned moue. "Don't get caught."

2 March 1618

She'd done as La Celestia instructed, but with unfortunate results. Alessandra looked with dismay at the ambassador. The sleeping draft had taken hold much faster than she had expected; she'd had no time to lure him into bed. They had taken supper in his private rooms at the embassy; even before he'd finished his beefsteak, he'd passed out in a wing chair next to the dining table, in full sight of his desk and the *damaschina* chest where the code book was kept. She was seated opposite and had been watching his steady breathing for some time now, but fear kept her rooted to the chair. What if he woke up? She shivered, thinking what the marquis might do if he discovered her rifling his desk. Then she recalled La Celestia's warning: If you don't steal the book, you'll hang along with the Spanish. She imagined the rough sisal noose scratching at her throat, so tight it burned, the terrible choking feeling. She'd heard that it was considered a mercy when a man's neck was broken instantly by the rope; worse was the slow suffocation that some endured. A sobering vision of herself so gruesomely dispatched—purple faced, tongue lolling, legs thrashing in vain—brought her back to the task at hand. The sleeping draft wouldn't work forever. She must hurry.

She carried a taper across the room and in the candle's light examined the desk. It was an intricate affair, with more than a dozen small drawers on the credenza-style top, and another long, narrow drawer beneath the parquet desktop. She tried the largest first, finding nothing but sheets of writing paper and a few fresh quills. The smaller drawers, too, held writing accoutrements: inks, wax, powder. Finally, a glint of metal: the tiny brass key fit perfectly into the locked chest.

She extracted the book carefully. It was compact in size, not much larger than her hands, and bound in a wine-colored morocco. With an eye on the slumbering marquis, Alessandra turned the pages. The book was written in Latin, but seemed to make no sense at all, being composed of random words, sentences, and quotations she recognized from Cicero, Virgil, Seneca. *Inhumanitas omni aetate molesta est,* she read: Inhumanity is harmful in every age. *Nullum magnum ingenium sine mixtura dementiae fuit:* There has not been any great talent without an element of madness. What could it mean? How did the marquis use this book to formulate a code?

She started as a sharp knock sounded at the door. She dropped the book, scrambled to pick it up, then quickly tucked it inside the velvet purse she'd brought with her that evening, setting it on the empty chair with her shawl.

She cracked the door open slightly. Bedmar's manservant, Pasquale, stood in the hall. "There's a messenger here for the ambassador."

"The marquis is sleeping."

"But he insists—"

"He does not want to be disturbed."

"It's urgent." From out of the shadows came a familiar voice. Antonio pushed past Pasquale, who slipped away into the dim recesses of the corridor. As he stepped inside, he brought the cool, damp air of the Grand Canal with him, along with the aromas of roadside taverns, horses, beds made of straw. Underneath, his natural scent was tangy and sweet, like apple cider.

"Sleeping?" Antonio said. He took in everything at a glance: the fireside table set for two, the remains of their dinner, the bottle of wine, Bedmar slumped in his chair, head thrown back, lost to the world. "Hard to believe." His eyes roamed over her gown, cut low in the courtesan's style, aureoles peeking over the lace neckline. "Especially as you're such a fetching sight."

The words were complimentary but his snide delivery was not. She hadn't seen Antonio since Carnival, and he exhibited little of the charm she remembered; he seemed tense, distant, angry. For weeks, she had imagined that the viscount harbored intimate feelings for her, and many times she had wished for his return to Venice—but not now, she thought with dismay. Not tonight.

"I must admit, when I first saw your face at the door, I expected quite a different scene," he went on in the same cutting tone. "Shouldn't you be playing the lute for your lord, seducing him with your voice, delighting him with your . . . skills?"

She could see that he was travel weary, but what right did he have to be so contemptuous, so cruel? "The ambassador's the worse for drink."

Antonio walked closer to Bedmar and studied his slack-jawed face. "I've thought the marquis many things, but I never thought him a drunkard." He looked suspiciously at Alessandra.

"The wine is strong."

"Is it?" He picked up Bedmar's glass and sniffed, then raised it to his lips.

Alessandra instinctively moved toward him, her hand raised in warning. "It is not very good."

He looked at her levelly. "But it does the trick, obviously." He slowly put the glass down. "Just what are you up to?"

"Nothing." Alessandra picked up her purse and wrapped her shawl around her shoulders. "I've had a note from Bianca. I must go home."

"Why in such a hurry?" Three strides and he had crossed the room, blocking the door.

"It's an urgent matter."

"Ahhh."

She stood before him, wondering if he noticed that she was trembling. "You must let me pass."

"Tell me, what would I find if I looked in your purse? The marquis's gold, his jewels, his silver?"

"You misjudge me."

"So prove me wrong."

They looked at each other solemnly. She wished she could unburden herself of her secret, but the viscount was a Spaniard in Ossuna's and Bedmar's service. Why should she imagine that their brief time together would overcome his devotion to duty? Surely catching a thief in the ambassador's quarters would be a coup for him. She stole a glance at the sword hanging at his side, the dagger secure in his belt. And there's another weapon, she remembered, a stiletto concealed in his sleeve.

"I cannot."

"What will you do when the ambassador discovers your crime?" he asked, his voice low, confidential.

"There is nothing to discover."

"Your lack of fear will be your death."

She couldn't tell if his words were a warning or a threat. Unexpectedly, Antonio stood aside and opened the door for her. "I'd take the back stairs, if I were you."

Chapter Seventeen

In the clear, early morning sunlight, against a backdrop of verdant garden and glistening lagoon, Andrew Kent stood half bent with hands on knees, breathing raggedly. He'd reached the end of the Riva fully six strides ahead of Claire—but then he was considerably taller than she was, and his Nike running shorts revealed well-defined legs, the sign of a dedicated runner. Still, when he had first appeared alongside her as she was bounding up the steps of the Ponte dei Greci, she'd imagined that she could leave him behind. At least, she had thought as she picked up her pace, he would get the idea that she'd rather jog alone. Instead, he'd run right past her.

The gauntlet had clearly been thrown, so Claire turned on the juice and dashed ahead of Andrew Kent. That was all it took to ignite a flat-out race, one that didn't end until the Riva did, at the edge of the public gardens.

Andrew was clearly winded, but Claire wasn't doing much better. She wondered if the confetti-like spots she saw when she closed her eyes meant that she should sit down, but damn if she would let him see her falter. The man was just too competitive. When he finally raised his head and opened his mouth to speak, she was fully expecting him to gloat.

Instead, he said:

"Pirates?"

"Pirates?" Claire repeated, surprised.

"Pirates." He paused for a few deep breaths. "You said . . . you were working . . . on Adriatic . . . pirates."

"And your point?"

"Yesterday I asked to see the Rossetti Letter"—he was breathing more normally now—"and I was told that you have it."

"You were checking up on me?"

"No, I simply wanted to see it again. But in doing so I reached the inescapable conclusion that you are also researching the Spanish Conspiracy. Why you felt compelled to lie about it I can't possibly begin to imagine, and I don't really care, but I would like to see the letter."

"You want to see the letter."

"Not for long. I just need to check something."

"I'll trade you, then—the letter for the diary."

"Alessandra's diary?"

"Of course."

"I haven't finished with it yet. I'm leaving Venice on Saturday, though, so you can look at it next week."

"I'm leaving on Saturday, too."

"In that case, I suppose we could trade for a half hour."

"Half an hour? How extraordinarily generous of you."

"I'm not fully awake yet, but I believe I detect a strong note of sarcasm in your voice."

"I can't read the entire diary in half an hour."

"That's the most I can offer. I'm under a lot of pressure to produce a book outline by next month, and I haven't been having an easy time of it; in fact, it's not going very well at all."

For a moment, Andrew Kent looked the way he had prior to his lecture: unsure of himself, even vulnerable. Maybe, Claire considered, he was human after all.

"The truth is," he went on, "I have book offers, but what I don't have is a book. I don't know what the problem is; maybe it's because I haven't written on Venetian history before, or maybe it's the sophomore curse, or maybe it's"—he stopped short, suddenly self-conscious. The kinder, gentler Andrew disappeared as quickly as he had appeared, and the one who invariably raised her hackles returned in full force. "The thing is, that diary could provide the key to—well, to everything, and I can't just hand it over to you indefinitely. My work is too important."

"You really are a *fondamentum equi*, aren't you?"

He looked at her as if a second head had suddenly sprouted from her shoulders. "Did you just call me a horse's ass in Latin?"

"I can say it in Greek, if you prefer."

"I don't understand why I deserved that."

"Because it didn't once occur to you that perhaps my work is important, too. Maybe I don't have publishers waiting breathlessly for every word I write, or prize committees lining up to give me awards, but I can assure you that my work is just as important to me as yours is to you. For you, it's just another book, but this is my dissertation. Everything else that happens in my life depends on this one thing. So unless you're willing to loan me the diary for a day, I don't think I'll show you the letter."

"First of all, there's no such thing as 'just another book,' as you shall quickly discover should you ever attempt to write one. And second, I only want to see it for a moment."

"No deal."

"That's just unbelievable," Andrew sputtered. "You're ridiculously competitive."

"I'm competitive? I'm not the one who nearly gave myself a coronary trying to outrun a girl."

"I didn't *try* to outrun you, I did outrun you. By at least twenty meters."

"Twenty meters? I don't think so."

"When I reached the end, you were way back there." He pointed to a spot farther back on the Riva, then began walking toward it. Claire followed him.

"I wasn't there," she insisted, "I was over here."

"I distinctly recall that when I turned around, you were right here, by this bench."

An elderly, black-clad widow slowly hobbled past, and briefly considered the strangeness of foreigners. She was of the opinion that all of them were lunatics of one sort or another, but these two were more barking mad than most: each was yelling at the other and pointing quite vigorously to a spot on the ground.

"*. . . lessons with the music master Signor Alberigo proceed apace. He says I must practice much more if I am to learn Spinacino's* Ricercai *. . .*"

Claire looked up from Alessandra's diary, put down her pen, and briefly rubbed her eyes as Gwen appeared at her side and hopped up to sit on the edge of the reading-room table.

"In a chair, please," Claire said automatically.

"Francesca is so cool," she said as soon as she was properly seated. "She just taught me a whole bunch of Italian swear words."

"Told you this would be an educational trip."

"And a couple of gestures, too."

"So you can offend the hearing impaired as well?"

"I don't think you have to be deaf to understand them," Gwen said earnestly. She scrunched her eyes as she considered further. "Or even Italian. She also told me how to get to that store with all the fake designer stuff."

"Hmmm," mumbled Claire, turning her attention back to the diary.

"Don't you want to buy something new to wear on your date with Giancarlo?"

"Maybe."

"Oh, come on. You can't wear the same clothes you've been wearing."

"If I get done with this early enough, we'll go."

"Cool. So where is he taking you?"

"I don't know yet. He's going to leave a message at the hotel."

"What did he say last night? Did he tell you he's not engaged anymore?"

"All he said was that he wanted to explain and he asked me to have dinner with him. It was nice of Stefania to invite you to the movies so that we could go out," she added.

"Yeah, she's really nice. So when are you going to be finished with this?"

"Gwen—"

"Sorry. I know I'm not supposed to bug you, but I don't have anything to do, and Francesca just left for lunch."

"Isn't there something in that backpack of yours to keep you occupied?"

"I left my iPod at the hotel. So what's that you're writing?"

"I'm translating this diary."

"That's the courtesan's diary?"

"Yes."

"Weird. It looks a lot like my diary. It's the same color leather and it's all beat up and stuff. She wrote this letter, too, right?" Gwen picked up the Rossetti Letter.

"Don't touch that."

"Sorry." Gwen peered over Claire's shoulder and read aloud from her notebook. ". . . *I have mastered many of the works of Canova da Milano, which Signor Alberigo says are more appropriate for performance by the fair sex. Apparently they do not rouse the senses as do Spinacino's compositions* . . ." Gwen paused, puzzled. "Why doesn't she write about something interesting, like her friends or her boyfriends or something?" she asked.

"I've been wondering that myself." Claire sighed, feeling frustrated. The diaries seemed to be leading nowhere, and the Italian edition of Fazzini she'd had such high hopes for was not to be had. As soon as Claire had come into the library that morning, she'd requested it, and Francesca had given her the bad news: Fazzini's *Diary* had been destroyed in a flood. That's why, the librarian explained, she'd given Claire the English version in the first place; they no longer had the Italian edition. Francesca thought there might be another copy in a library in Rome, but the Marciana hadn't had one since 1993. They'd lost a lot of books that winter, she'd said sadly.

"What does this have to do with the conspiracy thing?" Gwen asked, still reading Claire's notebook.

"Nothing directly, but I was hoping it would tell me more about the kind of person Alessandra was. Then I might be able to figure out if she was acting on her own, or if she was spying on the Spanish for the Venetians."

"I thought the English guy said that the Spanish didn't do anything."

"So you were listening."

"Not by choice."

"Yes, that's what he said, but I think he's wrong. Although I'm not going to prove it with this," she said, shutting the diary. Claire swiveled around in her chair. Andrew Kent had his nose buried in some ancient tome, and his table was stacked with books that hadn't been there the day before. What was he on to? She noticed with irritation that he wasn't reading Alessandra's second diary.

"Can't spare it for more than a half hour," she muttered, turning around again. "He's probably ignoring it just to annoy me."

"What's the problem?" Gwen asked.

"Andrew Kent has Alessandra's other diary. That's the one I really need."

"Oh, that reminds me. Francesca said something about that. I was supposed to ask you if you were using your . . ." Gwen thought hard for a moment, then said, "feminine power."

"Not in the way she envisioned, I'm sure," Claire admitted glumly.

Gwen glanced at the diary in front of them, then looked over at Andrew Kent's table. "You need the little book that looks just like this one?"

"Yes."

"Do you *really* want it?"

"Yes, I really want it, but he's never going to give it to me, not now."

"We could liberate it." Gwen's eyes had a curious sparkle to them.

"Are you suggesting that we steal it?"

"No, just borrow it for a while. If we switch it with this one, he won't even know that it's gone."

"I beg to differ."

"I beg to differ?"

"I beg to differ."

"I don't even know what that means, 'I beg to differ.'"

"It means I disagree with you."

"Then why didn't you just say, 'I disagree with you'?"

"Because I said 'I beg to differ.'"

"No one says that."

"I say that."

"No one normal says that."

"Be that as it may, Andrew Kent is most definitely going to notice that we took that diary."

"Okay, but maybe not right away. In the meantime, you can read it. And if he does figure out that he's got the wrong book, you just tell him that it was a mistake." Gwen looked at her with enthusiasm, which Claire hoped sprang from a sincere desire to be helpful rather than from kleptomania. "It really does work," Gwen added.

Claire sighed. She had only two more days in Venice, after all. "So what do we do?"

"You have to distract him. Stand on the far side of the table and talk to him, and I'll switch the books."

"Come on, then, before I lose my nerve."

"Not so fast. You need to be a little more distracting." Gwen rummaged in her backpack and took out a lipstick. "Put this on. And let me fix your hair. That braid thing is a little too Heidi, if you know what I mean." She took the tie off the end of Claire's braid and fluffed her hair around her shoulders. "And this." She unbuttoned the top button on Claire's blouse.

"What the hell are you doing?" Claire protested.

"Making you look more distracting. Be sure to bend over really low when you pick up stuff off the floor."

"What's going to be on the floor?"

"Everything."

Chapter Eighteen

She couldn't afford a new pair of shoes, too, Claire thought wistfully, gazing through the boutique window at an array of strappy high heels. Not to mention that she didn't have any more time to shop before her date with Giancarlo. Evening shadows were slowly settling into the charming cobblestone lane where she stood; from somewhere nearby, unseen within the maze of tiny streets of San Marco, a church bell marked the half hour. It was a shame, because the black evening shoes on the left would be perfect with her new dress. She shifted her focus from the footwear displayed inside the store to her reflection in the glass and adjusted a spaghetti-thin shoulder strap. The dress was slinky, formfitting, and undeniably sexy: a bold, warm red, with simple lines and a stunning effect. She never would have bought it without Gwen's prompting. In fact, it had been Gwen who'd spotted it in the window of the store that Francesca had told them about.

"I don't look good in red," Claire had said.

"My mom says that all women look good in red," Gwen replied. "It just has to be the *right* red."

When Claire had stepped out of the dressing room, she could tell from Gwen's expression that it was the right red; in fact, it was the right everything. The teenager pronounced it a "killer" dress, which Claire was made to understand was a positive endorsement.

Even the shop assistant had been bountiful with her praise. But there hadn't been time to buy shoes before going back to the hotel so that Gwen could meet Stefania.

Claire looked down at her worn-at-the-heel pumps. She really should replace them, as they undermined the whole effect. Of course, considering what she was wearing, it was entirely possible that Giancarlo would never look at her feet. She still had another twenty minutes or so before she had to meet him at the restaurant; she could at least pop inside the boutique and ask the price.

"Did you think I wouldn't notice?"

Startled, Claire turned around. Andrew Kent stood before her.

"Have you ever thought about beginning a conversation by simply saying hello?" she asked, exasperated.

"Hello. Did you think I wouldn't notice?"

"Notice what?"

"You know very well what—that you switched the two diaries. You and your young accomplice. Was it really necessary for her to knock all of my books off the table?"

"She's fourteen. It's an awkward age."

"Humph. In case you're unaware of this, stealing historical documents belonging to the Italian government is a crime punishable by very steep fines and a rather lengthy imprisonment, which I don't think you would much enjoy. I suspect that it wouldn't be good for your academic career, either."

"Don't you think you're overreacting? We didn't steal the diary, we just borrowed it for a while. If it bothered you so much, why didn't you say something this afternoon?"

"I didn't realize what you'd done until a couple of hours later, and by then it was almost time for me to go."

Claire remembered how surprised they'd been by his early departure. They'd raced up to the librarian's desk, where Gwen had just managed to exchange the diaries before Francesca placed Andrew's stack of books behind the counter. "All of this could have been avoided if you'd simply agreed to let me read it," she said.

"The point is that you don't have the right to take things from people whenever you feel like it."

"You don't have the right to hold on to books that you aren't even using."

"I do, as a matter of fact, as do you. I noticed that you had a few things on your desk that you didn't even glance at all day long. You were clearly too busy working with mine."

"You were watching me?"

"I wasn't watching you. You just happened to be in my line of sight occasionally. So tell me, did that additional bit of slapstick at the librarian's desk mean that you replaced my diary?"

"Your diary?"

"By that I mean the one that happens to be checked out in my name, and for which I am responsible."

"Yes, we put it back."

"Thank you." He was about to say something else, but then was silent. Andrew Kent seemed different this evening. Maybe it was the well-tailored dark suit and white dress shirt. No tie, but still he gave the impression of being dressed to the nines; he looked elegant, even dashing. He cleared his throat. "You look very—," he began.

The church bell rang again, and Claire was reminded of the time. "I'm sorry, I've got to be going."

"Are you on your way to Ca' Rezzonico?"

"Ca' Rezzonico?" she repeated.

"Yes."

"No."

"I thought because of your . . . the way you're . . . the red . . . I mean to say, there's a program of chamber music there tonight. Not quite as majestic as La Fenice, but impressive nonetheless."

"No, I'm going out to dinner."

"Oh. I see." His brow furrowed. "With Giancarlo Baldessari?"

"Yes."

"Of course." His mouth resolved into a little smirk, and it annoyed her. Why was her dating life any business of Andrew Kent's? Was he smirking because he thought she was too old for Giancarlo? Because he didn't like Giancarlo? Because he didn't like her?

"I really must go," said Claire, backing away. "Good night."

"Did you notice anything odd about the Rossetti Letter?" Andrew asked suddenly.

Claire stopped. She was going to be late, but curiosity compelled her to retrace her steps. "You know what it is, don't you?"

"The letter is dated March, but in it she writes that she knew about the conspiracy much earlier, in January. That thing about the letters between Ossuna and Bedmar. That's a two-month discrepancy."

"I knew there was something strange about it. I should have caught that."

"If she suspected something in January, why did she wait two months before informing the Great Council? If she was a patriot, as is commonly believed, why didn't she expose the conspiracy right away?"

"Maybe she wanted to be sure of the facts before turning them in."

"You think that she was spying on the mercenaries."

"It's possible."

"No one in their right mind would put themselves at such risk. If they had discovered her spying, they would have killed her."

"Perhaps she was willing to take that risk in order to keep Venice free of Spanish tyranny. And for all we know, they did kill her. No one knows what happened to her after the conspiracy ended."

"If anyone killed her, there's no evidence of it. As for risking her life to fight Spanish tyranny, it's rather unlikely, don't you think? People are rarely that altruistic."

"I agree with you that people don't usually put their lives in jeopardy for the greater good. But sometimes they do. History is filled with stories of people who stood up for what was right simply because it was right, even if it meant great personal sacrifice."

"I can see that you'd like to believe this conspiracy is all about her heroism, but that's a naive—"

"What do you think it's about?"

"The Venetians were threatened by Ossuna, and they wanted Bedmar out of Venice. The Council of Ten did what was politically expedient."

"You think the letter is manufactured evidence."

"I'd say it's the seventeenth-century equivalent of planting drugs in the glove box."

"And Alessandra was just a pawn in a plot hatched by the Ten?"

"The letter is proof of it."

"And how do you jump to that conclusion?"

"Girolamo Silvia was embroiled in a political battle with Dario Contarini, his hated rival. Contarini was one of Alessandra Rossetti's lovers. By choosing Alessandra Rossetti to write that letter, Silvia killed a number of birds with one stone. Not only does he slander Bedmar and Ossuna, but Contarini is tainted as well, by the implication that his mistress is involved with the conspirators. Contarini's political fortunes fell dramatically after this episode. He was dismissed from the Signory, and lost all chance of ever becoming Doge."

"I still don't understand how the letter can be proof of all that."

"Because the only possible explanation for this letter is that Silvia used Alessandra Rossetti for his own ends, to slander Bedmar and to taint Contarini's reputation by association. Otherwise, why have her write the letter? There's no evidence linking Alessandra to any of the conspirators."

"Perhaps all the evidence has been destroyed. You know, the other possible explanation is that the letter is exactly what it seems, a warning from a concerned citizen about a possible attack on Venice."

"And how in the world did she learn of it? Divine inspiration?"

"I don't know, but it's entirely possible that she saw or heard something. She wasn't sequestered, after all. She had eyes and ears and a brain. I really do take umbrage—"

"Take umbrage?"

"To assume a feeling of pique or resentment."

"I know what it means. It's just that one seldom hears anyone say that anymore."

"One seldom hears anyone refer to themselves as 'one' anymore."

"I wasn't specifically referring to myself," said Andrew huffily, "I was using the indefinite singular pronoun, as is grammatically correct."

"As I was saying," Claire continued, "I take umbrage with your assumption that she had no will of her own and that she could not have brought down the conspiracy by her own actions. Why is that so difficult to believe?"

"I don't believe that there was a Spanish conspiracy in the first place, so it's not possible for her to—"

"You don't believe there was a Spanish conspiracy because you're married to this belief that all of her actions were directed and controlled by men—"

"I'm not *married* to any—for god's sake, we're talking about four hundred years ago, when women's lives were remarkably different from what they are now. You can't take today's beliefs and feminist principles and wantonly apply—"

"*Wantonly?* I'm not *wantonly* doing any—"

"*Wantonly* apply them"—Andrew's voice rose to match Claire's—"just because you wish it so. The worst mistake a historian can make is to take modern assumptions and retroactively apply them to the past."

"But what you're doing is equally wrong. You're blindly following a tradition that says because women didn't leave behind voluminous records of their thoughts and deeds, then they didn't have any thoughts and deeds—they were just standing on the sidelines while history was made by men. Just because a woman didn't have a vote doesn't mean that she didn't have an informed opinion. It doesn't mean she was incapable of thinking or acting."

"I never said anything like that. You're twisting my meaning in a completely idiotic manner."

"So now you're calling me an idiot?"

"I was not, I was only saying—"

"That you think I'm an idiot."

"No, that is not what I think. I think you're the most argumentative, obstinate, infuriating, exciting, and fascinating woman I've ever met."

His words seemed to hang in the still air for a moment, a moment of abrupt and embarrassed silence. What a strange thing for Andrew Kent to say. There'd been nothing premeditated about it; it had come out in a rush, as if he'd been thinking aloud. They stared at each other, both at a loss for words. The fading light made a thin, golden halo at the edge of his hair. His eyes were a soft, deep, velvety brown, she noticed, and had lost their usual judgmental glare; instead, he looked abashed with the realization of what he'd just said and his obvious wish that he hadn't just said it. Andrew took a breath, as if he were about to speak again, and then the church bell began chiming the hour.

"I have to go," Claire said, not waiting for Andrew's good-bye before hurrying off down the lane, relieved to be away from him. She was already a few narrow, nameless streets farther on before she realized that if Andrew Kent's short but impassioned speech had been spoken by anyone else, it would have been very romantic.

Chapter Nineteen

CLAIRE AND GIANCARLO dined on the terrace of the Ristorante alle Beccherie, which overlooked a small canal and the ancient palazzo on the opposite side. Tiny white lights entwined within the branches of the terrace's sheltering tree glimmered on the water's surface, and reticulated golden reflections shimmered and rippled on the palazzo's ochre-colored exterior. The restaurant itself, with its arched stone walls and dim pools of light, made her think of a secret cavern, perhaps the hiding place of saints or thieves, and when she had commented on their evocative surroundings, Giancarlo told her that it was formerly the catacombs of a church.

"Isn't there a Venetian word for those reflections?" Claire asked.

"*El sbarlusego,*" Giancarlo said. "It simply means 'the shining.' Or *el sbarlusega,* for 'something that shines.'"

"It's magical."

"I remember lying awake at night when I was a boy, watching the light on the ceiling. Sometimes it was so bright, I couldn't sleep. The full moon on the Grand Canal can be almost as dazzling as the sun." Giancarlo speared another forkful of *fararona con la Peverada* and gave her one of his heart-palpitating smiles; Claire took refuge in a sip of light, crisp Bardolino.

Arriving late had had its benefits. When she walked into the restaurant, she'd seen Giancarlo checking his watch and looking worried, and it had bolstered her confidence tremendously to know that he would have been sincerely disappointed if she hadn't shown up. Then he'd spotted her and smiled. With the way he had of seeming to focus on her absolutely, he walked from the bar where he sat and met her at the door, greeting her warmly with a kiss on the cheek and touching her back lightly as they followed the maitre d' to their table. He'd pulled out her chair, held her hand as she sat down, then ordered a bottle of wine to be brought right away. Claire remembered something Meredith had said, about how Italian men made you feel like a woman, and she'd thought, Okay, I get it now.

But that feeling had its drawbacks: it made her self-conscious about the whole *dateness* of the evening, her new dress, her strange sense of anticipation, the unspoken promise of shared intimacies. Suddenly it was all vastly discomforting, like standing on the edge of the Grand Canyon. She felt like a woman, like a woman was supposed to feel with a man—but for the first time in eight years, the man wasn't Michael. It had been two years since they'd split up, but still she felt odd, as if the feelings Giancarlo inspired were a betrayal of Michael, of her own emotions, or of marriage itself. Which she recognized was stupid, incredibly stupid, but she couldn't quite shake it off.

And underneath that was a simple, elemental fear. This is how it all starts, isn't it? she thought. First, you're attracted, then you let yourself like someone, you tell them all your secrets, they tell you theirs, you start trusting them, and before you know it, you're in love, and god help you!

"I must tell you how sorry I am about the other night," Giancarlo said.

"You don't have to explain." It would be better if they didn't get too personal, she decided. Really, why begin anything more than a simple, uncomplicated friendship? She was leaving in two days, anyway.

"But I want to," Giancarlo replied. "Natalie and I are not engaged. We were, but we aren't any longer. The reason I could say nothing is because I haven't yet told my family. I didn't want that to be the way I would break it to them. My mother especially is very fond of Natalie."

Claire looked into his eyes. Giancarlo appeared about as guileless as it was possible to be. Just because Michael was untrustworthy doesn't mean that all men are, Claire reminded herself. It's entirely possible that Giancarlo's telling the truth. "You still haven't told them?"

"I'm working up to it. It isn't easy. Our families are very close. Natalie hasn't told her family yet, either."

"So what happened? Why did you break up?"

"We wanted different things. She was ready to settle down, have a family right away, and I'm not so traditional."

"You don't want to have a family?"

"Someday, yes, but I don't want to live the same life as my parents and grandparents. Natalie is happy to always be in Venice, always with the families, doing the same things, seeing the same people. Venice is my home, but I don't want to live here forever. I don't even want to be always in Italy. Here, my work concerns only the past. Architecture in Venice is all about history, about restoration, about reconstructing buildings that are centuries old. I am much more interested in the future. In modern architecture. I am in love with the New World."

"The New World?"

"Yes, America, and especially New York. That's the city for me. Everything's happening twenty-four hours a day; so much excitement, so much nightlife. I'm what we call a night"—he searched for the word—"bird. No, owl. Do you have that expression? A night owl?"

"Yes."

"There isn't much for me to do here. But New York! Theaters, art galleries, nightclubs. Didn't you say that you lived there for a few years?"

"While I was at Columbia. Now I live near Boston."

"But New York was wonderful, yes?"

"I guess. I was so busy with school . . . and I didn't have a lot of money, and plays are really expensive . . . and I lived way uptown, near the university, which is far from the theater district . . ."

"So you did not see many plays."

"No. Or go to many nightclubs."

"But Boston is very exciting, too, yes?"

"Yes, it is. It's my hometown, so I probably take it for granted a bit, but it's got a lot of the same stuff New York has—just not nearly so much of it. But I don't actually live in Boston, I live in a little town about an hour away."

"It's still America."

"I don't think it's the America you have in mind. It's very quiet."

"And you like that?"

"Most of the time." She glanced around. "Honestly, though, I like this much better. I guess you could say I'm in love with the Old World."

They shared a smile at their incompatibility. "Maybe we can teach each other about the things we take for granted," Giancarlo said.

"Yes, we could."

"So if I come to America, you will let me take you out to plays?"

"Even nightclubs, if you're so inclined."

"And while you are here?" Giancarlo asked. "What is it that you would show me?"

"We're sitting in one of the loveliest spots in all of Venice. All you have to do is look around."

The waiter came over and Giancarlo convinced her to share a dessert with him. While he was ordering, she tried to imagine Giancarlo in New York, in Boston, in Harriot; tried to imagine him walking through her front door, standing in her kitchen, sleeping in her bed. It was difficult to picture him shut in on a dreary winter afternoon, or walking through a few feet of snow to the General Store. But there was summer, too, with sailing and hiking, and of course Boston and Providence offered restaurants and nightlife and cultural events. Giancarlo would like that, certainly.

"And you?" he asked when the waiter had left.

"Me?"

"Do you have a boyfriend in this little town where you live?"

"No."

"Really? And you've never married?"

Oh god, here it was, what she'd been dreading. It crossed her mind that she could simply say, "No," and not have to answer any more questions; but no doubt Giancarlo had heard his mother's disquisition about the strong possibility of terrorist attacks on never-married, thirty-plus women, and for reasons surpassing her own understanding, she could not allow herself to be lumped in with that group.

"I'm divorced. We split up two years ago."

"I'm sorry. How did it happen?"

"We just grew apart, I guess. My mom was seriously ill, and I spent a lot of time away from New York taking care of her."

"Your father wasn't there to help?"

"My dad died when I was still a baby. So it had always been just the two of us, me and my mom. I think Michael felt I was choosing her over him. I don't know, maybe that was true, but in a situation like that—she was dying—you don't think about it in those terms. You just do what you have to do. And so we . . . grew apart."

Giancarlo looked at her sympathetically. Claire was silent for a moment; then inhaled sharply and let her breath out slowly.

"That's not exactly true. I mean, the part about my mom is true, but the growing apart part isn't. The truth is, my . . . Michael, my husband . . . he fell in love with someone else." She laughed softly and shook her head. "I've never said that out loud before." She tried it out once again. "He fell in love with someone else. There it is."

"I find that very hard to believe."

"It's true. Although I suppose you could say that we wanted different things. I wanted to stay married, and he wanted to go off to Florence with Renaissance studies Laura."

"Renaissance studies Laura?"

"The day of my mom's funeral, Michael was there, of course, and after it was all over and everyone had gone home, we were in the kitchen trying to figure out what to do with the three thousand casseroles my mom's friends had brought over, and he said, real casually, like it was no big deal, 'You remember Laura? In Renaissance studies?' and I knew. I just knew."

"You knew he was in love with her?"

"Well, I knew he had slept with her. And then he said, 'She got a Fulbright to study in Florence and I'm going to go with her.' Just like that. And by the way, I want a divorce and you can move your stuff out of the apartment while I'm gone. He didn't say it like that, but that was pretty much the gist of it."

"And what did you say?"

"I didn't say anything. I punched him in the nose."

"You hit him?"

"Yes." Claire couldn't tell if Giancarlo was impressed, appalled, or amused. Perhaps he was a bit of all three.

"Do you have a history of violence?" He sounded serious, but he was grinning.

"No! I'd never hit anyone in my life until then."

"And since?"

"It hasn't become a habit."

"Just wondering if I should learn how to protect myself."

"Only if you ask for a divorce on the day of my mother's funeral."

"That can't possibly happen again, can it?"

"There's always a silver lining."

It was true she'd never hit anyone before or since; in fact, her reflex action had surprised her almost as much as it had surprised Michael. She had, however, methodically cut every one of his neckties into tiny pieces the day she'd moved out of their Upper West Side apartment, but this she chose not to share with Giancarlo. Probably best not to paint a picture of herself as a *Fatal Attraction*–like harridan on the first date, she figured. Or on any date.

"Giancarlo, I've been wondering . . . I mean, there must be many beautiful women in Venice . . ."

"Yes, and you are one of them."

Claire blushed; she hadn't been angling for a compliment. "Thank you, but I was just wondering why—"

"Because right away, I liked you. You are so different from the women I usually meet. Not superficial. When you told me you were a historian, I knew that you were intelligent, and I said to myself, 'I want to know more.' I like that you're American. American women are so independent and exciting."

She'd been called exciting twice in one night. She should wear red dresses more often.

"And I thought you must also be nice because you brought your little sister along," Giancarlo added. "Well, I thought she was your little sister. How do you like being a chaperone?"

"Let's just say I'm glad it's a one-time job. We got off to a rocky start, but it hasn't been too bad since then. Meeting Stefania was a huge help."

"I thought it might be. And for Stefania, too, it's very nice. Most of her friends have already gone away for summer holidays."

"And honestly, Gwen was an angel all day today. Well, there was one thing she did that wasn't very angelic, but I asked her to do it, and it helped me a lot, so I can't really say it was bad. But she never even complained about going to the *biblio*—" Claire stopped. *An angel all day.* Oh, no. She had a sudden, hollow, nervous feeling in the pit of her stomach. "Giancarlo, tell me something . . . was tonight your idea?"

"Tonight?"

"The two of us going out together."

"Well . . ." He looked uneasy as he admitted, "Stefania called me yesterday after she got home from the Lido and told me that Gwendolyn said you wanted to see me again before leaving Venice. I'd wanted to ask you, but until she told me this, I didn't think you would say yes."

"I think we've been played."

"Played?"

"For fools. Misled. Maybe you should try calling Stefania."

Giancarlo dialed his cell phone and held it to his ear without speaking for a moment, then hung up. "Her voice mail's on," he explained. "Maybe she turned the phone off during the movie." He sounded nonchalant, but there was concern in his eyes.

Claire checked her watch. "It's time to be getting back to the hotel, anyway."

Chapter Twenty

THEY ARRIVED AT the Bell'acqua a few minutes before eleven. Claire went straight to the front desk. The key to their room was still nestled in its cubbyhole, and the clerk confirmed that Gwen had not returned yet. Claire was just about to ask Giancarlo if he wanted to sit down and wait for the girls to arrive when Stefania ran in the front door.

"Is she here?" she asked them, breathless and frantic.

"Gwen?" Claire asked as Giancarlo said, "Why isn't she with you?"

They could see Stefania's panic rising as her eyes darted between them. "She—she got lost on the way back from the movie."

"How could she get lost when you were with her?" Giancarlo asked.

"I don't know. I stopped for a moment to look in a shop window and then she was gone."

Gone, as in vanished? Claire thought. As in kidnapped? She's the daughter of a rich man, after all. What ever happened to that Red Brigade, anyway? "I thought you said Venice was safe at night," Claire said to Giancarlo, unable to keep the accusatory tone completely out of her voice.

"It is," he replied firmly. "Where were you when this happened?" he asked Stefania.

"Dorsoduro."

"What were you doing there when the movie is playing in San Polo?"

Stefania didn't answer, just looked frightened.

"Tell me the truth, Stefania, what were you doing tonight?" Giancarlo demanded.

"You can't tell Mamma and Papa." Her eyes were wide and pleading.

"I'm not going to tell anyone, just tell me what you were up to."

"We were with some friends."

"Marco?"

"Yes . . . and Nicolo."

"Our cousin Nicolo?" Giancarlo looked confused.

"Yes."

"Ah, of course," he said, comprehending. "You all met on the beach yesterday. So where were you tonight?"

"At Nicolo's friend's house."

"Was it a party?"

"No, just the four of us."

"What happened?"

"I don't know! Nicolo said that she got upset and ran out of the house. He went after her, but he couldn't find her."

"What the hell did he do? I'm going to kill him."

"He said he didn't do anything wrong. You know Nicolo—he's not such a bad guy."

"It's true, he's not so bad," Giancarlo said to reassure Claire. "Where were you and Marco while this was going on?"

"We were in another room," Stefania said pointedly.

"Never mind, I don't want to know. So where is this house, and where are Marco and Nicolo?"

"It's near San Sebastiano, on Calle Balastro. Marco and Nicolo are out looking for her."

"I'll ask the clerk to call the police." Giancarlo walked over to the front desk.

Stefania looked encouragingly at Claire. "I'm sure she'll come back here to the hotel," she said.

"You were a long way from here. I don't think she'll know how."

Christ, Dorsodoro. If Gwen went in the wrong direction, she'd end up at the boat harbor. She wondered if the docks in Venice were as seedy as they were everywhere else in the world. It was no place for a teenaged girl to be wandering around alone, especially at night. It had never occurred to Claire that there would ever be a time when Gwen would be on her own, and she thought of all the things she might have done to prepare her for it, but hadn't. She hadn't taught her how to call the Italian emergency number, hadn't taught her the Italian word for police. If Gwen saw a sign with *carabinieri* on it, how much chance was there that she'd know what it meant? Claire hadn't even thought to make sure that Gwen carried one of the hotel business cards so she'd have the name and number of the hotel with her at all times.

Gwen having been rather sweet all day just made Claire feel worse. Sure, she'd had an ulterior motive for being on her best behavior, but still, they'd had a really pleasant day together. Yes, she talked too much and she couldn't sit still for more than five minutes, but Claire was getting used to having her around. Successfully switching the diaries had given them a shared sense of accomplishment (and a fit of the giggles, once Andrew Kent had left the reading room). Claire would be the first to admit that her behavior had been less chaperonelike than it should have been, but it was hard to regret it; she'd never had that much fun in a library before. Shopping and getting ready before going out for the evening had been fun, too; it made Claire remind herself to have a daughter one of these days.

If anything happened to Gwen, it would be entirely her fault, Claire thought. She should have seen through that little charade the girls had put on the previous evening, and she probably would have, if she hadn't wanted to go out with Giancarlo. How would she find the words to tell Gwen's parents? How would she live with herself?

At eleven thirty, she was sitting in the lobby while Stefania talked on her cell phone to Marco, who was searching near San Sebastiano. Two policemen stood at the desk, studying Gwen's passport and filling out a form. *A missing person. She's a missing person.* What had Nicolo done to upset Gwen? If Giancarlo didn't kill his cousin, Claire thought, she might do it herself.

Giancarlo knelt down in front of her. He spoke gently. "We're going to find Gwen, I promise. The police are looking for her, and Marco and Nicolo are going back over the route they took from Campo Barnaba this evening."

"They were at Campo Barnaba?"

"They met Stefania and Gwen there, and then they walked to Nicolo's friend's house."

Claire stood up. "I'm going over there."

"You don't want to wait here?"

"Campo Barnaba is one of the only places in Venice that might seem familiar to her. I think that's where she is."

The driver of the small motorboat turned off the engine after they entered the Rio Barnaba, and let the boat sidle quietly up to the *campo* steps. The square was bright under a waxing moon. The white facade of the Church Sant Barnaba, which took up most of the east side of the square, glowed with a ghostly luminescence. The moonlight made everything pale, silvery, and sharp; even her footsteps on the pavement sounded abrupt, urgent.

Giancarlo waited in the boat as Claire scanned the empty *campo.* The shops were all closed, and the umbrellaed tables of the Caffé Alfredo had been taken in for the night. What if Gwen weren't here? Campo Barnaba was Claire's only hunch. Claire felt fairly certain that Gwen would remember their conversation about it. Of course, she would have to have found it first . . .

"Claire?" Gwen's quavering voice came from somewhere within the arched doorway of the church.

Oh thank god. Relief flooded over her. "Gwen!" Claire rushed across the square. Gwen sat in the darkness, hunched against the cold stone wall. She looked up at Claire with a tear- and mascara-stained face. "Are you all right?" Claire asked as she knelt down next to her.

Gwen nodded slowly, sniffed, and wiped her nose on her sleeve. "I got lost."

"I know. You did right to stay here, though. It would have been harder to find you if you'd kept walking around."

"I was hoping you'd remember."

"I remembered. I'm just so glad you're all right. We were all really worried." Claire looked over to the motorboat. "Come on, why don't we go back to the hotel."

Gwen peered across the *campo.* "Is that Giancarlo in the boat?"

"Yes."

Her chin quivered and she made a little gasping sound. "I'm too embarrassed," she said as the tears started to flow once more.

"Gwen, what happened? Did Nicolo do something to upset you?"

"No, it's not his fault."

"Then why did you—"

"I just decided I wanted to go, that's all." Gwen began to cry in earnest. "I thought I would go back"—sob—"to the hotel"—gasp—"but then I got loooost . . ." The last word merged into a long wail, in which her eyes scrunched up and her mouth stretched into an open grimace, much like a disturbing Carnival mask Claire had seen.

She took a pack of tissues from her purse and gave one to Gwen. "I still don't understand why you left."

Incomprehensibly, Gwen began crying even harder: her chest heaved with violent sobs, interspersed with a strange sort of hiccuping. She wiped her nose with the tissue and turned to Claire, her lips trembling. "He doesn't love meeeee . . . ," she cried.

"Nicolo? But you've just met him."

"Not Nicolo. Tyyy-lerrrr." The scrunchy Carnival-mask face appeared again, along with a copious flow of tears.

"Tyler? Isn't he your boyfriend at home?"

"He's not my boyfriend. He made out with me and then he dumped me and he won't even talk to me and now he's going out with Tiffany Havermeyerrrrr . . ." She paused just long enough for a few gasping breaths. "Tiffany's really pretty and blond and skinny and everybody at school knows that he kissed me and then dumped me and then he started going out with her. But I just can't believe he likes her better than he likes meeeee," she sobbed.

"I'm sure that's only because he doesn't know you very well."

"He likes Tiffany 'cause she's older and she'll do more stuff."

"What stuff?"

"You know, sex stuff." Gwen took a few ragged breaths and the tears seemed to subside a bit.

"You mean he dumped you because you wouldn't—"

"He said I was too young and not experienced enough. I thought that maybe if I got more experience . . ."

"That's why you wanted to go out with Nicolo?"

"Not the only reason. I like Nicolo . . . but then we started kissing, and I started thinking about Tyler, and about how he was probably kissing Tiffany . . . like, they're probably making out all the time."

"You can't know that for sure."

"But that's what it seems like."

"Yes, I know what you mean," Claire admitted. How many times had she had to blot out a vision of Michael and Laura?

"And then I just started crying," Gwen said. "And I was embarrassed and I didn't want Nicolo to see me crying, so I left. And then I got looost . . ."

And we're back to where we started. Claire took a few more tissues from the pack. "Any guy who dumps you because you don't want to 'do stuff' is just an asshole."

"He is?" Gwen sniffed and wiped her eyes.

"Duh! You shouldn't have anything to do with him."

"But I'm in love with him." Gwen hiccupped and a small, high-pitched sob escaped her. "Why am I in love with an asshole?"

"Millions of women have asked themselves that very same question. I'm afraid there isn't a good answer for it."

"But I can't stand it if he'll never be in love with me, too."

"Oh, Gwen," Claire sighed. "I know it hurts. One of the most difficult things to learn is that you can be very much in love with someone and he might not love you back."

Gwen rubbed the last of the tears away. "Has that happened to you?"

"Yes."

"What did you do?"

"Left New York, changed schools, shut myself away, and buried myself in my work. But I'm not saying that was the right thing to do."

"So what's the right thing?"

"Maybe everyone has to figure that out for themselves. But right now I would say it's to . . . live life. Meet more people. Believe that there'll be someone else, because . . . because there just has to be."

"But what if there isn't?"

"I promise you there will be." Claire caught Gwen's eye, held her gaze. "I promise." She waited a moment, until Gwen nodded, almost imperceptibly. "You ready to go back?" Claire glanced over at Giancarlo and the waiting motorboat. "Come on, let's go for a ride. It's not a gondola, but it is a boat."

The Moon

3 March 1618

THE RIO DI Santa Ternita, where La Celestia had asked Alessandra to meet her, was a tiny canal near the Arsenale. Alessandra huddled inside the *felze* and tucked her hands inside her cape, her cheeks stinging with the cold, as Nico steered the gondola through the maze of dark, narrow waterways that were common in this part of the city. Light from the newly risen, waxing moon slanted across inky black water and sparkled off the gondola's silver *ferro* as the bow slowly turned. Alessandra raised her head and sniffed; the bitter smoke from the Arsenale's furnaces was always present here.

Her nerves felt raw, stretched to the breaking point. She hadn't slept and her day had been riddled with anxiety. Although she had successfully delivered the code book to La Celestia the night before, Antonio's arrival had unnerved her.

What if the viscount revealed his suspicions about her to the ambassador? She wanted to believe that Antonio would be discreet, but even his silence might not keep her safe. It was quite possible for Bedmar to realize on his own that more than the wine had been at work on him. Would he check to see if the book was missing? She worried that she had left something in his rooms out of place, and went over her actions in her mind. Had she closed the top of the chest, and locked it again? Had she returned the key to its proper drawer? Had she left the candle on the mantel, where she'd found it? Even though she had distinct memories of all these tasks, her fear rose to torment her, causing her to believe that she had overlooked some crucial detail. And tonight she had to retrieve the book from La Celestia and put it back. The thought of going through it all again filled her with dread; but if she did not, Bedmar would discover the robbery and her fate would be sealed. No, her only hope was to follow through with the entire scheme.

They turned into the Rio di Santa Ternita. The buildings seemed to close in on them as they penetrated farther into the canal, and the stark shadows grew deeper. Soon Alessandra saw La Celestia's gondola up ahead, moored to a post on the right. Nico let their boat drift to a stop directly behind it. The lantern at the front of the courtesan's gondola threw a circle of dull yellow light over the prow, but the craft appeared empty; Moukib was not at his post on the stern. Nico offered his hand to help Alessandra onto the *fondamenta,* and from there she stepped down into the bow of La Celestia's boat.

She drew back the curtains covering the *felze.* When she saw La Celestia, she smiled in spite of herself, overcome with admiration, amusement, even a little envy. Worry had kept Alessandra from sleeping so much as a wink, and here was La Celestia peacefully napping. Nestled in the shadows where the moonlight did not reach, the slumbering courtesan lay back against a group of plump velvet pillows, one arm elegantly arrayed across the cushions, as if she hadn't a care in the world.

Alessandra stooped to enter, then reached out and gently shook her arm. "La Celestia?"

The courtesan fell backward, parting the curtains on the other side of the *felze* and landing on her back on the floor of the boat, her face turned up to the sky. Alessandra screamed. Moonlight streamed down upon La Celestia's pale skin and the wide, bloody gash at the base of her throat, so deep it had nearly severed her head from her body.

Alessandra scrambled outside, panicked and afraid. Her scream had brought Nico running, and he stood on the *fondamenta* looking with horror at the sight of La Celestia's mutilated body. Drained of its life fluid, her skin was so pallid it appeared as cold and inert as marble. Nico held out his hand to Alessandra. "We must leave here at once," he insisted.

"Wait," she replied, remembering the book. She had to step over La Celestia's body to duck back under the *felze*. As she turned over the cushions, she realized with revulsion that they were soaked with the courtesan's blood. Her stomach heaved. She covered her mouth with her hand, quickly jerking it away again. Her palm was wet, her hands and her dress smeared with blood. It occurred to her that if the book were similarly soiled, it would do no good to return it. She kept looking, regardless, afraid to depart without it. Within a few minutes, she had searched the entire cabin. The book was not there.

A bone-deep fear settled into her. What on the surface appeared to be a random crime was not, Alessandra was certain; La Celestia had been murdered for the code book. Had someone wanted it badly enough to kill for it, or had Bedmar discovered the theft? If the marquis knew that Alessandra had stolen the book, why hadn't he come after her first? It was probably just a matter of time before he did, Alessandra realized. And not much time, at that.

"Who killed her?" Nico asked when he saw Alessandra emerge from the *felze*.

"The marquis, I believe, or one of his men. Unless someone paid off Moukib quite handsomely."

"Her gondolier? It wasn't him." Nico nodded at the entrance to a narrow alley leading off the *fondamenta* and Alessandra saw what she'd missed earlier. Moukib lay on the ground, his knees curled into his chest, a pool of blood forming a wide circle around him.

"He's dead," Nico said. "We must away. And you must take steps to protect yourself."

Calm yourself, Alessandra thought as Nico rowed the gondola into the Rio di San Martino, on their way to the *bocca di leone*.

It had been Nico's idea that she write a letter detailing what she knew of the Spanish ambassador's crimes and deliver it to the Great Council. She hadn't been able to think of anything better, although she wasn't exactly sure how it would help her. "It will save you from the noose," Nico had said; but would it save her from the marquis? If he could kill La Celestia, surely he could kill her, too. Nico had offered to deliver the letter himself, but Alessandra had insisted that it was her responsibility, even though the sinister maw that waited for her in the courtyard of the Doge's Palace filled her with foreboding.

Her hand went to the letter tucked inside the small pouch tied at her waist. Soon, the marquis would know who had exposed him, and her life would be in even greater danger. But her own safety was not her only concern. What of Antonio? His association with the ambassador and the duke of Ossuna implied that he was also a part of their plot, and yet she would not want him to be implicated. She hoped that the viscount was already gone from Venice, but even distance might not be enough to protect him. Venetian justice had a wide reach, and was rightly feared. Naples was well within the jurisdiction of the council's assassins.

But how could she do other than what she had set out to do tonight? If only to avenge La Celestia's murder, she would have taken this risk, but La Celestia had assured her that the Republic was in peril. It was Alessandra's civic duty to place the letter in the lion's mouth. If she failed, many more lives could be lost.

They turned into a waterway that circled west, toward the Piazzetta dei Leoncini. A single gondola with a red lantern at its bow glided slowly toward them. One of its occupants, an elegant courtesan with a feathered headdress, wet her rouged mouth with her tongue and held out her hand in silent invitation. After turning into a wide, bright canal, they were swallowed by the shadow of a bridge and disgorged again, and all at once there was music and light and laughter, a riot of color and costume, as the crowds along Calle Canonica pressed into the Piazza. Nico halted the gondola and exchanged a wordless look with Alessandra before she stepped onto the *fondamenta* and rushed away.

The Piazza was bright with torchlight, alive with music and festivity. Alessandra pressed through the crowds, a somber figure among the revelers. She summoned her courage and moved toward the Porta della Carta, the high archway that led to the palace courtyard, then abruptly stopped, startled by something that had caught at the edge of her vision.

Between the two great marble columns at the entrance to the Piazza San Marco, a dead man hung limply against a background of starless sky. His limbs were broken, his face bloodied, his bruised flesh barely covered by dirty, tattered rags. Not one of the many costumed revelers below took notice of him.

Stirred by a gust of wind, the hanged man turned slowly on the cord that had snapped his neck. Light from a bonfire below animated his blank, staring eyes; flickering shadows played across his mouth and turned his death's grimace into a grin. Alessandra stood transfixed, as it appeared that the hanged man was still alive. She imagined that he spoke to her: *It could be you at the end of this rope, if you do not deliver that letter . . . but here is the fate of the one you love if you do.*

I am damned with the Devil's own choice, Alessandra thought, shaking her head to rid herself of the illusion. Her step was slow as she walked toward the Porta della Carta, and slipped through the archway into the shadowed, silent courtyard.

Chapter Twenty-One

Claire was awake before sunrise. Working at the alcove desk by the light of a small lamp, she looked over her notes from the day before.

Alessandra's second diary, which they'd "liberated" from Andrew Kent the previous afternoon, hadn't yielded the sort of material she'd hoped for. What she needed more than anything else was some kind of link between Alessandra and one of the conspirators named in the Rossetti Letter, but every source she'd found so far led to a dead end. If only that Italian edition of Fazzini's *Diary* hadn't been destroyed. She was fairly certain that she could procure a copy of it through the Harvard Library once she got home, but that wasn't going to help her now. Yesterday, Claire had read the English edition once more and checked the dates of Fazzini's report of the courtesan's debut and Bedmar's mention of a party at La Celestia's, and deduced that they had both occurred sometime in June 1617. An interesting coincidence, but still it was a long, long leap to make from that to a connection between Bedmar and Alessandra, especially since Claire didn't have any evidence that La Sirena and Alessandra were one and the same.

And Alessandra herself wasn't helping at all. Her dairies were remarkably unrevealing, almost pointedly so. Alessandra's second diary seemed very much a continuation of the first, filled with the prosaic details of her daily life.

Had a pleasant visit from the charming Signora Bognolo, Claire read. *She asked for a donation to help educate the orphans of Santa Maria dei Dereletti; she hopes to begin a* sala di musica *there. I gave of a few ducats and two dresses . . .*

Claire hadn't had enough time to translate the entire diary but, knowing she was on borrowed time, she'd skipped through it and selected passages from throughout the book. Even in the days preceding the conspiracy's exposure and demise, there was nothing that referred to Bedmar, his cohorts, or to any suspicious activities. How could the conspiracy transpire right under Alessandra's nose and she not write about it? It was as if it hadn't even happened.

As if it hadn't happened. Claire sighed. Maybe Andrew Kent was right after all. Clearly he'd spent time in Venice before this, digging around and finding nothing that could be considered definitive evidence of a Spanish conspiracy. What had he said in his lecture, that history would tell lies? Perhaps he was right, and the historians who had previously related the tale of the Spanish Conspiracy were propagating a fiction, knowingly or not. It was a relatively commonplace occurrence: theories and even facts that had once been considered incontrovertible were found to be false, unfounded, and history was rewritten; that's what kept historians in business.

But hadn't Andrew Kent admitted that he was having trouble writing his book? Actually, he'd said the *outline* of his book—which meant he was a long way from finishing it, or even from coming up with a solid hypothesis. Claire remembered the frustration in his voice, but the glimmer of hopefulness that memory inspired was short-lived. If she couldn't find the evidence she needed to support her own telling of the Spanish Conspiracy, she'd have to revise her dissertation, and whether or not Andrew Kent wrote a book would be beside the point. Revising would mean another year of work, perhaps two, and unless she got a generous grant or yet another student loan, she wasn't sure that she could afford to keep going. She'd have to get a job before her Ph.D. was completed—what were the chances that she'd then be able to finish it?

Claire stretched, tried to push such depressing thoughts from her mind, and absently picked a postcard up from off the desk. It had a photo of the Lido's long, golden beach on the front, Gwen's handwriting on the back:

Dear Shannon:

Venice very cool after all. Met a boy named Nicolo, even cuter than T. Can't wait to tell you everything!

Claire placed the postcard writing side down again, as she had found it, and tried to remember being fourteen, when meeting a boy on a beach was just about the most exciting thing that could happen. Or maybe telling it to your best friend later was the best part. *Your best friend.* Claire had always had a best friend; ever since grade school, she'd had someone to tell "everything" to. Come to think of it, every woman she knew had someone to whom she told most of her secrets. Yes, of course. Every woman had someone.

It felt odd to be without Gwen, Claire thought as she climbed the gilded staircase to the Marciana. Funny how she'd so quickly become accustomed to having the girl loping along at her side. But this worked out best for both of them, as she still had a lot of work to do and Gwen hadn't been especially thrilled to spend another day in the library.

They were just about to go downstairs to breakfast when Stefania had called and asked if Gwen would like to come over for the day, explaining that she was grounded for getting home past her curfew the night before. Gwen was enormously relieved that Stefania didn't hold her responsible for her temporary loss of freedom, and was eager to rejoin her friend, no doubt to rehash the dramatic events of the previous evening. Before they left to go to the Baldessaris', Claire created a mini survival kit—a hotel business card, a map of Venice, a phone card, a guidebook, and a list of the police and emergency phone numbers—that she insisted Gwen keep with her.

"Stefania says her mom isn't letting us out of the house," Gwen protested. "I'm not pinning this to my shirt." She waved the small, safety-pinned slip of paper on which Claire had written the *biblioteca*'s phone number. "I'm not eight."

"Then keep it in your pants pocket."

Gwen rolled her eyes.

"In case you lose your backpack," Claire explained.

"I'm not going to lose—"

"In case someone steals your backpack."

"I don't think Stefania's mom is letting us out of her *room*. And by the way, Stefania says her mom doesn't know that she saw Marco last night, so don't say anything."

"How can she be so sure her mom doesn't know?" Claire didn't think much got past Renata, especially where her children were concerned.

"Because Stefania said if she knew, she'd be grounded for the rest of her life, not just two days."

But when they got to the Baldessaris' house, Claire had the distinct impression that, while Stefania's mother might be ignorant of the details, she'd come to an accurate conclusion about the general circumstances of the night before. Upon their arrival, the two girls had almost immediately dashed upstairs, leaving her alone with Renata, not a situation she had been anticipating with pleasure.

"Thanks for letting Gwen stay with you for the day," said Claire, aiming for the fastest conversational route to "good-bye." "It will make it much easier for me to work."

"It is nice for me, too. In fact, I encouraged it," Renata said. She sounded almost friendly; her antipathy toward Claire seemed to have been turned down a notch. Perhaps the problems of her youngest child had made her forget about the problems of her eldest. "I don't know if you know what it's like to have a fifteen-year-old moping about the house all day, but I can assure you, it's very unpleasant. I thought if Gwen came over, it might take Stefania's mind off the terrible tragedy that is her life," she said, with gentle sarcasm and a smile.

Claire smiled back. "I guess it's tough, being fifteen."

Renata laughed. "Apparently, it is terrible. But don't worry, they're not going anywhere, and I will be here as well. So there is no chance of anyone getting lost."

Oh yeah, she knew, Claire had thought.

After consulting Francesca, who assured Claire that she could have the necessary documents quickly brought from the archives, Claire walked out of the Marciana and to the Riva, and then through the front door of the Hotel Danieli. The second part of her plan would be considerably more difficult than the first.

At the desk, she asked the clerk to ring Andrew Kent. With any luck, he'd be alone and would agree to meet her in the lobby. It was bad enough that she was going to have to swallow some of her pride in order to talk to him. She certainly didn't want to do it in front of Gabriella.

"I'm sorry, he's not answering," the clerk said, hanging up.

"Do you know if he went out jogging, by any chance?"

"I haven't seen him this morning, but I just came on duty a few minutes ago. Why don't you try the restaurant?" He pointed to a wide doorway.

In the dining room, Claire found Andrew Kent seated alone, finishing a late breakfast and reading the newspaper, broken glasses set slightly askew on his face. "Good morning," she said.

"Oh. Hello." He took off his glasses and hastily put them in his pocket. "What are you doing here?"

"May I sit down?"

"Of course."

Claire launched in without preamble. "Have you ever thought about reading her letters?"

"Whose letters?"

"Alessandra's."

"I've read a few, but they don't seem to be of any consequence."

"Have you found anything in her diary that explains why she waited two months before revealing the conspiracy?"

"No. In fact, there doesn't seem to be much of anything at all in either one of them. For a courtesan who had some powerful lovers and who must have been privy to at least a few secrets and intrigues, the diaries are remarkably tedious. It's like reading the journal of a country wife. 'Planted squash in the garden on Tuesday.' 'Got fitted for a new gown to wear to the marchioness's party.' She goes to church every Sunday and always finds something illuminating in the service. But most important, nowhere in it did she write 'Spaniards plotting to overthrow the Venetian Republic.'"

"Did she write, 'Today the Council of Ten asked me to write a letter'?"

"No."

"The diaries don't support your conclusions at all, do they?"

"Nor yours."

"What if she didn't put anything important in them on purpose?"

Andrew downed the last sip of coffee. "I'm not following you."

"What if she wrote the diaries with the expectation that they would be read by other people? For instance, if she was ever taken to court, those diaries could be important evidence. Only thirty years before, Veronica Franco was charged with witchcraft by a former servant. Obviously it was a lie, but still she had to defend herself before a judge. Even though she was successful, it couldn't have been easy. Alessandra would have known about that. After all, the government was quite happy to have the courtesans about—they brought in millions of ducats in tax revenue every year—but courtesans didn't have the same legal protections as other Venetian citizens. Maybe the diaries were Alessandra's way of creating some protection. Anyone who read them would quickly see that she led a blameless life: no devil worship, no clandestine meetings, no impious thoughts. Even her lovers are never mentioned."

"So you're saying that she created a kind of smoke screen—a facade of propriety?"

"Either that, or she's the most insipid, boring, and abstinent courtesan who ever lived."

Andrew nodded thoughtfully. "That's very clever."

"Thank you."

"I meant of her."

"I didn't see you figuring it out," said Claire, a bit frostily. "Anyway, that's not what I came to tell you. The Marciana has twenty-eight letters that Alessandra wrote between January and March 1618."

"What do you expect to find in twenty-eight letters? In those days, people of consequence wrote two or three letters every day. How much do you think you're going to discover by reading twenty-eight?"

"But all of these letters were written to women."

"And your point is?"

"Every woman has someone she tells everything to, a confidante, a best friend. It could have been a friend from childhood, or another courtesan—but there's got to be someone."

"That may be so, but it doesn't necessarily follow that Alessandra wrote anything revealing to her confidante. Maybe she saved her secrets for when they were together."

"But it's possible. You have to admit that much."

"Yes, it's possible. But why are you telling me?"

"I thought you might want to work together on this."

His eyes narrowed. "Really? Why?"

If there was ever a time for womanly wiles, this was it. "Well, um, because you're the best," Claire began. "You're the expert on the conspiracy. Of course, you don't believe there was a conspiracy, or at least not a Spanish conspiracy, but you know what I mean. You were nice enough to tell me about the discrepancy in the Rossetti Letter. And I'm sure I could learn so much from working with you—"

"You can't translate twenty-eight letters in one day by yourself, can you?"

"No."

Andrew tossed his napkin on the table and stood up. "All right, then. Let's go."

Chapter Twenty-Two

CLAIRE AND ANDREW KENT sat across from each other at a table near the center of the library. Between them was a pile of over two dozen four-hundred-year-old letters, each encased in its own protective plastic sleeve.

Claire looked up from the letter she was translating—she was already certain that it was not the enlightening missive she was looking for—and stole a glance at her colleague. He was lost in concentration, eyes fixed on the document before him, now and then looking away just long enough to check his notebook and the translation that seemed to flow from his pen. He bit his lower lip as he worked, and occasionally, quite unconsciously it seemed, brushed an unruly lock of hair from his eyes or pushed his glasses farther up the bridge of his nose.

He'd put those glasses on with a look of pique, she recalled; she had been amused and even a little touched by this fleeting moment of vanity. Was it simply because they were broken, or did he think they made him seem older? Not that he was old; late thirties at most. His face was actually very nice, she thought as she considered it, even handsome, especially when he was unguarded and wasn't being pompous or critical. Like the way he'd looked last night, when he'd said . . . what he'd said. She wondered for a moment if he'd been drinking. Not that he had seemed intoxicated, but for the life of her, she couldn't imagine the man who was now sitting across from her saying anything like that to her ever again.

Amazing how he could sit only three feet from her and not notice her at all, she thought with growing irritation. She gazed steadily at his forehead and willed him to look up. He didn't. Well, it really shouldn't surprise her that he was immune to her silent yet undoubtedly mesmeric influence. They'd already spent half the day together and he hadn't said a word about why he'd said . . . what he'd said. In fact, he hadn't mentioned last night at all, hadn't even offered a neutral opening sally such as, "It was nice running into you yesterday evening" or "Thought any more about the Rossetti Letter?" or any such thing that might have eventually led to a conversation about his remark. It was as if he'd completely forgotten about it, indeed, as if it had never happened at all. Well, if he wasn't going to say anything about it, she certainly wasn't going to say anything about it. Maybe if she stared at him long enough, though, he'd look at her and say—

"You finished with yours yet?" he asked, briefly glancing up and making an impatient gesture toward the letter lying in front of her.

"Almost," said Claire brusquely, returning her attention to the letter and translating the remaining few words.

"Well?" He rubbed his forehead.

Claire cleared her throat and read from her notebook. "'Please send the velvet and the brocade over at once. The two muslin dresses are not required until after Lent. Also please advise about matching shoes for the velvet gown. Yours sincerely,' et cetera, et cetera." She flipped the letter over to look at the direction. "Simone Montecelli, on the Merceria."

"Her dressmaker."

"Apparently so. And yours?"

"'My dear Isabella,'" Andrew read, "'Such delight you afforded our grateful party on Tuesday—as you could see, my escort was entranced by the sumptuousness of your arrangements and the exquisite cuisine which you provided.

"'The program of entertainments was also quite diverting—tell me, where did you find so many talented dwarfs? Their antics were so amusing I thought I would break from laughter . . .' shall I go on?"

"No."

"I thought not. I think we can reasonably assume that this letter to the baronessa di Castiglione was written only to fulfill a social obligation."

"Still, either of these women could have been a close friend."

"A dressmaker?"

"Why not? Hairdressers are traditionally women's confidantes, why not a dressmaker?"

"You think that shopping list of dresses is somehow revealing?"

"No, but maybe there's another letter."

"Or, here's a thought. Perhaps it's in code," said Andrew, lowering his voice and leaning closer. "'Muslin dresses' actually means 'armed legions.'"

"That's very clever."

"Thank you."

"I meant of her. And making jokes is not helpful."

Andrew sighed and put his pen down. "I think we're wasting our time here."

"But we've only gotten through twelve letters so far." Claire sorted the stack of documents. "Instead of working on them in chronological order, why don't we see if one of these looks as though it's addressed to a friend instead of a tradesperson." She turned the letters over to study the recipients' names and addresses. "How's this sound? 'Signora Barberigo, Castello.'"

"Could be, I suppose."

Claire pushed the letter across the table. "How does it start?"

Andrew read through the first sentence, then translated it for her. "'I require two dozen of your finest confections . . .' Signora Barberigo is a baker."

"What about this one?" Claire took up another letter and read the name of the addressee. "'Signora Giovanna Donatella.'" She handed it to Andrew.

"But this is addressed to Padua, not Venice."

Claire thought for a moment. "In the first diary—the one written before the conspiracy—Alessandra mentions a cousin in

Padua. Maybe they grew up together in Venice. Maybe they were best friends. Then . . . they grow up, Alessandra becomes a courtesan, Giovanna gets married and moves away . . ."

"But they continue to tell each other everything?" Andrew finished for her.

"Yes, exactly!"

"You have a vivid imagination, don't you?"

"You say that as if there's something wrong with it."

"Only because our job is to discover the truth, not make it up."

"I'm simply putting forth a hypothesis. All we have to do is translate that letter and find out if there's anything to it."

Claire skimmed a few other letters while Andrew worked on the one to Padua. After twenty minutes or so, he stopped, looked up at her, and distractedly ran his fingers through his hair.

"Be prepared to be disappointed," he said, and pushed his notebook with the translation over to her.

She bent her head and read:

My dearest Giovanna:

My apologies for such a long delay between letters. My delight in receiving your last knows no bounds; such a journey they must make between Padua and Venice!

Alas, for the moment I have not plans for similar travail, but remain safe at home, wanting only the happiness your company brings.

My garden is my sanctuary, although it will not bloom until May. Now is the best time to be preparing the ground for what is needed: a pomegranate or pear tree for Nico, a strawberry plant and sunflowers for Bianca, and a wild climbing rose for myself.

More soon. Your loving cousin, Alessandra

"Not exactly gripping, is it?" Claire said.

"No."

"But it does establish that Giovanna is her cousin."

"Yes."

"You're just dying to say 'I told you so,' aren't you?"

"I wasn't going to use those words. But I must point out that this letter is dated March 1, 1618 . . . and please turn your attention to the second paragraph, in which she writes—"

"'I remain safe at home,'" Claire completed the sentence for him. Of course she had noticed it; Alessandra had written that she was "safe" during the very time that the conspiracy was gathering force. "Are you sure your translation's correct?" she asked, reaching across the table for the original.

"Of course I'm sure," Andrew replied, slightly offended.

"Perhaps she was lying, so that her cousin wouldn't worry about her."

"You're grasping at straws."

"There's another, you know."

"Another what?"

"Another letter to her cousin." Claire pushed it over to him. "I think we should translate this one, too."

"Meaning that I should translate it?"

"You're faster."

"You're not going to give up, are you?"

"No."

Andrew scanned the document. "This one's longer than the other. It's going to take a while."

Claire worked on a few of the shorter letters—like the others she'd already translated, they were related to the daily needs of the Rossetti household—until Andrew had finished with Alessandra's second letter to her cousin. He handed his translation to her with a sigh; evidently he wasn't finding much enjoyment in the courtesan's epistolary style.

My dearest Giovanna—

I long for the time when we shall meet; it has been too long since all of us were together. Months have passed since we were at Burano, have they not? Longer since summer in Marghera.

I recall pleasant childhood memories most often at night, and your family is what I think most of. It is a shame that it is yet March, and still three months to go before the sixth month, when we shall join together, with such transport of joy as befits such long-lost friends, for I often feel the loss of not being four cousins together.

I often regret that I have no dear sister, but that would only strain my allegiance to my favorite cousin, and you know well to whom I refer. Do not think this is a compliment, for it finds its source and its cause in your goodness. But I am not the only recipient of your gracious generosity—is it possible to count them all?

Until next we meet again, a kiss to you—Alessandra

"It's clear Alessandra was very fond of her," said Claire.

"Excessively, I'd say."

"But it doesn't help at all, does it?"

"I'm afraid not."

Claire studied the letter. It was dated March 5, 1618, only one day before the date of Alessandra's letter to the Great Council. Perhaps she should start thinking of that as her *alleged* secret letter; Claire's search for Alessandra's confidante had only helped to confirm Andrew Kent's version of events.

"What's this?" She pushed the letter across the table, and pointed to a strange mark under Alessandra's signature.

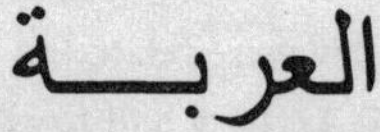

"I have no idea . . . blotting the quill, perhaps?" Andrew offered.

"I don't think so." Claire picked up the first letter. It was more smudged with time and less defined, but there was a similar dotted squiggle underneath her signature.

"It looks like—," Claire began.

"Arabic," Andrew said.

"You know how to translate Arabic, by any chance?"

"No. You?"

"No." Claire glanced around the library. "Maybe someone else in here knows how." She stood up.

"What are you going to do? Get up on the table and yell, 'Is there an Arabic speaker in the house?'"

"No, I'm going to ask Francesca."

"Who's Francesca?"

"The librarian."

"You really think she would know?"

"It can't hurt to ask."

Claire popped over to the counter, spent a moment huddling with Francesca, then sauntered back. She took the letters from the table and gestured for Andrew to follow her to the librarian's desk.

"Don't tell me, there really is someone?" he asked.

"Yes."

"Who?"

"Francesca."

Chapter Twenty-Three

"EVEN THOUGH THIS word, 'العربـــة,' is harder to read"—Francesca indicated the smudged Arabic word on the first letter—"the meaning is clearer. An *araba* is a wagon."

"A wagon?" asked Claire.

"An ancient wagon, a type that's been around since biblical times."

"What was it used for? Goats or livestock or something?"

"No, for transportation. It's a small wagon, pulled by donkeys. People stand up in it. It looks much like a chariot."

Claire exchanged a glance with Andrew, who looked as perplexed as she felt.

Francesca picked up Alessandra's second letter, dated March 5. "This one, 'النّاســك,' is a little more difficult to translate. It means someone who is alone . . . who is a loner. It also has a secondary meaning, which seems odd—someone who eats nothing but honey."

"Like John the Baptist," Andrew said.

"Yes, perhaps that's what it means—a wise man, a philosopher, or a kind of saint or sage, but most important, someone who lives outside of society." Francesca smiled apologetically. "That doesn't help much, does it? If you like, I can call the professor I studied with and ask her if she could look at this for you. She might be able to tell you more, but I don't know how soon she could do it, perhaps not until next week."

Andrew looked askance at Claire. This was your idea, he seemed to be saying, it's your decision.

"No, it's not necessary," Claire said to Francesca. "We thought . . . well, I'm not sure what we thought, but I don't believe another translation would make a difference."

They took the letters back to their table and sat down, silent and thoughtful. Claire was disappointed, even though she couldn't say for certain what she'd been hoping for. She felt a peevish frustration; the morning had started out so optimistically, but all their work had been a waste of time. Worse than a waste of time, actually; translating Alessandra's letters had only helped to make the hypothesis her dissertation was based on look rather flimsy. She wished she hadn't asked Andrew Kent to help her.

"You didn't really believe it was going to be some sort of code breaker, did you?" he asked.

How could he read her so easily? "I know it's far-fetched, but Venetians were known for the ingenious methods they used to encrypt their correspondence. And not just official government correspondence. Merchants used codes in their business letters, too, to protect their trade secrets and their financial transactions. Alessandra's father was a merchant. If she learned Arabic from him, she might have learned some encryption techniques as well."

"Yes, except that Alessandra's letters are not encrypted. If they were written in code, it would be obvious—it would all be gibberish."

"Encryption wasn't the only way to pass secret messages. The late sixteenth and the early seventeenth centuries were a time of intense intelligence gathering: Walsingham in England, Cardinal Richelieu in France, the Council of Ten here in Venice. A wide variety of methods were employed, and the spies—who often served as diplomats—were always looking for new ways to keep their secrets secure en route. And consider this: if Alessandra sent out a letter written in code, it would be obvious to anyone who intercepted it that it contained a secret message. Even if it couldn't be deciphered, it would still arouse suspicion, wouldn't it? Perhaps that was too risky. Perhaps she had to make them seem like normal letters."

"I think we've just officially gone through the looking glass of historical research. By your account, nothing is what it seems: the diaries are an elaborate hoax, and the letters contain what—invisible ink between the lines? Tell me, if we read the Rossetti Letter backward, will it say, 'Paul is dead'?"

"Now you're just being absurd."

"I'm being absurd?" Andrew picked up the letter dated March 1. "I don't know very much about ciphers, but I just don't see how this could be some sort of secret message—unless it was a huge anagram, which would have been enormously difficult to create."

"There were much simpler methods than that. For instance, some people used a template, which was essentially a piece of paper with holes cut out of it. When you placed the template over the letter, the words that showed through the holes comprised the secret message."

"So both the sender and the receiver had an identical template."

"Yes."

"And without it, it's not possible to decipher the letter."

"Not reliably. I admit I was hoping the Arabic word would be some sort of instruction."

"Like, read only the words beginning with *q*?"

"Something like that, I guess."

"But why put the key right in the letter?"

"Venice was a cosmopolitan city, but there couldn't have been that many people between here and Padua who read Arabic. Maybe she felt using a foreign language was disguise enough. But if it really is a key, then I suspect that this word, 'wagon'—and whatever the other word is—may have meant something only to the two of them. It could refer to something else that is actually the key."

"In which case, there's no way for us to uncover any code contained herein."

"No."

Andrew rubbed his chin thoughtfully. "I just remembered something . . . do you know the story about Sir John Trevelyan?"

Claire shook her head. "No."

"He was a royalist who was held prisoner in Colchester Castle after being sentenced to death by Oliver Cromwell. While he was there, he received a letter with a hidden message that told him how to escape. I think the method used was every third letter after a punctuation mark—when he put them all together it spelled out 'panel at east end of chapel slides.' He requested an hour of solitary meditation prior to his execution, and obviously used his arcane information wisely, as he made a successful escape and lived to tell the tale."

"I thought you didn't know much about codes."

"I don't, but I've always remembered that anecdote because it's one of the few instances in which we can say with certainty that prayer saved a man's life." He paused. "It's still a bit of a mystery, though. To this day, no one knows who sent Trevelyan the letter, or knows how he knew the encryption method."

"It sounds as if he knew the method in advance of receiving the letter, which may well be the case here." She looked at Alessandra's two letters and sighed. "Without the correct key, there's really no way to decipher them. We could try it a dozen different ways—the third letter following punctuation, the fourth letter following—and come up with a dozen different results. But we could never be sure if any of them were right."

"Or even intended, in the first place."

"Have you been humoring me?"

"No, I was honestly curious, and I like puzzles. It would have been exciting if we'd found something, wouldn't it? And it was a lot more interesting than reading her diaries." He glanced at his watch. "Good lord, it's after four already. What do you say to an extremely late lunch?"

"It really wasn't a bad idea," said Andrew as they stood at the bar of a tiny corner café a few blocks from the Piazza.

"What wasn't a bad idea?" Claire scanned the gleaming bottles of liqueurs and spirits along the back wall of the old-fashioned bar and wondered if she should try a shot of something with her ham and cheese *panino.* It might take some of the sting from her disappointment.

"Reading the letters."

"I don't know how you can say that. It didn't produce anything worthwhile, and we wasted a whole day."

"You had a hunch—a good one, I think—and you followed through on it. As for not producing anything—that's the way it happens, more often than not. I didn't think it was such a bad way to spend the day. I got to avoid working on my lecture."

"You mean you don't know what you're going to say tomorrow?"

"Not entirely, no. Like you, I had a hunch—that the Rossetti Letter wasn't exactly what it appeared to be—but I haven't found enough evidence to support it."

"What will you do?"

"Talk about what I know for sure, and hope that the Q and A will be brief." Andrew stopped to pull a ringing cell phone from his coat pocket. "Yes? Oh, hello," he said, with some surprise. "I'm sorry, I forgot to call you earlier. Did you have a good day at the conference?"

Gabriella, Claire guessed. She felt uncomfortable eavesdropping, so finished her cappuccino and wandered across the small lane to look in the window of the shop directly across.

"No, I spent the day in the Marciana . . ." His voice drifted faintly across the lane. "I'm going to work on it now. I'm afraid I won't be able to join you right away . . . perhaps later . . ."

Claire wondered how Gabriella would react to being stood up for the evening. Probably not well. Judging from the apologetic tone of Andrew's voice, not well at all. She peered through the shop window at a jumbled array of Venetian arts and crafts and New Age paraphernalia: carnival masks, string puppets, and perfume bottles from Murano were mixed with winged cherubs, Buddha statues, Asian gongs, and Tibetan prayer wheels. Meredith would like one of those perfume bottles, she thought, slipping through the curtain of beads that covered the doorway, and into the shop's patchouli-scented and slightly mystical atmosphere.

As Claire's eyes adjusted to the dimly lit interior, she scanned the small, one-room boutique for a display of perfume bottles, but her attention was caught instead by two colorful posters hanging on the back wall. At first, she was engaged by the medieval-style art; not until she walked closer did she realize that she was looking at reproductions of the sun and the moon cards from a tarot deck. Next to the two posters was a bookshelf filled with tarot decks of various design, and next to that, a third poster, which depicted, in smaller size, each of the twenty-two major arcana cards from the same medieval-style deck.

Of course. A smile spread across Claire's face as she turned and ran outside.

"Where'd you disappear to?" Andrew asked.

"Come with me." Claire beckoned, and Andrew followed her into the store.

"What's going on?" he asked.

"There." She led him over to the tarot posters, and pointed at the third one, with the twenty-two cards pictured on it. "It's from the tarot. Look at this." She pointed to a card in the second row from the top.

"'*Il Carro*,'" he read. "The Chariot."

"And this one," she said, pointing again, "the Hermit. Doesn't that fit Francesca's translation of *baran*?"

"Yes, I see, but how does knowing what the word refers to make any difference?"

"The cards are *numbered*." Claire pointed to the bottom of the two cards, where the numbers seven and nine figured prominently, then took a deck from the shelf and put it on the counter in front of the cashier.

Andrew understood her intention. "The library closes in twenty minutes."

"Then we'd better hurry."

Chapter Twenty-Four

"How do you want to begin?" Andrew asked. "Every seventh letter, or every seventh letter after a punctuation mark?"

They sat next to each other, Alessandra's two letters to her cousin and the tarot deck between them, the green glass lamps at each end of the table softly gleaming. Francesca worked quietly behind the counter, alone in the only other circle of illumination in the darkening room, her face aglow with the aquatic light emanating from her computer monitor. It hadn't been easy to persuade her to bend the rules to keep the library open for them, but in the end she had, somewhat reluctantly, agreed to give up a few hours of her Friday evening in support of their quest.

"Why don't we start with words instead?" Claire suggested. "Say, the seventh word in each line?"

"Not all of the lines have seven words."

"Just the ones that do, then."

He quickly wrote down the translation: *delay bounds and not wanting it time or for myself.*

"Even if the words were moved around, it doesn't seem like it would make much of a message, does it?" he asked.

"No," Claire had to agree. "What about every seventh word from the beginning?"

Again, it took only a few minutes for Andrew to translate: *such delight bounds between moments travail only garden not best for pear and climbing.*

Claire's heart sank. She'd felt so excited, so certain that the tarot cards held the key to the code. "Are you sure that's right?"

Andrew sensed her chagrin and looked at her sympathetically. "Yes, I'm sure. It's not newsworthy, but it is kind of poetic, isn't it?"

"Like a badly written fortune cookie."

"We can still try individual letters," he proposed.

Claire studied the document. *Talk to me, Alessandra.* "Try every seventh word without the salutation. Start here, at 'My apologies.'"

Andrew put pen to paper once more. When he was done, he sat back in his chair, his hand raking through his hair in a gesture of amazement.

"Oh my god," Claire whispered as she read what he'd written:

delay your journey Venice not safe your sanctuary may be needed: Nico, Bianca, myself.

Claire turned to him. "Are you sure that's right?"

"Are you going to ask me that often? Because if you are, you could do this by yourself, you know."

"I just want to be certain."

"That's every seventh word."

"But could it be some sort of fluke? A coincidence?"

"Let's look at the other letter."

Claire scrutinized the tarot cards spread on the table. "The Hermit is the ninth card."

"Nine it is, then."

She watched over his shoulder as he wrote.

Meet . . .

Marghera . . .

four . . .

With each new word, she felt her excitement increase; when the message was finally written out in its entirety, they looked at each other, stunned and perplexed.

Meet us at Marghera night of March sixth transport for four no allegiance to a cause only to a

"Only to a *what*?" Claire asked. She pulled the letter closer. "Where's the last word?"

"It's not there. Look," he said, pointing to the last line. "'*But I am not the* only *recipient of your gracious generosity—is it possible* to *count them all? Until next we meet again,* a *kiss to you—Alessandra.*' There are only four words after it, not nine."

"It doesn't make any sense. Are you absolutely *sure*—"

Andrew shut her up with a look. "Maybe the last line doesn't make sense, but the rest does. I should have realized before that the bit she wrote about 'summer in Marghera' was odd. No one ever spent more time in Marghera than was absolutely necessary; it wasn't a retreat like Burano. Marghera was just a dreadful little *terraferma* village where people hired boats to row them over to Venice. It was one of the main points of departure from the mainland, and the main point of entry, especially if one were going to Padua."

"And March sixth—that can't be a coincidence."

"Yes, the same date as the Rossetti Letter."

"Which does make sense. She drops the letter in the *bocca di leone,* then leaves town right away, because she knows as soon as the council reads it—"

"All hell will break loose."

"And she'll be in danger from Bedmar and his cronies. This is amazing. With these two letters, I'm sure I can prove that there really was a Spanish conspiracy, and that Alessandra was the one to expose it!" Claire's exultation came to an end as soon as she saw the expression on Andrew's face; it was rather as if someone had pulled a chair out from under him just as he was sitting down. Suddenly she didn't feel like gloating. "I'm sorry, I wasn't thinking."

"You have nothing to be sorry about," he said evenly. "One of us was going to be right, and the other was going to be wrong. Honestly, I've suspected for some time now that I was heading toward a dead end."

"Do you think Alessandra went to Padua?"

"This seems to indicate that, but we can't be sure this letter was received, or even sent. It doesn't have any postal markings, as do the others."

"And why transport for four?" Claire asked. "In the earlier letter, she mentions sanctuary for herself, Nico, and Bianca. Do you have any idea who the fourth would be?"

"No. I was wondering about that, too."

They traipsed over to the counter to retrieve their other materials. They looked in vain for Arabic words on the other letters, then Andrew cracked open Alessandra's second diary. "The last entry's dated March second," he confirmed. "So it's possible that she left town on the sixth."

"Or someone killed her."

"So now you're certain she was murdered?"

"Hoddy insisted that he read something in Fazzini about a courtesan being murdered around the time of the Spanish Conspiracy. It could have been Alessandra." Claire opened up Alessandra's earlier diary, hoping that at least some of it had been encrypted like the letters, then quickly snapped it shut, suppressing a strong desire to scream. She turned from Andrew and slowly opened the book just a little, as if she might see something different from what she'd seen the first time. No, it was no different.

Claire stood up and, carrying the diary, walked a few paces toward the librarian's counter, then peered hard at the shelves on the wall behind it. The place where her books and documents had been held was completely empty; so was Andrew's. She looked back to the table: no, there was nothing on it that looked like the diary she held in her hand. She walked over to the wall of windows where there was more light and opened the diary again.

Instead of Alessandra's spidery script, Gwen's round, girlish handwriting met her eye. *. . . I saw T. today after algebra, he said hi hope everything's cool with you. He was wearing that blue shirt . . . Horton gave us so much homework today . . . T. sat at my table at lunch he was with his friend Danny . . . T. is the cutest boy I've ever . . .*

She snapped the diary shut again and turned around. How in the world had Gwen's diary ended up in place of Alessandra's? Claire thought back to the day before, when Gwen had switched Alessandra's two diaries for the second time, as Andrew was leaving the library. After Gwen had returned the diary they'd taken from him, she'd slipped Alessandra's first diary into her backpack. Claire hadn't asked for it until they were leaving, then she'd added it to her stack of books and given it back to Francesca. Gwen must have had this, her own diary, in her backpack, also—and had mistakenly handed it to Claire. Gwen's and Alessandra's diaries were just close enough in appearance that no one had noticed the mix-up. Unfortunately, this meant that Alessandra's first diary was still in Gwen's backpack.

It was an exceptionally bad place for a four-hundred-year-old book owned by the Italian Republic. Claire imagined it crammed in among the chocolate candy and the sticky tubes of hair gel and lip gloss; it would probably sustain more damage during its few hours in Gwen's backpack than in the previous three hundred years of its existence. The only thing worse would be if she had somehow lost it. And who was going to believe that they'd taken it out of the Marciana by accident? What had Andrew said—steep fines and a lengthy imprisonment?

Claire found herself back at the table, standing over Andrew, Gwen's diary gripped tightly in her hands.

He looked up. "Haven't found anything new so far," he said. "No Arabic words, anyway. Anything interesting in that one?"

"Just the same old boring stuff," Claire said with a little laugh, which sounded unnaturally shrill to her ears. She hid the diary behind her back. Andrew looked at her strangely. "May I borrow your phone? Need to call Gwen," she explained.

"Haven't you called her three times today already?"

"I told her I would check in again."

He gave her his cell phone and she backed away from the table. "Don't want to disturb," she added, turned and sprinted to the library door, then went out into the hall.

Claire felt somewhat calmer once Gwen had confirmed that Alessandra's diary was where she had thought it was, but she hadn't expected Gwen to be so opposed to the plan she suggested.

"But it's my diary! I don't see why you have to leave it there."

"Because if I don't, someone might notice that Alessandra's diary is missing. Not a word to Stefania about this, okay? It's only for one night. We'll bring Alessandra's diary back first thing in the morning and switch them."

"I don't want anyone to read my diary."

"No one's going to read it, not even me."

"'Cause it's personal," Gwen went on. "Personal and private."

"Yes, I understand." She didn't add that she couldn't be less interested; no doubt the whole diary was filled with stories of her beloved "T." T for Tyler, of course. *T for Tyler.*

"Gwen, I have to go," Claire said. "I'll be over there to pick you up in an hour or two, okay?"

"But, Claire . . ." Gwen stopped, and Claire heard Stefania's voice in the background. "Stefania says that Giancarlo called. He left a message for you at the hotel."

"I'll call him," Claire said distractedly. "See you soon."

T for Tyler. Claire felt strangely lightheaded with the beginning of an idea so shattering it hadn't quite formed into words yet. *No allegiance to a cause, only to a . . .* If she was right, it would change everything, her own theories and Andrew Kent's. Earlier accounts of the Spanish Conspiracy would be turned upside down, around, and be regarded in an entirely new light. *No allegiance to a cause only to a . . .* If she was right—and she had a sudden certainty that she had never been more right about anything . . .

She rushed back to the table where Andrew was still working and picked up Alessandra's letter of March 5. She read it through once, quickly, but that was all she needed.

"It's not 'a' cause," she said.

Andrew looked up from the manuscript he was reading. "What?"

"The Italian word for 'a' is '*un.*' What if this isn't meant to be read as a word, but as initials? 'No allegiance to UN's cause, only to UN.'"

"U N . . ." Andrew mused. She could almost see the gears turning. The light of comprehension was just beginning to dawn in his eyes when she spoke.

"Utrillo-Navarre." Claire took the chair next to him, and they looked at each other steadily, as the implications of what she had said settled over them.

"Alessandra knew Antonio Perez," Claire said quietly. She looked at the letter once more. *Allegiance only to un.* "Not only did she know him, she was in love with him."

Chapter Twenty-Five

"IT EXPLAINS HOW she knew about letters between Ossuna and Bedmar," Claire said. "We know that Utrillo-Navarre was one of their messengers—among other things. This could also explain why she waited until March to expose the conspiracy. The two-month discrepancy in the Rossetti Letter."

"Yes, perhaps she delayed until she could arrange their escape from Venice," Andrew agreed.

"Utrillo-Navarre must have been the fourth person in their party. She's saying as much to her cousin—'allegiance to UN'—as if to warn her in advance that she's not giving aid to the enemy—"

"But to her lover. Except that we know their escape didn't turn out as planned, did it?"

"No," Claire said. "I'd hoped for a happier ending."

"Falling in love with Ossuna's swordsman may have precluded that. What if she didn't know what Perez was? What if she never made it to Marghera?"

"I thought of that, too."

"There is another possibility, although I know you won't like it," Andrew said. "This could have been an elaborate ruse of Alessandra's. She feigns love, offers to help him escape—and all the while, she's planning to betray him."

"You're right, I don't like it. For one thing, it doesn't add up. Why bother writing a message in code—'allegiance to UN'—if she didn't sincerely care about him?"

"I only say it because"—Andrew sifted through the documents on the table until he found the Rossetti Letter—"because this letter doesn't seem as if it were written in haste. Certainly not like something written by someone who was planning to leave Venice the same day."

Claire remembered thinking something similar, when she'd read it. Her thoughts whirled: Alessandra, Antonio Perez, Bedmar, Ossuna, Silvia, the letter. She reached for the large, morocco-bound *Great Council Minutes, March 1618* and turned to the entry for March 6: *Alessandra Rossetti, bocca di leone Palazzo Ducale.* Something clicked.

"Andrew, isn't there another *bocca di leone* in the Doge's Palace? Besides the one in the courtyard, I mean."

"I think there's one in the Sala della Bussola, the compass room."

"Isn't that right next to the Sala de Trei Capi?"

"Yes."

Claire sat back in her chair, silent and thoughtful. She didn't like what she suspected, or how this last piece of the puzzle changed the picture. As she told her version of events to Andrew Kent, she watched his expression become increasingly solemn.

"Yes, I see," he said, when at last she was finished. "So you're saying we were both wrong."

"And both right, too," she added.

Outside Caffè Quadri, a classical octet played American standards as Claire and Andrew slowly walked through the Piazza, heading for the Baldessaris'. Claire was going to pick up Gwen; Andrew hadn't said precisely, but she suspected that he was meeting Gabriella there.

Along with the music, the air buzzed with the constant murmur of conversation from the crowded tables outside Caffè Quadri and Caffè Florian. The Basilica was ablaze with light, its jumble of spires and domes haloed against the night sky. Directly above them, small, sharp stars glittered.

This is my last night here, Claire thought. I can't believe it's almost over. "I've seen so little," she said.

"Pardon?"

She hadn't realized she'd spoken out loud. She felt her face flush. "Just sorry that I have to leave tomorrow."

"Me, too. It is amazing, isn't it?" With a slight movement of his head he managed to indicate the Piazza and, by extension, all of Venice. "Although 'amazing' doesn't really do it justice. Whenever I try to describe Venice, I always end up speaking in clichés."

"Before I left Harriott, I'd read that Venice was 'magical' or 'like a fairy tale' so often that I had begun to believe that the Venetian Tourist Board had discovered a way to brainwash people on their way out. And then I arrived here and found myself thinking, 'It's magical—like a fairy tale.'"

"Perhaps they brainwash people on the way in."

"So much for originality, anyway. But what strikes me most is how intense and alive it is—and how sad it would be if it were turned into a museum-city, as some people have suggested."

"I agree, that would be a shame."

They continued walking toward the west end of the square and soon left behind the light and sound of the Piazza for the small, shadowed streets of San Marco. They'd been walking along in companionable silence when Andrew suddenly said, "I believe I owe you an apology."

Claire looked up at him, surprised. "For what?"

"The day we met at the airport. I think I may have been rather . . . ah . . . rude."

"I hardly noticed," she lied.

"Now you're not only goading me, you're lying. You were just as bad in return—all that blather about the Italian police. Hah." Andrew sounded miffed, but he wore a crooked smile.

"Would I really have been taken away by the militia for trying to go through the EU line?" Claire asked.

"I haven't any idea. I've never seen an American try to sneak through it before."

"Oooh! And you said!"

"That's why I'm apologizing. I know I behaved badly, but there were extenuating circumstances."

"Such as?"

"I'd just spent two days in Amsterdam, where I was giving a seminar. When I arrived, I discovered that my luggage had gone to Athens instead, and later I found out that my hotel room was in the midst of an entire wing of vacationing Bulgarians, who apparently slept all day, since they spent the entire night crashing beer steins together and singing. Then, on the plane here, the fellow next to me broke my glasses."

"On purpose?"

"I don't know how it happened exactly. He must've got up, I fell asleep, took them off and put them on his seat without even knowing it, then he came back, and—"

"He sat on them?"

"I'm afraid so. By the time I arrived here, I'd had almost no sleep, I'd been wearing the same clothes for three days, I couldn't see very well, and I was about to give a lecture based on a book I was writing except that I hadn't written it because I couldn't figure out how. So . . . I am sorry, but I hope you'll understand."

"I do understand. My trip here wasn't all that pleasant, either."

"I should have realized."

"It's okay. Your apology is accepted, as long as you'll accept mine for that 'horse's ass' remark."

"Of course. But I must say, no one's ever insulted me in Latin before. It was rather intriguing. Tell me, do you only curse in a dead language?"

"No, I can swear like a sailor in Greek, as well."

"So you're fluent in the classic languages?"

Claire shook her head. "I only know the expletives."

"Really? How does one learn just that? Is there a book, or a CD or something?"

"No, there's no book," said Claire, laughing. "But it's easy, really. Just marry a classics scholar and you can learn only those words and phrases you find truly indispensable."

Andrew looked perplexed. "So, your . . . husband? . . . is a . . . ?"

"Ex-husband," she corrected him. "He's an assistant professor of ancient history at Columbia." *And his girlfriend has an office down the hall.*

"That's a rather marginal skill, though, isn't it, knowing how to swear in Greek and Latin?" Andrew said. "Although I suppose it could be quite useful if you're ever in Athens—"

"Or in ancient Rome," Claire pointed out.

"Indeed." He paused. "What are you planning to do once you get your degree?"

"I'd like to teach. Ideally—in my wildest fantasy, I suppose—I would be a professor at Harvard."

"Any chance of an offer?"

"Oh, no. It's almost impossible to get a job there. It's just that my ex was hired at Columbia, and it's a big deal, really, very prestigious . . ."

"And you wanted to show him up."

"Yes. Silly, isn't it? I'll probably end up at some little college in the Midwest."

"I don't think it's silly at all. I'm sure you'll be an excellent teacher. You certainly got through to your—is she your niece?—with that story about Casanova."

"Thanks. Gwen isn't my niece. I'm her chaperone." Claire could see that a clarification was necessary. "Gwen's parents needed someone to bring her to Europe for a week, and I wanted to attend this conference but couldn't afford it, so we struck a deal."

"Do you act as a chaperone often?"

"Isn't it obvious that this is my first time?"

"On the contrary, you seem to be doing fine. Well, apart from allowing her to become inebriated on the plane."

"I didn't allow it! I fell asleep, and she wandered off."

"Trouble, is she?"

"She's a teenager. I think trouble is considered 'age appropriate.'"

"I have a nine-year-old boy who's already more than I can handle. Please don't tell me it's going to get worse."

"I'm sorry to be the bearer of bad news, but things get pretty complicated when adolescence hits."

"In my experience, they're complicated right from the start."

"So you wouldn't describe your son as sweet, shy, and perfectly normal?"

"Stewart? I can honestly say that he's completely and absolutely none of those things."

"What do you do with Stewart when you travel?" As soon as she asked the question, she realized that Andrew would know she'd been talking to Hoddy about him. How else could she know that he was a widower?

Thankfully, Andrew simply gave her a brief, inscrutable look and ignored the slight faux pas. "He stays with my parents."

"Do you worry about him?"

"I do worry . . . but not about Stewart so much as about everything within a five-mile radius of him. At the moment, I'm worried about my parents . . . their house . . . their car . . . their dog. To quote one of his tutors, Stewart has a great capacity for mayhem."

"Mayhem?"

"The staff at Stewart's former school voted him 'Most Likely to Build a Nuclear Bomb in His Own Basement.' Of course I told them that I was careful to keep the plutonium in a very high cupboard, well out of his reach, but they suggested that we find another situation for him."

"Your son was kicked out of elementary school?"

"Not kicked out exactly, but it was agreed that it would be better for Stewart, and for everyone else, if he were in a different learning environment. And it's true, he's much happier now. He's at the university."

"Cambridge has a school for children?"

"No, actually, he's attending the university—Trinity College, my alma mater."

"I thought you said he was nine."

"He is."

"And he's attending Cambridge?"

"With tutors, of course."

"Of course."

"Well, you see, he's, ahh, well, he's considered advanced for his age."

"He's a genius."

"Apparently so."

"You must be very proud."

"Yes, although since he became passionately interested in rocket science, it's difficult to distinguish between pride and fear for one's life." Andrew stopped at a wrought-iron gate. "Here we are." He opened the gate to the Baldessaris' courtyard; they walked through it to the front door and knocked.

Andrew turned to her. "You know, what you said that night in the restaurant meant a lot to me."

"What did I say?"

"How even the smallest stories were important, if they provided some insight into humanity."

"You mean I wasn't making a fool of myself?"

"Not at all. I'd been so discouraged with this book, and with my work, and I'd begun to feel that it was meaningless. You were so passionate, you reminded me of how I felt when I first started."

"I did?"

Andrew moved closer. "I was thinking . . . are you going to be at my lecture tomorrow?"

"Of course."

Just as Andrew opened his mouth to speak again, the door opened. Gabriella stood in the doorway. Her thousand-watt smile dimmed noticeably when she saw Claire. It gave her an odd feeling, as if Gabriella had interrupted an intimate moment, even though they'd been doing nothing more than standing there talking. Gabriella had that same sort of radar that Renata did, and at the moment it was set on full power and trying to detect any sign of closeness between the two of them. Of course there was nothing to detect, but Claire had a feeling that it wouldn't matter. She knew at once that she'd managed to ensure Gabriella's lifelong enmity, just by showing up on the doorstep with her boyfriend.

"Darling!" Gabriella said to Andrew, taking his arm as they stepped inside. "And, Carrie, what a surprise."

"We were both at the library all day," said Andrew, by way of explaining their combined presence at the Baldessaris', "and Claire needed to come over to pick up her—charge—so . . ."

Good lord, Claire thought, he's just making it worse. He actually sounds guilty. Maybe he could sense that radar, too, although in Claire's experience men never seemed to notice when a woman was metaphorically hanging a big "Hands Off" sign around their necks.

"It's the funniest thing," he went on, "Claire happens to be working on the Spanish Conspiracy, too . . ."

No, he hadn't noticed at all. Gabriella's eyes gleamed with proprietary fervor and a smoldering animosity. Thanks very much, Andrew, Claire thought. Good thing she was leaving tomorrow and wouldn't see either of them again; she suspected that the receiving end of Gabriella's wrath was a very dangerous place to be.

Chapter Twenty-Six

"I DON'T SEE why you're so worried," said Gwen as she and Claire hurried across the Piazza.

"A few years in prison is a pretty good reason to be worried." A flock of pigeons turned in the air above them, and a flurry of argent wings glinted in the sunlight. They'd gotten a late start this morning, and the Piazza was already filling with tourists. They had only about five minutes in which to switch the diaries at the Marciana, if they were going to get to Ca' Foscari in time for Andrew Kent's lecture.

"Why didn't you come over to Stefania's yesterday and get it?"

"By the time I realized what had happened, it was too late. The library was already closed—officially, anyway. I wouldn't have been able to put it back."

"I think a judge would understand that it was just a funny accident."

"What did you do yesterday, study for the bar? I hate to contradict you, but I don't think judges are swayed by 'funny.' Although," Claire said, smiling slyly, "it occurs to me that if you took the fall for me, I could probably beat the rap."

"Huh?"

"You're a minor, so they couldn't put you in prison. They'd probably just garnish your allowance for the next twenty or thirty years. You'd do that for me, right?"

Gwen snorted. "I beg to differ."

Claire grabbed the handle to the *Marciana*'s front door and pulled, but it didn't budge. It was locked, she discovered after a few more unsuccessful tugs. For the first time, Claire noticed a gold plaque on the wall near the door, with an engraved list of the library's hours on it: it didn't open until eleven on Saturdays. Claire stifled an urge to speak loudly in Greek and Latin.

"We're going to have to come back later," she said.

"But my diary!" Gwen protested.

"No one is going to read it," Claire assured her. "No one is even going to touch it. But we can't wait here for the library to open or I'll miss the entire lecture."

Ca' Foscari's grand salon was packed; every seat had been taken by the time Claire and Gwen arrived, and people stood around the periphery of the room. They found a space near the front, to the right of the stage. Not far away, Maurizio, Gabriella, and Andrew Kent stood closely together, conferring in low voices. He'd looked at Claire only once, when she'd first walked up to the front and settled against the wall, but hadn't smiled or acknowledged her. It was probably just as well, she thought, with Gabriella standing right there. She wondered if he'd had time to pull his notes together and write his lecture, or perhaps he was confident enough to speak extemporaneously. Would he use what they'd discovered yesterday, or would he stick to the research he'd done before? She realized that she felt a bit nervous for him; there were an awful lot of people here. That the lecture was starting late only added to the general feeling of anticipation.

Claire occupied herself by looking around for Giancarlo. They'd spoken by phone the night before, after she and Gwen had gotten back to the hotel. As soon as Claire had left the Baldessaris', she'd known that she wasn't up for another evening out. Happily, Giancarlo had understood her desire for a quick dinner, a leisurely bath, and a long night of sleep. They had agreed to meet here, at Ca' Foscari. She and Gwen didn't have to leave for the airport until five, so there was plenty of time for lunch and sightseeing. She was wondering how she would explain a quick but necessary trip to the Marciana as Maurizio Baldessari walked onto the stage.

"Welcome everyone to Andrew Kent's second lecture on the Spanish Conspiracy against Venice," he said, "or, after Tuesday's lecture, what might hereafter be known as the Venetian Conspiracy against the Spanish." Gentle laughter rose from the audience. "He has quite a bit of material to cover, so he tells me, and has asked me in the interest of brevity to dispense with the formal introduction. So without further ado, Andrew Kent."

Andrew stepped up to the podium and thanked the applauding audience. "On Tuesday I finished my lecture with a quote from Shaw: 'History, sir, will tell lies, as usual,'" he began. "But of course it's not history per se that tells lies, it's people who tell lies. When we try to piece together the truth of an event such as the Spanish Conspiracy from four hundred years on, it's helpful to remember that the patina of time does not make the written word any more reliable. Even more so than usually, we must not take everything we read at face value.

"Reading between the lines, finding the motivations and reasons behind the bits of printed matter we have left to us requires skills we don't often think about as research skills, precisely, although we use them all the time to a greater or lesser degree: hunch, intuition, even imagination.

"Researching the Spanish Conspiracy has put these skills to the test, but only in the past week have they been rewarded. These latest discoveries are going to upset a few apple carts, one of which is my own. Was it a Spanish conspiracy or a Venetian conspiracy? The answer to that question is more complicated than I had thought. But as it turns out, I'm not the person most qualified to explain it."

Andrew turned away from the microphone and looked at Claire. Along with everyone else, she waited for Andrew to continue speaking; instead, he beckoned for her to come up on stage.

Claire shook her head vigorously. Andrew looked at her quizzically, and summoned her on stage once more. The people in the audience, curious and restless, murmured and craned their necks to peer in Claire's direction. Everyone was beginning to realize that something strange was going on. Wasn't Andrew Kent giving this lecture?

"One moment, please," Andrew said, then strode across the stage, down the steps, and over to Claire. By the time he reached her, the room was buzzing with whispers. Gabriella looked on with surprise and thinly disguised hatred.

"Come up to the stage with me," he said calmly. "I'll introduce you, then you can give the lecture, all right?"

"I'm not sure I can."

"I thought you wanted to be a professor. You'll be lecturing all the time."

"That may be true, but the first time I spoke in public, I fainted."

"You can't be serious."

"Completely. I passed out."

"So you're a little gun-shy, are you? Well, that won't do at all. I'm sure you've heard about getting back on the horse and all that."

"Yes, but—"

"All you have to do is tell the story just like you told it to me last night. I promise you, you're not going to faint."

"How do you know?"

"You'll have to trust me on this. If you forget something, just look at me and I'll prompt you." His gaze was calm and encouraging.

If she could give a lecture to such a large crowd, she reasoned, facing Hilliard would be a breeze. She nodded her assent and handed her tote bag to Gwen. She followed Andrew across the floor, her palms damp, her mouth suddenly as dry as if she'd swallowed sand.

As the two of them stepped up to the stage, the murmuring in the room swelled and seemed to combine with the buzzing in her head. She watched as Andrew returned to the podium and introduced her, but didn't comprehend a thing until he turned toward her, smiling, and then she sensed the sound of applause, as if from a great distance. It was as if it were all happening in a slow-moving dream, the kind of dream from which you awoke with your heart beating wildly, and struggling for air.

Claire stepped up to the podium, the audience a rustling, blurred mass in front of her. She gripped the edges of the stand to steady herself, then looked to the right of the stage: Giancarlo was there, standing with Maurizio, Andrew, and Gwen. He smiled warmly as he caught her eye, but Claire couldn't look at him for long; he just made her feel more nervous. Gabriella, standing next to him, didn't appear angry anymore; instead, she seemed her usual self-satisfied self, her arms folded across her chest and a complacent, even pleased look on her face. She's sure I'm going to embarrass myself, Claire thought. In fact, she's counting on it. Well, she decided, she wouldn't give her the satisfaction.

Claire turned to the audience in front of her. One hundred faces looked back, quiet, expectant. She moved her mouth closer to the microphone and felt the strange sensation of her lips brushing its perforated surface, smelled its tangy metallic scent.

"The Rossetti Letter—," she said, and her voice resounded around the room, startling her with its volume. Her head jerked back momentarily; then she regained her composure and began again.

"The Rossetti Letter lies at the center of the Spanish Conspiracy," she said. "For four hundred years, it's been considered a cornerstone of the case against the Spaniards in the conspiracy of 1618; recently, however"— she glanced in Andrew Kent's direction— "this assumption has been challenged. Did Alessandra Rossetti write it to expose the Spanish Conspiracy or to create the Spanish Conspiracy? The following account should answer that question."

The Devil

3 March 1618

ALESSANDRA TURNED AWAY from the hanged man and slipped into the courtyard of the Doge's Palace. She walked slowly around the perimeter, keeping to the shadows near the walls. As she moved away from the Piazza, the torches lighting the courtyard grew scarce, and the sounds of Carnival faded to an indistinct but steady roar that echoed faintly inside the stone quadrant.

Set into the wall at shoulder height in the courtyard's far corner, the bronze plaque of the *bocca di leone* shone dully in the dim, flickering light. Its relief depicted not a lion's but a man's face captured in a grotesque grimace, his eyes wild with pain, his mouth a black chasm. She ran her fingers over the engraved words below it and read the inscription: *For secret indictments against those who commit crimes, or collude to hide their income.*

She reached into her purse for the letter. Where would it go, she wondered, once she fed it to this gluttonous orifice? Far below in the bowels of the palace, was there a man seated in a frigid cell who waited for communiqués such as this to fall into his lap? More likely her letter would fall into a locked box, and would not be collected until morning.

She turned the letter over and brushed her thumb across the raised wax seal. She knew she had no choice but to drop it into the lion's mouth; if she did not, La Celestia's murderer might never be brought to justice, and the possible consequences to Venice were too terrible: the sacking and pillage of the city, hundreds dead, the Republic under the rule of the Spanish king. Half the populace of Venice would be considered heretics, and she would be among them: a burning pyre would be her end.

And yet she hesitated. What would happen to the viscount? The fearsome prophecy of the hanged man resounded in her ears: *If you deliver that letter, here is the fate of another.* But surely he would not be harmed by her disclosures; she wasn't even certain that he was involved in Bedmar's plot. Yet she could not deny the terrible feeling that if she dropped the letter in the lion's mouth, she was sealing Antonio's destiny as well as her own. The consequences of her letter would, in one way or another, divide them forever.

All at once the letter was plucked from her fingers and a man's hand covered her mouth. It happened so quickly she had no time to gasp with surprise. Her attacker wrestled her arms behind her back, gripping her wrists in one strong hand. He then took his hand away from her mouth, but the relief she felt was fleeting, for instantly the steely point of a knife pressed sharply against her ribs.

"This is aimed at your heart," he said. "If you cry out, you will be dead within seconds."

They traveled far from the city center, snaking through the labyrinthine canals of Cannaregio, journeying into the secret, sordid neighborhoods of Venice, where the darkness grew ever darker and each canal shabbier and more sinister than the last. A place where the groups of armed citizens who patrolled the city streets during Carnival refused to go, and gangs of cutpurses hid beneath bridges. Menacing shadows crept alongside them as they cautiously progressed through the ever more turbid waterways.

He'd bound her wrists with rope as soon as she was seated in the gondola. He sat next to her on the cushioned bench, his arm in a relaxed curve behind her, but his hand still gripped the sharp blade with which he had threatened her. His face was covered, like her own, by a Carnival mask. Of course she knew who he was, and had known, from the moment she heard his voice in her ear. Her second impression was equally certain: *He means to kill me.*

He hadn't said a word throughout the entire journey. Alessandra was silent, too. She did her utmost to remain calm and take stock of her situation and turned to look at the gondolier standing behind them. He was one of the marquis's *bravi,* of course, surly, squat, and bald, with a grisly scar in the place where his left eye should have been. She judged that he was shorter than herself, but he appeared as though he were chiseled out of stone. With every stroke of the oar, his arms seemed to swell to twice their normal size. A former galley slave, Alessandra guessed. No chance she'd be able to defend herself against one of these men, much less two. She couldn't throw herself over the side, either, not with her wrists bound, not while wearing this heavy costume. She'd drown before she could swim away. She glanced down at the dark, viscous water of the scum-covered canal. If it was her fate to drown, at least let it be in the lagoon, she thought, not here.

She didn't know if it was stupidity or pride that kept her from begging for her life; perhaps it was both. Half her mind held foolishly to the belief that her captor intended her no harm, that there was some other purpose in this scheme; the other half, the rational half, knew that he was capable of murder. But was he capable of killing her? If that were true, then she would not, could not, give him the pleasure of seeing her beg for her life. She would rather die.

"Here," he finally uttered, pointing to a crumbling archway. They glided through the portal and into the low-ceilinged ground floor of a small, decrepit house. He took a lantern from under the gondola seat, lit it with a wick from the lantern on the bow, then yanked Alessandra to her feet.

He pulled her from the boat and across a stone floor, then up a flight of stairs. The door at the top was weathered and warped, and he opened it with a violent shove. Gripping her by the arm with one hand, carrying the lantern with the other, he guided her through it and along a narrow corridor until they came to what looked to be the main room, dark and shabby though it was.

The few sticks of furniture were covered in dust and the heavy window coverings were moth holed and moldy. It was clear that no one lived there; possibly no one else had entered in years. If he left her body there, Alessandra thought, chances were that by the time she was found, there'd be nothing remaining but bones.

He set the lantern down and took off his mask. Then he reached out and lifted Alessandra's mask from her face and pulled it over her head. For a moment he said nothing, just leaned against the table in a relaxed manner and turned her mask over in his hands. She was instantly aware of his confident strength, his restrained power. He acted nonchalant even though he was not, she realized; if she made a move toward him, or if anyone burst through that door, he would be on his feet, sword in hand, before she could blink. When he looked back at her, she felt the full bore of his black eyes.

"I am sent to kill you," Antonio said. "But I expect you know that by now."

"Yes." She met his steady gaze with her own, unwilling to show her fear. "You were sent by Bedmar?"

"Yes."

"Did you kill La Celestia, or did the marquis do it himself?"

"I know nothing of this. Who is La Celestia?"

"A friend of mine, another courtesan. I found her only hours ago with her throat cut."

"I'm afraid I cannot help you on that score. I only know that the marquis wishes you dead."

"Doesn't he have the nerve to do it himself?"

"I believe he thinks your murder may incriminate him. Too many are aware that he is your lover. He has gone from the city, just to put a fair distance between himself and your disappearance."

"So you volunteered for the job?"

"Not exactly, but my skills in this sphere are highly regarded."

"And how do you plan to do it?"

"To kill you?" Antonio looked amazed at her forthrightness,

then confused. "Would you not prefer to plead for your life instead?"

"I will not give you that satisfaction."

"I have known men twice your size who had not half your courage," he said with a little smile.

"You should count yourself among them, since you prey on those weaker than yourself."

The smile left his face. He moved behind her and began untying her wrists.

"We have very little time," he said. "You must take off your clothes."

"Killing me isn't enough? You mean to humiliate me as well?"

Antonio picked up the lantern. "We have very little time," he repeated, more urgently. He walked a few paces farther into the room and swung the lantern around. Alessandra gasped when she saw what it illuminated.

On a low couch was a woman clad only in her undergarments. Even before she saw the bruises that ringed her throat, Alessandra knew that she was dead. Except for the dried spittle that flaked at the corners of her mouth, the woman resembled a life-size doll, with long ringlets of gold hair and wide blue eyes that were fixed in an everlasting stare. Her fair complexion bore patches of vivid paint, the unnaturally rosy cheeks and rouged lips of a prostitute. Her dress was draped across her feet.

"Take off your clothes and put on that dress, then help me dress her in your costume. Already she grows as stiff as a plank."

"Did you kill her?" Alessandra asked.

"I purchased her from the morgue." His voice was low but contained a banked anger. "If everyone else in the world, including that cretin downstairs, wants to believe me capable of murdering defenseless women, so be it, but I would not have you think so."

"But she was murdered."

"Not by me. She was found in a doorway not far from here, I believe. Don't look so shocked, it's more common than you think. There are ten thousand whores in Venice—surely you've noticed that not all of them live as well as you do." He regarded her impatiently. "You must hurry."

She stripped off her costume and put on the dress. It was tattered and dirty, but the fit was close enough when she laced it tight. Alessandra held her costume out to him. He didn't take it; instead, he lifted the dead woman by the shoulders and nodded to Alessandra to slip it on over her head. They threaded her arms through the sleeves, then rolled her onto her side to pull the costume underneath her and over her legs. Alessandra placed her mask over the dead woman's face.

"Is she supposed to be me? Don't you think someone will notice when they take off the mask?"

"The gondolier's the only one we have to convince, and he hasn't seen your face."

"Isn't he going to ask why you brought me here—why you didn't just slit my throat out in the lagoon?"

"I told him I'd taken a fancy to you."

"Why go to all this trouble just for him?"

"He'll report back to Bedmar, that's why. That reminds me—your jewels. I'm afraid you'll have to give those up, too." Alessandra took off her pearl earrings. "Do you think the marquis will recognize these?" Antonio asked.

"He might."

"Good. I'll make sure he gets them," he said as he attached them to the dead woman's ears.

"If you meant to spare me, why did you stick a knife in my ribs and frighten me half to death?"

"I needed you to come with me without making a fuss. There may have been others watching in the Piazza."

"You could have told me."

"There was no time for a discussion. There isn't time now, either. I'm going to take her down to the gondola. Wait at least five minutes before you leave." He withdrew the dagger from his belt. "It's little protection, but here's my knife. I've arranged for a link boy to light your way to an inn not far from here. He's waiting for you in the *campo.*"

"To an inn?"

"I don't think it's safe for you to go home."

"I've no money with me."

"Everything's been paid for. You must leave the city as soon as you can. Do not tarry; the marquis is at his villa on *terraferma* for the next few days, and you must not be here when he returns. Do you have somewhere to go?"

"Yes." Alessandra looked at the dead whore. "What are you going to do with her?"

"Take her out to the lagoon." He said no more, but he did not have to, for Alessandra knew the rest: bags of rocks would be tied to her hands and feet, and she would not be seen again.

"Why are you doing this? Saving my life, I mean."

His eyes flicked over her and quickly looked away. "You saved mine once," he said simply.

He felt a sense of obligation, then, and nothing more. Alessandra didn't know whether to laugh or cry, and for a moment she felt as if she might do both at once. With the dead woman in his arms, Antonio turned away and walked out the door. Alessandra felt a sharp, burning pain in her chest, as if he had plunged the knife in after all.

With its wood-paneled walls and brass fixtures, Alessandra's room at the Cannaregio inn reminded her of the captain's quarters of her father's lost ship. It wasn't elegant, but it was clean and cozy, with a well-kept fire and an arrangement of simple furnishings: a four-poster bed tucked under the eaves and a small dining table near the hearth. She looked around with approval as she sat down at the writing desk, then gazed out the window to the canal three stories below.

I am safe, Alessandra wrote in a note for Nico and Bianca, *but we must leave Venice at once. Pack a chest with my traveling things and one for the two of you. Convey them here to the inn as soon as you are able. Bring the keys to Giovanna's house in San Polo, where we will stay until we arrange passage out of the city.*

She dusted the paper and sealed it, then stood to ring for the servant. As she crossed the room, she realized that she was weak from exhaustion. How long had it been since she'd slept? As soon as the valet had carried off her missive, she sank down on the bed and closed her eyes, but the visions that arose in her mind kept her awake. The leering grimace of the *bocca di leone*, the nightmarish sight of La Celestia's brutalized body, the marquis as she'd last seen him: a sleeping giant who would rise and seek his revenge. Would she be safe from him now? Would Antonio's ruse work, or was it only a matter of hours before Bedmar found her?

Her thoughts kept turning back to Antonio, to his strange and indifferent behavior, the contradictory nature of his actions. He'd saved her life—for the moment, at least—yet seemed to resent doing so. She thought of his stiff-necked manner earlier and felt that unfamiliar ache inside her breast again.

A persistent knock woke her from troubled dreams. Alessandra cracked the door open. In the hallway, a servant girl bobbed her head and curtsied. "You have a visitor, miss."

Antonio's pale countenance appeared in the shadows behind her. Alessandra opened the door wider to let him in. "You seem surprised to see me," he said as he stepped into the room.

She shut the door behind him, pausing before facing him, afraid that her emotion was too evident in her eyes. She had longed to see him again, so much so that she hadn't allowed herself to hope. But now that he was here, she felt something other than the happiness she had expected, something more complicated and less clear. "I thought you'd be away as soon as your unpleasant work was done," she said.

"I've come to retrieve my knife and to give you this." He held up the letter he'd taken from her, noticing the writing accoutrements on the desk as he did so. "But I see you are prepared to write another." Antonio bristled with an impatient energy. He seemed as if he were on an errand he found distasteful, almost as if he were there against his will.

She'd had no such intention, but his blunt, purposeful attitude irritated her. The coldness in his voice felt like a slap, and her voice rose in anger.

"I'm prepared to do whatever's necessary to protect Venice," Alessandra said.

"Even if it means putting yourself in greater danger?"

"Is that possible? Already you tell me it is not safe to go home, that I must leave the city."

"Yes, it's possible. You don't realize what harm you do with this."

"You've read it, then?"

"I don't need to read it to know what is in it. 'The Spanish ambassador and the duke of Ossuna conspire together against Venice, the viscount of Utrillo-Navarre conveys their secret plans . . .'"

"So you admit that it's true?"

"I admit nothing, but I can see that you believe it. It would be better for you to leave Venice and forget about this entirely."

"You seek to protect yourself?"

"Not only myself."

"Your co-conspirators?"

"After our escapade earlier tonight, I have left all behind, most especially my co-conspirators, as you call them." Antonio strode about the room, then peered out the window. "There is nowhere for me to go except away from Venice, and that isn't easy when Bedmar's men are looking for me."

"Why would they be looking for you, when you serve him?"

"Bedmar thought I was the means to a perfect murder. His plan was for me to kill you—and for me, the murderer, never to be seen again." Antonio tossed the letter on the writing desk.

"He intends to kill you, too?" Alessandra's anger was overcome by anxiety. What would she do if any harm came to him? It was too unbearable to contemplate, but she did her best to preserve her unruffled demeanor. Why should she reveal any tenderness to a man who was acting so coldly toward her?

"The marquis has grand ambitions," Antonio explained. "He won't allow anyone to stand in the way of his political career. Whether he succeeds or fails in this latest scheme, he will not want any witnesses to his treachery."

"All the more reason why I should take that letter to the Great Council. I refuse to spend the rest of my life in fear."

"You do realize that if you deliver that letter, I will be marked, too."

"I did not mention you."

"I doubt that will make any difference."

"Why do you try to dissuade me when you know that the Republic is in danger? Do you believe that your life is worth more than the lives of all the innocent people in Venice?"

"From the accounts I've heard, all the innocent people in Venice could fit easily inside a gondola." He mustered an ironic smile, which Alessandra did not return. "I think I may put your mind at rest, however—the thing you fear is not likely to come to pass. There are so many mercenaries in Venice at present that even the most obtuse of your senators must have noticed that something's afoot. Ossuna presses forward recklessly and Bedmar behaves with insane confidence. There are spies everywhere. This plan of Ossuna's will be uncovered long before his ships set sail. It will be thwarted and the consequences will be severe."

"And what about you? What will you do?"

"Is that concern for my person after all?"

"I admit to being curious, that is all."

"If Ossuna is defeated, my fortunes will fall along with his. I'll have to leave Naples certainly, and look for new employ. Or perhaps I'll go home to Navarre, collect what paltry rents I can, marry a rich widow, and settle down." He cocked an eyebrow at her.

That he could speak so casually of joining his life with another's made his very presence painful to her. Alessandra kept her voice as light as she possibly could. "You're so well suited for the life of a country squire, I'm surprised you did not think of this long ago."

His wounded expression confirmed that her barb had hit its mark. "And what will you do when this is over and you return to Venice?" Antonio asked. "Go back to your chosen trade?"

He does not need a blade, he can kill me with his words. "My chosen trade? Do you think this is the life I would have chosen had I a choice?"

"You could have married." His voice was low, accusatory.

"Married? I had no dowry, no money. I had only my house, and was in danger of losing it for want of the taxes I owed upon it. No one marries a merchant's daughter without money."

"What about the convent?"

"You mean imprisonment."

"At least it would have been honorable."

"As honorable as you, who carries out the orders of a madman?"

"I find more honor in doing my duty than in being one of the most popular courtesans in Venice, listed in a book with a price next to her name!" Antonio paced, unable to contain his rage.

She felt the same sharp pain in her breast as she'd felt earlier. Her voice fell to a whisper. "Why do you hate me so?"

He stopped and looked steadily at her. "You think it is hate?" He stood so close she could touch him if she wished. He looked away and spoke harshly, as if he were not speaking to her, but to himself. "It is not hate, it is torment." He looked back at her. "I cannot—" He stopped, and for a moment looked as if he could not go on. "I cannot bear to think of you with those . . . those men. With any men."

In his stricken appearance, Alessandra saw what Antonio was unwilling to say. "Is this a declaration of love? If it is, it is ungenerous and cruel. You do not declare your feelings, yet you tell me you are jealous and persecute me."

"Persecute you? How?"

"By telling me of your plans to marry."

"Little chance, I should think, that you would leave Venice and become the wife of a poor viscount, and move away with me to my scrubby patch of land. Or did you think I would stay here and live off your munificence?"

"I don't know. I haven't thought—"

"I have, and there's nothing to be done." His voice was hoarse, his eyes clouded with pain. "How can I declare my feelings when I have nothing to offer you?"

"You must think very little of me if you think that all I care about is money."

"A singular creature—a courtesan who cares nothing for money."

"You do not believe me?"

"I think it's easy to say you care nothing for money now, when it is of no consequence. But later, when your fine clothes are in tatters and your jewels are long gone—"

"I have lived most of my life without fine clothes and jewels."

"But you have not lived in the country in Spain, without a neighbor for miles and nothing more than a village to visit on a Sunday. What of society, of a city full of amusements and beautiful things to buy?" Alessandra could not answer. "You see, I have thought about it."

"So that's it, then? An unbridgeable breach?" Although they were standing close together, Alessandra felt as though they'd moved miles apart. "You would color our future so black that it cannot exist."

"Perhaps . . . perhaps if things were different than they are right now, these obstacles might have been overcome. But now . . . don't you understand? What future can there be for a hunted man and a woman who is soon to be a refugee?"

"This is the only outcome you can envision?"

He didn't answer, just stared at her, his black eyes wide. Suddenly she understood. "You don't expect to live."

"I think it unlikely that I will leave Venice."

"You would give up so easily?"

"I simply say what I believe to be true."

"It can't be true. I refuse to believe it. We can go away together. I have money saved . . . there must be a way . . ."

"She cries," he said with wonder. He stepped closer, bridging the distance between them, and gathered her in his arms.

She brushed her tears away and looked up at him. "Why do people say love makes one happy? This is the most terrible thing I have ever felt."

The fire had burned low, but Alessandra could still see reminders of everything she would rather forget: the letter that lay on the desk, unopened; Antonio's sword, a slim shaft of light as it leaned against the chair over which he had draped his clothes. Too soon the night would end and the morning would dawn; what new terrors would the day bring?

A few hours is all we have, Alessandra thought, moving closer to Antonio as they lay on the bed, feeling the warmth of his bare skin all along her own. He was all muscle and sinew, but his hands were softly caressing as they ranged over her body. She shivered a little as her eyes met his.

"Can it be that you're uneasy?" he said with a solemn smile. "I would not have imagined . . ."

It was true she felt tremulous, even anxious. She'd never felt so vulnerable before. "Not uneasy, but . . . how is it that I cannot hide from you? As if you can see into my soul, and see everything that I am."

"Perhaps because with you, I am unmasked, too." Antonio touched his fingers to her lips, then brought his lips to her lips, holding her closer and enveloping her in a deep kiss. Then for a long time they did not speak, but communed only by the touch of their hands, their intertwined limbs.

"You are very quiet," Antonio said.

Alessandra touched his face tenderly. "I am afraid that I won't see you again after this."

"Now is not the time to be thinking of that."

"You will depart in the morning, then?"

"I'll stay long enough to help you leave Venice."

"And after?"

"I don't know. I fear my presence will only put you in danger."

"I don't believe that."

"We might be followed by Bedmar's men. What if I cannot save you?"

"Then I will save you. You must come with me to Padua."

"We shall see," he said, and silenced her with a kiss.

She hadn't understood how powerful sex could be, what it meant to yield not just her body but her heart and soul to another person. For the first time, she understood how completely she'd kept her distance from her lovers, how she'd managed to conceal her true feelings. Only now, when she was incapable of hiding, did she realize how little her soul had been touched by any man.

She looked down on Antonio from above. His face appeared younger in the dusky light, his eyes wide and dark, speaking volumes. She wanted to tell him that it was different with him than with anyone else, but words felt beyond her reach now, surrendered as she was to sensation.

Antonio's hands gripped her hips hard, digging into her flesh. Although he was underneath her, he moved her exactly as he wanted, as they wanted, driving her with a relentless rhythm that was pushing her closer to complete dissolution. She uttered a soft, anguished moan. Her nipples were tight and hard, and she had a sudden urge to feel them rubbing against his chest. She bent down to feel her body upon his, to bury her face in his neck.

"No." He gently pushed her upright again. "I want to watch you, to see the moment overtake you." He caressed her breast, then brushed her nipples brusquely, as if he knew she craved his touch exactly there. She felt a violent twinge of pleasure in her womb. His hand moved farther down, stroking her stomach and her thighs, then he pressed his thumb against the nub at the top of the cleft between her legs.

She cried out as the first of the long, wracking spasms struck her, shaking her with such intensity she felt as though she would break apart. Words tumbled unbidden from her lips. She heard herself moan, and closed her eyes.

"Look at me," Antonio said, his voice low and hoarse. Alessandra opened her eyes and faced his frank stare as she trembled, out of control. A shadow crossed his face and his breath quickened, coming in ragged, rapid gasps. He pulled her against him so fiercely that he drove himself deeper, then deeper still. Alessandra felt herself responding with a gathering power, which would unleash again with renewed force.

Antonio's head lifted off the bed and his body curved toward her, as if he'd been wound tight with an invisible spring. A great groan, from the depths of his soul, escaped from his lips. He ground his hips so tightly into hers that it left her breathless, and in that moment she felt him pulse inside her, followed by his warm release. He gave a strangled cry and fell back, bucking underneath her, reaching deeper and deeper inside, until she climaxed again in great, shattering waves.

She fell upon him, feeling his arms enfold her, their breath mingling, their hearts beating wildly. Antonio stroked her hair. "My love," he murmured, "oh, my love."

Across the room, the logs in the fireplace crumbled into ash and embers, and the shadows shifted and grew deeper. Too soon those shadows would disappear and it would be morning. Alessandra held Antonio tight and resolved to commit every detail to memory: the scent of his skin, the touch of his hands, the feel of his stubbled cheek against her face, the warm pressure of his lips. Even now, in the peacefulness that followed frenzy, she could sense the lion's mouth waiting for them, its black chasm opened wide, yawning, cavernous, ready to engulf them both.

The Stars

4 March 1618

SEATED NEXT TO her in the gondola, Alessandra felt Bianca shivering as they pressed slowly forward into the fog-shrouded canal. The weather had turned so gloomy that the *ancone* were already lit, though they were few and sputtered with damp. Vague shapes, unnatural and dreamlike, loomed in the murky distance, then gradually resolved into solid forms as they approached: a gnarled mooring pole, a boat's curved prow, a grinning gargoyle, a stone bridge. Even Paolo, only a few feet behind her at the stern, looked eerie and indistinct, and the cadenced splash produced by his measured rowing was muffled.

"It's too quiet," Bianca whispered. "It's still Carnival, for a few days. Why are people not celebrating?"

"It's the fog," Alessandra said. But it seemed odd to her, too, and for some reason she had answered Bianca in an identical whisper.

Nico and Antonio had gone on ahead, taking the larger of the two chests to her cousin's vacant house in San Polo. There they could stay hidden until they had hired a barge to take them to Marghera.

She'd composed a letter to Giovanna that morning, which Nico could take to the post as soon as the trunks were upstairs. With luck, Giovanna would be there to meet them at Marghera the following night. It would not be well if she were late. As eager as they were to leave Venice, it wouldn't do to wait at the *terraferma* village for long; they might be even more vulnerable there.

The other letter, the one she'd written to the Great Council, had been destroyed. Late last night Alessandra had awakened, stiff with cold. She turned and realized she was alone in the bed; Antonio was no longer there.

Moonlight shone in the windows and left diamond-shaped patterns of light on the floor. The entire room seemed transformed into strange configurations of metallic brightness and fathomless shadows. For a moment she wondered if she were dreaming, if Antonio himself had been a dream.

Then she saw him. He was sitting on a footstool in front of the hearth, his naked body bathed in the ruddy glow of the embers. She thought of calling to him, then she saw what he was doing. Silently she watched as he opened the letter she'd written to the council and read it through. When he was done, he held the corner of the paper to the embers until it caught fire. The light from the sudden burst of flame illuminated his face, his enigmatic expression. With the letter pinched between his thumb and forefinger, he let the fire devour it until he could hold it no longer, and threw the last flaming bit of it into the grate.

Then the morning arrived, and soon after it so had Nico, Bianca, and Paolo, and they'd had no time to speak of it. But why had Antonio burnt the letter? Who was he protecting? Could it be that he still served Bedmar and the duke? Alessandra resolved to question him as soon as they arrived at Giovanna's house.

They turned into the Rio dei Frari. Through the mist Alessandra saw the dark shape of a fortified door open to the canal. She looked back at Paolo, then pointed ahead. "That house there."

Paolo steered the boat through the archway. The gondola that Nico and Antonio had arrived in bobbed in the water next to the stone slab of the ground-level storerooms. Alessandra's wooden chest was still in it.

Why had Nico and Antonio gone upstairs and left the chest behind? Alessandra felt a fleeting irritation. "Nico!" Bianca screamed, standing up and rocking the gondola wildly. As she bolted from the boat, Alessandra saw what had prompted her sudden outburst and scrambled out after her. Nico was slumped facedown on the stairs leading up to the house. They rushed over and knelt beside him. Alessandra saw the bloody gash on the back of his jerkin and turned him over. Bianca convulsed with tears as they saw the blood that covered his chest and the wound where the sword had entered and run him through. The trickle of red that ran down from the corner of his mouth was still wet, but Nico's face was contorted in a silent, stilled agony. They were too late to save him.

"No!" Bianca sobbed and threw herself upon him. "No, not my Nico!"

Stunned and bewildered, Alessandra reached to comfort Bianca. She gasped as a strong hand gripped her shoulder and another grabbed her arm, lifting her to her feet. Paolo forcefully turned her away from her sobbing maidservant and pointed across the room.

"By the Virgin," Alessandra exclaimed as she saw the dead *bravo* lying near a group of old wine barrels. Paolo pointed again and she saw a second man, floating facedown in the water. The gondolier pulled at her arm, and gestured toward the boat.

"It isn't s-safe."

"Bianca, we must go," Alessandra said.

Tears streamed down Bianca's cheeks as she turned to her mistress. "My lady, what has happened?"

"I don't know, but I fear a trap. We must leave at once."

They got back into the gondola and Paolo rowed them outside, into the canal.

"Signorina Rossetti." A man's voice came from out of the fog. A gondola blocked the canal; through the mist she saw that it was filled with the red-and-blue-liveried soldiers of the Missier Grande, the Council of Ten's special police force. "Signorina Rossetti," the voice said again, "you must come with us."

* * *

His attire marked him as Venetian, but he was unlike any Venetian Antonio had ever seen. The man who faced him in the Crooked Alley of Secrets reminded him of the Mongol slaves he'd seen in Sicily—except for the blue eyes that peered out from his wide, angular face with an intensity that chilled Antonio's soul. This man was no one's menial, clearly, but a confident swordsman of his own age or thereabouts who advanced toward Antonio with a long, shining rapier pointed right at his heart.

At first Antonio had thought that the five men who'd set upon them at Giovanna's house were thieves lured by the sumptuous chest they carried in their gondola. He'd killed two of them, but once Nico had fallen, he'd made his escape rather than face three alone. He had imagined that the thieves would stay there, to carry off the goods, and hoped that he would be able to find and warn Alessandra before she arrived at the house. He'd had the surprise of his life when they followed him instead.

He'd dispatched one quickly, and had given the slip to another, but this pale-eyed creature had dogged his steps all through the back alleys of San Polo. At the very moment Antonio had thought he'd finally lost him, the ruffian had dropped down right in front of him, as nimble as an acrobat, and as menacing as a snake.

"Antonio Perez," he said, with a slight accent that gave a sinister edge to his voice. "I have long been desiring your acquaintance."

"And who are you?" Antonio raised his sword.

"Batù Vratsa. I'll be taking you to the Doge's Prison."

"You'll have to kill me first."

"If you insist."

Antonio stepped back as Batù advanced, looking for a place that would give him more room to maneuver but finding none in the narrow passage. His opponent held his sword with confident grace. The air whistled as he slashed it back and forth, equal parts threat and opening sortie. Their gazes locked and Antonio saw the intention in Batù's eyes a split second before he sprang forward, anticipating his attack with a rapid parry. The clanging sound of clashing steel echoed off the stone walls. Antonio lunged, aiming for Batù's chest. His foe dodged the rapier easily, with a sudden twist and a leap to the left that brought the point of his sword even closer to Antonio.

What Antonio had seen of his challenger already, in his first attack at Giovanna's house, had been impressive, but now he began to understand just who he was up against. Batù moved with a sure-footed skill and an extraordinary agility, unlike any sword fighter he'd ever seen. Antonio surpassed him in size, but he perceived that this wasn't likely to help him much. This was no brawling, bludgeoning combatant—this was a man who could slip a sword into a man's side with such lightning rapidity that he'd be dead without ever seeing the blade.

This time Batù made the first strike. Antonio realized how close he came to feeling the blow, barely shielding himself with the flat of his sword. Don Gaspar had taught him always to look into his opponent's eyes, but with this one, he found himself also following the deadly blade as it flashed in the air around him. As his own rapier clashed with the other, he felt as though he were fending off two attackers instead of one.

They parried the length of the alley. Antonio went on the offensive, lunging with his weapon held high, and sliced in a downward curve. His blade connected with his adversary's left shoulder, stripping away the sleeve and leaving a deep cut. It was a wound severe enough to make a man cry out and back away—but Batù seemed to feel it not at all. Instead, a smile flickered across his mouth and he countered the blow with a ferocious rally that pushed Antonio's back against a wall.

He could not gain an advantage where he was, so rolled to his side and Batù's sword came into contact with stone instead of flesh. The setback threw off his antagonist for only a second, but it was enough for Antonio to rebound with a powerful thrust that Batù evaded with only inches to spare.

"I see your reputation is justified, Viscount," Batù said. "But mine will be greater when it is known that I am the man who brought you to your knees."

"You speak precipitately. As you see, I am still on my feet."

Batù came back at him with fury, repulsing Antonio's next thrust and whipping his thin rapier in a figure-eight motion that suddenly and surprisingly left a red, horizontal slash along Antonio's cheek. His eyes were instantly stinging and his face burned as though it were on fire. He could feel blood running down his cheek, as if the skin had been stripped away like a glove peeled from a hand. He clenched his jaw and resisted the urge to touch his face; he suspected the wound felt worse than it actually was. And anything that distracted his attention from the task before him would surely bring about his death. It would require all his skill and every faculty he possessed to best this monster.

They were both breathing heavily now, their chests heaving, their breath rising like steam, mingling with the foggy air. They circled each other slowly, looking for advantage. Batù's blade flashed again, a furious, slashing razor. Antonio deflected his jabs and parries, but he couldn't deny that his attacker was getting the better of him.

I cannot die, Antonio thought grimly, strengthening his resolve. If I die, who will protect Alessandra?

Batù attacked once more, pushing Antonio back along the alley. Then, with a running start, Batù launched himself, pulling his dagger from his waistband in midair, and flew at Antonio with a blade in each hand.

Antonio's first impulse was to back away, but a sudden intuition told him that to do so would place him exactly in his attacker's range, where the knives would find their intended mark. So he stepped forward instead, ramming his left shoulder into Batù's chest. His foe's dagger came down in a slashing motion that scraped Antonio all along his back, but the move had been effective in keeping him free of the rapier thrust, and the force with which he crashed into Batù sent him reeling back to land on the ground. But even this setback did not deter his deadly opponent. Without missing a beat, Batù threw his dagger straight at Antonio's chest. With a slash of his sword, Antonio intercepted the flying blade; an equal motion to the left engaged Batù's rapier and disarmed the prone swordsman. In one final, fluid move, Antonio thrust his sword into the vulnerable indentation at the base of Batù's throat, running him through the neck until he felt the tip of his weapon connect with stony ground.

He stayed long enough to watch his adversary's body buck in its death throes, to see those strange blue eyes open wide with a look of terror, and then, slowly, to see the light in them fade and go out.

Antonio glanced up and down the narrow alley. Which way had he come? Blast these Venetians and their tangled streets, he thought as he set off to find his way back to Giovanna's house and Alessandra.

The Tower

5 March 1618

It was a setback, certainly, but perhaps he could find a way to turn it to his advantage, Girolamo Silvia thought as he climbed the Giants' Staircase leading up from the courtyard of the Doge's Palace. La Celestia's murder implied that all his best-laid plans had come to nothing, but he couldn't be sure until he found out what had happened to Bedmar's code book. Perhaps the girl had retrieved the book before La Celestia had been so unhappily dispatched. If she'd returned it to the ambassador's room, then he might still be able to decode the ambassador's correspondence, as long as Bedmar had not discovered the deception. If the marquis had gotten wise, then the copy he'd had made of the book would be no use to him now, of course, as the ambassador would never use the original again.

But who had killed La Celestia? Already Silvia feared that he would never know for sure. She had too many enemies: lovers jealous of the loss of her affections, courtiers angry about their gambling losses, courtesans looking to rid themselves of their greatest rival. Of course Silvia suspected Bedmar—hadn't La Celestia been afraid of the ambassador's reprisals?—but his inquiries had revealed that the marquis had been at his *terraferma* villa for the past two days. The damned Spaniard certainly knew how to keep his hands clean, removing himself from the city like that. That, combined with the ambassador's diplomatic immunity, meant there was little chance that Silvia could implicate him. No doubt the marquis had sent one of his *bravi* to do the job, but Bedmar was no fool; the murderer would be gone from Venice by now, or dead himself.

Silvia gazed across the courtyard, watching the senators who gathered around the two bronze wellheads in the center, the scurrying figures of magistrates, lawyers, secretaries, and scribes. Batù should be here already, he thought, and his quarry locked up.

The previous night, Batù had shown up at Silvia's palazzo with the news that Antonio Perez had been spotted in Cannaregio. The senator had told his disciple that the viscount's arrest was critical: Utrillo-Navarre was known to be Ossuna's most lethal swordsman, and he had met with Bedmar at the Spanish embassy only a month ago. His capture could provide the necessary link between the duke and the marquis. He's slipped through our fingers before, Silvia had said, and Batù had promised to bring him in. But where was he?

Silvia looked to his left and saw Ottavio, his personal secretary, hurrying along the colonnade to greet him. The very sight of the pale, chubby-cheeked young man irritated him, as always. The little favors required for political gain are often more irksome than the large, Silvia reflected.

"Good morning, Senator."

"Where's the whore?" he barked.

"Which one, sir?"

Silvia sighed. *Face like a turnip and a brain to match.* If Ottavio weren't his cousin's son, he would have tossed him out on his ear ages ago.

"The courtesan Rossetti."

"She's in the *pozzi.* Number eight."

"Have her brought up to the Sala dei Tre Capi," he said. "I'll be along in a while."

He hoped that the girl could provide some answers. But even if she couldn't, Silvia had already thought of a way in which she would be very useful.

* * *

Silvia stood outside the Sala dei Tre Capi and peered through a peephole. The courtesan was seated in a chair that sat alone in the center of the room. This room was usually reserved for meetings of the Three, not interrogations, but Silvia disliked going down into the ground-floor prison; he suffered too much from the cold and wet.

Alessandra Rossetti was a handsome woman: thick gold hair, a fair countenance and figure. Younger than he'd imagined, though he could see the wear and worry in her face. She hadn't slept, of course. No one slept well in the Doge's Prison. After a few days, prisoners were usually so debilitated by anticipation and fear that confessions were easily achieved. But the courtesan had been here only one night. Unfortunately, Silvia couldn't afford to wait any longer.

He entered and made his way to the riser at the back of the room, where three chairs sat on a dais, and settled into the middle chair. The courtesan looked at him warily. She's no fool, he thought; she's guessed that this room belongs to the Three. Her intelligence would work in his favor—he could use her fear to obtain her compliance.

"Signorina Rossetti, I am Senator Silvia. I'll be the only person speaking with you today."

She relaxed a little. "Why am I here?"

"I ask the questions. You answer them." She looked chastised, but not afraid—not yet, anyway. "Where is the book?"

"What book?"

"The book you stole from the Spanish ambassador."

She started with surprise. "It was you who was behind it?"

"Just answer the question."

"I don't know where it is."

"You did not put it back in the ambassador's room?"

"No."

"And why not, when you were told that this was an essential part of your task?"

The girl was silent. He could see the confusion in her face. "Answer me."

"I could not put it back because . . . because La Celestia did not have it."

Silvia rose from his chair and approached the girl. "La Celestia was discovered yesterday in a very unfortunate condition—her throat was cut so deeply that her head was very nearly detached from her body. But I see this is not a surprise to you. Did you kill her?"

"No, of course not. She was my friend."

"And when did you see her last?" The courtesan did not answer. "After she was killed?"

Reluctantly, Alessandra gave a little nod. "I was meeting with her in order to retrieve the book. When I got there, she was already dead. The book wasn't there."

"You looked for it?"

"Yes."

By the bloody Virgin. Silvia took a moment to collect his thoughts. Bedmar must have gotten wise, he realized. Who else would have stolen the book, once he'd killed her? Damn him to Hell. Silvia knew he couldn't implicate the marquis in La Celestia's murder, but he could pursue another path to the ambassador's ruin, perhaps an even better one. And this young courtesan would help him do it.

He turned back to her. "So your friend, as you call her, was brutally murdered, and yet you did nothing—did not call for help, nor alert the authorities. Why is that?"

"I was afraid."

"Of what?"

"That whoever killed her would kill me, of course."

"You could have at least written a letter for the *bocca di leone*—"

"Do you really believe that would protect me?"

Silvia studied the set of her mouth, the way her shoulders rose with tension. He could see that she was not telling all. "Has anyone ever told you that you're not a good liar? You may be able to fool a dimwit, but I will have nothing less than the truth. Trust me when I say I have ways of getting at the truth that you would not like at all. Now, why did you not tell anyone of La Celestia's murder?"

"As I said, because I was afraid." No, she was not a good liar.

"Do not toy with me. I think you protect someone."

The girl dropped her eyes from his face.

"Yes, I think that's it. The Spanish ambassador has bought your loyalty, has he not, in the same way his Spanish gold has bought up half the Venetian army?"

"That is absurd."

"That is the truth, I am sure. Bedmar plots to overthrow the Republic. I think you are as deeply involved in his intrigue as the mercenary captains whose service he has purchased. You will hang along with them once your treason is known—"

"No!" She rose to her feet, her eyes darting, her cheeks flushed. Silvia smiled a little as he saw the panic take hold. "How can you accuse me of such a thing? I am a loyal Venetian citizen, the daughter of a citizen. I would never—"

"Sit down," he commanded. "Another outburst and the guards outside will take you back to your cell—or to someplace worse."

She sat. Silvia could see that her panic had turned to fear. *Good. Very good.* Now maybe he would get somewhere.

"Are you familiar with the punishment for treason?" Silvia asked. "As you probably know, traitors are hung in the Piazzetta by their feet, but that is the least of their sufferings. By the time that happens, they are already dead. What transpires before that is slow and agonizing. In fact, you would probably go mad with pain long before you died."

He stood up and walked closer to her. He noticed a strong, rapid pulse at the base of her throat. He could feel her anxiety, smell her fear. "I see you're beginning to understand the position you're in," he said. "You are luckier than most, however. I'm going to offer you a way out."

She didn't speak, just stared at him, wide-eyed.

"All you must do," he continued, "is write a letter outlining the ambassador's plot."

"I have already told you that I know nothing of this plot except what I was told by La Celestia."

She's dissembling again, Silvia thought. Why? "That matters little. My information comes from other sources. I'll tell you what to write."

"If you have other sources, why do you require my assistance?"

"First of all, because Bedmar is known to be your lover. And because, as you said, you are a citizen, and the daughter of a citizen. A courtesan, yes, but one who is known for her piety, her charity, and her discretion. I've heard you are educated, if that is possible for a woman. A letter from you will be far more persuasive than one from one of the wretches who has revealed the conspiracy among his compatriots. In fact, as they are all illiterate, I don't think it would be believed at all. They can't even write their own names, much less the names of those men who will be identified in this letter."

She turned pale. "Are you asking me to implicate men who may very well be innocent?"

"Innocent? To a man, they are rogues and scoundrels and worse."

Her face grew paler still. "But surely you cannot condemn men until you are certain they have committed a crime."

"It seems to me that a loyal Venetian citizen such as yourself would care more about securing the safety of the Republic than the fate of a few Spaniards and Frenchmen."

"I do. I do, but you are asking me to be a party to the deaths of men I know nothing of."

"Tell me, are you protecting your Spanish lover? Is he just too good to give up?"

She gave a start, and for a moment looked as though she might be ill, then recovered. "You mean Bedmar."

"Of course."

"I do not love him, if that is what you think."

"Then I suggest that you write this letter. It will save your skin—literally."

She trembled, and gripped the arms of the chair. "I will not do it."

"I can force you." He took one of her hands in his, then twisted her wrist until she cried out in pain.

She wrenched her hand away. "If you break my hands, I will not be able to write, will I?"

"There are other parts of you that are equally vulnerable."

She shuddered again, and held on to the chair as if to still her shaking. Then she stood and looked him in the eye.

"I will not do it."

We shall see, Silvia thought. We shall see.

Perched on the bench in the center of her cell, Alessandra pulled her knees closer and wrapped her arms around them. The puddle of water that had formed at the end of her cell abutting the Rio del Palazzo had grown to cover the entire floor and was rising with the tide. Although the prison wasn't old—it had been completed around the time she was born—it had already been dubbed the *pozzi,* or the wells, as the cell floors were under water more often than not. She knew that the tide would subside in a few hours, but the effect was disconcerting—like being inside the dark, dank hold of a slowly sinking boat.

Her cell was dark and windowless. There was a small window in the corridor, but she could not see it unless she stood at the iron gridwork door, and the daylight that came through it was diffuse and gray. A small torch was mounted on the stone wall outside her cell, but its faint light was barely enough to illuminate the corridor. Here, it would always be night. Already, she'd lost track of how long she'd been there. Since she'd arrived, the only glimpse of daylight she'd seen was when they'd marched her across the Bridge of Sighs to the palace and the Sala dei Tre Capi.

She heard the sound of light, quick footsteps approaching. Not the guard's, certainly; the Missier Grande soldier who stood at the end of the hall was large enough to fill the doorway. Her curiosity was satisfied when Bianca appeared at her door.

"I've brought some victuals, my lady," said Bianca, and pressed the small, napkin-tied bundle of food through the bars.

"I'm not hungry."

"You must eat it anyway." Bianca's voice was dull with grief; Alessandra was pained to see how haggard and worn she looked.

"Will you be all right, Bianca?"

"Do not worry about me. We brought Nico home. I am preparing him." A few tears escaped and rolled down her cheeks.

Alessandra reached through the bars and held her hand. "I'm so sorry. I don't understand what happened."

"It was not your fault, my lady."

"I will always believe that it was."

"Nico would not want you to blame yourself." Bianca sniffed and rubbed at her eyes. "Now, you must eat."

Alessandra forced herself to take a bite of the fried fish and corn cake that Bianca had brought. Her maidservant glanced over at the guard who stood at the end of the hall, to make sure he was out of earshot. "Many rumors are flying about the town just now," she said softly.

"Tell me what you have heard."

"There is a great exodus from the city. The taverns and the bordellos have emptied, and the mercenaries are leaving in droves. The Missier Grande is rounding up foreigners and anyone connected with the marquis. Some say that the Canal of Orphans runs red with blood—that it is filling with the bodies of those the Missier Grande carries away."

"And the viscount?"

"There is no word."

"Bianca, I know that you are fond of Paolo, but do you think he might have given us up to the marquis? How else to account for what happened at Giovanna's house? I fear his allegiance is with Bedmar."

"Paolo?" Bianca said incredulously. "Paolo would never do such a thing, he is a loyal Venetian. He will never work for the ambassador again." A look of pique, followed by sympathy, crossed her soft, round face. "My lady, have you not noticed? Paolo loves you fiercely. He would die before betraying you. And he would be in this prison now, too, if I had not forced him to come away with me by reminding him that you shall have need of him now that Nico is gone."

The guard ambled over and, towering over Bianca, said that it was time for her to leave. Bianca slipped him a coin. "Five more minutes?" she asked. The guard nodded and stood there. "In private," she added. He walked back to his post at the end of the hall.

"You must speak to Senator Valier, and to the bishop," Alessandra said. "Tell them where I am, and that Senator Silvia is threatening me with—," she stopped; telling Bianca anything more would only upset her. "Just tell them Silvia is threatening me. Ask them to intercede for my safety. Can you do that?"

"Of course, my lady. I'll go at once upon leaving here."

"When you get home, go to my room. Behind the painted chest you'll find a secret place where I keep some coins. Take what you need to see that Nico is well buried."

Bianca began to cry again.

"Hush, do not upset yourself further," Alessandra said. "All will be well."

The guard returned to take Bianca away. Alessandra waited by the door of her cell until she could no longer hear their footsteps. She hoped that her words had reassured Bianca. To herself they sounded hollow, without conviction.

"I've been a fool." Girolamo Silvia stood in the somber torchlight outside her cell. For a moment, she thought he might be admitting that he'd made a mistake by imprisoning her, even that he was apologizing. But when she stood and walked closer to the door, she saw this was an idle hope. The senator's heavy-lidded eyes were filled with anger and resentment. Alessandra felt the same revulsion she'd felt on their first meeting. He was a disagreeable man; the aroma of frankincense that clung to him did little to mask his smell of decay, his foul breath.

He nodded to the guard. "Take her."

Take me where? she wondered. To the Court of the Room of the Cord?

The guard opened the door of her prison and pulled her out into the hall. He hurried her along musty corridors lined with dark cells, where condemned men moaned and stirred in the shadows. They turned a corner and the guard marched her to a cell at the end. He unlocked the grated iron entry, pushed her in, and slammed the door behind her.

Inside, all was darkness. Something large moved in the corner. Alessandra jumped back against the door. The mass moved again and her heart quieted a little. It was only a man, she saw, a man lying on the narrow bench, his face to the wall. Then, with a groan, he turned and she saw that it was Antonio.

"Good God," she whispered, horrified. His face was a mess, the left eye swollen shut, lower lip crusted with blood, a deep cut along one cheek. She rushed to him. "What have they done to you?"

It took him a moment to reply. "I'm not sure, exactly." Speaking seemed to cause him pain. "I lost track."

"Can you sit up?"

"If you help me."

He winced in agony as he leaned against the wall. "I think a few of my ribs are broken."

"Anything else?"

"My wrist." His forehead was clammy with sweat. "Could you bring me some water?"

She dipped her hands in the bucket near the door and carried it to his mouth. "What happened at Giovanna's house?" she asked.

"We were set upon by some men. Apparently they had tracked us from the inn and then tried to trap us inside your cousin's house. Nico was killed."

"I know, we found him. Were they Bedmar's men?"

"No, they were Venetians. The marquis was right to leave the city when he did. I think his time in Venice is coming to an end much sooner than he expected. That might bode well for you . . . although your being here is not a good turn of events. What happened?"

"I was taken at Giovanna's house."

"Are you are all right? You have not been hurt?" He turned his head a little, to peruse her face with his good eye.

"I am well."

"I'm sorry about Nico. He fought ably; I'm sure I would not be alive if he hadn't been there to help. I got away, but I had to face one of the men again. After that, I went back to your cousin's house. I waited for some time, then went to the Rialto, thinking you might have gone there to hire a barge. That's where the Missier Grande discovered me. Took three of them to bring me in, though." He smiled wanly, then grimaced with pain.

"Tell me something," Alessandra began. "Last night . . . why did you burn the letter?"

"To protect you, of course. Bedmar already wishes you dead. What do you think will happen if he discovers that you have betrayed him to the Venetian authorities? I fear he will never rest until he has his revenge."

They both fell silent as they heard footsteps approaching. "Do not let on that you care for me," Antonio said in a harsh whisper. "It will make it worse for you."

The footsteps stopped in front of the door and the odor of frankincense wafted through the bars.

"Your Spanish lover," Silvia said. "I should have realized right away who you were protecting." He beckoned to Alessandra. "A word, signorina," he said. "And not a word from you," he added, addressing Antonio, "or I'll have you taken to the Court of the Room of the Cord at once."

Alessandra moved to the door. "You see the kinds of things that can happen in this prison," Silvia said, his voice low but clear. "Are you ready to write that letter now?"

"You don't dare threaten me with torture," she said. "Senator Valier would never allow it." Alessandra wondered if Bianca had been able to deliver her message; if she hadn't, her bluff might well be worthless.

"Not you, my pretty one," Silvia said. He tilted his chin toward the back of the cell. "Him."

Alessandra stiffened. *Holy Mother of God.*

"The longer you refuse," Silvia went on, "the more he suffers."

"No," she said in a strangled voice.

"All right then," said Silvia, snapping his fingers. "Guard!"

"No." She threw herself against the door and spoke to the guard, now brandishing his keys. "Stop, please."

Silvia nodded to the guard to step back. "So?" he asked.

"He's committed no crime," Alessandra protested.

"Conspiring to overthrow the Republic is the most reprehensible crime there is."

"But you can't possibly have proof of this."

"I don't need proof, my suspicion is enough. You are an ignorant girl who knows nothing of political matters, or of the many threats our Republic faces. I will do what must needs be done to keep the state strong—and I tell you that I need that letter." He glanced once more at Antonio. "This Spaniard is nothing to me. I would just as soon torture him as not. Perhaps he shall suffer something especially painful first, before he loses consciousness."

"No . . ." Alessandra could feel herself shaking. "No, you mustn't do this, I beg of you. I will do as you ask. But . . . I will not name him in the letter, and you must take him away from here. I must see you do that first."

He gazed steadily at her. Already, there was something triumphant in his stare. "You will have to implicate others."

Others. Others who would suffer even more than Antonio had. It was an impossible dilemma, but Alessandra knew she would go mad if they hurt him. She looked at the senator, smugly waiting for her answer.

"So you would make me a murderer, then?"

"And his savior," Silvia said with a nod at Antonio.

"Alessandra, no," Antonio said. "Don't do it." His voice was slurred. The cut on his lip had opened and blood dripped from his chin. He didn't seem to be aware of it.

"I will not have you die here," she said to him. It was no use pretending that she would do anything other than make this unholy pact with Silvia. He had known she would agree to it even before she did, known that she would sacrifice anything, anyone, to save her lover. In her heart, she was already a murderer, and she knew it beyond a doubt when she looked into the senator's face. *If I had a weapon, I would kill him now, without remorse.*

But there was only one way to get Antonio out of here.

"I will do it." Her face was wet. She touched her cheek. She was crying.

The senator's face contorted disagreeably. She supposed it was a smile.

Inside the cell, there was no day, no time. Alessandra drifted in and out of sleep. Once she thought that Silvia had come to stand outside her door, then decided that it must have been a dream. Once she awoke to find a little brown mouse only inches from her face, nibbling on the last crumbs of her corn cake. But none of this bothered her. She could rest now.

He was away.

They'd allowed her to watch from a room in the palace as Antonio had been helped into a gondola and rowed out to the lagoon. They were taking him to Malamocco, where he would board a boat for Spain. The ship's doctor would tend his wounds. He would be safe.

He would be safe, and she would never see him again.

Then they'd taken her back to the Sala dei Tre Capi, where Silvia waited next to a table neatly laid out with sharpened quills, ink, and sheets of parchment. She had thought he would be flush with victory, but instead he seemed to be suffering from a great fatigue, or a deep sadness. A soldier of the Missier Grande never left the senator's side. Alessandra wondered if he'd seen her murderous intent earlier, if he'd intuited how much she wanted to kill him. Odd. She no longer cared. She no longer felt anything, not fear, not hope, not even abhorrence at what she was doing. Silvia spoke and she wrote down his words as if he were her tutor and she still at lessons.

Even when she had to write the names of the men, the French and Spanish adventurers, as Silvia called them, her hand barely faltered, though she knew she was drafting their death sentence. She could not say with certainty that any were guilty of a crime.

And when she was done, they'd brought her back here. No word or clue as to how long she would be held. Perhaps forever. The senator had said she was never to speak of what he had forced her to do. Perhaps this was his way of making sure—she would live out the rest of her life here, in the darkness and the damp, marking the days by the ebb and flow of the tides.

She heard whispering at the end of the hall, then the guard appeared at her door, jangling his keys.

"Out," he said.

"Where are you taking me?" she asked as the huge man gripped her arm and led her along the hallway. He didn't answer, simply kept moving forward, propelling her along as easily as a normal man would a child. They walked through the prison corridors, up a short flight of steps and then down again. They were moving away from the Bridge of Sighs, Alessandra realized, away from the palace. But where, then?

At last they came to a large, fortified door. Sentries stood on each side. The guard gave a slip of paper to one of the sentries, who looked it over, then nodded to the other. They unbarred the door and pulled it open. The guard pushed her through, out onto the Riva degli Schiavoni and into the solemn grayness of the overcast morning.

Bianca waited for her. "Thank heavens, you're safe," she said, embracing her.

"What has happened?" Alessandra asked, stepping back.

"The bishop sent word that you would be released today. We've come to take you home." At the base of the Ponte della Paglia, Paolo waited in the gondola.

Bianca offered Alessandra her arm, but she didn't take it. Instead, she looked past the Ponte della Paglia to the Piazzetta and the twin columns that marked the entrance to Venice, then began walking up the steps of the bridge.

Bianca clutched at her. "No, my lady. You must not go there."

Alessandra shook her off. She continued walking, slow but determined, down the steps on the other side and past the Doge's Palace. Bianca and Paolo watched her with concern. The heavily clouded sky pressed low. The Piazzetta and the Piazza were deserted, and had that peculiar, forlorn feeling that always descended upon Venice the morning Carnival ended. Colored feathers and bits of costume lay on the ground and skittered about in the wind like bright confetti. The square was empty, except for the three dead men who dangled from the gibbet between the columns.

They had been hanged by their feet, the punishment for treason. As Silvia had said, they were already dead by the time they were strung up, but gravity had distended their faces, giving them a gruesome appearance and exacerbating the marks of torture that had been inflicted upon them. At each end, she was certain, were two of the men named in her letter, although she had never seen them before: one was a Spanish *bravo* with a silver hoop in one ear, the other a French corsair, a captain's insignia on the breast of his leather jerkin.

And, hanging in between them, Antonio.

Alessandra's knees buckled and she sank down onto the cold stone of the Piazzetta, her skirt billowing out around her. She was too stunned to cry or to cry out. A seabird hovered high overhead and its plaintive call seemed to echo within her, as if her very soul had shattered.

Years later, she would remember it just so: the three hanged men, herself on her knees, Bianca standing on the bridge, quietly sobbing, Paolo waiting faithfully in the gondola, the empty Piazzetta. As if she'd seen it from above, all of it together, frozen and unchanging, in an eternal tableau.

Chapter Twenty-Seven

"We knew from Venetian records that Antonio Perez was one of the men hanged that day," Andrew explained to Maurizio and Gabriella after Claire's lecture had ended. The four of them stood near the stage as the audience streamed out the doors.

"But his name isn't included with the others in the Rossetti Letter," Claire added. "In fact, Utrillo-Navarre was the only known conspirator who wasn't mentioned, an oversight no previous historian had ever been able to explain. When we discovered that Alessandra and Antonio were acquainted, and possibly intimately involved, this omission seemed even odder. We concluded that Alessandra was trying to protect him."

Claire looked around the room with satisfaction. She hadn't fainted, hadn't even faltered, once she'd gotten started. Then there'd been all that applause at the end, and not just the polite kind, either. This lecturing business might turn out to be fun after all.

"Which prompted the question: if Alessandra was trying to protect Perez, why would she write this letter at all?" Andrew said. "That, combined with the two-month discrepancy and the tone of the letter, led us to believe that it was dictated to her. The final piece fell into place when Claire remembered that there was more than one *bocca di leone* in the Doge's Palace, and that it wasn't outside in the courtyard, but inside, in the Sala della Bussola, the compass room right next to the Sala dei Tre Capi. When Alessandra wrote the letter, she was *inside* the Doge's Palace, and most likely a prisoner. These discoveries seem to indicate that the Rossetti Letter was coerced; however, it's also evident that Bedmar and Ossuna were planning something—although we may never know precisely what it was."

"So, although we can say with certainty that there was a Spanish conspiracy," Claire said, "there was also, as Andrew believed, a Venetian conspiracy to create a Spanish conspiracy. Girolamo Silvia knew that Bedmar and Ossuna were plotting against Venice, but he didn't have enough hard evidence to prove it, so he created what he needed. At the same time, he blackened the reputation of his political rival, Dario Contarini. It was a huge political coup for him. It's clear that Alessandra Rossetti was Silvia's pawn," said Claire, looking at Andrew. "An unwilling one, perhaps, but still a pawn."

"It seems certain that both sides were culpable in the events of that year," Andrew said, "but I think Claire deserves much of the credit for this deduction."

"You can't be serious," Gabriella said. Her normally deep, sensual voice sounded peevish. "You've been working on this for months now, and suddenly she shows up and after a couple of days together, you're willing to share your sources and credit her with your conclusions? Not to mention allowing her to give your lecture. What are people going to say about that?"

"Frankly, I don't care what people say about it," Andrew said.

Gabriella responded by shutting Claire out of the conversation with a turn of her shoulder and an appeal directed at Maurizio. "I think Andrew's being much too charitable, don't you?" When she didn't get an answer from Maurizio, she turned to Andrew and for a moment looked as though she were going to demand an explanation for his largesse.

"I simply did what I thought was right," Andrew said.

"Exactly what did you do to make him act so generously?" she asked, turning a withering gaze on Claire. "I hope you can prove that your dissertation is based on your own research, and I mean yours alone. I don't think examining committees look favorably on people who 'borrow' from other historians. I'm sure the head of your department will be very interested to learn that both of you were working in the Marciana at the same time."

Claire was so shocked that she was at a loss for words, just as Maurizio and Andrew seemed to be. Gabriella's insinuation was obvious: that Claire had seduced Andrew into giving her more credit than she deserved. Maurizio looked at Claire and Andrew as if considering whether there was any truth to Gabriella's accusation. She couldn't blame him completely. After all, he'd seen them show up together rather late at his house the night before, and then he'd witnessed Andrew give up the limelight to her—not a common occurrence, she was sure. Andrew appeared stunned for a moment, then roused himself.

"You really are going too far, Gabriella," he said. "It wasn't like that at all."

"Why don't you tell me what it was like, then."

"We were working together."

"Working? Is that what it's called?"

Claire had heard enough. "It's curious that you think Andrew would be so susceptible to being used in that manner," she said. "We were simply working together. If you can't accept that, then I'm sorry for you. And"—Claire knew she shouldn't, but she couldn't resist—"sorry about your show being canceled, by the way."

Before Claire turned away, she saw Andrew look at Gabriella with complete surprise. So he hadn't known. She left them and walked out of the salon.

Claire stopped on the landing at the top of the staircase. Her confrontation with Gabriella had left her shaken, but whether it was from anger or apprehension she wasn't sure. Clearly Gabriella's need for Andrew Kent to succeed was immense. It would have been sad, even pathetic, except that Gabriella could do her serious harm. Just the suspicion of unethical behavior could be damaging. The competition for jobs, and the subsequent pressure to produce a spectacular dissertation, was so fierce that some people did incredibly foolish things: she'd heard of a student whose paper was based almost completely on sources that turned out to be of her own invention, another who stole archival documents and sold them online to help finance his degree. The examining committees had heard it all before, and Claire suspected that they were inclined to believe the worst. All Gabriella had to do was make a phone call or mail a letter.

She took a breath and felt her anxiety subside a little. It wasn't all that likely that Gabriella would do something so spiteful, was it? In any case, it certainly wasn't something Claire wanted to worry about today. Indeed, she had a lot to celebrate. She'd completed her research, she'd given a successful lecture, and now, she firmly decided, she was going to forget about it and enjoy herself. She had in mind a leisurely lunch and, as a surprise for Gwen, a gondola ride. All she had to do was collect Gwen and find Giancarlo and they could be away from here.

She spotted Gwen walking across the foyer and then outside, carrying Claire's tote bag over her shoulder along with her backpack. Strange, she thought as she descended the stairs, that Giancarlo had left before her talk was over. She'd noticed him at the beginning of the lecture and a few times while she was speaking, then suddenly he wasn't there anymore. Perhaps he was out on the patio, where Gwen had just gone.

Claire walked outside. A few small groups had gathered on the patio, but neither of her companions was among them. She turned into Calle Foscari, the lane that bordered the university building, and nearly ran into a man embracing a tall, beautiful woman with long black hair.

It took her a moment to realize that the man was Giancarlo. When her confusion had cleared, her first impulse was to turn and walk away. Then the couple noticed her, and drew away from each other.

Giancarlo turned to face her. "Claire, I'm sorry, this isn't what—"

The woman said something in Italian, so fast that Claire couldn't catch it, although it was obvious that she was upset and angry. And then, to Claire's surprise, she ran off.

"Oh my god," Giancarlo said. "This is not . . . Natalie is not . . . I mean, she's very . . ." He looked down the lane after her. "I'm sorry." Then he ran off, too.

Well. This day was turning out to be spectacularly different from what she had expected, and now her date for the afternoon had abandoned her for his erstwhile fiancée. Claire turned around and walked back to the patio. Gwen stood on the opposite side. She spotted Claire and waved frantically.

"Claire!" she called. "Don't go over there!"

Too late for that, Claire thought, and began walking toward her. Gwen ran across the patio just as Maurizio, Andrew, and Gabriella were coming out the door. Claire couldn't see if Gwen tripped or collided with them, but she did see what happened next: Gwen's bags went flying, and all their contents spilled out—Claire's notebooks and pens and guidebooks, Gwen's hair gel and makeup and candy—and Gwen ended up on the ground, unhurt but embarrassed. Claire helped Gwen stand up as Maurizio and Andrew retrieved the scattered items. Alessandra's diary had landed at Gabriella's feet. Gabriella looked down curiously for a moment, then bent over to pick it up. She opened the cover and flipped through the pages, her expression becoming more indignant the longer she looked at it.

"What are you doing with this?" she asked Gwen.

"It was in my bag, not hers," Claire said.

"This belongs to the Marciana." Gabriella's eyes flashed triumphantly at Andrew. "I told you she couldn't be trusted."

Surprised and confused, Andrew turned to Claire for an explanation.

"It was an accident," she said. "It got mixed up with Gwen's diary. We didn't mean to take it out of the library, of course." While Claire was trying to explain exactly how it had happened, Gabriella disappeared into a small *carabinieri* office just across Calle Foscari. Everyone looked up with surprise when she came back with a young officer in tow.

"Gabriella, I think you're being a bit hasty," Andrew said.

"Are you going to deny the evidence before your very eyes?

Something like this doesn't get into someone's purse by accident. I say she can tell her story to the magistrate." Gabriella turned to the *carabinieri* officer and began speaking in Italian. Claire caught most of it: priceless Italian artifact, the recent rash of thefts from Italian libraries, foreigners responsible. The policeman, who couldn't have been more than twenty-two, laconically nodded his small, flat head in solemn agreement. He seemed so accustomed to taking orders that he did her bidding without protest, as if a woman commanding him to arrest another woman happened every day.

He turned to Claire. "You must come along with me," he said, and motioned her toward the *carabinieri* office.

Gwen didn't say a word, but Claire saw her eyes grow wide. Then she bolted from the patio.

"Gwen!" Claire started to run after her, but the officer held her back.

Andrew leaned down to speak into her ear. "Stay here and talk to the police. I'll get her." Then he ran off, too.

Chapter Twenty-Eight

Claire peered through the grimy windows of the tiny *carabinieri* office in vain: outside, Calle Foscari was empty. She'd assumed that Gwen and Andrew would be showing up within minutes, but at least twenty had crawled by without any sign of them. She resisted an urge to pace and took a seat next to one of the policemen's desks, her thoughts whirling. Why had Gwen run off? And why hadn't Andrew brought her back yet?

She told herself to stay calm. Gwen had a guidebook and the hotel business card with her; she knew that if she were ever lost, she should ask for help getting to the hotel. But why did she run? Because she was afraid? Had she thought Claire was serious when she'd made that remark about Gwen taking the blame for her? No, surely not. Perhaps she went to call her father. Claire wondered if she'd even be able to reach him; he was en route from Nice to Paris today. She had mixed feelings about getting him involved, anyway. It was true that a rich man like Edward Fry could come in handy in these sorts of situations, but she would be mortified if he found out about this. Claire wasn't even sure how to refer to it: arrested? apprehended? held? Whatever it was called, Claire reckoned she'd be lucky if she got out of this stuffy little office in time to catch their evening flight out of Venice; the wheels of justice turned slowly in Italy. She didn't want to think about what would happen if she and Gwen weren't at the Paris airport to meet Gwen's father and his new wife.

At least Andrew had a phone with him. Claire decided to call as soon as Maurizio and Gabriella stopped talking long enough to give her his number. They'd both been glued to a cell phone from the moment they had all walked in the door. Claire had no idea who they were talking to, but she caught a few of Gabriella's words: " . . . our heritage . . . international problem . . . enforce the law . . . Rome, also . . ."

The police station was so unassuming that if it weren't for the rather medieval, iron-barred cell in the far corner, no one would ever know that it was anything other than a nondescript office, one containing a few gray metal desks and a row of battered file cabinets. A couple of ancient floor fans whirred and swung laboriously from side to side without doing much to disturb the close air. The two young policemen sat quietly at their desks.

Maurizio hung up and came over to perch on the desk near Claire. "I was just speaking to the director of the Marciana," he said quietly. "He told me that taking a book out of the library carries an automatic fine."

"How much?"

"Two thousand euros."

"Oh, dear." She wasn't sure she had that much in her bank account, and somehow she didn't think this would be covered under Edward Fry's miscellaneous expense fund. She might need Meredith's help after all. "If I pay it, will I be free to go?"

"The director says he can't make the decision as to whether or not to press criminal charges."

Criminal charges? "But you don't believe I took the diary on purpose, do you? It was stupid, yes, but I didn't steal it."

"I'm afraid that what I believe doesn't matter much. If it weren't for this rash of thefts, it wouldn't be such a problem. But as it is . . ."

"But I'm not involved with that. I can prove it."

"Can you prove it in the next hour or so?"

"Probably not, but no one can prove that I am."

"Italian criminal procedure is much different from American. We don't require proof of a crime for someone to go to jail. Sometimes suspicion is enough, and then the case is investigated once the suspect is . . ." He trailed off, not wanting to say the words.

"Behind bars?" For the first time Claire felt afraid. Maybe Gwen had done the right thing, running off like that.

Gabriella sauntered over to them. "He'll be here momentarily," she said.

"Who'll be here?" Claire asked.

"The investigating magistrate," Maurizio replied. "He'll talk to you and decide if there is any reason to issue an arrest warrant."

"Oh." Her voice sounded unnaturally high-pitched.

"I think it would be best if you postponed alerting your colleagues in the press, Gabriella," Maurizio said. She looked up from her perusal of her cell phone's personal directory. "At least until after the magistrate's decision. It might not turn out like you think." He spoke calmly but there was a warning in his tone, and Claire had the impression that he was reminding Gabriella of some past mistake. Whatever it was, it worked, and she snapped her phone shut, frowning petulantly.

Claire asked Maurizio for Andrew's phone number. She knew Gabriella had it, but she was loath to ask her for anything. If not for Gabriella, she wouldn't be in the police station, she was sure. Andrew and Maurizio may have been surprised, even shocked, to discover that she had taken Alessandra's diary from the Marciana, but she felt sure—well, pretty sure, anyway—that they would have believed her explanation and then allowed her to discreetly return it. Even though he hadn't uttered a word in support of her innocence, and had by all appearances remained completely neutral, Claire suspected that Maurizio was sticking around to make sure that Gabriella didn't make things worse than they already were—by calling the six o'clock news, for instance, with a late-breaking story about an international theft ring and, of course, a heroic retelling of how she had apprehended one of the thieves.

"Gabriella?" Maurizio said. She dutifully handed over her phone, with Andrew's number already up on the screen. Claire pressed a button and it dialed automatically.

"Yes?" Andrew's voice was barely audible, what with the static and the sound of a revving motor in the background.

"It's Claire. Where's Gwen?"

"She's right here with me. We're on our way back."

"Back from where?"

"Be there in . . ." His last words were lost in static and noise.

"I like my Saturday lunch best of all," said Armando Corregio, the investigating magistrate, his voice tinged with a querulous sense of loss. "On Sundays, Signora Corregio insists on cooking roast beef. Her roast beef is like shoe leather. I like my Saturday lunch best of all."

Honestly, Claire thought, Signor Corregio looked as though he'd never met a lunch he didn't like. He wasn't obese so much as stupendously solid around the middle. The suspenders holding up his summer-weight slacks were stretched to their limit; she imagined that when he took them off, they went flying across the room like a huge rubber band. The magistrate's face was round and smooth, with a thick layer of fat under the skin, like an ocean-dwelling mammal. He wore his dark hair slicked neatly back, and sported the slender mustache of a Victorian-era dandy.

"We're very sorry to have interrupted your meal," Maurizio began.

"My *Saturday*—"

"Yes, your Saturday meal . . . but if you can give us just a few minutes of your time and listen to Miss Donovan's story, I'm sure you'll find"—his eyes briefly went to Gabriella—"that there's no reason to begin proceedings."

"Signor Magistrate!" Gabriella interrupted. "That woman was discovered with this book, a priceless artifact of Italian history." She held up the diary as if it were a Bible and she were about to lead an evangelical service.

"Yes, but it seems to have been an honest mistake," Maurizio argued.

"Quiet, please." Corregio sighed and shifted grumpily in his chair, which was about half the width necessary for his girth. He nodded at Claire. "Can you make it quick? If I can get back in less than fifteen minutes, I won't miss the soup."

Claire searched his face, unsure of where to begin. Corregio didn't look like someone with a sense of humor. She suspected that he'd just as soon tell the officers to take her away if it would expedite his quick return home. "Well, you see, it was just an accident, really. I was working with the diary in the Marciana, and—"

Just then, Andrew, Gwen, and Francesca rushed in the door, slightly out of breath, as if they'd been running. Andrew quickly took in the scene: the two policemen, Claire in a chair facing the magistrate, Maurizio and Gabriella looking on.

"Before you begin any questioning, you should know there's been a terrible mistake," Andrew said.

"It's all my fault," Francesca chimed in. "I've made a terrible mistake."

"Terrible mistake," Gwen echoed.

Dumbfounded, Gabriella, Maurizio, and Claire stared at the three of them. Maurizio was the first to recover his poise. "This is Signor Corregio, the investigating magistrate," he said. "Perhaps you should explain further. You could begin," he said to Francesca, "by telling us who you are."

"Yes, of course." She smiled. "I am Francesca Luponi, head librarian at the Biblioteca Marciana," she said to Corregio. "You see, Gwen was showing me her diary . . ."

Eager to help, Gwen took her diary from her backpack. "See? It looks a lot like that old one, 'cause I spilled Coke on it once, and I dropped it in the road a couple of times, and once this guy on a bike ran over it—"

Andrew gave Gwen a warning glance and she abruptly stopped speaking.

"Gwen was showing me her diary," Francesca continued, "then Claire brought her materials to the desk and somehow when I was putting them all away, I mixed up the diaries and gave them the wrong one."

"But she said that she and this girl mixed it up themselves." Gabriella pointed at Claire while addressing the magistrate. "She already admitted that she took it!" She turned to Andrew. "Do you actually believe this?" she asked, waving her hand at Francesca.

"It seems that there's been a . . . a terrible mistake," he said. "When I caught up with Gwendolyn here, she told me what had really happened, but she said that Claire told a different story because she didn't want Francesca to get in any trouble. I thought that it was best for us to proceed to the Marciana to inform Francesca of what had transpired, and being the very nice person she is, she insisted on coming here to put things to rights. So, apparently, it was all just a—"

"Terrible mistake," Gwen and Francesca said.

Good god. Gwen and Francesca had concocted this ridiculous story, and somehow managed to convince Andrew Kent to go along with it. Three faces—Andrew's, Gwen's, and Francesca's—looked guardedly hopeful; two faces—Gabriella's and Signor Corregio's—looked as though Francesca's confession hadn't quite registered yet, and the questions they sought to form remained formless. Maurizio seemed to be smiling, rather enigmatically, to himself. Claire kept her face as blank as possible lest someone notice that the terrible mistake was actually a terrible lie.

Corregio looked from Francesca to Maurizio. "Does the director of the Marciana know about this?"

"Yes, I spoke to the director just a few minutes ago," Francesca said. "Once he heard that I was completely to blame, he said that he would like to extend his apologies to Miss Donovan, and said that he would be very sorry if an American was arrested or in any way slandered because of a mistake made by an employee of the Marciana, as it could become an international incident and reflect badly on us all." She smiled prettily at Signor Corregio.

"Yes," the investigating magistrate muttered. "Yes, indeed. A very bad reflection that could be." He stood up, checked his watch, and rubbed his ponderous belly. "Well, well. I think we're all done here. A terrible mistake. If I leave now I might get home in time for the pasta. *Arrivederci.*" He eased his bulk out the front door and walked off down the lane.

Gabriella turned to Andrew, openmouthed with rage. "How could you? You know very well they're lying."

"Gabriella, what does it matter? The diary's going back to the library. It was a mistake. There's no reason to carry on like this."

"How would you feel if English historical documents were being stolen? If someone took your precious Magna Carta out of the British Museum?"

"This hardly compares to that. And it wasn't stolen, it was an accident. Why don't we just let it be?"

Gabriella looked around the room defiantly. "We'll see about that." She flounced out of the office.

Andrew and Maurizio exchanged a glance. "I'll take care of it," Andrew said, and walked out after her.

The moment they were gone, the atmosphere in the room lightened considerably. Claire looked at Gwen and Francesca in amazement, and they smiled back broadly. "I don't know how to thank you," Claire said. "But, Francesca, I don't want you to get in any trouble. Perhaps I should speak to the director myself."

"It isn't necessary," she replied.

"But you took the blame for all this, and it's not your fault."

"There is no need to worry," Maurizio said with a smile. "I don't believe Signor Luponi will fire his own daughter for making a little mix-up like that. Would he?" he asked Francesca.

"Oh, no."

"What do you mean, daughter?" asked Claire, confused.

"My father is the director of the Biblioteca Marciana," Francesca confirmed. "As was my grandfather before him. I have excellent job security, although I would hate for this to happen again." She smiled, but her eyes were serious.

"It will never happen again," Claire promised.

"I think it's best for us to leave here quickly," Maurizio said to Claire. "I'll take you back to your hotel, then go with Francesca to return the diary to the library."

They all left the *carabinieri* office for the nearest *traghetto* stop. As they walked out of Calle Foscari, Claire saw Andrew and Gabriella at the far end, standing close together and talking. She couldn't hear what they were saying, but Andrew seemed to have a calming effect on Gabriella. She was still speaking excitedly, but with less vehemence than before. Andrew's hand gently rested on her arm as he looked earnestly in her eyes, attentively listening. Maurizio noticed Claire glancing back at the pair, and walked closer to her.

"Please excuse our contessa. I know she did not behave very nicely, but she does mean well. This is none of my business, I know, but a word of advice: it might be wise if you didn't spend any more time alone with Andrew. Gabriella is not an understanding girlfriend. And she is very powerful within certain circles in Italy. She can make a lot of trouble when she wants to."

"Not that I was planning to spend any more time with him, but I do appreciate your advice. And thank you for watching out for me. I don't know what I would have done if you hadn't been here to help."

"Don't speak of it. I have a vested interest, after all. I would much rather that you be free to speak at the conference again next year instead of locked up in jail. What do you think?"

"About coming back? I would love to, of course."

They reached the *traghetto* crossing. Maurizio stepped down into the boat and extended his hand to help them board. Claire let the other two go ahead of her, and was still standing on the stone terrace when she heard footsteps behind her.

"Claire."

She turned. Andrew stood a few feet away.

"I never had a chance to tell you how good your lecture was," he said.

"Thanks."

"I'm really sorry about all this. Gabriella can be a bit overzealous."

A bit? Claire thought, but held her tongue. "It's okay," she said, wishing she were completely sincere. Instead, she was thinking that it must be nice to have two men willing to make excuses for you. Ah, well. They'd done a fine job standing up for her, too; she might as well be a good sport about it. Anyway, there was something else on her mind, and this was her last opportunity to find out.

"Now that the research is done, how long will it take you to write your book?" she asked.

"Hmmm. That's a good question." He clasped his hands behind his back and peered at the ground for a moment. When he looked up, his expression was serious. "I don't see how I could possibly finish it until well after you've written your dissertation. After all, I'll need to quote from it—quite a lot, I should imagine."

Claire smiled, relieved and grateful. Her dissertation could be completed without worry of competition, or redundancy, and then it would be cited in his book. "That's—that's just—great," she stuttered happily.

"You will send it to me soon, I hope."

"At Cambridge?"

"Trinity College, yes. You can find my email address on the university website." He paused. "You know, we still don't know what happened to Alessandra after the conspiracy ended."

"That's true. I wish we'd been able to find out," Claire admitted.

"I have a friend at the University of Padua. Perhaps I'll give him a call and see what he can turn up." Andrew checked his pocket for a pen and paper. "Write down your email address, and if he comes across anything of note, I'll have him send it on."

Claire jotted down the information for Andrew, then joined the others in the *traghetto.*

"What was all that about?" Gwen asked.

"Just work stuff." As the boat moved out into the canal, Claire realized that she hadn't thanked Andrew—for his help, for the lecture, for everything. She turned around to call to him, but he was already gone.

Chapter Twenty-Nine

GWEN LEANED BACK in the gondola seat and turned her face up to the sun with a satisfied smile.

"This is awesome," she sighed as the colorful houses of the Rio di San Giuseppe slowly glided past.

Claire agreed it was a brilliant outing and more than compensated for the dramatic events of the day. After they'd checked out of the hotel and stowed their luggage in the lobby, she'd surprised Gwen by taking her out to the nearest group of gondole and asking her to choose a gondolier. It was Gwen's idea to make a tour of the sights mentioned in Claire's lecture. Good thing she had chosen a young and apparently tireless gondolier for their extended journey.

Claire regretted that she hadn't spent all her time in Venice traveling by gondola. It was, of course, the way that the city was meant to be seen, but the obvious truth felt like a revelation. The arterial canals gave the city light and life; it was as if Venice opened before them like a blossoming flower, revealing its true beauty and hidden secrets. The constant movement—of undulating reflections in the water, of their forward progress through sunlight and shade as they slipped momentarily under the arch of an ancient bridge and out again, of the teeming boats in the larger canals or the flapping laundry hung high above the smaller waterways—was interspersed with kaleidoscopic images of sun-drenched stone facades, cascading red begonias in blue window boxes, fat orange cats lazily sunning themselves upon stone steps, and was accompanied by the wonderful aromas of cooking food and the sounds of conversation and music floating down from high, arched windows.

The gondolier stopped rowing as they reached the end of the canal near the lagoon, and the boat glided to a gentle halt.

"That's Alessandra's house?" Gwen asked.

"Yes," Claire affirmed as she took her camera out of its case.

"Wish we could go inside."

"Me, too." Claire took a few photos of the house and its surroundings.

"Where to next?"

"The Rio del Palazzo and the Bridge of Sighs."

"That's where the prison is, right?"

"Right."

"Then to the Piazzetta, where Antonio was hanged, then to the Canal of Orphans, where all those guys were drowned."

Claire felt gratified by Gwen's interest in the Spanish Conspiracy, and chose to overlook her morbid fascination with the places where the more gruesome episodes had occurred. "Yes, and then to Campo Barnaba," Claire said.

"This is totally cool."

"It's the least I could do to repay you for springing me out of the clink. Tell me," she said as the gondolier began rowing them toward the lagoon, "how did you get Andrew Kent to go along with that story you made up?"

"I didn't make it up."

"Who did, then?"

"I don't know. When I saw the police taking you away, I decided to call Francesca. I knew she would understand that I would never leave my diary behind on purpose. Then Andrew caught up with me, and when I told him what I wanted to do, he decided that we should go over there to talk to her. So we took a motorboat to the Marciana, and then Francesca called her dad, and he was talking on the phone to him in Italian—I mean Andrew was talking in Italian, and then he and Francesca talked, and then she told me what to say."

"It was incredibly nice of her to go out on a limb for me, even if the director is her father."

Gwen shrugged. "I don't think she was the only one who convinced her dad to go along with it. She told me later that Andrew promised him he'd donate money to the Marciana restoration fund."

"He what?"

"He made a donation. He promised to bring them a check this afternoon."

"How much of a donation?"

"Three thousand euros."

"Three thousand euros?"

"Why are you yelling?"

"Three thousand euros!"

"I don't know what you're all excited about. It's a charity. It's tax deductible."

Claire groaned softly and put her head in her hands. Three thousand euros? Andrew Kent had been primarily responsible for Signor Luponi's acquiescence, without which she could still be sitting in that *carabinieri* office, or worse. And she hadn't even said thank you.

They wheeled their luggage behind them as they walked along the Riva to the San Zaccaria vaporetto stop and to the end of a line waiting for the airport-bound boat. Claire turned to look at the Piazza one last time. This was the busiest hour of the day, with crowds thronging the Riva and filling the tables in the Piazzetta. A masculine hand rose above the constantly moving masses and waved in her direction. A moment later, the person belonging to the hand appeared: it was Giancarlo, pushing his way through the crowds. Striding alongside him was a tanned, dark-haired young man whose good looks rivaled his own. She knew they were together because she saw Giancarlo cuff him on the head, as if urging him to keep up. More incredible still, they were both holding floral bouquets wrapped in cellophane.

Gwen followed Claire's speechless gaze into the crowd and

gasped. "Nicolo!" she screeched. She turned to Claire. "Oh my god. What am I gonna do? What am I gonna say?"

Claire had been wondering much the same thing herself. "Just smile and say, 'Thank you for the flowers.'" Her voice was calm despite the fluttery sensation in her stomach.

In an instant, Giancarlo and Nicolo had arrived and were standing before them.

"Ciao," Nicolo said to Gwen. He seemed to be having a difficult time looking up from his feet.

"Hi," said Gwen, blushing to the roots of her hair.

"I'd hoped to catch up with you sooner, at the hotel," Giancarlo said to Claire, "but Nicolo wanted to come along, and so . . ." He touched her arm and tilted his head. They moved a few feet away from the tongue-tied teenagers. "I hate that I've spent so much time apologizing to you, but this morning was not what it looked like. Natalie and I are not getting back together. It's true she's not very happy right now, and I don't know what to do about that, but I would really like to see you again."

"But I'm leaving now. I have to take Gwen to Paris to meet her father."

"And after that?"

"I'm going home."

"Do you have to?"

"What do you mean?"

"If no one's waiting for you there, why don't you come back here?"

"That's a lovely idea, but I can't afford to stay in Venice any longer."

"You could stay with me. My flat is not nearly so nice as my parents' house, but there's room enough for two."

Claire looked into Giancarlo's face and remembered the breathless excitement she'd felt when she'd first met him. There was no denying that he was one of the handsomest men she'd ever met, perhaps would ever meet.

"That's an incredible idea," she finally said. "I mean, it sounds wonderful, but I don't know if I—well, I don't know."

"Will you think about it?" he asked.

"Of course."

"Call me from the Paris airport and let me know what you decide." He handed her the flowers. "So you don't forget."

They looked at the younger couple near them. Gwen and Nicolo were talking; evidently they'd gotten over their initial shyness. Jesus, he was a good-looking kid, Claire noticed. Must be quite a gene pool these Baldessaris sprang from; she'd never seen such a beautiful family.

Claire motioned Gwen aside for a quick tête-à-tête. "I bet there aren't any other girls at your school who can say they've got an Italian boyfriend."

"Nicolo's not my boyfriend," said Gwen, glancing around to see if Nicolo had overheard them. "I mean, we only went out once, and it didn't turn out very good."

"You don't necessarily have to share all the details," Claire replied. "I'm just saying that when you go back to school in September, I'm sure that a story about a—how would you describe him?"

"Drop-dead gorgeous."

"A story about a drop-dead gorgeous Italian guy you met in Venice will make everyone forget about what happened with Tyler."

Gwen looked hopeful for a second, then reality hit. "Sure, except that no one's going to believe me. I mean, look at him. No one's going to believe that someone like him would like someone like me."

"You believe that Nicolo likes you, right?"

"I dunno," she said, shrugging.

"Well, you should! If he didn't like you, he wouldn't have come to say good-bye."

Gwen brightened noticeably for a moment. "Still," she continued, "just because I know he does, and you know he does, doesn't mean that anyone else will believe that he does."

"Oh, I think they'll believe you," said Claire, taking out her camera once more. "Because I'm going to take some photos of you and Nicolo, then you're going to make a really big enlargement of the best one and put it up on the wall of your dorm room where all your friends can see it—including Tyler."

Gwen's eyes grew wide with delight as she contemplated Claire's devious plan. "You rock!"

"That's good, right?" Claire asked.

"It's great."

Claire turned to Giancarlo. "Do you mind if we act like tourists for a moment?"

"Be my guest," he said graciously.

She nudged Gwen. "Stand with Nicolo over there, with the palace in the background," Claire said. As she aimed the camera, Nicolo shyly draped an awkward arm around Gwen, who smiled radiantly.

"She wasn't trying to kill him," Gwen said. They had just passed over the Alps on their northwest trajectory to Paris. Claire turned away from the airplane window and her contemplation of the wrinkled green earth far below.

"What?"

"My mom. Everyone thinks that she tried to kill my dad, but it's not true."

"She was just trying to . . . hurt him?"

"He had just bought this new, really expensive golf cart. That's what she was aiming at."

"But she shot him in the foot."

"Well, she's not a good shot! She's my mom, you know, not a sniper or whatever. Sorry. I'm not mad at you. It's just that everybody else said that she was upset because my dad was getting married again."

"And what did she say?"

"She said that the wedding had nothing to do with it. She said that he had destroyed her belief in love, so she decided to destroy his belief in golf." Gwen shrugged. "I don't know, though."

"You think there's more to it?"

"It's just that my parents got divorced a really long time ago—I mean, I don't even remember when my dad lived with us. But my mom hasn't had a boyfriend since, even though she's really pretty, and kind of funny, and a great dresser. My dad had like four or five girlfriends before he met Helen. But my mom—it's like my dad was the only guy for her. And the weird thing is that when they're together, all they do is fight. I don't understand why they got married in the first place, they're so different."

"It's harder for some people to move on," Claire said. "Divorce can be devastating, even when it seems like it's the right thing to do."

"Yeah, but it's been, like, nine years."

"Oh. That is kind of a long time. When you see your mom again, why don't you tell her what you just told me?"

"What, that she should get over my dad?"

"Maybe not that, exactly, but you could tell her that it's okay with you if she has a life of her own, if she goes out on dates. Maybe she's been worried you wouldn't like it."

"Except that I can't imagine who she'd go out with. They'd have to be really great, and she says there aren't any good men left in Boston."

"There is that little issue, yes."

"If only she could find someone as nice as Nicolo. We exchanged email addresses," Gwen confided. "He promised to write to me."

"That's terrific," Claire said as the seat belt light came on and the captain announced the start of their descent. "Although," she added as she buckled up, "who knows what Paris will bring. Another brief encounter, perhaps?"

Gwen snorted. "If my dad's anywhere nearby, it'll be brief, all right." She fastened her seat belt. "So, do you know anything about Paris?"

"Like what?"

"Like cool places to go."

"What do you mean by cool?"

"Like historical places where people were killed and stuff. Are there any places like that in Paris?"

"As it turns out, you're in luck," Claire replied. "You see, there was this little thing called the French Revolution . . ."

Chapter Thirty

EDWARD AND HELEN FRY waited at the end of the Alitalia wing of the Charles de Gaulle airport, just beyond the crush of people streaming out of the gates into the main terminal.

Gwen was the first to see them. "Dad!" she squealed and for a second Claire worried that Gwen's mad dash would end much like her sprint across the Ca' Foscari patio that morning, but she managed to pass through the crowds without mishap. She embraced Ed Fry with such force that he wobbled unsteadily, regaining his balance only after planting his cane firmly on the floor.

The newlyweds appeared tanned and relaxed. In their casual yet conservative attire, they looked every bit the Bostonians, as if they'd just come from Sunday brunch, or a boat ride on the Charles. Helen had a natural, unadorned attractiveness that, after Gwen's tales of her designer-clad mother, took Claire by surprise. She'd fallen victim to stereotype, thinking that a man as wealthy as Ed Fry would have married a trophy wife, but Helen struck her as clear-eyed and commonsensical. They exuded a calm happiness.

Gwen was already talking a mile a minute by the time Claire joined them and introduced herself to Helen.

"We took a gondola all over Venice and we went by the courtesan's house and the prison and the place where they hang people and this really awesome canal that was full of dead bodies and bones and stuff," Gwen rattled on.

"I'm so glad you had a good time, honey," Ed replied, patting her shoulder. "So everything went fine, then?" he asked Claire.

"Fine," Claire nodded briskly. "Absolutely fine." She saw a look of relief on Gwen's face. Helen briefly wore just the slightest expression of amazement, one that was quickly and politely suppressed.

"Dad, Claire told me about some really cool places to go in Paris. I was thinking that maybe tomorrow—"

Ed and Helen exchanged a look.

"I've got a ten o'clock tee time tomorrow at this course called St. Quentin something or other," Ed Fry said.

"Yvesline," Helen added.

"It's one of the top-rated courses in France," he explained.

"Dad!"

"Just this once. I won't be playing again while we're here, I promise. It was the only time available."

"Did he play golf every day when you were in Nice?" Gwen asked Helen.

"Only twice," Helen said. "You owe me ten dollars."

"Oh, man," Gwen moaned, but she didn't seem unhappy.

"We had a bet," Helen explained to Claire. "Gwen thought he'd be on a golf course every day. Anyway," she said, turning to Gwen, "save your ten dollars for tomorrow. It looks like it's going to be just you and me, during the day, at any rate. What do you want to do? Go shopping, I suppose?"

Claire got the impression that Helen would rather spend the day having oral surgery.

"Well . . . actually . . . Claire told me about some places, like from the revolution," said Gwen, glancing at Claire to make sure she got it right.

"Oh?" Helen seemed surprised, but intrigued.

"Yeah, like where they had the guillotine—what's that called?"

"The Place de la Concorde," Claire said.

"And there's this prison, where they kept people before they cut their heads off."

"It's the Conciergerie, on the Île de la Cité," Claire filled in.

"And this underground place; I *have* to go there."

"The Catacombs." Claire took a sheet of paper from her bag and gave it to Helen. "I've written everything down. I'm sure you can find the details in any guidebook."

"How interesting," Helen said sincerely, smiling as she looked over the list. "Sort of a 'reign of terror' tour. Certainly more fun than pawing through racks in the junior department at Galeries Lafayette." She caught Claire's eye. "Thanks."

Claire took a few more items from her bag. "Here're some things you left behind in the hotel room," she said, handing a small sack to Gwen. "And some postcards you bought, that lipstick I borrowed, and a little gift."

"It's beautiful," said Gwen, unrolling the velvet scarf Claire had found in a shop on the Merceria. "But I didn't buy anything for you."

"You didn't have to. Well . . ." She shifted uncomfortably from foot to foot. Why were good-byes so awkward? "I should check in for my next flight." She shook Edward Fry's hand, offered a heartfelt "Nice to meet you" to Helen, and smiled at Gwen one last time before she headed back in the direction they'd come from.

"Claire!" Gwen ran after her. Claire stopped and turned around. Gwen threw her arms around her and hugged her tight. "Thanks." Gwen released her, but stood there, silent and thoughtful, for a moment longer. "Don't go home," she said.

"You mean back to my boring life?"

"Giancarlo really likes you. I know he does, Stefania told me. You're going to call him, right?"

"Yes."

"When you get back, you have to tell me what happened."

"Sure," Claire said, smiling.

"And don't forget to send those photos. I can't *wait* till September. Well . . . ciao!"

"Ciao," Claire called after her. Instead of the relief she'd expected to feel upon returning Gwen to her father, she felt a pang of regret, even a little envy, as she watched the three of them walk away and blend into the crowds. She suddenly felt too aware of everything she'd lost when Michael left.

Claire turned and began walking back to the Alitalia wing. She didn't know much about Helen, but she guessed that her age was closer to Ed Fry's than to her own—late thirties, maybe forty. Chances were that Helen was divorced, but she obviously hadn't given up; here she was, newly married, moving on, moving forward, trying again. What was the advice she'd given Gwen? Live life, meet more people? Advice she hadn't taken herself. No, she'd retreated from everything, had become . . . that description still nagged at her . . . *secret and self-contained, as solitary as an oyster.*

Claire stopped in her tracks as she remembered where she'd read that line: in *A Christmas Carol.* It didn't refer to a romantic heroine wandering around on the moors, or something equally poetic; it was a description of Ebenezer Scrooge, she realized with wry dismay, and laughed out loud. She should have known that comparing herself to an oyster wasn't good. Gwen was right, Meredith was right: it was time to get out of her little house and get on with her life. But where exactly, and with whom?

In the center of the hallway, two rows of seats flanked a bank of telephones. Opposite the phones, floor-to-ceiling windows overlooked the tarmac and a line of jets parked at the gates. Claire sat down in one of the chairs and mulled over her options as she watched an Alitalia 727 taxi into place.

Don't go home, Gwen had said. No one's waiting for you there, Giancarlo had reminded her. It wouldn't be so difficult, would it, to rebook her ticket and go back to Venice? Claire had never done anything so impulsive in her life, and although she was fairly convinced that it was time to start, she wasn't finding it easy. She fervently wished that she could be one of those people who simply shrugged off lingering doubt, but she never had been, and probably never would be.

Too many things nagged at her conscience. She wouldn't be able to finish her dissertation in Venice, not without her computer and the notes and files and books she had at home. She'd worked on it for so long, and she was finally so close to completing it. It was foolish to let herself get sidetracked, even for a week or two, especially by someone as distracting as Giancarlo. But that wasn't the only thing holding her back. She suspected that, in spite of his protests to the contrary, Giancarlo's relationship with Natalie was unresolved, and she was certain that Renata would not be welcoming.

None of these things would have mattered too much if she were in love with Giancarlo, but she wasn't. It was an admission that caused her considerable discomfort. He was intelligent, handsome, rich, gainfully employed in a profession he seemed to be passionate about, and from all indications he was a sincere and sincerely nice person. If she couldn't fall in love with Giancarlo Baldessari, what hope was there for her? Like Deirdre Fry, had her belief in love been so destroyed that she couldn't fall in love again? If she didn't want Giancarlo, what was it she really wanted?

She knew that she would have to call Giancarlo and tell him she wasn't coming back, but what would she say? She supposed she could use the pressing demands of her work as an excuse. While it was true, it was also true that she could delay a week or so without much consequence. A novel idea occurred to her: what if she were honest and said that she thought they would be better friends than lovers? Why did a relationship between a man and a woman have to be all or nothing? Wouldn't it be nice, if she returned to Venice next year, for them to meet again as friends?

She went to the phone, took a credit card from her wallet, and then, with growing dismay, set about reading the instructions for the telephone's use. Numerous minutes later, she finally had Giancarlo's business card in one hand and was dialing with the other when she saw a familiar face among the crowd. She blinked a few times: surely her imagination was playing tricks. But as he walked closer, she saw that it was him. Unmistakably him. She slowly hung up the phone and waited. He didn't recognize her until he was about ten feet away. Still not wearing his glasses, she noticed.

He stopped as soon as he saw her, and the most amazing sequence of emotions animated his face: utter surprise followed by astonishment and then a subdued delight.

"Hello," Andrew said.

"Hello," Claire replied.

"Hello," he said again.

"Is that all you're going to say?"

"I thought you didn't like it when I didn't say hello."

"That's true, but most people quickly follow it up with something else."

"I'm just so surprised to see you. This is so odd. I was just thinking about you."

His confession caused a strange palpitation in her chest. Andrew Kent was thinking about her? She waited, curious to hear his innermost thoughts.

"So . . . Gwendolyn's back with her parents?" Andrew asked, shifting his satchel from one hand to the other. "All safe and sound?"

Not quite the sentiments she was expecting to hear. "Yes."

"And you? You're not staying in Paris, are you?"

Good lord. Were they going to make small talk until it was time for her to board the plane? Funny, but earlier that day she'd been thinking it was important to see him again, and now she couldn't remember the reason. "No, my flight for Boston is leaving soon."

"I rather thought you'd be going back to Venice."

"No."

"Ah."

Was she imagining it, or did he seem relieved? She could have sworn that when he'd said, "going back to Venice," there'd been a twinge of regret, even jealousy, in his voice.

"You see, I was thinking . . . ," Andrew said hesitantly, "just wondering, really . . ."

Oh, go on, get on with it, Claire thought impatiently. If you're going to ask me something, then *ask*—

"I'm sure you'll have plenty of other offers, but I thought . . . you see, we have a spot open for a guest lecturer this fall, and I was wondering if you'd consider it."

It took a moment for his words to sink in. Her thoughts had been traveling on a completely different track. "You're offering me a teaching position? At Cambridge?" she asked incredulously.

"The pay isn't fabulous, and it's only for a year, but . . ."

"You're offering me a job."

"Did I say something that you didn't understand?"

"You're offering me a job?"

"I am speaking English, yes?"

"You can do that, just like that?"

"You'll have to be approved by the hiring committee, but as I'm the head of the committee, and there are only three of us, I think I can swing the votes." Andrew waited for her reply, but Claire was speechless. "I'm sure you'll want some time to think it over . . ."

"No. I mean yes."

"Which is it?"

"No, I don't need to think it over, and yes, of course I'd love to teach at Cambridge." She decided so quickly that she surprised herself, but it was everything she'd ever wanted, and more. "So you would recommend me?"

"With confidence."

Claire wondered if Andrew's reasons for offering her a job were strictly professional. She couldn't tell, not with that English reserve of his. As he gave her his card and explained that she should get in touch with him in a few weeks, he was all business. And then she remembered why she'd wanted to see him again: to thank him for going to such lengths to get her out of trouble, and to ask why. Did he habitually cough up thousands of dollars to save women in need, or had he made a special effort for her?

"This afternoon," Claire began, "Gwen told me about what happened while I was in the police station, and she said—"

"Darling," Gabriella purred as she strolled up to Andrew and slipped her arm through his. She carried a shopping bag from the Chanel duty-free store. "Well," she said, smiling coolly at Claire, "I should have known we'd run into you again. Andrew, I'm beginning to think you're being stalked."

"Gabriella . . . ," he warned.

"Are you staying in Paris?" Gabriella asked Claire, ignoring him.

"No."

"No need to alert the French archives, then."

"Why don't you meet me at the baggage claim?" Andrew said to Gabriella. "I'll be along in a minute."

"We haven't time," Gabriella objected. "We're running late for our dinner with Bertrand as it is."

"I'm sorry, it seems I've really got to be going," Andrew said to Claire. "But you will get in touch, then?"

"Of course," Claire replied. It wasn't until they started walking away that she remembered what she'd wanted to say. "Thank you!" she called after Andrew, but she wasn't entirely sure if he'd heard.

Chapter Thirty-One

CUP OF TEA in hand, Claire had just walked out of the kitchen when she saw Meredith arrive on her front porch and knock on the door.

"I've only got a few minutes before I have to be at school," Meredith said as she stepped inside, "but I wanted to find out how the trip went."

"It was great, actually."

Meredith stared at her oddly. "Are you going somewhere?" she asked.

"No, in fact, I'm going to be working nonstop for the next month, and then I meet with Hilliard to hand in my dissertation. All that's left is the oral exam and I'll have my degree. Can you believe it?"

"That's terrific. But . . . how come you're dressed like that?"

"Like what?

"You're not wearing your pajamas."

"Oh." Claire laughed. "I threw them away."

"And about time, too. Where'd you get that green blouse? It's pretty."

"It's a souvenir from Gwen. She must have slipped it into my suitcase before we left."

"So how was it? With Gwendolyn, I mean."

"Well, at first it was . . ." Claire checked herself. No reason to go into all of it, was there? "It was great. We had a really good time together."

"What happened with that professor? Did you meet her? Did you find out about her book?"

"First of all, she turned out to be a he, and second, he offered me a job."

"You mean a real job? A teaching position?"

"Yes."

"Where?"

"At Cambridge, as a guest lecturer for a year. It starts in September."

Meredith looked at her, wide-eyed. "Good lord. That's fabulous!" She smiled wickedly. "Michael is going to eat his heart out."

"I know." Claire grinned back.

"So you're going to be gone for a whole year?"

"I'll be back next summer."

"What am I going to do without you for so long? A week was bad enough. I didn't have anyone to jog with, and I went out on this horrible date with a doctor."

"A doctor?"

"I thought it would be a nice change from the artistic types I usually go out with. Well, it wasn't. The very first thing he said to me after we sat down to dinner was, 'For such a tall woman, you sure have short, stubby fingers.' It took every ounce of self-control I had to keep from replying, 'For such a young man, you sure are bald.' And it just got worse from there. Do men actually believe that being insulting is some kind of courtship ritual?"

"Only the psychotic ones."

"Anyway, it was terrible, and I didn't have you to talk to."

"Summer school only lasts six weeks, right?"

"Yes."

"Maybe you should take some time off after that and go to Venice. After all, there are Italian men in Venice."

"You don't say."

"Hordes of them, all gorgeous." Claire paused, then smiled.

"Although there's one in particular I think you would like very much."

A week later, Claire received an email from Federico Donato, professor of history at the University of Padua.

> Andrew Kent asked me to get in touch with you regarding any information I could find regarding Alessandra Rossetti. We have nothing definitive here; however, in 1988, a graduate student wrote a paper on a woman named Alessandra Calieri, a resident of Padua in the early seventeenth century, whom she believed was born in Venice at approximately the same time as Alessandra Rossetti. The author of this paper made some claims that they were one and the same person. Intriguing idea, although it was never proven beyond a doubt. Apparently Alessandra Calieri and her husband were well-known illustrators of their time—botanical studies and so forth. There are only a few surviving examples of their work, but I can mail or fax copies, at your request.

Of course she'd write back and ask him to send them along. She'd like to read that graduate student's paper, too. Maybe the paper, combined with the coded letters Alessandra had written to her cousin, would be enough to prove that she'd gone to Padua after the conspiracy ended. Solving the mystery of Alessandra's disappearance would make a very nice ending for Andrew Kent's book. She forwarded the email to him, with a note that she'd be in touch soon.

And then she got back to work on her dissertation. If she were going to finish it by next month, she had no time to waste, and Claire was determined to meet her deadline.

After all, she had a lot to do before she left for England.

The World

12 September 1621

THE *AURORA*, A 600-ton French galleon on the final leg of its present journey, smoothly pitched over the gently rolling waves of the open ocean. Alessandra stood on the starboard side of the quarterdeck, enjoying the brisk, sea-misted air. This spot on the deck just above her cabin had been her favorite post from the beginning, during their journey south along the Adriatic, through the Strait of Otranto and into the Ionian Sea, and now, southeast across the Mediterranean. From here she could see most of the 140-foot ship stretched out before her and could view the activity on deck without being in anyone's way.

She watched as a group of sailors climbed the ratlines to unfurl the mainsail, which had been trimmed the night before when a storm appeared to the east. But the morning had dawned clear, with a steady wind, calm seas, and a sky of vibrant blue. The crew scurried about with a pleasant sense of purpose. She hadn't decided yet if the crewmen were the keepers of the galleon, or if it was the other way around: sometimes she thought of them as small, parasitic creatures clinging to the rough brown hide of a giant sea beast that creaked and groaned as it swam through the waves. At night, trussed in canvas slings, the men were rocked to sleep inside its great belly, like a hundred Jonahs inside a whale.

She understood why her father and brother had been drawn to

the road of the sea. A turn of the ship's rudder and they could go anywhere: Greece, Turkey, Syria, Jerusalem, Tunisia, Sicily, Spain, or west through the Strait of Gibraltar to Portugal and across the Atlantic to the New World. She felt exhilarated, alive and free as never before, felt alive as she'd never expected to feel again after the events of three years ago.

Once they'd buried Nico at the Church of San Giuseppe, she, Bianca, and Paolo left for Padua. She couldn't stay in Venice; her memories of Antonio were too painful, and she still had reason to fear Bedmar's and Ossuna's retribution. But soon after they were taken in by Giovanna and her husband, Lorenzo, she had received news of the conspirators' fates.

The Spanish ambassador was brought before the Great Council for an angry confrontation in which he was accused of "ignoble deceits." Bedmar swore to the Doge in the presence of the Senate that "as the nobleman I am, and by the chrism on my forehead," he knew nothing of the matters with which he was now being charged. But he had made a hasty exit from Venice almost immediately afterward, and no one expected him to return. The last Alessandra had heard, the marquis had become a cardinal and was serving in the Netherlands.

Shortly after the conspiracy was brought to an end, Ossuna's palace in Naples was attacked by an angry mob, and the duke burned in effigy. Ossuna was recalled to Madrid, where he was thrown into jail and, for the next two years, until he died, protested his innocence in the Venetian affair.

Jacques Pierre was arrested onboard the *Camerata* and executed by its Venetian admiral. Arturo Sanchez and Nicholas Regnault had been hanged along with Antonio. The fate of the others mentioned in her letter was unknown. They may have met their end in the Canal of Orphans, as so many did; or they may have escaped the city.

Girolamo Silvia adopted La Celestia's daughters, who as the heirs to their mother's and to Silvia's fortunes became the most desired match among the Venetian nobility, in spite of the fact that they were some years away from being of marriageable age. Silvia prospered after the conspiracy was exposed and ended. His political status increased, until the winter of 1620, when a sudden illness unexpectedly took his life. Rumors persisted that he had caught a fever from the contaminated blood of a Turkish spy he had tortured; others whispered that poison had hastened his end. Mourning for the senator was brief and perfunctory.

In the weeks following her own flight from Venice, Alessandra desired no one's company except for Bianca's, her cousins', and Paolo's, who stayed on with them in Padua. Even after the three of them moved into their own domicile, a small villa surrounded by gardens, she remained a recluse, spending her days in silence, taking no comfort in her usual pursuits. Paolo was her most constant companion. With his skillful pen, he often captured views of Padua to share with her. Every day he urged her to draw, bringing her the gilded box that contained her inks and charcoals and paper, until one morning she proposed a pact: she would draw if he would read aloud to her one hour each day.

During that long summer, they whiled away the daylight hours together in the garden, sketching the plants and the flowers and each other, she learning his silent language, he strengthening his voice. One evening, Giovanna and her husband came to visit and Lorenzo exclaimed over their sketches and insisted on taking a few to show his friend, a publisher of books that were widely used at the university. Soon they had a commission to create illustrations for a series of volumes that would document the local flora.

It took them nearly a year to complete them all, and in that time Alessandra discovered the joy of true employment. It was a pleasure to be contributing to the edification and greater knowledge of all, to draw with a purpose beyond her own amusement, to earn a living with her mind, her talent, and her craft. With this satisfaction came the certainty that she would never return to her former life.

Paolo also flourished. He was now a man of twenty-four, confident, secure, tirelessly industrious. After the botanical books were printed, they received many offers; Paolo's precise rendering caught favor and was in great demand. Sometimes Alessandra worked with him, and sometimes Paolo was sent far afield on his commissions, to Verona, to Florence, once even to Rome.

Gradually, Alessandra realized that she was in love with him. Perhaps not with the same kind of passion she'd felt for Antonio, but with a quiet, steady love that grew deeper with time and gathered strength from the pleasure they found in their mutual endeavors and from the tenderness with which Paolo always treated her. Soon after they were married, they were offered an extraordinary commission: a trip to Egypt to document the wonders of the Nile Valley, of which many people had heard but few had seen. Alessandra recalled her father's stories of that magical land, and they had accepted at once.

Alessandra rested her arms on the thick wood rail of the ship and looked over the ocean with deep wonder and satisfaction. What sights they would see! What treasures they would behold! The date palm and the camel, the white-robed followers of Mohammet, the minarets and the mosques, the colossal pyramids rising from a sea of sand. She was brought back from her reverie when she spied Paolo on deck, walking toward her. He had become a handsome man, almost unrecognizable from the scrawny youth she had first seen rowing Bedmar's gondola. Sometimes, like now, she felt that she was seeing him for the first time, and her heart never failed to leap a little.

Paolo approached and offered his cloak. She shook her head.

"But the air is cold, my love."

"I don't mind, I find it refreshing."

"Captain Fournier says he can't recall a woman who adapted to life onboard ship so well as you. I believe he admires you."

"He also admits that this has been an uncommonly happy voyage. Yesterday he mentioned that he'd never seen the weather so clear at this time of year."

"He just told me that if we continue at this pace, we should sight land in two days."

"Did he say where?"

"If we keep true to our course, we should see it there, just right of the bowsprit." He pointed across the sea. Her gaze followed, skimming over the water to where the sky met the edge of the earth and resolved into a thin, silvery line. The vision filled her with awe at the immensity of the world and the vast, unknowable future. Not long ago, her life had ended—and she had discovered that a life could end, and still continue, and still be utterly surprising and unpredictable, with the capacity for wonder and joy and love. She had discovered that a heart, once broken, could be healed.

She felt Paolo's arms enfold her, and she readily accepted their familiar comfort. He was her willing partner on this journey, yet she knew that at times he longed for the Serenissima's watery world, its labyrinthine canals, its delicate rippling light, just as she did.

Someday they would go back to Venice; someday, after the old memories were replaced by new memories and all the ghosts were put to rest. But for now their future lay ahead, and she held her gaze steady on the place it would appear: there, just there, on the shining horizon.

Author's Note

Although *The Rossetti Letter* is a work of fiction, the Spanish Conspiracy against Venice is a real event. It has been written about and debated by historians and others ever since Paolo Sarpi, author of *History of the Council of Trent* and Venice's official historiographer, summed up his thoughts on the conspiracy in a memorandum to the state in the early seventeenth century.

Accounts of the Spanish Conspiracy typically follow a similar narrative, although the particulars often vary. In May 1618, the duke of Ossuna and the marquis of Bedmar were accused of planning an attack on Venice "from within and without": Ossuna with his fleet, Bedmar with a newly recruited mercenary army. The plot was ended precipitously when one of the mercenaries revealed all to the Venetian Senate. Three of the mercenaries were hanged in San Marco—strung up by their feet, the sign of treason. The Venetian government gave no reason for the executions, but the sight of the hanged men quickly emptied the city's inns and lodging houses of the *bravi,* soldiers, and sailors whose numbers in Venice had recently increased. By some accounts, three hundred of these French and Spanish soldiers-of-fortune were subjected to Venetian justice and were drowned in the Canal of Orphans; other chronicles mention only three so ruthlessly dispatched.

Bedmar was summoned by the Senate for a fractious meeting in which he was accused of "ignoble deceits"; even though he proclaimed his innocence, he soon left Venice and never returned. Ossuna's reign in Naples also came to an unsavory end. He was recalled to Spain, accused of seeking to make himself "king of Naples," and died in jail two years later.

Although Bedmar and Ossuna's complicity has never been established beyond doubt—the basis for the belief in their culpability ultimately lies with Sarpi's pro-Venetian view of the events—it seems clear that they were by no means innocent of the desire to stage a coup against Venice. The facts of the Spanish Conspiracy have been long debated, and it's possible that no one will ever be certain of exactly what happened. I have attempted to give an accurate portrayal of the Spanish Conspiracy, insofar as those events are known. For the purposes of fiction, however, I changed the timing of the deaths of the three conspirators, moving forward to March 1618 what actually occurred in May of that year.

But with its lack of definitive evidence, the Spanish Conspiracy still offers an unsolved mystery, which has allowed for much invention on my part. With the exception of Ossuna and Bedmar (and minor characters Jacques Pierre and Nicholas Regnault, French mercenaries who are often mentioned in accounts of the conspiracy), all the characters in the novel—including Alessandra Rossetti, Antonio Perez, La Celestia, and Girolamo Silvia—are fictitious, as are the situations in which they are involved. However, the characters' lives, concerns, and milieus are rooted in research of the period. In re-creating the world of seventeenth-century Venice, I was greatly assisted by a variety of sources.

Regarding the Spanish Conspiracy, I am deeply indebted to Professor Richard Mackenney for his erudite and fascinating article, "A Plot Discover'd?: Myth, Legend and the 'Spanish' Conspiracy against Venice in 1618," collected in *Venice Reconsidered: The History and Civilization of an Italian City-State 1297–1797* (Johns Hopkins University Press, 2000), which first posits the intriguing idea that the "Spanish" conspiracy was a feat of statecraft engineered by master propagandist Paolo Sarpi. Other accounts of the Spanish Conspiracy can be found in *Venice; an historical sketch of the Republic* (Putnam, 1893) and *The Venetian Republic* (J. M. Dent, 1902) by Horatio F. Brown; *Venice and the Defense of Republican Liberty: Renaissance Values in the Age of the Counter Reforma-*

tion by William J. Bouwsma (University of California Press, 1968); *New Cambridge Modern History,* volume IV (Cambridge University Press); and *A History of the Italian Republics* by JCL Sismondi (Anchor Books, 1966). There is also a brief mention in Will and Ariel Durant's *The Story of Civilisation,* part VII (Simon & Schuster, 1961).

For general Venetian history, I found those stalwart classics, *Venice—A Maritime Republic* by Frederic C. Lane (Johns Hopkins University Press, 1973) and *A History of Venice* by John Julius Norwich (Knopf, 1982) to be most helpful. The *Diary of John Evelyn* (Oxford University Press, 1959) and Michel de Montaigne's *Diary of a Journey to Italy in 1580 and 1581* (Harcourt Brace, 1929) provided enlightening first-person accounts of travelers to Venice in the sixteenth and seventeenth centuries. Tim Moore's *The Grand Tour* (St. Martin's Press, 2001) contrasted the author's hilarious twentieth-century Venetian pilgrimage with that of seventeenth-century wanderer Thomas Coryate. I was often inspired by the incomparable *The World of Venice* by Jan Morris (Harcourt Brace, 1993), an evocative, multifaceted exploration of the city's past and present.

Lynne Lawner's *Lives of the Courtesans: Portraits of the Renaissance* (Rizzoli International, 1991), Patricia Fortini Brown's *Private Lives in Renaissance Venice* (Yale University Press, 2004), and Margaret Rosenthal's and Catherine Stimpson's *The Honest Courtesan: Veronica Franco* (University of Chicago Press, 1993) were invaluable sources on Venetian courtesans. Also, *The Book of Courtesans* by Susan Griffin (Broadway Books, 2001) and *Elegant Wits and Grand Horizontals* by Cornelia Otis Skinner (Houghton Mifflin, 1962) offered anecdotes and insights into the world's oldest profession. On the flip side, Mary Laven's *Virgins of Venice* (Viking Press, 2002) provided a compelling examination of Venetian nuns and convents.

Acknowledgments

My sincere thanks to everyone who so graciously read and commented on this work: Briana Baillie, Marianne Betterly-Kohn, Claudia Michelle Betty, Bruce Cobbold, Lauren Cuthbert, Karen Hronek, Amanda Jones, Danielle Machotka, Kate McClain, Megan McLaughlin, Cynthia Phillips, Chelsea Tiffany, and Alison Wright. I am also indebted to Professor Richard Mackenney for his help and advice regarding the Spanish Conspiracy, Venetian history, and historical research. All errors, inaccuracies, and improbable fictions, etc., are solely my own. I owe a debt of gratitude to my parents, Don and Laurie Phillips, for their unflagging love and support over the years. My thanks also go to Mary Evans, agent par excellence, and to Maggie Crawford, who from the beginning saw the book's potential and who so skillfully—and diplomatically—made it better. Everlasting love and thanks to Brian Beverly, for his support, encouragement, and belief. A special thank-you to Diana Cobbold and Linda Watanabe McFerrin, for the camaraderie, the commiseration, and, of course, the chocolate.

Prologue

29 June 1670
the Palace of Saint-Cloud, Paris

Urgent to the Rue de Varenne, Paris

The Royal Doctors give her over and so do all that see her. Princess Henriette-Anne took to her bed this morning with a Sickness some say is Poyson. She convulses and screams and clutches her Belly sobbing—it is a Piteous thing to Witness. Most suspect her husband, the Duc d'Orleans, and his lover, the Chevalier de Lorraine, whom King Louis banish'd to the country only a Fortnight ago. But the King will never condemn his scandalous Brother, even though his sister-in-law is now Torment'd by the most excruciating Agonies.

Mors certa, hora incerta, yet all goes on as Before. The courtiers mill about Henriette-Anne's apartments, engaging in idle Discourses, as if this Night were no different from any other. Not one of these tricked-up Peacocks has a care that the Princess's sincere Piety and youthful Beauty will soon be Lost; tho' I must confess that her beauty has quickly Wither'd, with the repeat'd clysters and the copious Vomits. The French courtiers—it is a simple task to distinguish them from the English, for their excess of Lace and overbearing Scent reveal them at once—can barely conceal their Astonishment, that a young noblewoman would Suffer so indelicately; and they continually sniff their perfum'd handkerchers to mask the Stench that accompanies Death. The Princess's bedchamber, tho' it is grand and overlooks the Palace gardens and the Seine, smells like a charnel-house.

The English contingent (who are known to you) are more stoic and less Afflict'd. Tho' I detect a Panic amongst them that cannot be attribut'd to any gentle Sentiment for the Princess. I am almost certain that they are not waiting upon her because she is King Charles's belov'd sister and King Louis' belov'd sister-in-law, but have remain'd in France on a secret Purpose; the Discovery of which may well Benefit you.

The efficient overseer of Henriette-Anne's bedchamber, Madame Severin, is as always present. Tonight she is perch'd at the Princess's bedside, as ominous as a Tower raven, alert to every Sigh and Tremor her mistress makes. Henriette-Anne's fatal Distress has made Madame Severin the very embodiment of Despair and Melancholy, or so it appears; yet not long past I chanc'd to hear a Quarrel between them, of which I will disclose more when we meet. The Princess's Maids are as mournful as the Matron; they huddle in the corner, red-eyed and fearful, knowing they will be without Employ or Benefactress once their Lady is still and cold.

Only one, the pretty little Breton Louise de Keroualle, seems unconcern'd with her Fate. Perhaps the Attention given her by King Charles at Dover was not Lost upon her. De Keroualle is not clever, but she is comely and very Ambitious. She makes much of her Virtue, but I have heard rumors of a past Liaison with the Comte de Sault, a dull Rogue if I ever knew one, and she is poor. Even if she became maid-of-honor to the Queen she could not make an auspicious Match in France. If lured to England, I believe she will be amenable to offers of something less than Marriage. Use her and use her well.

I must bring this Missive to a close — more later.

It is now past Three of the clock. Madame Severin has risen and call'd for the Bishop—the End is near. But no; the Princess motions her back to the Bed, rising on one unsteady Arm to utter a few hoarse

Words. Madame Severin looks into the crowded room, her black Eyes uncommonly bright in the candlelight.

"Monsieur Osborne," she says, her voice rough with grief.

The courtiers react with perplex'd bewilderment, a suppress'd ripple of Protest, even outrage. Why Roger Osborne? The Englishman is not a favorite. A friend to King Charles and to Henriette-Anne, to be sure, but someone who arriv'd late to the Royalist cause. Has the princess forgotten his Parliamentarian past, his work for Cromwell? Perhaps all that matters is that Osborne forgot it quickly enough once Charles was restor'd to the throne.

Osborne steps out of the crowd, a man of middle Years in unfashionable dark clothes and a cheap Periwig. He kneels at Henriette-Anne's bedside, then leans forward to hear her weak rasping Voice. As she murmurs his eyes grow wide and he shakes his head. Whatever Task she is assigning him, he does not want it, though by refusing he risks a charge of Treason. Henriette-Anne becomes agitated. Madame Severin moves closer, ready to end their dangerous Interlocution. The Princess waves her away, then tugs a weighty gold Band from her finger. She presses it into Osborne's palm. He stares at it as if he has never seen a ring before.

When he looks up he has the Countenance of a man who has heard something deeply disturbing. The Princess utters a grievous Sigh and falls back onto the bed, her body buckling in pain. Madame Severin summons the Bishop and the room breaks into a Commotion as the courtiers make way. The Bishop rushes to the bed, but it is all for naught: the Princess's rattle is loud enough for most to hear that she has Dyed. A shock'd Gasp fills the room and the courtiers stop their twittering. The ring falls from Osborne's hand and rolls along the floor, a golden streak of Light. Finally it collides with the wall and falls to one side, wobbling on the rim in ever faster Revolutions, its metallic singing filling the sudden Silence.

Your dear Friend and my Angel the Princess Henriette-Anne is gone. Her Radiance was too early extinguished. I will say only this, *Letum non omnia finit:* death does not finish everything.

I remain your most Humble & Obedient, &c.

One

London, November 1672

She leaves her house on Portsmouth Street carrying a wood box with a smooth ivory handle and tarnished brass fittings. It is late afternoon in early November. The street is deserted and cold, and the sunless ground sprouts scaly patches of hoarfrost; with each step her pattens crack the thin ice to sink into the mud beneath. At the top of Birkin Lane she hoists the box to gain a firmer hold—it is heavy, and she is slight—and the constant dull ache behind her eyes becomes a throbbing pain. She has learnt, to her dismay, that the least occurrence can precipitate a headache: a sudden movement, a sound, even a sight as innocent as birds' wings fluttering at the periphery of her vision. She considers setting the box down, unhitching its scarred metal latches and searching its neatly arranged collection of bottles and vials until she finds the one that she desires. It is late, however, and she is in a hurry. She continues walking. The small streets she passes through are little traveled; she encounters only a few others who, like herself, appear anxious to reach their destination. Hers is an alley near Covent Garden, and the decrepit attic room of a house that was once grand. As she crosses Middlebury Street her breath appears as puffs of white vapor that linger long after she has gone.

When she reaches the Strand she stops, confronted by a street teeming with people, horses, sheep, and snorting, mud-caked pigs that root in the gutter. The autumn evening is brief and precious, a time for gathering the last necessaries before going home, and the shops and street vendors are briskly busy. The air is blue with coal smoke, rich with the aromas of roasted meat and onions. Underneath is the ever-present odor of the sewer, a narrow, open gutter in the center of the road, where the pigs scavenge. The morning's storm washed away some of the sewage, but the gutters of London are never completely clean. In between the piles of gnawed bones and bits of offal are orphaned puddles of rainwater that shine like mirrors, reflecting nothing but overcast sky.

She pushes back the hood of her cloak; long locks of unruly dark hair break free. In the crush of scurrying people, the limpid brightness of the paned shop windows, the copper lanterns haloed against the darkening firmament she senses a feeling of contentment tantalizingly within reach. All Hallows' Eve is approaching. This is her favorite season, or once was. In the chilled grey hour before the November night descends she has always felt a kind of magic. When she was younger she imagined that this feeling was love, or the possibility of love. Now she recognizes it for what it truly is: longing and emptiness.

"Mrs. Devlin." A voice rises above the street noise. "Mrs. Devlin? Is that you?"

"Yes," she replies, recognizing the short, ruddy-faced woman in a cotton bonnet and a thick apron who pushes through the crowd to reach her. She remembers that the woman is a goodwife to a Navy minister, remembers that she lives with her husband in St. Giles near the sign of the Ax and Anvil, remembers that the woman's mother had suffered an apoplexy and then a fever. It takes her a moment longer to remember the woman's name. "Mrs. Underhill," she finally says, nodding.

"We never properly thanked you, Mrs. Devlin," Mrs. Underhill's flushed face gets rosier, "seeing as we couldn't pay you."

"Do not trouble yourself. You owe me nothing."

"You're very kind," the goodwife says with a small curtsy and bob of her head. "I tell everyone how good your physick is. My mother's last days were more easy because of you."

She remembers Mrs. Underhill's mother. By the time she'd been summoned the elderly woman was as frail as a sparrow, unable to speak, barely able to move, and delirious with fever. More than a year has passed, but she suddenly recalls holding the woman's emaciated body as if it were only moments ago. "I'm sorry I could not save her."

"She'd lived a long life, Mrs. Devlin. She was in God's hands, not yours." Her words carry a gentle admonishment.

"Of course," she says, closing her eyes for a moment. The pain in her head has grown stronger.

"Are you all right?" Mrs. Underhill asks.

She looks into the goodwife's eyes. They are clear, green, ageless. She briefly considers telling her about the headaches and the sleeplessness. Mrs. Underhill would understand.

"I'm fine," she says.

"That's a funny one, isn't it?" Mrs. Underhill smiles, relieved to be unburdened of the thought that a physician could take ill. "Me asking after a doctor's health. And you with a whole case full of physick," she adds, looking at the wood box. "I suppose you of anyone would know what medicines to take." She peers across the Strand at one of the street vendors. "Pardon my hurry, but I should be on my way. If the master doesn't have his oyster supper every Friday…"

They take their leave of each other. As she departs the Strand for Covent Garden, a wintry, soot-filled wind strikes her face. The sky is darker now and the sense of tranquility she momentarily felt has disappeared as if it never existed. Inside her head, a bouquet of sharp metal flowers takes root and blossoms. The headache is here to stay, for hours, perhaps days. The medicine case bumps hard against her leg. Many times she has thought of purchasing a smaller, lighter one, but she has not done it. She would never admit it, but she believes that the medicine case itself has healing power. She is aware that this is a superstition with no basis in fact; indeed, she has ample evidence to the contrary. The boy she is on her way to see, a seventeen-year-old apprentice stricken with smallpox, will most likely die before the night is over. For days she has followed Dr. Sydenham's protocol, providing cool, moist medicines where others prescribe hot and dry. The physician's radical new method seems to offer a slightly improved chance of a cure, but she knows that only a miracle will save her patient now, and she has long since stopped believing in miracles. The most she can do is ease the boy's suffering. *Ease suffering.* So she was instructed, but it hardly seems enough. Just once, she would like to place her hand on a fevered cheek and feel it cool, to cradle an infant dying of dysentery and stop its fatal convulsions, to give medicines that cure rather placate disease. To heal with her hands, her knowledge, and her empathy. Even a small miracle, she believes, would redeem her.

When she looks up from her ruminations she sees that night has fallen. A coach has stopped at the end of the lane, its outer torches lit. The bald coachman sits with straight-backed posture and pulls on the reins, as if he'd just brought the horses to a halt. She slows her pace. Something about it bothers her, though there's no precise reason for her concern; it's only a common hackney. The door creaks open, a man steps down to the street. He looks at her with a gaze so direct it feels both intimate and threatening, as if he knows her and has a personal grievance with her. She is certain she has never seen him before. He is dressed like a man of quality, but his stance and beefy body are more suited to a tavern brawler.

She's close enough that he hardly needs to raise his voice when he speaks. "Mrs. Hannah Devlin, daughter of Dr. Briscoe?" he demands. His voice is hard, without finesse, and her first impression is confirmed: he's a brute in expensive clothes. She braces herself, her right hand dipping toward her skirt pocket and the knife concealed there, a knife she wields with more than ordinary skill. Before her fingers touch the weapon she is seized from behind. The ruffian's accomplice wraps his thick arms around her waist and lifts her off the ground so quickly and effortlessly she doesn't have time to think about the strangeness of it all. The first man grabs the medicine case from her and shoves it inside the coach; the other immediately hoists Hannah through the door after it. She lands on the hard seat facing the back, knocked out of breath. Even if she had been able to speak, being confronted with the person who calmly sits across from her would have shocked her into momentary silence.

"Mrs. Devlin," he says. It's both a greeting and a chastisement.

She regards him warily. Lord Arlington, Secretary of State, is the king's most trusted minister and the most powerful man in England, after the king. His periwig has more grey in it than she recalls, but his air of self-importance and the small but pretentious black bandage across his nose, covering a scar won fighting for Charles I, is the same as ever.

"You carry your father's medicine case," he comments. "How sweet."

Arlington had once been a friend of her father's, but that was many years ago, before they had become enemies. She dislikes hearing him mention her father, even in such a cavalier manner. Arlington raps his gold-tipped walking stick on the ceiling and the coach lurches forward.

"Where are you taking me?" Hannah asks.

"To Newgate," he says, settling back and letting his walking stick fall to the side. "You're under arrest."

The Worst Thing I've Done

By Ursula Hegi

On the east end of Long Island a young woman deals with the aftermath of one reckless choice that changes everything . . .

Friends since childhood, Annie, Jake and Mason had a special bond that transcended all other relationships. When Annie's parents die on her and Mason's wedding night, the three friends decide to raise Annie's infant sister, Opal, together. But Annie's closeness to Jake and Mason treads a dangerous line. Entangled relationships develop between them as Annie struggles to be both a sister and a mother to Opal. And then on one fateful night, the friends step over a line that has shocking, unforeseen consequences.

Beautifully written and brilliantly vivid, this shockingly frank and riveting novel of friendship, love and death will resonate long after each character tells their story. *The Worst Thing I've Done* is a subtle and haunting novel that poses the darkest of moral dilemmas.

'Hegi's unusual, original talent is a delight'
Independent on Sunday

ISBN 978-1-84737-094-5
PRICE £11.99

Ursula's Story

By Sandra Howard

From the author of the acclaimed *Glass Houses* comes a captivating new novel: the story of a woman whose marriage break-up makes headline news, while she tries desperately to keep her family together and forge a new life for herself . . .

Ursula's story opens on the morning of her ex-husband William's wedding. The press call her first thing, demanding she share her innermost feelings with the world at large. Her three children cannot restrain their excitement. After all, it isn't every day that their father marries a government minister, and the Prime Minister and half the Cabinet are to be among the guests.

Ursula, herself embarked on a shaky new relationship with Julian, a local antiquarian bookseller, sees how hard their 11-year-old daughter Jessie has taken the break-up. Her father's favourite, she has put up walls, closed doors and turned to Julian for support. But Julian himself is hard to read, his absences from their lives ever more prolonged and unexplained. Are Jessie's defences strong enough to protect her, when a threat to her life catches Ursula completely off-guard?

ISBN 978-0-7432-8556-8
PRICE £12.99

Black Mulberries

By Caitlin Davies

Family secrets. Sibling rivalry. Passionate love affairs. Dangerous obsessions.

Four women take turns to tell their story.

Nanthewa, the matriarch determined for her son and daughter to live the lives she's planned for them – despite what they might want for themselves.

Kazi, Nanthewa's beautiful, wilful daughter who defies her mother to follow her lover abroad. From an isolated Scottish castle to the catwalks of Paris and Milan, Kazi's life will follow a very different path to the one she had imagined.

Petra, the daughter of a Great White Hunter who harbours a childhood passion for Kazi's brother, Isaac. Now a successful journalist, she's returned home to uncover the truth about a story no one wants revealed.

And **Candy**, Nanthewa's troubled granddaughter, who sees and understands more than anyone knows.

Set against the lush, wild landscape of northern Botswana, *Black Mulberries* is the unforgettable tale of two feuding families whose destinies are intertwined.

ISBN 978-1-4165-2254-6
PRICE £6.99

Stone Cradle

By Louise Doughty

'All of us are born into a stone cradle but some of us have the sense to climb out of it . . .'

Clementina Smith is just a young girl when she gives birth to her illegitimate son, Elijah. Others have been put out on the highroad for less, but Clementina's mother and father stick by her and Elijah grows up greatly loved by his small but tight-knit family. But then he meets a non-Romany girl . . .

From the farms of the Fens in the 1870s through the back-streets of Victorian Cambridge to modern-day Peterborough, *Stone Cradle* charts the history of three generations of one extended family. How do Travellers adapt to a century that no longer needs them? And what is everyone to do, when two women in a family can hardly stand the sight of one another?

Wonderfully readable, funny and sad, *Stone Cradle* is a masterful evocation of the lives of two women confronting the changes of the twentieth century. Vivid, compassionate and beautifully written, it confirms Louise Doughty as one of the major writers and storytellers of her generation.

'A compulsively readable story, both informative and moving'
Daily Mail

ISBN 978-0-7434-4039-4
PRICE £7.99

POCKET
BOOKS